OTHER LIVES AND OTHER WORLDS

Other *Lives &*
Other *Worlds*
PHILOSOPHY AND MODERN FICTIONS

STEPHEN R.L. CLARK

Angelico Press

First published in the USA
by Angelico Press 2025
Copyright © Stephen R.L. Clark 2025

For information, address:
Angelico Press, Ltd.
169 Monitor St.
Brooklyn, NY 11222
www.angelicopress.com

ppr 979-8-89280-066-2
cloth 979-8-89280-067-9
ebook 979-8-89280-068-6

Book and cover design
by Michael Schrauzer

Contents

Preface

In my most recent book, *How the Worlds Became*, I addressed ancient stories drawn largely from Egypt, Greece, Mesopotamia, and the North, to show their philosophical grounds and implications. Towards the end of that work, I began to draw also from modern speculative fictions, especially those of Lovecraft, Tolkien, and Stapledon. Those authors were notable for the work they put into devising whole worlds and histories in which to stage their stories.

My interest in speculative fiction of this sort goes back to my childhood reading of fantasy and science fiction, and I have often found inspiration there for past philosophical enquiry, most openly in my Read Tuckwell Lectures at Bristol University in 1994 (published as *How to Live Forever* [London: Routledge, 1995]), in my study of Chesterton as an early SF writer (*G. K. Chesterton: Thinking Backwards, Looking Forwards* [West Conshohocken, PA: Templeton Foundation Press]), and in sundry papers for philosophical journals, some of which were republished in the collection *Philosophical Futures* (Frankfurt: Peter Lang, 2011). Others of my past papers—which some critics might also think indebted to science-fictional analyses both of animal nature and our own political prospects—have been collected as *Animals and their Moral Standing* (Routledge, 1997), and *The Political Animal* (Routledge, 1999). I have lightly revised most of the other papers that follow here, and expanded a few (especially chapters six and thirteen). The effect, as I only saw as I re-read the papers, is a prolonged examination, from 1983 to 2022, of the apparent conflict between the world as we are compelled to think it and our need for faith in the reality of humane values. How shall we manage to live in a world that appears to deny our values? Olaf Stapledon imagined his "Last Men" in despair:

> Many million, million selves; ephemeridae, each to itself,
> the universe's one quick point, the crux of all cosmical
> endeavour. All defeated! It is forgotten. It leaves only a

darkness, deepened by blind recollection of past light. Soon, a greater darkness! Man, a moth sucked into a furnace, vanishes; and then the furnace also, since it is but a spark islanded in the wide, the everlasting darkness. If there is a meaning, it is no human meaning. Yet one thing in all this welter stands apart, unassailable, fair, the blind recollection of past light.[1]

Or else, perhaps, that very image of entire defeat is itself the product of an Imagination that transcends the failure. How do we even know to imagine "Darkness" and World's End without any faith in Reason? The papers that follow are my long attempt to fight "the long defeat" — in faith that we (or someone) shall after all survive.

Modern speculative fiction — or so we all prefer to think — is better supported by respected, "scientific" investigations than were the older stories. Some science fiction writers, indeed, profess to be writing entirely within a scientifically grounded framework, and expect that what is now "science fiction" will soon be simply *realistic* fiction, on a par with any stories set within our present familiar world. Other writers select less well-supported theories and possibilities, imagining what it would be like to travel between star systems, or encounter wholly alien species. Some imagine even more distant possibilities — that we might have access to our own past realities or to wildly alternate histories, that we are currently living in an artificial dream, or that our species was seeded by galactic engineers only a few thousand years ago and is still being observed and managed by our makers. All these imaginings resemble past mythologies, and all allow us to conceive what we might be, and what laws or norms we should obey, or hope to see obeyed.

Such speculations, of course, need not demand belief. They may, indeed, inoculate their readers against too ready acceptance of wild stories about past alien interventions, secret conspiracies, or utopian prospects. We know that they are fictions — and this may also have been true of our ancestors' attitudes to *their* mythologies.[2] Lucian spoke for himself, but perhaps also for many earlier poets:

---

[1] Olaf Stapledon, *Last and First Men* (Harmondsworth: Penguin, 1972 [1930]), 605.

[2] See Rodney Needham, *Belief, Language and Experience* (Chicago: University of Chicago Press, 1973); Paul Veyne, *Did the Greeks Believe in their Myths? An essay on the constructive imagination*, trans. Paula Wissing (Chicago: University of Chicago Press, 1988).

Though I tell the truth in nothing else, I shall at least be truthful in saying that I am a liar. I think I can escape the censure of the world by my own admission that I am not telling a word of truth. Be it understood, then, that I am writing about things which I have neither seen nor had to do with nor learned from others — which, in fact, do not exist at all and, in the nature of things, cannot exist. Therefore, my readers should on no account believe in them.[3]

They are fictions, but they may also contain more serious speculations about our worlds, and motivate both moral action and further scholarly or scientific enquiries. At the least they may serve to remind us that we should also be *willing* to doubt the truth even of "realistic fictions" and currently respectable theories. Pyrrhonism — the refusal to give secure assent even to common sense and scientific dogma — may not be an entirely helpful life-style: there are some truths, especially *moral* truths, that we ought not to doubt, and even *cannot* doubt without a perverse imagination.[4] But it does allow us to distinguish our own selves from even our most confident "beliefs": challenges to those beliefs and theories are not necessarily attacks on our own intelligence or integrity. Correspondingly, we may make our speculations public so as to let them survive, mutate, or perish on their own. We often do not even know what it is we have succeeded in saying until there has been time for others to hear and (mis)interpret it.

A further corollary of a partly Pyrrhonist attitude is that we can abandon the need to "prove" a proposition before it is endorsed as a subject of enquiry. That imagined need is itself a weapon in debate — used, for example, in the initial response to Charles Darwin's speculations about "natural selection" as the chief engine of evolutionary change. Because Darwin could himself produce no clear case of the emergence of any new species by such gradual, cumulative change over many successive generations, nor offer any clear account of the way such inheritance (with modifications)

---

[3] Lucian (2nd century AD), "True Story," 1.4: *Works*, vol. 1, trans. A. M. Harmon (Cambridge, MA: Harvard University Press [Loeb Classical Library], 1913), 253.
[4] See "Living the Pyrrhonian Way," in *The Science, Politics, and Ontology of Life-Philosophy*, eds. Scott M. Campbell and Paul W. Bruno (London: Bloomsbury, 2013), 197–209.

worked, his critics were able to disparage the hypothesis as one without "empirical" foundation. What could not be proved in present-day experience should not, they suggested, be made public even as a speculative alternative to other imagined theories, especially if it might so easily be interpreted in ways damaging to public morale. Thomas Huxley himself, later known as "Darwin's Bulldog," had rejected Robert Chambers's similarly speculative account of evolutionary change—essentially, that the same inherited form would be realised in very different phenotypes according to environmental needs[5]—not many years before, with a degree of venom that even he later somewhat regretted.[6] Alfred Russel Wallace, the co-author of the theory of natural selection, had a more favourable view of Chambers's suggestions:

> I do not consider it a hasty generalization, but rather as an ingenious hypothesis strongly supported by some striking facts and analogies but which remains to be proved by more facts & the additional light which future researches [sic] may throw upon the subject. It at all events furnishes a subject for every observer of nature to turn his attention to; it thus furnishes both an incitement to the collection of facts & an object to which to apply them when collected.[7]

To prove—or disprove—any idea, it is first necessary to make the idea attractive enough to warrant the efforts involved in developing it further till it can be checked against relevant evidence and controlled experiment. "What is now proved was once only imagined."[8] Much that is now disproved—or at least made less attractive as a work in progress—was once the most respectable

[5] This is not obviously false: see John Maynard Smith, *Evolutionary Genetics* (Oxford: Oxford University Press, 1998), 11, describing the distinct phenotypes of *Daphnia*; see my *Biology and Christian Ethics* (Cambridge: Cambridge University Press, 2000), 49.

[6] See Robert Chambers, *Vestiges of the Natural History of Creation* (Leicester: Leicester University Press, 1969 [1844]); and Joel S. Schwartz, "Darwin, Wallace, and Huxley and Vestiges of the Natural History of Creation," *Journal of the History of Biology* 23 (1990), 127–53.

[7] Wallace to a colleague (December 28, 1845): cited by Schwartz, "Darwin, Wallace and Huxley," 141. See also Alfred Russel Wallace, *The Wonderful Century: Its Successes and Its Failures* (London: Swan Sonnenschein, 1898), 137.

[8] William Blake, "The Marriage of Heaven and Hell," plate 8: *Complete Writings*, ed. Geoffrey Keynes (London: Oxford University Press, 1966), 151.

idea. In either case there is often no other way to progress than to make the best of a project, whether that is conceived as a "scientific" program or a "religious" life. It is not even always ridiculous to identify with an obviously invented fantasy of good government and almost magical competence: *Star Trek*, from its beginnings in Gene Roddenberry's imagination, offered hope for the future.[9] An aphorism widely (and mistakenly) attributed to Aristotle has some merit: it is the mark of an educated mind that it can entertain a proposition and see what follows without believing it. It is wise, on the other hand, to remember that such merely "entertained" propositions may infect our reason, for good or ill, so that we end by believing them after all! They are, after all, "familiar"!

Speculative fiction may offer us goals to strive for. It may even, like older mythologies, build living presences within our souls that may advise and inspire, or punish. Asking ourselves what Spock or Kirk or even Buffy would do may invoke an internal voice and image almost as well as prayer to more familiar angels.[10] Whether such imagined voices are genuinely Other, and not merely our own fantasies, is not a question to be answered quickly. Whether imagined worlds are only ever virtual is also an open question. And both these questions are ones that I have attempted to address in the chapters following. As always, I also acknowledge the support and criticism of friends and family, students, fellow scholars, editors, and reviewers. My thanks also to the Universities of Liverpool and Bristol for continuing to provide me with library resources, and virtual habitations, as Emeritus Professor of Philosophy and Honorary Research Fellow in Theology and Religious Studies. I owe special debts to Edward James, David Seed, Colin Stanley, and Gregory Swer for requesting, and inspiring, the original papers. And to my wife, Gillian Clark, for her constant care and support.

---

[9] See Lance Parkin, *The Impossible Has Happened: The Life and Work of Gene Roddenberry, Creator of Star Trek* (London: Aurum, 2016); Daryl G. Frazetti, *Anthropology of Star Trek: Exploring core cultural concepts* (California: CreateSpace, 2016).

[10] See Grant Morrison, *Supergods: what masked vigilantes, miraculous mutants, and a sun god from Smallville can teach us about being human* (New York: Spiegel and Grau, 2011).

ACKNOWLEDGMENTS

Taylor and Francis, and the editors of *Inquiry*: "Waking-up: a neglected model for the After-life," *Inquiry* 26 (1983–84), 209–30.

Cambridge University Press and the editors of *Philosophy*: "Orwell and the Anti-Realists," *Philosophy* 67 (1992), 141–54.

David Seed and Liverpool University Press: "Alien Dreams—Kipling," in David Seed, ed., *Anticipations: Essays on Early Science Fiction and its Precursors* (Liverpool: Liverpool University Press, 1995), 172–94.

Edward James, Farah Mendlesohn, and the Science Fiction Foundation: "Psychopathology and Alien Ethics," in Edward James and Farah Mendlesohn, eds., *The Parliament of Dreams: conferring on Babylon 5* (Reading: Science Fiction Foundation, 1998), 153–62.

George Ellis and Templeton Foundation Press: "Olaf Stapledon (1886–1950)," in George Ellis, ed., *The Far-Future Universe* (Radnor, PA: Templeton Foundation Press, 2002), 355–70.

Eric Symes Abbott Memorial Fund: "Deep Time: does it matter?," at Westminster Abbey on Thursday 10th May, 2001 and subsequently at Keble College, Oxford: https://www.kcl.ac.uk/dean/assets/pdf/esa-lecture/16th%20esa%20lecture%202001.pdf (accessed July 30, 2024).

Springer and the Editors of *Metascience*: "Review of Robert Markley, *Dying Planet: Mars in Science and the Imagination*," *Metascience* 15 (2006), 561–65: https://doi.org/10.1007/s11016-006-9042-0.

Colin Stanley: "*The Mind Parasites*: Wilson, Husserl, Plotinus," in *Around the Outsider: essays presented to Colin Wilson*, ed. Colin Stanley (Alresford: O-Books, 2011), 42–62.

Andrew Moore and Taylor and Francis Publishers: "God, Reason, and Extraterrestrials," in *God, Mind and Knowledge*, ed. Andrew Moore (London: Ashgate, 2014), 171–86.

Anna Tomaszewska and *Diametros*: "Changing Kinds—Aristotle and the Aristotelians," *Diametros* 44 (2015), 19–34.

Colin Stanley and Cambridge Scholars: "Lovecraft and the Search for Meaning," in *Proceedings of the Colin Wilson Conference*, ed. Colin Stanley (Cambridge: Cambridge Scholars, 2017), 10–45.

Gregory Swer and *Philosophical Journal of Conflict and Violence*: "New Histories of the World: Spenglerian Optimism," *Philosophical Journal of Conflict and Violence*, 6.2 (2022), *Oswald Spengler's International Influence: from The Decline of the West till the Present Day* (ed. Gregory Swer).

1.
Waking Up
A NEGLECTED MODEL FOR THE AFTERLIFE[1]

DREAMING OUR LIFE AWAY

In my first published volume, based around my doctoral thesis, I composed the following analogy, which was duly published, as an aside, in *Aristotle's Man*:

> Suppose it is possible to guide men's dreams. Suppose we submit a number of men to our device: as far as we are concerned they are lying on their beds, plugged into our oneirotokon. As far as they are concerned (with whatever qualifications about the possibility of thinking while asleep) they are engaged in the common pursuit of a bear. They are enduring and partly inventing a shared dream which they take to be waking reality. We make it seem to them that one of their number dies: they dream-bury his dream-body and forget. But he, the identifiable being that was asleep and dreaming, merely wakes up. Waking to life eternal, by analogy, is waking from a masquerade, to find that reality of which this world is no more than a copy — as Plato said.[2]

As no reviewer troubled to comment on this passage, and as no one (so far as I know) has developed the analogy further, I was reduced to performing these tasks myself. This at least enabled me to confess that the *oneirotokon* is a not unfamiliar science-fictional

---

[1] First published as "Waking-up: a neglected model for the After-life," in *Inquiry* 26 (1983–84), 209–30.
[2] *Aristotle's Man* (Oxford: Clarendon Press, 1975), 170.

device, employed, for example, by Roger Zelazny in *Dream Master*, and by Samuel Delany (my immediate source) in *The Fall of the Towers*. James Tiptree Jr. also seems to employ this or a similar idea in "Beam Me Home" *(10,000 Light-Years from Home)*, in which a young American is strongly influenced by Star Trek, joins the air force in order to get into the space program, and ends his terrestrial life as a pilot in Vietnam. In a final, despairing conversation he reveals to a friend that he has for years half-believed that someday he would be recalled to "the star-ship Enterprise," or its equivalent, from a period of ground duty on a primitive planet. Since the story *is* science-fiction, rather than a merely psychological novel, his hope or fancy is fulfilled. His death is an awakening back "home" amongst the clean and courteous citizens of a Galactic Federation. Obviously enough, the story encapsulates many suggestive ideas, about the American dream, the nature of "belief," and the role of "extra-terrestrialism" as the new religious form of the Western world that has (as Martyn Skinner prophesied way back in the 1950s)

> Led to a wide revival of belief
> In presences and beings ultrahuman
> Pervading earth, and seen in glimpses brief
> As deities once were by Greek and Roman.
> In other words, through scientists' acumen,
> Mars, Venus, Jove returned to men's experience
> In shapes of Martians, Jovians and Venerians.[3]

Doris Lessing's quartet, *Canopus in Argos*, also testifies to the religious strength of extra-terrestrialism, and uses a very similar model for the survival of earthly death. All these themes would be worth further development. At present I am concerned chiefly with the model of survival, that it is as if we were to wake up from a shared dream and find our original natures that we had before our births. As a further historical comment, I should remark that the analogy took shape in my mind during the 1960s, when it was fashionable in philosophical circles to insist that bodily continuity was an essential element in personal identity. On this view, discarnate spirits could not be reckoned to be persons at all, still less "the same persons" as those who had died. Peter Strawson

---

[3] M. Skinner, *The Return of Arthur* (London: Chapman and Hall, 1955), 2.1.35.

had commented that it was wise of the Christian Church to insist on the resurrection of the body, rather than putting any reliance on a purely "spiritual" immortality.[4] Philosophers had gone on to doubt that any "recreated" bodily person could possibly be the "same person" as (perhaps) she initially supposed herself to be. What was to stop the Almighty creating two or more immortalized dopplegangers of the deceased? Neither would be more truly identical with the formerly existing person than the other, and so neither could reasonably be considered as anything more than a replica. It began to seem that neither spiritual immortality nor bodily resurrection could provide a coherent basis for personal immortality. This debate culminated in the Parfitian analysis of split-brain cases or the problems of rational amoebae,[5] and led many to suppose that personal identity in any case was not a variety of strict identity at all: all we ever had was some sense of backward and forward psychological continuities, founded (as it happens) in the physical nature of our bodies and the universe. If the Almighty willed it, similar continuities and connections could be made by other means, but it hardly mattered whether He did or not. Our ordinary concern for survival or future well-being was the product of irrational impulse. The true philosopher would experience a variety of Buddhist enlightenment, in the recognition that there was no self. As most professional philosophers, being human, manage not to give a real assent even to their own theories when these conflict too radically with common sense, the pursuit of fame, tenure, higher pay, and pension rights has not noticeably diminished! Since then, it has been the computer-program model which has most enlivened philosophical discourse. Instead of taking the hardware as central to personal being, adventurous thinkers concentrate on the software. Perhaps computers, suitably programmed, will one day give undeniable evidence of conscious being. Perhaps we are just such computers—or rather, just such computer-programs. I am the set of routines and sub-routines that get this body moving in appropriate ways. If the whole complex program were to be preserved and re-embodied I would live again, whatever the embodiment was like. Maybe my new life (in half a million years)

[4] P. F. Strawson, *Individuals* (London: Methuen, 1959), 116.
[5] D. Parfit, "Personal Identity," *Philosophical Review* 80 (1971), 3ff.

will consist in directing the motions of a silicon-based, artificial, space-explorer—if our remote descendants have the technology to rediscover or rewrite the program that now moves this carbon-based, free-range academic.[6] The physical embodiment of the program itself is perhaps a skein of ribo-nucleic acid, but I am not essentially that skein, any more than I am this body: I am an abstract possibility that exists as long as there is the possibility of using "me" to do something. Perhaps I need not even be re-embodied: I can enjoy a ghostly existence in the circuits of a tenth-generation computer (the Japanese are currently working on the fifth generation) that also houses indefinitely many other personoids. The last term is Stanislav Lem's, and several speculations of this kind, by Lem and others, can be encountered in Dennett and Hofstadter's collection *The Mind's I*.

In this new age of extravagant speculation, the question whether any sort of personal immortality even makes sense seems rather old-fashioned. If the current models of selfhood are inadequate—as they surely are—then the old Cartesian alternative has a certain charm. And there was never any difficulty about supposing that the Cartesian ego was immortal if one could believe in it at all. If the computer-program models are, after all, adequate, then immortality, of a somewhat etiolated kind, is theoretically obtainable by human, extraterrestrial, or divine technology. So my excuse for returning to the question must be that neither Cartesian nor computerized immortality seems to be what anyone would want. I hope to show that my model of personal being and immortality can allow that there is some truth in both the other models: my consciousness does not consist in any material performance, and my being Me is a matter of degree, of how far the Idea of Me is embodied over time. It does not follow that my immortality will lie either (as program-modellers would allow) in the world of our present experience, or (as Cartesians are perhaps required to imagine) in self-enclosed splendour, having no grasp of the existence of any finite others. That any suitably-programmed computer might turn out to be conscious, simply in virtue of its publicly discoverable capacities,

---

[6] This is indeed the standard form of interstellar "travel" in Frederik Pohl and Jack Williamson's *Farthest Star;* in Greg Egan's *Schild's Ladder;* and in Tony Daniels's *Warpath*.

is the necessary condition for a technological survival. If being conscious is something more than being appropriately responsive (and reflective) then there will always be something—"what it is like to *be* a bat" or a Video-Genie?—that is on the far side of the traditional epistemological divide for any consciousness but its own, and which we have not the foggiest of ideas how to produce. At first sight it seems clearly possible that some cleverly-programmed automaton should be able to deceive us all into thinking that it was conscious, even self-conscious, and that it understood what it was saying. If Dennett is correct, no such deception is possible, since that automaton would indeed be conscious in the only way to which we could ever put a name, the only way we ourselves could be conscious. Cartesian consciousness is a figment. If this view is strictly unbelievable, as I confess I find it, we must try to give some account of what it misses. Searle has suggested that consciousness is a causal power of the brain, or the cerebral cortex, not identical with the activities that might be replicated by an automaton.[7] On Dennett's view, he points out, a room which contained a mono-lingual English speaker and a sufficiently large collection of algorithms would be said to understand Chinese if appropriate ideograms were handed out on demand—the room, that is, would understand Chinese. I do not feel that Dennett has made any sufficient answer to this challenge—his answer, indeed, amounts to an admission that the room *would* understand Chinese, but that the algorithms would be very complicated indeed and that makes it easier to believe. But Searle's own position seems to be a weak one. Why should we suppose that the brain as such has any such causal property? That I at least am conscious in more than Dennett's sense, I am as convinced as ever Descartes or Augustine were.[8] But I know of no theoretical reason why brain tissue should have this odd property: the relation between the merely molecular and the mental remains a wholly unintelligible one, to be recognized only as a brute fact of experience. But it is no part of my experience that all and only cerebrating beings are *conscious*. I have evidence

[7] J. R. Searle, "Minds, Brains, and Programs," *Brain & Behavioral Sciences* 3; reprinted in D. C. Dennett and D. R. Hofstadter, eds., *The Mind's I* (Brighton: Harvester, 1981), 353ff.
[8] "Descartes' Debt to Augustine," in M. McGhee, ed., *Philosophy, Religion and the Spiritual Life* (Cambridge: Cambridge University Press, 1992), 73–88.

that they are conscious, but this is not logically compelling, and rests only on my brute conviction of likeness, that I am one of a kind: the kind, that is, of subjects. I recognize that "conscious" is the word for what I am because I can recognize that others are conscious: but my consciousness is immediate to me in a way that others' consciousness is not. Searle's account therefore seems to lack both theoretical and empirical justification, and leaves us with the ancient problem: "what is it that is conscious?"[9] And with this preamble I return to the analogy of my *oneirotokon*. What can be said for or against the possibility that the real cause of my conscious experience lies elsewhere than in the world of our present experience? Could it be that I am not what I thought I was, not a terrestrial body, not a cerebral cortex?

TALKING ABOUT INVISIBLES

Can my story be ruled out as merely nonsensical? Is it, as some philosophers have contended, quite impossible to wonder whether all our present experience is dream-like, all our conceptual apparatus subtly misleading? Can we not even raise the possibility that earthly death is not the real end?

At first sight it seems ridiculous to deny that one might raise this possibility: after all, I am raising it now, and those who would object to my doing so clearly have some notion of what possibility it is that I am raising. The sort of metaphysical imperialism which would deny us the right to examine our ideas in a new light is the death of intellect. What could ground the sheer rejection of my story? The language in which I have expressed it employs terms which we have learned through experience. I know what it is to be dreaming, or to have dreamed. I know what it is for someone to be killed. I know what it is to discover that I have been mistaken, and what it is to be chased by a bear. The meaning of these terms is settled by what their correct use is in the linguistic community of which I am a part. Being a

---

[9] In the original version of this paper I here referred to my presentation, "Could Consciousness Evolve?," at a Thyssen Conference in 1982, which I expected to see published in the conference proceedings. It was judged too distant from the main themes of that conference, and appeared instead as a chapter of *From Athens to Jerusalem* (Oxford: Clarendon Press 1984; Brooklyn, NY: Angelico Press, 2019), which was founded around my Gifford Lectures at Glasgow in 1982.

bear just is being the sort of thing that is regularly called a bear by English speakers. Being genuinely dead just is the condition of never coming back, being no more. Being awake just is being in a position to exchange views with others and check on what has been happening in our temporary absence. The dead do not survive; the wakeful are not dreaming. We cannot use words which we could only learn, only apply, in one context in order to cast doubt on their genuine applicability. Someone who says that to wake is to dream and to dream is to wake to life eternal is contradicting herself, since dreaming and waking are opposites.

But is it not obvious that we can describe the position of my *oneirotokon*'s patients? They think they are chasing a bear, and their usage of the term "bear," their respective images of what it is they think they are chasing, may not be very far from the uses of our waking world. Is it not obvious that this might be our position too, relative to some yet more wakeful world? We dream that we can cause others to dream, but our apparent wakefulness is as distant from the truth as theirs. The problem is familiar to epistemologists as the sceptical argument that our experiences are compatible with their really being caused by a bunch of neurologists busily stimulating a brain in a vat: in so far as we do not know that this is not the truth of the matter, we cannot continue to claim really to know the truth of any ordinary information about the world. If I really knew that I was typing here I would know that it was not the case that I was a brain in a vat being stimulated to produce the experience of typing. I do not know that I am not a brain in a vat, and so I do not know that I am really typing.[10]

The full examination of this very powerful argument would take me too far afield. What is of significance is that some philosophers, notably Putnam,[11] have chosen to argue that the vat-brains could not themselves intelligibly suspect that they were vat-brains, since the property they could know by the term "being a vat-brain" would only be the property actually displayed by such entities of *their* experience as were made to seem to them to be vat-brains. In their language only a few vat-brains exist (the transcendental

---

[10] P. Unger, *Ignorance* (Oxford: Clarendon Press, 1975); K. Lehrer, "Why not Scepticism?," *Philosophical Forum* 1 (1970–71), 283–98.
[11] H. Putnam, *Reason, Truth, and History* (Cambridge: Cambridge University Press, 1981); see R. Nozick, *Philosophical Explanations* (Oxford: Clarendon Press, 1981).

neurologists have caused them to suppose that they are conducting just such experiments as the neurologists actually are...). Most of them are not vat-brains, as they understand the terms. It is not possible for them to understand the claim that really they all are. Correspondingly, we cannot really envisage the possibility that *we* are vat-brains, even if (in some transcendental sense) we are.

One point about this argument is worth remembering. If once we admit the possibility that the world of our experience does not reveal the truth, it is unreasonable to expect that the Real World will contain all and only such creatures as we have (perhaps) been conditioned to imagine. Why should there be neurologists or brains or vats at all? There might be: it is not impossible that our dream is rather like the Real World. But it is also not impossible that it is not. Extraterrestrials and callous scientists are part of our mythology, as gods and demons once were. It may be that we have no ready images, nor even any space in our minds, for what really is.

Two objections to the Putnamesque case seem to me to be definitive. First, it ignores the theoretical, explanatory function of language. Second, it ignores the metaphorical power of the human imagination. If we accept the account of language favoured by such objectors we should have to agree that, for example, being-a-witch simply consists in being the sort of thing that is regularly called a witch by competent English-speakers. On such terms those reformers who denied that there were any such things as witches would have had a hard time: they would have been denying, falsely, that anyone was ever called "witch" by English-speakers. It would have been similarly difficult to deny the existence, as such, of dephlogisticated air. If current usage is to define what can be said, no rational critique of that usage could ever get started. As it happens, reformers were able to deny that the terrified old women who were tortured, burnt, and hanged were really what the populace considered them to be; they did not have the natures, powers, plans, and dispositions attributed to them. It is similarly possible that the things to which we casually refer are not what we imagine them to be. We do not merely give names to classes of experience, we theorize about them. If we say that someone is dead, we cannot be supposed to mean only that she is in that condition which competent English-speakers call "dead": we mean that she is what our theory of death requires her to be. Our theory may be wrong, and we may all be misapplying it.

Delany's *oneirotokon* differs from mine in that a dream death is the signal for a real death:

> The computer [singles out] soldiers to be killed by random choice. Then, when the choice has been made, by controlled suggestion the dream is manoeuvred into some situation that will allow death. Then the cell in which the soldier is lying is electrified, his body is incinerated, and the cell is ready for another drugged madman.[12]

Delany's unfortunates are right to judge that there is such a thing as extinction, and even right (contingently) to suppose that real extinction is the fate of those they reckon to have died. But the real causes of their experience lie elsewhere, and there is no necessary link between death and the second death. Other imaginable tales allow that there is no such thing as death at all, although people do go through the event that we call "dying," just as there is no such thing as dephlogisticated air, although there is a gaseous stuff which Priestley and others would have called by that name, and no such thing as *pneuma* even though every biologist from Aristotle to Harvey took the thing for granted. In so far as what we say about our experience embodies one theory or another we may be wrong, either to believe that the theory has any application at all, or to believe that it is rightly applied where we now use it, or where we first thought of it. Even if we learn the term "dream" from our terrestrial experience of waking up with apparently delusive memories (that our parents teach us to disregard), it is not unimaginable that one or other of those very dreams was our one meeting with the Things that Are.

> Once I dreamed that I was a butterfly, and then awoke to find I was a man. Now I do not know if I am a man who dreamed he was a butterfly, or a butterfly dreaming that he is Chuang Tzu.[13]

It is not enough to reply that Reality shall henceforth be taken to be the agreed system of discourse, so that only those things are "real" which we can induce others to cooperate in imagining.

---

[12] S. R. Delany, *The Fall of the Towers* (London: Sphere, 1971 [1962]), 2:229 (chapter 13).
[13] Chuang Tzu, *Musings of a Chinese Mystic*, trans. H. A. Giles, with an introduction by L. Giles (London: Murray, 1906), 49–50.

Anti-realism of this kind is an understandable response to radical insecurity, as well as an example of humankind's readiness to ignore the non-human universe we inhabit. But even if it did not matter, for practical purposes, whether life is a dream or not, there is at least an imaginable possibility that Chuang Tzu's suspicions were correct—though the dreaming "butterfly" may be a stranger beast than we imagine here. Another piece of SF of the early 1950s postulated that human beings were the grubs of the true inhabitants of interstellar space, and earthly death an awakening to that celestial maturity:

> Now and again one [grub] more daring than the rest might have sneaked from the hiding place of its own grub-conditioning and peered furtively into the dark and seen a great, bright-eyed moth like a nocturnal butterfly beating gloriously through the endless night. And it would cower down, sorely afraid, totally unable to recognize—itself![14]

It is easy to smile at this piece of grandiloquence, but the author's imagined worship of a beatified humanity, set against the indifference or hostility of Nature and of other species, is only a more dramatic version of fashionable humanism. And he was at least innocent of the merely bourgeois conviction that humankind as it now experiences itself to be is the sole heir of the ages, or the sole measure of reality.

Our present waking experience may be structured by concepts that reflect the true life to which we have a chance of waking. The geometrical circles of our acquaintance are, as Plato argued, enough to remind us of the celestial Circle, even though they cannot be the sources of our geometrical knowledge. But we can also regard our trans-empirical theorizing as the product of our metaphorical imaginations. Until recently, fashionable philosophers were chary of metaphor, of any attempt to use language to convey thoughts for which it was not first designed. But even in our present lives it is by metaphorical extension of concepts that we devise new theories of a useful kind. Sometimes we may even extend them to cover cases which we had at first classified as just the opposite: we can treat the act of polishing a piece of metal as

---

[14] Eric Frank Russell, *Sentinels from Space* (London: Museum Press, 1954), 207; see also B. Shaw, *The Palace of Eternity* (London: Gollancz, 1970).

the making of many tiny scratches, even though "polishing" was hitherto considered as merely removing scratches.[15] We can consider a geo-stationary satellite that seems to hover over the earth to be, instead, a projectile forever falling towards the earth—and missing it. We can consider that our waking lives are only a slightly more coherent, common dream, instead of the mere opposite of dreaming, and look towards an ideal lucidity when we shall know as we are known. "It's concealed from other men what they do when they're awake, just as they forget what they do sleeping."[16] Whether we are, as Plato held, remembering the concepts that we used in Real Life, or simply using some empirical idea "as a condensed program for the exploration" of some other, unfamiliar area,[17] does not greatly matter. It is enough that the attempt to prove the dream-model radically unacceptable is unconvincing if we are to retain any grasp on the notion of Reality as such, or acknowledge the power of metaphorical inquiry.

But suppose that the dream-model is unacceptable for another, though related reason? Are there any such events as dreams at all? At first sight the question seems ridiculous, since practically everyone would admit to having had many dreams. But it would hardly be reasonable for me to entertain doubts about the real truth of other customary claims and yet be credulous of the claim that most of us do genuinely dream! Perhaps, as I hinted earlier, "to have dreamed" is only to awake with delusive memories that sometimes, in the first moment of our waking, knit themselves into a coherent story. The main philosophical argument for this position, of course, has been that supposed dream-events are immune to falsification. There is no way in which I can discover even that I have misreported the dream-events, let alone that anyone else has. My dream-model, strictly speaking, is immune to this criticism, since there is a shared dream-world and a computer program against which to check any particular participant's claims. One hunter can claim that it was he who struck the final blow, and the others meaningfully disagree, even though in fact no one struck such a blow, but only intended and seemed to do so, and the dream-bear collapsed because the dream required it to (and woke

---

[15] D. A. Schon, *Invention and Evolution of Ideas* (London: Tavistock, 1967), 30.
[16] Heracleitos 22B1, in Hermann Diels, *Die Fragmente der Vorsokratiker*, ed. Walther Kranz (3 vols, Zürich: Weidmann, 1996), 1.150.
[17] Schon, *Invention*, 64.

up in the Real World). This fact may itself lead some commentators to deny that the *oneirotokon*'s victims are really "dreaming," and also to suggest that the ordinary "waking world" cannot really be a *dream*: it is simply too well organized, as well as being publicly verifiable. My suspicion is that it is not after all as well organized as systematists suppose, but I would be willing to concede the term: let it be that the *oneirotokon*'s victims are not strictly dreaming, but only suffering a collective delusion, and that our waking world is not a dream, but a delusion (at least in part). Little hangs on the word. But I suspect that even our dreams are not wholly unreal.

That there actually are present experiences which will be reported later as dreams is difficult to demonstrate. I do remember such events, and some of us seem to remember that they were lucid dreams: the one who has woken up reports that even in the dream she knew or suspected that it was a dream. It is also not uncommon for people to report that they dreamed that they had woken up, and maybe woke up to many different layers of dream before at last they "really" woke (if they have woken yet). I have no proof that any of this is so, but I doubt that verificationism can show that it is not. Realism about our dreams, that there are true propositions about what we dreamed even if we have forever forgotten what they are, seems as viable as realism about unknown areas of the universe, or numbers too great ever to have been contemplated. But in any case, if the model of many-layered reality which I am sketching has any force, then even apparently unshared dreams (which most of us have nightly) are open to view. They are not merely private, but accessible in principle to suitably skilled dream-divers.

The idea that there are dream-worlds, even with only one present inhabitant, need not be given any very strong sense in order to expound the dream-model. My story can be told purely in terms of identical or nearly identical delusions. We need not suppose that there is any shared space within which dream-figures meet. It is merely that what is experienced by any dreamer may be reflected in the experience of others. They are "really" in separate vats or cells, and their imagined positions in the imaginary realm which is the set of their delusions bear no systematic relation to their "real" positions. On the other hand, this metaphor of shared space may be taken, more realistically, to mean that there are nested spatio-temporal systems, accessible to each other only through the experience of those who dream-dive, but related by the causal chains that determine their existence.

Weaker or stronger readings of the "dream-world" metaphor may go with slightly different attitudes to the question of identity between dreaming and waking selves, a point to which I shall be returning. What I need to emphasize first is the question of causality. My dreamers suppose that it is the bear which leaves traces in the undergrowth, that it is their own wit and strength which ensure the kill, that their bodies are sustained by the bear-meat that they eat. None of this is true-in-fact, but they can rely upon the customary associations of events in order to make their future plans. Life within the dream-world, so to call it, follows the rules of Humean causality. All conjunctions are equally unintelligible, merely matters of brute fact, that might as easily go otherwise. Hume's analysis of causation followed the ancient pattern of mystical occasionalism: according to the Mutakallimun ordinary "causes" were merely occasions. The one true cause was Allah,[18] in whom Hume did not believe. Berkeley was truer to the tradition, concluding that our notion of causation was found in doing and willing, so that no idea, no object of sense, could be a cause. Ideas were rather the language that the one God chose to speak with us, or the fantasy game in which we were enmeshed.[19]

Those ordinary dreamers who have reported lucid dreams, in which they were convinced that they were dreaming, do not seem to have established this conclusion by trying to pinch themselves. Sometimes they can point to a distinct incongruity which roused their suspicions (e.g. the dreamer's wife suddenly dissolves into a cloud), but it is more usual for people to become suspicious before they notice the oddity (if indeed they ever do locate a specific incongruity). One route to lucidity seems to be to begin thinking critically about why one is acting as one seems to be, why things are turning out this way or that. It is when no intelligible answer is forthcoming that the conclusion "so this is a dream" becomes compelling.[20]

True wakefulness, in short, is associated with a grasp of intelligible connection, and the lack of it. It is possible for us to seem

[18] S. L. Jaki, *Science and Creation* (Edinburgh: Scottish Academic Press, 1974).
[19] G. Berkeley, *Alciphron*, in *Works*, ed. A. A. Luce and T. E. Jessop (Edinburgh: Nelson, 1950), 3:149ff.
[20] C. Green, *Lucid Dreams* (London: Hamish Hamilton, 1968), 30ff.

to wake up many times: each apparent waking is associated with the conviction that we now understand what is going on. The philosophical discovery that no intelligible connection is to be found between any phenomenal event of our supposedly waking life, together with the conviction (which Hume lacked) that such intelligible causation is real, provides an incentive to conclude that this seeming wakefulness of ours is dream. Real causation, of an essentialist or a volitional kind, occurs where there is a genuine intelligibility, within a larger theory, about the connection between cause and effect. It is to that goal that scientific realists, who have not abandoned the quest for truth in favour of merely pragmatic methods, are aiming. So Grover Maxwell concluded that our ordinary understanding of the world, with its folk taxonomy and folk physics, is simply mistaken.

> We are in the position of savages who suppose that their god is angry when it looks like rain: the anthropologist had better take an umbrella with her when they say "Mombu is angry," but she is right to think that they are quite mistaken.

Real causation, for Maxwell, is discoverable by scientific inquiry. One day we shall know why things must be as they are, and then we shall have woken from the dream of life.[21] We do not see pretty colours, nor sense individuals of distinct kinds with distinct boundaries, because there are such things. What there is, is otherwise.

So science as well as philosophy may suggest that our present "waking" life has less claim on our final devotion than we might suppose. We shall of course forget this very quickly. Our own emotional attachment to what we seem to sense, and the eagerness with which our fellow dreamers punish those who stray too far from the consensus world, are usually enough to keep us safely sane:

> The sane person prides himself on his ability to be unaffected by important facts, and interested in unimportant ones. He refers to this as having a sense of perspective, or keeping things "in proportion"... A mentally healthy

---

[21] G. Maxwell, "Scientific Methodology and the Causal Theory of Perception," in I. Lakatos and A. Musgrave, eds., *Problems in the Philosophy of Science* (Amsterdam: North-Holland, 1968), 149ff.

person has made a value judgment in advance that no idea or experience can be qualitatively more important than those he already understands. He is able to rely on his defence mechanisms and can listen with a bland expression to people with unpleasant ideas.[22]

Sometimes we are reminded of our situation in a dream, but we usually prefer to rationalize the thought away. In 1958, Jung dreamt of flying saucers, shaped like the lens of a telescope or a magic lantern, and woke thinking, "We always think that the UFOs are projections of ours. Now it turns out that we are their projections. I am projected by the magic lantern as C. G. Jung. But who manipulates the apparatus?" In 1944 he had dreamt of a meditating yogi with his own face, waking with the thought: "Aha, so he is the one who is meditating me. He has a dream and I am it . . . When he awakened, I would no longer be." Jung goes on to describe the dream as a parable:

> My self retires into meditation and meditates my earthly form. To put it another way: it assumes human shape in order to enter three-dimensional existence, as if someone were putting on a diver's suit in order to dive into the sea . . . This reversal [of the relationship between ego-consciousness and the unconscious] suggests that in the opinion of the "other side," our unconscious existence is the real one and our conscious world a kind of illusion, an apparent reality constructed for a specific purpose, a dream which seems a reality as long as we are in it.[23]

By selecting a psychological label for the unknown origin of our experience, Jung makes it possible for us to receive his idea as an allegory of personal integration and human relations. But if true causality is not to be found in our ordinarily waking life, we should not so readily explain our experience as the product of the unconscious capacities of a biological organism of the kind with which we are currently acquainted. "The Unconscious" can either name a metaphysical reality, or merely the inarticulate capacities of a psycho-physical organism for self-deception. But if it names the former the title is unwarranted. *We* are not conscious of it; it

---

[22] C. Green, *The Human Evasion* (London: Hamish Hamilton, 1969), 12, 17.
[23] C. G. Jung, *Memories, Dreams and Reflections*, ed. A. Jaffe, trans. R. and C. Winston (London: Fontana, 1967), 355–56.

does not follow that *it* is unaware of us. Nor is it entirely safe to speak of *it* as my self, with whatever qualifications to distinguish my Self from my ordinary Ego-consciousness.

Perhaps I am after all the Red King's dream.

IMMORTALITY AND THE REAL WORLD

So far I have argued merely for the intelligibility of the supposition that our "waking" life is a false awakening, and noted various philosophical, scientific, and mystagogic reasons for supposing that supposition to be correct. The intelligible truth about things is not laid open to ordinary view. Some scientific realists may, in their charity, agree that this metaphor is not inappropriate, but add that there seems little chance of our ever waking up to experience things as they are, least of all at that moment when our earthly existence seems to end. "Men are asleep: they awaken at their death."[24] But maybe our life is a dream from which we do not wake. What can be said for Ibn Arabi's opinion, and what is the relation likely to be between my dreaming self and the awakened being?

Before attempting to answer these questions it is necessary to remark upon the proper grounding of belief. Academic sceptics, rationalists, and secularists regularly use the rhetorical device of demanding that "We" believe only those propositions which can be shown to be more probable than any available alternatives, and ration the degree of our belief in proportion with the rational evidence. There are several problems about this epistemological opinion, which this is not the time to explore. Briefly: there seems little reason to accept this claim. What we believe is very ill-defined, but if "belief" is understood as the acceptance of a thesis into our program of exploration and action, there seems no good reason to insist (except for polemical purposes) that we only entertain those suggestions that already strike us as more agreeable than their rivals. Why should we not, remembering the extent to which our prejudices colour our conception of the world, set ourselves to explore unfamiliar ideas, to build upon one thesis out of many, even if it be no more demonstrable from

---

[24] Ibn Arabi: H. Corbin, *Creative Imagination in the Sufism of Ibn Arabi*, trans. R. Manheim (London: Routledge and Kegan Paul, 1969), 208; see also P. B. Shelley, *Adonais* (Pisa, 1821).

the presently available evidence than any other? There are other good reasons for accepting a claim than that it is implied by theses we already accept, or than that it itself implies some set of those other theses. We enter theses in our program because they strike us as likely to lead to interesting results, or because they make intelligible sense of our lives, or because the alternative is worse.

> If we had an infallible intellect with its objective certitudes, we might feel ourselves disloyal to such a perfect organ of knowledge in not trusting to it exclusively, in not waiting for its releasing word. But if...we believe that no bell in us tolls to let us know for certain when truth is in our grasp, then it seems a piece of idle fantasticality to preach so solemnly our duty of waiting for the bell. Indeed we may wait if we will ... but if we do so, we do so at our peril as much as if we believed.[25]

The subjective probability that a given thesis is correct is not the only factor in deciding whether we should enter it in our program. We must also reckon the general usefulness of so doing, and the probable outcome of error. It is better to risk believing something which will do us little harm if we are mistaken, than withhold belief (or believe a proffered alternative) when error in so doing would create great harm. It is better to believe that babies are sentient individuals even if we are mistaken in so doing than to believe that they are not: for the harm we would thereafter do if we believed mistakenly that they were insentient is enormously greater than the harm we do, if any, if we mistakenly believe that they are. From which it follows that I do not need to show that the dream-model of our deaths is in itself more probable, given the available (dream-)evidence, than every alternative. I need show only that it is an option worth exploring. Correspondingly, I need to urge that a mistaken belief in this would at least not do more harm than a mistaken failure to believe. These tasks are difficult enough without complicating them by appeal to the irrational ethic of rationalism.

That there are felt to be incongruities and contradictions in our ordinary lives has been a great incentive to the pursuit of some more coherent vision. One available explanation is Borges's, that we have dreamt the world but left within it subtle traces of

---

[25] W. James, *The Will to Believe* (New York: Longman, Green and Co., 1896), 30.

unreason to remind us that it is a dream, that it is not the ultimate context of explanation.[26] An experienced universe that seems to point all ways at once (so that light is both a stream of particles and a wave-formation; matter both a pile of small, hard objects and the mere intersection of probability networks; humankind both flesh and spirit) is not implausibly regarded as a dream. If we are not what we supposed ourselves to be, the way is open to supposing that we are immortal dreamers, though the conclusion cannot be reckoned certain.

What could we be? In my original analogy the dreamers were correct (at any rate by our own standards) to suppose that there were bodies, spatio-temporal locations, and the like, and mistaken only in the details of their lives. "Really" they were asleep, and dreaming in the cells of the *oneirotokon*, but they would find no radical alteration in their whole conceptual structure when they woke. Their real selves were identifiable spatio-temporally locatable organisms. Is this analogy adequate to the immortalist case? Can we suppose that our Real Selves are bodily, even if they have rather different accidental properties? Perhaps in the true awakening I shall find myself to be a butterfly, but still a body.

If this were so, it might seem likely that even my Real Body is a mortal thing. To be a body, in our experience, is to be a thing composed of many separable parts that someday do their things. Decay, destruction is a consequence of our complexity: only simples shall survive for ever. But the conclusion is not certain: maybe our world, our dream-world, is a demonstration?

> "I will," said Fiorinda, "that this shall be the life of them, of every thing that breatheth the breath of Life in this new world of ours: to be but part of the waters as it were of a whirlpool, wherein is everything for ever neither produced nor destroyed, but for ever transformed: the living substance for ever drawn in, moulded to some shape of life, and voided again as dead substance, having

---

[26] J. L. Borges, "Avatars of the Tortoise," in D. A. Yates and J. E. Irby, eds., *Labyrinths* (New York: New Directions, 1964). "We (the undivided divinity operating within us) have dreamt the world. We have dreamt it as firm, mysterious, visible, ubiquitous in space and durable in time; but in its architecture we have allowed tenuous and eternal crevices of unreason which tell us it is false." Borges has Kant's antinomies and Zeno's paradoxes especially in mind.

for that span of time yielded its strength and purpose to that common sink or cesspool of Being . . . Every one that knoweth life in my world shall know also death. The little simplicities, indeed, shall not die. But the living creatures shall. Die, and dissipate as children's castles in sand when the tide takes them, but the sand-grains abide. Is it not a just and equal choice? Either be a little senseless lump of jelly or of dead matter, and subsist for ever; or else be a bird, a fish, a rose, a woman, 'pon condition to fade, wax old, waste at last to carrion and corruption?"[27]

Eddison's story is "a consecutive history, covering more than seventy years in a special world devised for Her Lover by Aphrodite, for whom (as the reader must suspend disbelief and suppose) all worlds were made."[28] Even in this imagined world there is death, though it comes not by decay. Our own world is created for a moment's wry amusement, and the lord and ladies of Zimiamvia, themselves the multiple incarnations of Zeus and Aphrodite, descend into it to know it from within. In yet higher mansions of Olympus the ones who dream us all may live in immortal flesh, having orderly motions and locations, but without any fear that things will run awry.

The story is, I think, intelligible, and matches our demands of heaven, that it be a realm where old friends meet in joy, and our bodies are ones that can fulfil our designs. Two features of it, though, deserve more attention. The first, that it is for amusement that the worlds are made. The second, that such ultramundane bodies are sometimes thought to be impossible compromises. On the first point, Eddison is aware how harsh it seems:

> That [these peculiar and inconvenient arrangements] are far from amusing to us, here and now, — that they daily, for some or other of their helpless victims, produce woes and agonies too horrible for man to endure or even think of — is perhaps because we do not, in the bottom of our hearts, believe in our own immortality and the immortality of those we love. If, for you and me as individuals, this world is the sum, then much of its detail (and the

[27] E. R. Eddison, *Fish Dinner in Memison*, ed. J. Stephens (New York: Ballantine, 1968 [1941]), 268–69.
[28] Eddison, *The Mezentian Gate* (New York: Ballantine, 1972 [1958]), xi.

whole in general plan) is certainly not amusing. But to a mind developed on the lines of the Mahometan fanatic's, the Thug's, the Christian martyr's, is it not conceivable that (short, perhaps of acute physical torture) the "slings and arrows of outrageous fortune" should be no more painful than the imagined ills of a tragic drama, and could be experienced and appraised with like detachment?[29]

What is the immortalist's attitude to earthly life? Suicide or mass murder might seem appropriate, but this "is essentially a shirking of the game She sets us."

The second issue is the credibility of immortal bodies, perfectly attuned to our desires and capable (why not?) of passing with the speed of thought from place to place. Such bodies, it has been held in discussions of Christ's resurrection, are impossible compromises, vulgar misconceptions.[30] The "astral bodies" favoured by occultists have earned similar scorn. By our standards such things are dream-like, less real than our solid flesh which creeps from one location to another and cannot occupy the same space as another solid. If too much flexibility is allowed to flesh it ceases to be the firm foundation of a spatio-temporal system in which bodies (and the persons that they manifest) can be reidentified. If too little is allowed, then the bodies of the Real Waking World present no advantage over the incongruous creations with which we are now linked, and we have that much less reason to believe in them.

On the other hand, we should not exaggerate the importance of the extremely rigorous rules we now endure. It does not seem to me impossible that there should be reidentifiable beings in a world where discontinuous motion was allowed (relative, that is, to the motions and presences of other beings in that or other worlds). And though such a body might seem dream-like to us (for that is our only present experience of anything like such freedom), it does not follow that it would be dream-like to itself. We can conceive that my oneirotokon's victims sometimes stir, and are momentarily aware of a Real Presence that intrudes upon their ordinary scene in flashes and unexpected motions. They will be like Abbott's Flatlanders in failing to see the real continuity between successive, discontinuous appearances in their world. We may also conceive

---

[29] Eddison, *Fish Dinner*, xxviii.
[30] D. Cupitt, *Christ and the Hiddenness of God* (London: Lutterworth, 1971), 144.

that in the higher realms entities may move discontinuously, as some physicists have imagined that electrons do. Maybe only in our dream-world is it necessary for an entity that moves from P1 to P2 to occupy successively an infinite number of locations in between. The imaginary world of sub-atomic physics does not seem to obey this inscrutable rule: why should the gods?

But though it is not inconceivable that the higher realms are bodily without being restricted in the ways that our world is, there does seem to be something incomplete about the vision. Such a waking world would contain very many of the same incongruities as ours, notably the merely contingent relationship between outward sign and inward consciousness. Even a perfectly expressive flesh would not be the same thing as the spirit it expressed. Thought and the object-thought-of would not be identical. What the laws of nature were would be as little deducible from self-evident principle as the laws of our world. Certainly the waking world would be more comprehensible than ours, would provide a good account of why ours is as it is, but it would not be final, would not be its own best explanation.

So it might be as well to wonder whether the final awakening would not be to a world "not stuffed with flesh and colours and a great deal more perishable nonsense."[31]

Present-day fashion looks askance at any suggestion of disapproval for the bodily. The healthy attitude to take to Brother Ass is one of appreciation, though rarely modulated into worship. Donne's declaration of delight, "Her pure, and eloquent blood/ Spoke in her cheekes, and so distinctly wrought,/ That one might almost say, her body thought," has been remembered, though its setting, a joyous lament for Elizabeth Drury's death, is forgotten:

> But thinke that Death hath now enfranchis'd thee,
> Thou hast thy'expansion now, and libertie;
> Thinke that a rustie Peece, discharg'd, is flowne
> In peeces, and the bullet is his owne,
> And freely flies: This to thy Soule allow,
> Thinke thy shell broke, thinke thy Soule hatch'd but now.[32]

---

[31] Plato, *Symposium* 211e. See W. K. C. Guthrie, "Plato's Views on the Nature of the Soul," *Entretiens Hardt* 3 (1955), 3–24.
[32] J. Donne, "Second Anniversary," *Complete Poetry and Selected Prose*, ed. J. Hayward (London: Nonesuch, 1967), 221, 219.

There is no good reason to think that every expression of dissatisfaction with our present or any imaginable flesh is the product of sexual immaturity. There are moments, including many erotic moments, when "one might almost say, her body thought," when one is so involved and present in the flesh as to recognize no gap between our inner and our outer being. But it is also true that we can be mistaken even in this, and that the fact that to our eyes a body seems to be, for example, erotically charged, is no final proof that the person whose body it is feels the same. Even in those moments when we are brought together by our bodies, we are held apart by them — which, presumably, is why Milton allowed his angels greater scope:

> Whatever pure thou in the body enjoy'st
> (And pure thou wert created) we enjoy
> In eminence, and obstacle find none
> Of membrane, joint, or limb, exclusive bars:
> Easier than air with air, if spirits embrace,
> Total they mix, union of pure with pure
> Desiring; nor restrain'd conveyance need
> As flesh to mix with flesh, or soul with soul.
> But I can now no more . . .[33]

But though Milton's astral angels do not strike me as an "impossible compromise," it has to be admitted that the effort to describe the angelic biology is a little comic, because it seems to be so far from any properly spiritual or religious point. The advantage of the Real World over ours is surely not simply that it is inhabited by astral amoebae. That an infinite number of angels can dance upon the point of a pin is not a consequence of their especially airy nature, but of the fact that they are simple intellects: they no more exclude each other than my *attention* excludes yours.

So what is the waking world, the real world, in terms of which all lesser realms of being must at last be explained? According to Ibn Arabi "one and the same being can exist simultaneously on entirely different planes,"[34] and "the identity of a being does not stem from any empirical continuity of his person; it is wholly rooted in the epiphanic activity of his eternal hexeity."[35] The

---

[33] J. Milton, *Paradise Lost*, in *The Poems*, ed. John Carey and Alastair Fowler (London and Harlow: Longmans, Green, and Co., 1968), 848–49 (8: 622–30).
[34] Corbin, *Creative Imagination*, 226.
[35] Ibid., 202. "Hexeity" is Corbin's preferred spelling of "haecceity."

miraculous teleportation of Sheba's throne was not movement, if movement requires continuity through infinitely many point locations, but a new creation, a new manifestation or epiphany of something held eternally in the divine intellect.

> It is the throne in respect of its hexeity, its individuation determined in divine knowledge, but not in respect of its existence as concretised before Solomon.[36]

Electrons and other particles "move" in similarly exotic ways. If there are genuine cases of telekinesis it would seem better to suspect some such explanation than to suggest that matter was converted into energy of a detectable kind and then reconverted into the shape from which it came (an alternative SF model that retains a physicalist bias, but no plausibility). The great Plato scholar, Lutoslawski, who advocated, by the way, that one look upon "feeding [one's] body as upon the feeding of any other animal entrusted to [one's] care," also supposed that it was an underlying Self that created or manifested itself in a string of persons.[37] The unity is not given empirically even in the higher realms of being. Even astral bodies are only the epiphany of the divine ideas.

If bodies and spatio-temporal locations can be regarded as only the constantly recreated expression of an underlying non-bodily, non-spatial realm, what are the "hexeities" which make us "one and the same" through many false awakenings? In my original analogy it was proposed that the dream-experiences were to be explained by reference to the *oneirotokon's* interference with the brains and bodies of its victims. But all physical "causation" turns out to be occasionalist; all physical laws are at best the habits of God or the gods. What should explain is a realm of being which is its own best explanation. We can wake up to that only if we are already there. Our present world requires us to suppose that things are at a distance from each other, that being is always being *something* that excludes all other beings. If we allow ourselves to consider the alternative we may begin to see what the Real World might be like. In our essences we are not distant from each other. Every manifested being is in the same celestial place, as every character of the congregation of voices we find in our

---

[36] Ibid., 238.
[37] H. L. Lutoslawski, *The World of Souls* (London: Allen and Unwin, 1924), 71, 201.

earthly dreams is in the same place. All that is required to "be elsewhere" in the space-time world is to find what mathematically or personally intelligible essence is mapped into the space-time world at that other representative point.

This notion too has received assorted science-fictional treatments: "hyperspace," the all-too-frequent recourse of interstellar travellers in a hurry, is the fashionable version of the ancient *alam-al-mithal*, from within which the active Imagination or the multiple layers of created and uncreated Spirit can body forth the objects that we see: "Every sensible thing has a created Spirit by which the form is constituted. This created Spirit has a divine Spirit, by which it is constituted."[38] Similarly, in a story of Poul Anderson's, the interstellar traveller's problem is to find the magic formula which is represented in the space-time world by one location. Once one is characterized accordingly one is instantaneously migrated there. The story, like many SF stories, has more resonances than the author can handle: the travellers are themselves deathless, except by accident, and encounter, on an extra-galactic world, a race who believe themselves alone to have dreamed the universe, that they alone are gods. The longer the travellers live the more each of them is absorbed into the Idea of himself, as each chooses to forget what is accidental and unimportant to his life. Unfortunately, the author can only represent this phenomenon by letting his central, three-thousand-year-old character talk like a stage Irishman, always revisiting the three-thousand-year-old grave of his childhood sweetheart, dead before the end of ageing.[39]

Science fiction writers, I believe, regularly catch hold of myths and images which our earthly predecessors would have recognized. If the myth can be decoded, I would offer this: each of us sleeping intellects is a partial embodiment of an Idea, a theme, which is being tried against the manifold of realms. Our identity lies in our approximation to, our explanation by the eternal hexeity, abiding beyond space and time in the divine Intellect, which is our Angel. When that Angel opens its eyes again, our life will end, if what we are has been too far removed from that essence.

---

[38] Abd al-Karim Jili: Corbin, 245.
[39] Poul Anderson's story, *World without Stars* (New York: Ace Books 1966), also includes a character who has lost his idea of himself, and falls victim to the extra-galactics' offer of this-worldly peace.

All that is trivial and irrelevant in us will be forgotten; only what always is will be remembered.

> Whence came the soul, whither will it go, how long will it be our mate and comrade? Can we tell its essential nature? When did we get it? Before birth? But then there was no "ourselves." What of it after death? But then we who are here joined to the body, creatures of composition and quality, shall be no more, but shall go forward to our rebirth, to be with the unbodied, without composition and without quality.[40]

On Philo's account the immortal soul is to be distinguished from the personality or personalities we enjoy in this earthly life: our death is the re-emergence of the new creature, a new creature who can come to light (a little) even in this age. The yogi of whom Jung dreamed did not have *Jung's* face: Jung resembled the yogi, just a little, as befits a dream.

That our present lives are far from amusing, as Eddison knew, can also be explained another way. The Divine Imagining[41] has many nightmarish possibilities ever present to it: we are the instruments and the arena of the divine grappling with those threats. The gods might have left the nightmares unredeemed, might have agreed that nothing of their divinity could be expressed in such dire forms. They do not agree, and the proper way for us dreamers to behave is to remember what our waking selves, the selves we are not now, determined to do.

Which leads me to the final point I have to make about this model. Those who profess to act upon the view that this life is a dream, and human individuals of very little moment, not unnaturally frighten the rest of us. We do not feel safe with them, because they will not consider our lives or theirs as important as we do. We may agree that this is an understandable attitude, especially in ages when all life is cheap. How else could we cope with the imminent prospect of death for ourselves and for our

---

[40] Philo, "On Cherubim," 114: *On the Cherubim. The Sacrifices of Abel and Cain. The Worse Attacks the Better. On the Posterity and Exile of Cain. On the Giants.* Translated by F. H. Colson, G. H. Whitaker (Loeb Classical Library 227. Cambridge, MA: Harvard University Press, 1929), 76–77; see E. R. Goodenough, *Introduction to Philo Judaeus* (Oxford: Blackwell, 1962), 115.
[41] D. Fawcett, *Divine Imagining* (London: Macmillan, 1921).

family but by investing our emotional energy in something out of this world? We could, of course, ignore it, and occupy ourselves with entertainment and personal relationships. That is, in fact, what most of us do. We persuade ourselves that this is the better course by letting ourselves believe that anyone who devotes less energy to our games is likely to be cruel or callous, if she is not simply crazy.

> How can I describe this generation? They are like children sitting in the market place and shouting at each other, "We piped for you, and you would not dance. We wept and wailed, and you would not mourn."[42]

People who do not respond to things in the way we think they should both puzzle and alarm us. Understandably so: but are we right to think them cruel or callous? If earthly life is but a dream, the moral might seem to be that it should be treated carelessly, and those who agree to reckon it a dream will be dangerous and careless companions. But is that the moral that such believers have in practice drawn? Who are the greater villains in our world? Those who recognize that they and those they meet are expressions of an underlying unity, that the route to awakening is through remembrance of the divine pattern which is to be embodied in these nightmare realms? Or those who reckon the joys of earthly existence things to be fought for and defended, who imagine that they are separate and potentially inimical beings who live only as long as they can find the earthly necessities?

When paranoids and manic-depressives claim to have nothing but kindly attitudes to all mankind, this is interpreted as a cover for their repressed hostility. Statements about their own motivation made by sane people should be regarded with a similar open-mindedness. It is always useful to try the technique of substituting opposites throughout — e.g. "Sanity is a particularly sadistic state, and any deviation from it would be marked by sensitivity, kindness and generosity."[43]

What is objectionable in murder is not the death of the victim, for death is no extinction of the theme that was being played in her, but the denial of our common root. Those who believe

---

[42] Matthew 11:16f.; Luke 7:32.
[43] Green, *Human Evasion*, 96f.

themselves to be dreaming, in the way that I have been describing, do not ignore their experiences or the symbols that they see of other dreamers. They welcome them as old friends, and delight in coming to a mutual remembrance of eternity.

> It is truly a greater beauty than that when you see moral sense [*phronesis*] in someone and delight in it, not looking at his face — which might be ugly — but putting aside all shape and pursuing his inner beauty. But if it does not move you yet, so that you call someone like this beautiful, you will not when you look inward in yourself be pleased with your beauty. It would be in vain for you to seek beauty when you are in this state, for you will be seeking with something ugly and impure. This is why discussions about these sorts of things are not for everybody; but if you have seen yourself beautiful, remember them.[44]

By way of very brief conclusion: it is not, I would judge, unreasonable or unethical to postulate as part of our working program that we are the dreams of our angels, who are in their turn the dreams of higher and even less bodily beings. What wakes up in us when we remember this is not indifference to the company we keep but a renewed delight in them and the ideas they represent. That things are genuinely as I have described them I cannot prove. That we should adopt only such theories as can already be demonstrated from the (apparent) information acquired under the influence of some other theory seems to me to be an epistemological rule of no plausibility whatsoever. We are entitled to adopt such programs as bring us some hope of increased liveliness: in short, such programs as wake us up.

---

[44] Plotinus, *Ennead* V. 8 [31]. 2, 39–47. This and all subsequent quotations of Plotinus's *Enneads* are drawn from A. H. Armstrong's seven-volume edition and translation in the Loeb Classical Library (Cambridge, MA: Harvard University Press, 1966–88).

2.
Rudyard Kipling's Dreams[1]

KIPLING'S KIM AND DOC SMITH'S

Once upon a time there was an orphan boy called Kimball, known as Kim, whose special gift was to impersonate, and communicate with, peoples of all kinds. He was also exceptionally skilled in map-making and mathematics. He worked undercover to maintain the peace against powers who wished to impose despotic rule upon a thronging multitude of different trades, and cults, and races, many of them addicted to vile drugs that brought bad dreams. A high point of his career was the day he first put on the uniform prepared for him, even though he often had to put it aside, and work in disguise. As identification (in or out of uniform) he carried a gem, obtained only from a master of illusion (to whose powers he was himself immune, or nearly so).

This boy, whom I have described with careful ambiguity, might either be the chief hero of E. E. (Doc) Smith's space opera (namely Kimball Kinnison), first encountered in *Galactic Patrol* (1937), or else Rudyard Kipling's Kim O'Hara, Friend of all the World.[2] The comparison, of course, is ludicrous: the Lensman series of which *Galactic Patrol* is a part is pulp fiction, ill-written and poorly characterised. Its sole merit (or at least its sole claim to fame) is that it expounds an ancient myth in

---

[1] "Alien Dreams — Kipling," in David Seed, ed., *Anticipations: Essays on Early Science Fiction and its Precursors* (Liverpool University Press: Liverpool 1995), 172–94.

[2] I know one other science-fictional Kim, in David Wingrove's epic, *Chung Kuo: The Middle Kingdom* (London: NEL, 1989), and its sequels: the reference is explicit, but that Kim is more like a debased Mowgli. Robert Heinlein's *Citizen of the Galaxy* (1957) has been compared to Kipling's *Kim*, but there is no detailed correspondence between the characters and plots.

scientific (and pseudo-scientific) imagery: namely the perennial war between "Good" and "Evil" (each epitomised in an alien race that struggles over human, and galactic, destiny). Kipling's *Kim* (1901) is probably his single greatest work, and one of the profoundest studies of human affection, religious sensibility, and India, in the English language. There are also detailed differences between the two. Smith's Kim is unselfconsciously dedicated to the active maintenance of the law, and ready to kill any number of enemies (unless they're female). Kipling's Kim may carry a revolver (a gift from the Afghan horse-dealer and secret agent, Mahbub Ali), but uses it only once, and not to kill. The bond of affection between boy and Tibetan lama has no real parallel in Smith, nor yet the lama himself. A structuralist comparison uncovers yet more illuminating differences. Smith's Kim is nursed through convalescence (in *Galactic Patrol*, and also in *Grey Lensman*, 1951) by his predestined bride; Kipling's by a mother-figure, the talkative Sahiba, whom he had charmed into supporting his adoptive (grand)father, the lama, years before. Kim O'Hara's red hair and Irish ancestry is transferred to Kim Kinnison's eventual bride, Clarrissa (*sic*). There are also hidden identities: consider Kim's colleague and occasional companion, who constantly professes his own cowardice in literary periods (namely Hurree Chunder Mookerjee, on the one hand, and Nadreck the Palainian on the other). Or Mahbub Ali the horse-dealer, with his blood feuds and feigned hostility to all idolaters, and Worsel the Velantian (a flying snake). It may even be that Smith intended his Kim's third companion, Tregonsee the Rigelian, as an echo of the lama: Rigelians can sense the world in the round, and themselves, their particular identities, as of no greater significance than any other's. If that comparison was intended, it falls flat, since the Rigelian is as much an active soldier as the rest, and there is no special or illuminating bond between Smith's Kim and this image of four-square enlightenment. Kipling knew more about affection, and more about the realities of soldiering, than Smith.

It falls flat, perhaps because — along with other critics — Smith misunderstood Kipling's Kim, or else because Smith really intended to convey a different message. Maybe Smith really thought that *Kim* was an adventure story, set in a strange land, where the young hero rises from poverty to high office in a possibly decent empire (which is the plot of Robert Heinlein's *Citizen of the Galaxy*). Maybe he meant to *contrast* his Kim with Kipling's more pacific hero. Kipling's Kim acknowledges the attraction of Mahbub Ali and the Game, but his heart is given to the lama, and the novel ends with their joint enlightenment, their release from the Wheel exactly in the moment that "the wheels of [Kim's] being lock up anew on the world without," and the lama returns from "the Threshold of Freedom." This is not, by the way, a sign of "Christian" or "Western" influence: it is standard doctrine in the "Greater Vehicle" of Buddhism, the Mahayana (of which the lama is a devotee). Although it is absurd to ask "what Kim did next," there are plenty of clues within the text to suggest that Kipling meant him to vanish into the wide world: at the very least the records of his secret service, mentioned in the text, are said to have been thoroughly confused, and Kim is greatly relieved to hand the Russian documents he has captured on to Mookerjee. Smith's Kim rejects the possibility of enlightenment, to ally himself instead with the flying snake, and rise to be (in all but name) a king.[3] "I will teach thee other and better desires upon the road," the lama said.[4]

Does the comparison still seem ludicrous? The fact is that Smith, like other writers of science fiction, knew Kipling's work, and often quotes it (most notably the Ballad of Boh Da Thone),[5] even if he misses much of Kipling's irony. He may even have believed that he too sought to reproduce the speech and understanding of common soldiers and unlearned multitudes, who deserved to be protected from the imperial ambitions of those who aim only at dominion. Even his occasional references to "the Supreme Witness" may be a deliberate echo of "the Great Soul which is beyond [and contains] all things." That he was a far less able writer and thinker than Kipling is obvious; likewise, that he sought to honour Kipling by echo, commentary, and imitation.

---

[3] This was the choice presented to Siddhartha Gautama Sakyamuni: whether to be World Ruler (even a wise and compassionate one), or else an Enlightened Saviour. See Peter Harvey, "Buddha and Cakravartins," in *Encyclopedia of Buddhism*, ed. Damien Keown and Charles S. Prebish (London: Routledge, 2013), 153.

[4] *Kim* (London: Macmillan, 1901), 24.

[5] *Rudyard Kipling's Verse, 1885–1926* (London: Hodder and Stoughton, 1927), 252ff.

KIPLING'S SCIENTIFIC ROMANCES

Some of Kipling's stories are unambiguously science fiction. In the future he imagines in "With the Night Mail" (*Actions and Reactions*) and "As Easy as A. B. C." (*A Diversity of Creatures*), the Aerial Board of Control has unquestioned responsibility for the transport system "and all that it implies," and is thereby saddled with the whole burden of planetary administration. "Theoretically we do what we please, so long as we do not interfere with the traffic *and all it implies*. Practically, the A. B. C. confirms or annuls all international arrangements."[6] In *Kim* the one admitted gift of the Government to all India is the train; in the later stories the train and its equivalents (especially the dirigibles that carry almost all the traffic of the Planet) are the sole but sufficient business of all the Government our descendants can endure. "In *Kim*, the rulers carry out their lonely arduous task in order that the *diversity* of the Great Trunk Road shall flourish."[7] That condition—anarchy tempered by despotism—lies on the far side of a world-wide rebellion against "Whatsoever, for any cause,/ Seeketh to take or give/ Power above or beyond the Laws."[8] It is especially a rebellion against mobs: "the Planet, she has had her dose of popular government. . . . She has no—ah—use for crowds."[9] In the second story of the pair, Kipling imagines a statue of a negro in flames, bitterly inscribed "to the Eternal Memory of the Justice of the People" (that is to say, lynch law). He did not live to witness what India now remembers as "the Holocaust"—the ten million murdered in the Partition Riots— but might justly have remarked that this was what he had feared. Those who would bind us to do all and only what "the People" say (especially as this is given voice by "the word-drunk") are as much the enemies of personal liberty, and responsibility, as any literal kings. Kipling's principled, and often misunderstood, antagonism to "democracy," and to a rhetoric of "human dignity," will concern me later. His particular imagined future has echoes in the alternate world imagined by L. Neil Smith in *The*

---

[6] *Actions and Reactions* (London: Macmillan, 1951 [1917]), 138.
[7] Angus Wilson, *The Strange Ride of Rudyard Kipling* (London: Secker and Warburg, 1977), 247.
[8] "McDonough's Song," in *Rudyard Kipling's Verse*, 546f.
[9] *A Diversity of Creatures* (London: Macmillan, 1917), 5.

Probability Broach:[10] there too people insist upon their privacy, detest politicians, and travel by enormous dirigible.[11]

Others of Kipling's stories employ devices that might easily be science-fictional. Investigation of circadian rhythms, and the impact of external tides, lies behind a study of the relationship of millionaire patron, medical researcher, and patient, in "Unprofessional" (*Limits and Renewals*). Angus Wilson suggests that the story might be contrived more convincingly "now that science fantasy has been so much developed," to make its central point about the importance of imagination in scientific theorising.[12] A similar point, that new discoveries may rest on *false* hypotheses, is made in "A Doctor of Medicine" (*Rewards and Fairies*), whose hero finds an answer to the plague because he believes "Divine Astrology."

> Dare sound Authority confess
> That one can err his way to riches,
> Win glory by mistake, his dear
> Through sheer wrong-headedness?[13]

For Kipling, the answer is yes. The useful and the true, as I shall observe below, are not quite the same—and some truths, perhaps, are deadly: witness the premature discovery of the microscope, celebrated in one of his most brilliant stories, "The Eye of Allah" (*Debits and Credits*).

In "The Ship that Found Herself" and ".007" (both in *The Day's Work*; ".007" is a newly commissioned railway engine!) machinery is given a voice, and allowed to work through folly to mature responsibility. In very many stories non-human animals act out the same progression from childishness to adulthood, or else secure a place for themselves within an uncomprehending human world: so in "The Maltese Cat" (*The Day's Work*), "The Bull that Thought" (*Debits and Credits*), and the stories of *The Jungle Books*.[14] There is

---

[10]　L. Neil Smith, *The Probability Broach* (New York: Ballantine, 1980).
[11]　Edgar Allan Poe had imagined a similar system, in "Mellonta Tauta": *Tales of Mystery and Imagination* (London: J. M. Dent and Sons, 1908), 294–306.
[12]　Wilson, *Strange Ride*, 333.
[13]　W. H. Auden, "The History of Science," in *Collected Shorter Poems 1927–57* (London: Faber, 1966), 306.
[14]　See also "In the Rukh," in *Many Inventions* (London: Macmillan, 1893). This story entirely refutes C. Scheerer's suggestion that "Mowgli at the end is a tortured youth," unable to conceive of a happy adult life ("The Lost Paradise of Rudyard Kipling": in H. Bloom, ed., *Rudyard Kipling's*

a pair of monsters from the deep in "A Matter of Fact" (*Many Inventions*). Ghost stories, tales of magic amulets, and Kipling's satires on the heavenly bureaucracy ("On the Gate," in *Debits and Credits*, and "Uncovenanted Mercies," in *Limits and Renewals*) could all be given science-fictional readings—especially with respect to the Galaxy created without the knowledge of Death, or mention of the wondering sigh of new-born suns a universe of universes away. All these stories, that is, could have been provided with a richer background in real or imaginary science—and many of their devices have been used since Kipling's day by less able, but better equipped, "science fantasists."

But though the devices have been more adeptly used, Kipling's work is richer in ideas, as well as in human insight, than most. "The Brushwood Boy" (in *The Day's Work*), for example, imagines how an ordinarily decent young head of school, and soldier, can also be a figure in another world. Kipling quite deliberately makes his hero innocent beyond belief: the perfect head of school, and subaltern, moved by different sorts of dream. On the one hand, "his training had set the public-school mask upon his face, and had taught him how many were the 'things no fellow can do'" (it may be that Smith's Kim owes something to this paragon). On the other, he inhabits a dream world, "beyond the brushwood pile," whose geography he shares with a woman he met, once only, when they were children. The mask cannot ever have been all he was, any more than Kim can ever simply *be* a sahib. But better wear that mask than the one worn by too many of Kipling's parsons (the Reverend Bennett, for example, in *Kim*), just because it does represent a truth about proper obedience, decency, and courage. The Brushwood Boy lies on the edge of what has since become known as "portal fantasy": a child stepping through into another world, or finding that she is already there, in some other guise.

In all these stories (and many others that lie quite outside the broadest limits of the nascent genre) is the sense of a world beyond, a world with different meanings, a world that does not bend to the wishes of the undisciplined, those of whom the Muslim Shafiz Ullah Khan is made to write "If they desire a thing they declare that it is true. If they desire it not, though

Kim [New York: Chelsea House, 1987], 75–85, 76). On the contrary, he is portrayed as a good husband, father, and forest ranger—and is depicted thus by Lockwood Kipling in his illustrations for *The Jungle Book*.

that were Death itself, they cry aloud, 'It has never been'" ("One View of the Question": *Many Inventions*). Those afflicted by this condition can perhaps be cured only by dreadful experience, like the bumptious atheist McGoggin ("The Conversion of Aurelian McGoggin": *Plain Tales from the Hills*), who found that "something had wiped his lips of speech, as a mother wipes the milky lips of her child." "By the time you have put in my length of service," said the Doctor, "you'll know exactly how much a man dare call his own in this world."

That sort of experience, by Kipling's account, was especially to be found in India, where "the climate and the work are against playing bricks with words." In Town, he suggests, a man may naturally suppose that there is no one higher than himself, and that the Metropolitan Board of Works made everything. In India, full of "a raw, brown, naked humanity" between the blazing sky and "the used-up, over-handled earth,"[15] it is all too obvious that everyone is under orders, from the Deputy to the Empress. And "if the Empress be not responsible to her Maker—if there is no Maker for her to be responsible to—the entire system of Our administration must be wrong; which is manifestly impossible." Critics often fail to hear the multiple ironies in this bland remark, because they have convinced themselves, by careful inattention, that Kipling was "a bully, and a defender of bullies." The fact is that he was certainly no uncritical admirer of the Raj and of its officers: what he did admire was proper obedience, truthfulness, and mercy. The Protestant chaplain and his wife, who betray Lispeth (to return in *Kim*, as the Woman of Shamlegh), deserve Kipling's censure (*Plain Tales from the Hills*), but we might also acknowledge that "by some mysterious rule-of-thumb magic, [the English] *did* establish and maintain reasonable security and peace among simple folk in very many parts of the world, and that too, without overmuch murder, robbery, oppression, or torture."[16] That they are now attacked (not quite unjustly) for the sins they *did* commit (especially in the aftermath of the "Mutiny") is a

---

[15] "The earth is iron and the skies are brass": "The Masque of Plenty," in *Rudyard Kipling's Verse*, 36.

[16] "England and the English," in *A Book of Words* (London: Macmillan, 1928), 181. See Nigel Biggar, *Colonialism: a moral reckoning* (London: William Collins, 2023) for a mostly even-handed discussion of the British Empire, its faults and virtues.

sign that they set higher standards for imperial control than any earlier empire.

That we lie under orders, and dare call very little even of our mind and memory "our own," does not imply that we are helpless. On the contrary, by learning humbly how the world works, we can work with it: machinery, which Kipling loved, did not exist to dominate, or to control the natural world, but to take a careful advantage of it.[17] What social changes new machines will bring cannot always be predicted: optimistic liberals expect, for example, that the train will help to break down caste boundaries, since "there is not one rule of right living which these *te-rains* do not cause us to break."[18] But it is equally true that trains allow a stricter segregation than the older ways, since "well-educated natives are of opinion that when their womenfolk travel . . . it is better to take them quickly by rail in a sealed compartment."[19] What happens does not depend on what "we" say, or want — but there is no security in refusing change. It is that intense interest in how things work, and the recognition that there are no secure boundaries in space or time or possibility, that marks Kipling as a true precursor of the genre.

INDIA AND BIG WORLDS

In *Kim*, and in the other Indian stories, there is a sub-continent of varied and conflicting cultures, an alien and dangerous climate, secret societies, forgotten histories, and unexpected powers. The habits of its natives constantly outrage the etiquette and ethics of its British visitors, who find their own behaviour judged to be cowardly, mean-spirited, hypocritical, unclean, or pretentious, even while they themselves find native behaviour treacherous, or homicidal.

> And if you cross over the sea,
> Instead of over the way,
> You may end by (think of it!) looking on We
> As only a sort of They![20]

---

[17] See my "Tools, Machines and Marvels," in Roger Fellows, ed., *Philosophy and Technology* (Cambridge: Cambridge University Press, 1995), 159–76 (reprinted in *Philosophical Futures*).
[18] *Kim*, 40: this fear was one of the factors in the Mutiny, which was therefore as much *in favour* of oppression, as against it.
[19] *Kim*, 91.
[20] "We and They," in *Rudyard Kipling's Verse*, 709f.

What is significant in this is that there are after all shared standards in Kipling's India: despite the manifold conflicts, courage and hospitality and oath-keeping are to be praised by all. Smith's heroes (and those of many other science fiction writers) must also respect almost entirely alien moral codes, while still maintaining their allegiance to deeper, would-be universal standards. The frequent failures of the British (and perhaps especially of Protestant pastors) derive from their conviction that the natives are *merely* heathen and could neither appreciate nor deserve fair dealing. Their occasional successes turn on their realisation that caste, race, and creed are simultaneously real and finally unimportant. The English, Kipling thought, had been made "akin to all the universe" by their mixed origin, "and sympathetic in their dumb way with remote Gods and strange people."[21] Kim is Irish by descent—but no-one would be able to tell this from his habits: he is an English type, and therefore ready to believe that "to those who follow the Way there is neither black nor white, Hind nor Bhotiyal."[22] Not only to those who follow the lama's Way: those who "go looking for *tarkeean*" (which is the password of the secret service) also lie beyond all castes. Kim even transcends the grand division between European and Asiatic (though it seems he remains afraid of snakes and sometimes requires flesh foods—neither of which failings strike modern readers as either especially European or especially admirable).[23] The deeper division in Kipling's world is between those who know and those who don't, those who see the true significance of action and those misled by appearances.

Some of the peoples encountered in India—the Hill-folk of Shamlegh, for example—know almost nothing beyond their own locale and speak of elsewhere as a mystery: "the hot terrible Plains where the cattle run as big as elephants, unfit to plough on a hillside."[24] Others travel between these places, on foot,

---

[21] *A Book of Words*, 181.
[22] *Kim*, 303: this is not, of course, the *only* English type.
[23] In the earliest known version he had other ingrained European habits, which Kipling fortunately eliminated on his father's advice, along with far too many patronizing comments on the lama: see M. P. Feeley, "The *Kim* that Nobody Reads," in Bloom, ed., *Kipling's Kim*, 57–74.
[24] *Kim*, 369.

horseback, or by train. The last functions as "a place outside all places," moving outside ordinary time between locations, lifting Kim and the lama from Lahore to Benares to Delhi. Travel around India, whether it is the lama's search around the holy places for his River or Kim's holidays, lays the foundation for that vision of the whole that the lama at last experiences, and that regularly appears in science fiction. Consider, for example, Valentine's visions in Robert Silverberg's *Majipoor* trilogy: Valentine sees all the lands of Majipoor in the world-mind, as the lama sees everything in the Great Soul.

So Kipling's lama:

> As a drop draws to water, so my soul drew near to that Great Soul which is beyond all things. At this point, exalted in contemplation, I saw all Hind, from Ceylon in the sea to the Hills, and my own Painted Rocks at Suchzen; I saw every camp and village, to the least, where we have ever rested. I saw them at one time and in one place; for they were within the Soul.[25]

And Silverberg:

> The water-king carried him effortlessly, serenely, as a giant might carry a kitten in the palm of his hand. Onward, onward over the world, which was altogether open to him as he coursed above it. He felt that he and the planet were one, that he embodied in himself the twenty billion people of Majipoor.... He was everywhere at once; he was all the sorrow in the world, and all the joy, and all the yearning, and all the need. He was everything.... Everything enfolded itself into That Which Is. Everything was part of a vast seamless harmony.[26]

Edward Said's comment on the passage from Kipling, that "some of this is mumbo jumbo, *of course*,"[27] would better apply to Silverberg's. The problem with invoking science-fictional representations of familiar philosophy is that it invites *scientific*—that is, materialistic—enquiry. What sort of energies are involved

---

[25] *Kim*, 411.
[26] Robert Silverberg, *Valentine Pontifex* (London: Gollancz, 1984), 339f.
[27] Edward Said, *Culture and Imperialism* (London: Chatto and Windus, 1993), 172 (my italics).

in Majipoor's telepathy and dream manipulation? What sort of species are the water-kings, enormous sea-mammals who think of themselves as gods (and may remind Kipling-readers of Small Porgies, risen to shame Solomon)?[28] Kipling's more familiar version allows his readers to suppose either that the lama is describing a personal, psychological event which also needs to be transcended, or that he really is attuned to that Great Soul which lies beyond the realm of physical science.[29] That metaphysical vision (which is not certainly ridiculous) is also Silverberg's, but genre conventions require him to imagine that there might be mechanical aids for its attainment, and mechanical manipulation of the Underlying World.[30] The dream-world of the Brushwood Boy with its sudden terrors may have formed part of the background to Majipoor's economy of dreams. There, too, Silverberg gives the appearance of an explanation for what, in Kipling, needs no gloss.

Silverberg's sequence of stories, indeed, offers another gloss and transformation. They begin, like *Kim*, with a meeting between a childlike older man fallen from high office and a street-wise boy, within a vast world of many species, Majipoor. But the older man, radiant with good will though he

---

[28] *Just So Stories* (London: Macmillan, 1908), 208ff. The sea monsters of "A Matter of Fact" are sadder creatures.
[29] See also Plotinus: "Let it look at the great soul, being itself another soul which is no small one, which has become worthy to look by being freed from deceit and the things that have bewitched the other souls, and is established in quietude. Let not only its encompassing body and the body's raging sea be quiet, but all its environment: the earth quiet, and the sea and air quiet, and the heaven itself at peace. Into this heaven at rest let it imagine soul as if flowing in from outside, pouring in and entering it everywhere and illuminating it: as the rays of the sun light up a dark cloud, and make it shine and give it a golden look, so soul entering into the body of heaven gives it life and gives it immortality and wakes what lies inert.... Before soul it was a dead body, earth and water, or rather the darkness of matter and non-existence, and 'what the gods hate,' as a poet says" (*Ennead* V [10].2, 1, 13–23, trans. A. H. Armstrong).
[30] Peter Hamilton's *Night's Dawn* trilogy (Macmillan: London, 1996, 1997, 2000; *The Reality Dysfunction; The Neutronium Alchemist; The Naked God*) and other episodes in his Confederation universe, provide the elements of a mechanical, naturalistic account for most elements of folk-religion, including ghosts, demonic possession, and a literal *deus ex machina*. The only "religious" character in those novels is an unrepentant Satanist.

is, must at last climb back into the Hills to power, and the boy remains peripheral. The pattern is at once repeated: later in the sequence another orphan child, encountered as a guide in the underground Labyrinth that is the seat of legislative power, is befriended, educated through immersion—via their recorded memories—in the lives of others, and transformed at last into yet another king, and Valentine's successor when the older man does what he most hates, but what he sees he must, namely, to use force against the world's enemy (a challenge or temptation that the lama refused). The identity and differences here are evident, but it is Majipoor itself that re-embodies Kipling's vision of open country. The one thing missing from Kipling's India is Ocean, and that is lovingly restored in Majipoor, in the shape of an unnavigable hemisphere of water. It is probably an accident that the story replicates a medieval theory: Gregory Palamas, writing in the late fourteenth century, insisted that our inhabited world is an island, the protruding section of a globe of earth contained within an immensely larger globe of water (echoing here the Egyptian myth that the primeval mound, Atum, emerged from ocean).[31]

"Big Worlds" like Majipoor offer the greatest opportunities and dangers for science fiction writers: opportunities because as many races, cultures, places as they wish can be encountered there; dangers because the opportunity may sometimes reveal the weakness of the author's imagination. Big Worlds can be literal globes, or some imaginable artificial world (Ringworlds or Dyson spheres), or else a galactic milieu traversed by interstellar magic (like Kipling's train). They can also be expanses of alternate histories: movement between the myriad possibilities of human history (what if Alexander lived longer, or the Battle of Tours was won by Muslims, or Babbage's computer worked?)[32] also allows that sense of open country, and of possibility, that Kipling also offered. Kipling's India (and India itself) is densely populated: for the other aspect of Big Worlds we look instead to Kipling's Africa, as it is described in "The Explorer" (1898):

---

[31] Gregory Palamas (1296–1359), *The 150 Chapters*, trans. Robert E. Sinkewicz (Toronto: Pontifical Institute of Mediaeval Studies, 1988), 9–14.
[32] On which possibility see chapter 12 below, on singular and plural futures.

"There's no sense in going further — it's the edge of
  cultivation,"
So they said, and I believed it — broke my land and
  sowed my crop —
Built my barns and strung my fences in the little bor-
  der station
Tucked away below the foothills where the trails run
  out and stop:
Till a voice, as bad as Conscience, rang interminable
  changes
On one everlasting Whisper, day and night
  repeated — so:
"Something hidden. Go and find it. Go and look
  behind the Ranges —
"Something lost behind the Ranges. Lost and waiting
  for you. Go!"[33]

Just out of sight, behind the Ranges, there is a new world waiting,
which the later comers will enjoy and till, but never really see as
the First Explorer does.

POLITICAL IDEOLOGIES

Kipling, of course, needed less creative imagination (in a sense)
than later writers: he had only to represent the actual castes, cults,
and races of the real Indian subcontinent, and the actual experience of exploration, in Africa and elsewhere. The probability
is that he really did just that: certainly, those critics who declare
that he knew and understood much less than he pretended, that
he only voiced the British prejudices of his day, themselves know
very little, and mostly voice the prejudices of a *later* day. But it is
obvious that Kipling cannot be called "politically correct." His
crimes are manifold: he believed, or seemed to have believed, that
British rule was generally beneficial, even if it was often foolish;
he believed that its follies rested with the word-drunk politicians
or the parochial pastors who could not understand the honour
of an alien culture; he mocked Democracy and Human Dignity;
he doubted, with good reason, that "natural humanity" could
be expected always to be kind. That he also mocked imperial
pretensions, and prophesied the fall of empires, seems to escape

---

[33] "The Explorer," in *Rudyard Kipling's Verse*, 103f.

the notice of his modern critics. Also, that he could hear — and voice — what the poor thought of patronage.

> God bless the Squire
> And all his rich relations
> Who teach us poor people
> We eat our proper rations —
> We eat our proper rations,
> In spite of inundations,
> Malarial exhalations,
> And casual starvations,
> We have, we have, they say we have —
> We have our proper rations![34]

He seems to have believed — like almost everyone until late in the twentieth century — that there were some *hereditary* virtues, that it was possible to breed, train, and educate honest and intelligent officials, so long as we also recognized the underlying natures of particular lines, and the possibility of going bad. Good breeding is a value, but far less than good education, and the effects of dangerous responsibility. Greatness could emerge from humble origins (as Kim emerged). But those who now deny that breeding counts for anything apparently believe that human beings are not animals, even though they will usually also mock the suggestion that they are real souls. If we are — biologically — animals, then it is irrational to insist that there are no distinctive lineages, or that every lineage can produce any human character or talent (as though Great Danes could be bred together to produce chihuahuas). If we are something more, then our character and talent cannot rest entirely on our physical inheritance, nor even on our early education. Kipling believed (if "belief" is what we should attribute to creative writers) both that we were animals and that there was something else in us than nature and nurture could provide (as there may also be for "animals"). He was prepared to suggest, as he does in "With the Night Mail," that we are our fathers (a fable given slightly different form in stories about reincarnation). He also insisted that each successive incarnation of the lineal type must find its own way in the world, and might transcend its ancestry.

---

[34] "The Masque of Plenty," in *Rudyard Kipling's Verse*, 35ff.

This image, of a soul embodied in a body that carried its own character and value, is what many Indians (then and now) believed. Such a belief, notoriously, helps people to endure what otherwise would be unbearable: by bearing this life, whatever it is like, and doing the duties of my line and station, I may secure a better life hereafter. If I "am" a sweeper (and should act as such), it is still true that I, the abiding Self, "am not a sweeper." When Kim asks "Who is Kim?," the answer cannot be that he is simply a sahib (even if, in another sense, he is): that is, perhaps, *what* but not *who* he is.[35] One conclusion, of course, might be politically correct. Anyone of us is the equal, essentially, of any other, for all alike are "souls seeking escape." Difference and inequality lie in the realm of appearance. But precisely because all such are mere appearances, we do not need to be troubled by them. "India is the only democratic land in the world,"[36] for riches and political station give no special kudos. Holy men, and even spurious holy men, have kudos, *because* they have no riches or political station. We all have duties to perform, the "highest" as well as the "lowest," and acquire merit by recalling who essentially we are, and who we deal with. Asking that those not bred and trained, in this life, for high office should be trusted with those duties is risky; forgetting that those bred and trained for lower offices can be, and often are, our spiritual superiors is sillier by far.

Critics are right to say that Kipling and other British writers of the time sensed an affinity between Indian castes and British breeding. We have forgotten that hierarchies, with stable lines of descent and occasional intermarriage, have been the norm in civilized societies. The idea (that we hardly act on) that there should be absolute identity of opportunity, and absolute equality of respect, would have been wholly strange to most of our ancestors, except perhaps for bands of hunter-gatherers (at any rate while they are prosperous). "Inequality and wretchedness were then to be found in society; but the souls of neither rank of men [noble or serf] were degraded."[37] Kipling was orthodox in this, as he was in his dislike (which now seems dangerous) of Germans,

---

[35] For an elaboration of this insight, see my "Who is God": *European Journal for Philosophy of Religion* 8.4 (2016), 1–22.
[36] *Kim*, 5.
[37] Alexis de Tocqueville, *Democracy in America*, ed. H. S. Commager (London: Oxford University Press, 1946), 9.

Russians, and such other "breeds without the Law" who fail to acknowledge their fragility, or put their trust in arms.[38] Science fiction writers now may be more self-conscious in their political imaginings, but they are often like Kipling in being "politically incorrect." Hierarchical societies, perhaps with kings, and ones that lay great stress on personal and family honour, often manifested in martial or magical arts, are common in the genre. One of the most completely realised of those societies is that of C. J. Cherryh's Mri, but Poul Anderson's stories constantly repeat the same idea, often with explicit reference to Kipling.[39]

Liberal democracies live in uneasy balance: correct ideology requires that any human individual (or every "rationally responsible individual") be the equal in dignity and opportunity of any other, but no substantive effort is made to break down the ties of family, talent, and association which impede the realization of this vision. Such efforts would, most probably, create their own gross inequalities (occasionally imagined in such dystopias as Orwell's *1984*, or "ambiguous utopias" like Ursula Le Guin's Anarres[40]). The best we can manage, we could say, must be to imagine loathly opposites of our own preferred society. We cannot wholly create the liberal ideal, but we can at least imagine what "*illiberal*" societies would be, and find occasional antidotes. Or perhaps we might decide instead that "liberal" societies are not an absolute ideal. It is understandable that serious representations of illiberal societies are found more often in science fiction than in "mainstream" writing. Seeming to approve (even for debating purposes) of caste-bound, hierarchical arrangements is a scandal best avoided by representing different castes (of the kind that Kipling's India contains, and India) by different *species*. Whereas it is politically incorrect — and dangerous — to wonder whether there are human sub-species having different talents, characters, and dignity, no-one need deny that there are, or might be, really different *species*. Species do not usually interbreed, and generally breed true: that is why they are species. Pretending, or believing,

---

[38] His "Recessional" (1897) was written to warn against the arrogance he detected in Britain's imperial ambitions.
[39] C. J. Cherryh, *The Faded Sun* (New York: Daw Books, 1978–79), published in three parts, subtitled *Kesrith*, *Shon'jir* and *Kutath*. For Anderson, see *No Truce with Kings* (1963), and *The Enemy Stars* (1968).
[40] Ursula Le Guin, *The Dispossessed* (New York: Harper and Row, 1974).

that there might be distinct human species (castes or classes or races) is too dangerous to conceive, except in metaphor.[41] Correspondingly, it may be possible to give a sympathetic ear even to *horrendous* ideologies, if they are conceived to be the thoughts of other species. Any number of imagined enemies of a Terran empire, or the Federation, are depicted as calmly genocidal, caste-ridden and callous, and yet admirable, as we might admire (but not approve) a cat. So Chesterton:

> It is enough for me to say here that in this small respect Japs affect me like cats. I mean that I love them. I love their quaint and native poetry, their instinct of easy civilization, their unique unreplaceable art, the testimony they bear to the bustling, irrepressible activities of nature and man. If I were a real mystic looking down on them from a real mountain, I am sure I should love them more even than the strong-winged and unwearied birds or the fruitful, ever-multiplying fish. But, as for liking them, as one likes a dog—that is quite another matter. That would mean trusting them. In the old English and Scotch ballads the fairies are regarded very much in the way that I feel inclined to regard Japs and cats. They are not specially spoken of as evil; they are enjoyed as witching and wonderful; but they are not trusted as good. You do not say the wrong words or give the wrong gifts to them; and there is a curious silence about what would happen to you if you did.[42]

Even Chesterton saw some danger in thus imagining the Japanese as alien beings—better to imagine alien beings directly—but there will often be some echo of the original racist conceit. We can imagine beings, that is, who cannot transcend their species, and who do have natural virtues: they may be elegant and honourable

---

[41] Once there were many hominin species: some of us rather relish the suggestion—partly supported by DNA analysis—that we are, or some of us are, the mongrel descendants of Neanderthal (if we are Europeans) or Denisovan (if we are Asians) intercourse; some of us prefer to continue to suppose—without any good empirical evidence—that those other extinct varieties were subtly inferior to our own true line, that "we" have survived because we were and are just "better."

[42] G. K. Chesterton, "The Elf of Japan," in *Miscellany of Men* (London: Methuen, 1912): https://www.online-literature.com/chesterton/2604/ (accessed September 15, 2023).

in all their dealings with each other, while openly indifferent
to all other kinds. Klingons (from *Star Trek*), Merseians (from
Poul Anderson's future history), and Larry Niven's Kzin are all
embodiments of the spirit Kipling saw in Shafiz Ullah Khan.[43]

That picture of a Muslim warrior prepared to feign a common cause with Hindus for as long as was needed to confuse
an ignorant Britain no doubt seemed shocking to those who
believed that all men of good will must obviously love each other
(a dangerously ambiguous diktat). Even now (after much evidence
to the contrary) it still seems clear to some of Kipling's critics
(who are also critics of the British Raj) that the insurrection of
1857 ("the Mutiny") must *obviously* have been the action of an
Indian Nation which (others might reasonably hold) did not
at the time exist. Perhaps the loyal soldier Kim encounters was
correct to say that the mutineers were moved to carve out little
holdings for themselves now that, they thought, the British were
defeated. What justified "rebellion" against government? Modern
nationalists (who cannot easily pretend that the British Raj was
uniformly harsher or more violent than past or present native
governments) insist that it matters that the Raj was "British," and
not "Indian." In one sense, Kipling agreed: he dreamed instead
of a native European elite, with some Eurasian backing, who
would preserve the peace of an independent India, a marvellous
Dominion, precisely because they were not parties to ancestral
feuds between castes, races, and religions. "The English" held
Zam-Zammah, the great bronze gun of Lahore, and the Punjab,
as Muslims and Hindus had before them, by conquest and current
duty. But the subjects of that Dominion would have as little to
do with Government as most subjects of the British Isles themselves: the *consent* of the governed matters for the legitimacy of
government, but not necessarily their "participation," by symbolic
vote, or by official duties. Consent might actually be withheld if
we were all expected ourselves to work as political leaders, or if
there were any prospect of our immediate rivals doing so.

It may be that these political ideas — assigning power and
authority chiefly to a caste or class or profession kept separate
from the masses (as Plato devised in his *Republic*) — are dangerous,

---

[43] "One View of the Question" (1890), in *Many Inventions* (London: Macmillan, 1893).

or foolish. But it is not obvious that we should therefore sweep them aside, or castigate an author brave enough to hold them up to the light. If they are dreams we choose to reckon nightmares, we should still examine them, and think it possible that we are ourselves mistaken. Two dreams stand opposite to Kipling in this matter. The first requires us all to participate in government rather than to be content with managing our own particular affairs in an order preserved by government. But why should we surrender our control of our own lives to get a trifling share in the control of all? Older liberals felt less affection for Government, and wished not to give it any power beyond what would be needed to keep the peace, to keep traffic moving, and "all that this implies." Modern liberals may attack the Government, but chiefly because they wish themselves to govern, and will interfere far sooner while denying that they have any right to do so. If Government controls all our lives, we had better get our word in; if it tries to control very little, we might prefer to get on with our own lives, and not interfere with others. The Prime Directive, according to Nadreck the Palainian, is "Ignore and Be Ignored"! In "As Easy as A. B. C." those throwbacks who profess allegiance to Democracy (that is, to Voting on every question) are almost lynched (and eventually saved to become a comic turn).

The second dream is Nationalism itself, and it is one that sits a little oddly with other dogmas of our day, even though in origin "Democracy" and "Nationalism" are one in demanding that "the People" — conceived as a unit — rule. With one voice liberals insist that there are no sub-species of humanity, that every individual is to be judged interchangeable in law with any other; with a second voice, they insist that people are defined by nationhood, that it is an offence to be governed, even if well-governed, by any but those of our own kind and nation. Kipling, more realistically, acknowledged the importance of national (and other) groupings, but for that very reason denied that we should trust our lives entirely to one universal government. Good government is to preserve the peace between castes, sects, and nations, so that different groups can live their lives in peace. Better perhaps to be governed by people who are themselves subject to the laws they enforce on others, but this rule can easily be twisted: so Puritans of one sect or another will enforce the laws they themselves wish to live by, whether or not their patient subjects do.

TRUTH OR DARE

"What should they know of England who only England know?"[44] Kipling's question rests upon his deep understanding of the oddities, in space and time, of English, British, European attitudes. Not knowing what the other options are, we fail to understand or to appreciate our own. The liberties we now enjoy, the demands we make upon each other and the world, are not "natural" to humanity.

> Ancient Right unnoticed as the breath we draw—
> Leave to live by no man's leave, underneath the Law—
> Lance and torch and tumult, steel, and grey-goose wing,
> Wrenched it, inch and ell and all, slowly from the King.[45]

Kipling detested those without the Law, the irresponsible and greedy. He also detested, and with sharper venom, those complacently convinced that they *deserved* their lawful liberties, and that no-one could challenge their virtue. The song of an "English Irregular, discharged," Chant-Pagan:

> Me that 'ave been what I've been—
> Me that 'ave gone where I've gone—
> Me that 'ave seen what I've seen—
> 'Ow can I ever take on
> With awful old England again,
> An' 'ouses both sides of the street,
> And 'edges two sides of the lane,
> And the parson an' gentry between,
> An' touchin' my 'at when we meet—
> Me that 'ave been what I've been?[46]

That irregular remembers open country, "An' the silence, the shine an' the size/ Of the 'igh, unexpressible skies." There is something greater than "awful old England"—even if that same England, properly appreciated, is also "Merlin's Isle of Gramarye."[47] It is that latter because, to the discerning eye, it is full of strange, remembered histories, as alien and exciting as any contemporary land "beyond the Ranges." Imagining or rediscovering different

---

[44] "The English Flag" (1891), in *Rudyard Kipling's Verse*, 218.
[45] "The Old Issue," in *Rudyard Kipling's Verse*, 294.
[46] "Chant Pagan," in *Rudyard Kipling's Verse*, 453.
[47] "Puck's Song," in *Rudyard Kipling's Verse*, 481.

times and places, we can identify the principles we choose to act upon and understand our own place better. That was why, so Kipling said, Cecil Rhodes arranged his "game" so "that each man, bringing with him that side of his head which belonged to the important land of his birth, was put in the way of getting another side to his head by men belonging to other not unimportant countries."[48] Kipling's grasp of what other countries *were* important was somewhat broader than Rhodes's.

It was also rather broader than that of many modern writers who think that their own "modernity" is obvious and universal (and so think nothing of insulting those whom they can identify as "fundamentalists," "primitives," or "Neanderthals"). The commonest ideological stance in contemporary science fiction is an atheistic humanism, although its devices are often those of a more ancient metaphysics. By this account there is no overarching Providence, nor any difference that is not essentially *physical*. At the same time, there is a residual conviction that there is, within the human species, something quite distinctive, that will triumph over every possible disaster. Why we should imagine that this might be true is difficult to see, unless that the occasional denials of it (for example, by H. P. Lovecraft or Stephen Baxter) make depressing reading.

Consider "The Bridge Builders" (in *The Day's Work*): British engineers, much hampered by corruption, incompetence, and disease, have constructed a great bridge across the Ganges. A flood comes down, and one engineer, marooned upon a sandbank with his Lascar subordinate, beholds, as in a dream, the conversation of the gods of India about his bridge. Mother Ganges and Kali demand that the bridge be broken; Hanuman and Ganesh explain that those humans who admire machinery, and riches, are, unknowingly, their worshippers, and therefore wish the bridge to stand; Bhairon speaks for the Common Man, and Krishna persuades Ganges that the bridge, in any case, will stand only for a while. Krishna then predicts that all the gods, save he, will end their days as "rag-Gods, pot Godlings of the tree, and the village-mark," as Wayland Smith had ended in *Puck of Pook's Hill*. Shiva concludes by reassuring all the gods that they will exist as long as Brahm dreams (a remark the Lascar interprets to mean that they are all the *engineer's* dream).

---

[48] "Work in the Future," in *A Book of Words*, 259.

There can be many readings of this text. Are bridges, trains, and all the rest, attempts to dominate the world of nature, or ways of enabling nature? Are all the achievements of the engineers bound, in the end, to pass? Will the bridges, if they fail, be constantly rebuilt, to higher standards? Are the engineers in service, unknowingly, to Hanuman the Ape? Or is it that the people are at last to deny such godlings as are only the priests' excuse for begging? Who is Brahm, who will one day—possibly to our misfortune—wake? There is no absolute conclusion in the story. On the one hand, Kipling insists in many stories on the virtue of curing and preventing pestilence, famine, war. On the other, there is little chance of any final victory (which might, if it occurred, itself be a disaster). Maybe we must do honour to the little gods, but the gods whose presence we desire are those of forgiveness, order, and affection. Many of his stories do suggest that there will, in the end, be mercy, even if we have no adequate account of what the world must be to provide for it, and even if events here and now often seem incalculably cruel.

The Ocean demands truth:

> Ye shall not clear by Greekly speech, nor cozen from
> your path
> The twinkling shoal, the leeward beach, or Hadria's
> white-lipped wrath.[49]

The same is true of machinery, which is "not built to comprehend a lie."[50] Machines may be "nothing but the children of [our] brain," but they work by courtesy of natural law, a law that does not allow them to "love or pity or forgive." The other law of our being, which *is* to forgive, demands something more than trust in our machines. For despite Kipling's insistence upon truth, there is something to be said for fiction. "Splendaciously mendacious rolled the Brass-bound Man ashore...." Language, indeed, begins with lies. "No one in the world knew what truth was till someone had told a story."[51] Kipling identifies the "pride, the awestricken admiration of himself" that the First Liar experienced "when he saw that, by mere word of mouth, he could send his simpler companions shinning up trees in search of fruit

---

[49] "Poseidon's Law," in *Rudyard Kipling's Verse*, 631f.
[50] "The Secret of the Machines," in *Rudyard Kipling's Verse*, 675f.
[51] "Fiction," in *A Book of Words*, 282.

that he knew was not there."[52] All we know of Truth comes down
to "That that is, is":

> But it is just this Truth that Man most bitterly resents
> being brought to his notice.... He desires that the waters
> which he has digged and canalised should run up hill
> by themselves when it suits him. He desires that the
> numerals which he has himself counted on his fingers
> and christened "two and two" should make three and
> five according to his varying needs and moods.... In
> other words, we want to be independent of the facts;
> and the younger we are the more intolerant we are of
> those who tell us that this is impossible.[53]

Most of us, indeed, will find that it *is* impossible.

> As surely as Water will wet us, as surely as Fire will burn,
> The Gods of the Copybook Headings with terror and
>   slaughter return![54]

Some (and who can tell beforehand who they will be?) will follow their dream, their fiction, their God away from what was
imagined to be unchangeably the case and find a new world
waiting. "These were men who intended to own themselves, in
obedience to some dream, teaching or word which had come to
them"[55]—and we had best not fight against them!

> I'll not fight with the Herald of God
> (I know what his Master can do!)
> Open the gate, he must enter in state,
> 'Tis the Dreamer whose dreams come true![56]

That dreaming, and demanding, presence refuses to accept Things
as They Are, or as they are seen to be. Kipling said of himself
that he "visualised [the Empire], as [he did] most ideas, in the
shape of a semicircle of buildings and temples projecting into
a sea—of dreams."[57] On the one hand, this is folly: "for every

[52] "Independence," in *A Book of Words*, 234.
[53] *A Book of Words*, 235.
[54] "The Gods of the Copybook Headings" (1919), in *Definitive Edition of Kipling's Verse* (London: Hodder and Stoughton, 1940), 793–95.
[55] *A Book of Words*, 243.
[56] "The Fairies' Siege," in *Rudyard Kipling's Verse*, 508.
[57] Cited, without reference, by James Morris, in *Pax Britannica* (London: Faber, 1968), 255.

dreamer whose dreams have been good ... there are thousands who have been a hindrance to themselves, an expense to their families and a nuisance to mankind."[58] On the other hand, it is the source of all improvements, and all mercy. So the lama pursues his entirely fictional River, till the world invents it for him. So science pursues "the dream of an essential unity of all created things, ... the boldest dream of all, that eventually Man might surprise the ultimate secret of his being where Brahm had hidden it, in the body of Man."[59] So the explorer follows God's Whisper:

> Then I knew, the while I doubted—knew His Hand was
>   certain o'er me.
> Still—it might be self-delusion—scores of better men
>   had died—
> I could reach the township living, but ... He knows what
>   terror tore me...
> But I didn't ... but I didn't. I went down the other side....
> I remember going crazy. I remember that I knew it
> When I heard myself hallooing to the funny folk I saw.
> *Very full of dreams that desert*, but my two legs took me
>   through it...
> And I used to watch 'em moving with the toes all black
>   and raw.[60]

Truth matters, but so does Fiction. And Kipling had reason to suspect that many who mocked fiction were themselves deluded. A grimy realism, "a ram-you-damn-you-liner with a brace of bucking screws," will never reach the Islands of the Blest that are achieved by "the old three-decker," the romantic three-volume novel.[61]

Science-fictional devices, I suggested, often flow from a more ancient metaphysics, which reflects this demanding dream, that we can lay our hands upon the engines of the world or pray down the gods. Telepathy and interstellar travel alike are often referred to some Other Place, where all places are coincident. If only we could enter that Place, in thought or body, we could exit it wherever we might please. All minds, and times, and places, are

---

[58] "The Uses of Reading," in *A Book of Words*, 93.
[59] "Surgeons and the Soul," in *A Book of Words*, 227.
[60] "The Explorer," in *Rudyard Kipling's Verse*, 104f. (my italics).
[61] "The Three-Decker" (1894), in *Rudyard Kipling's Verse*, 327ff., an image splendidly realised in Michael Scott Rohan, *Chase the Morning* (London: Futura Publications, 1990) and its two sequels.

a step away.[62] Again: the pattern of stars, and human history, are caused by the acts of fire-folk overhead: galactic empires, Elder Races, gods. Machinery itself can speak the thoughts of greater intellects than ours. We ourselves will one day speak the thoughts of greater intellects. All these dreams give shape to the demand that things be Different, and to the conviction that How They Are depends upon a dream.

> Read here:
> This is the story of Evarra—man—
> Maker of Gods in lands beyond the sea.

Evarra makes "four wondrous Gods," declaiming on each occasion "*Thus Gods are made,/And whoso makes them otherwise shall die.*"

> Yet at the last he came to Paradise,
> And found his own four Gods, and that he wrote,
> And marvelled, being very near to God,
> What oaf on earth had made his toil God's law,
> Till God said mocking: "Mock not. These be thine."
> Then cried Evarra: "I have sinned!" "Not so.
> "If thou hadst written otherwise, thy Gods
> Had rested in the mountain and the mire,
> And I were poorer by four wondrous Gods,
> And thy more wondrous law, Evarra. Thine,
> Servant of shouting crowds and lowing kine!"
> Thereat, with laughing mouth, but tear-wet eyes,
> Evarra cast his Gods from Paradise.[63]

The "two sides to [Kipling's] head"[64] ensure that he gave due weight to both convictions: that we cannot stand against the Truth, and that we sometimes must. There is perhaps a possible resolution of the conflict, in the notion that there is indeed a God who calls us out from former certainties, but also requires a proper reverence for ordinary life. The lust for something New and Different, something that the Squire and Parson will not understand, is an important force in science fiction, and in Kipling: the

---

[62] See, for example, Poul Anderson, *World Without Stars* (1966); Orson Scott Card, *Xenocide* (1992); Melissa Scott, *Five Twelfths of Heaven* (1986), and its sequels.

[63] "Evarra and his Gods," in *Rudyard Kipling's Verse*, 335–37.

[64] *Rudyard Kipling's Verse*, 568.

lust for something new, and the knowledge that it will happen whether we lust for it or not. Those old before their time, "the Old Men" of Kipling's poem, may forget the obvious:

> We shall not acknowledge that old stars fade or brighter
> planets arise
> (That the sere bush buds or the desert blooms or the
> ancient well-head dries),
> Or any new compass wherewith new men adventure
> 'neath new skies.[65]

Science fiction is a genre that has chosen not to forget the obvious, and is therefore more genuinely realistic than most "mainstream" stories. Kipling is a precursor of that genre, in the devices and plot-lines he contrives, in the pleasure he takes in alien worlds and new machinery, in the political ideas he uses India and elsewhere to explore, and in the philosophical concerns his fantasies reveal. Some authors of Kipling's day employed their talents to express a fear that there were things "we were not meant to know." "Kim laughed. 'He is new. Run to your mothers' laps, and be safe.'"[66] Others closer to our own have chosen only to despise those small and ordinary people, who are too tired, or dull, or timid to escape. Kipling, as far as I can see, did neither. He did not despise the ordinary (only the complacent) and ensures that Kim at last returns to his (and our) Mother's lap, "the good clean dust . . . the hopeful dust that holds the seed of all life."[67] It is the oldest things that are always new: Krishna and Mother Earth. And they are to be found, at last, in our familiar places, won back from despair, as Kim wins back the world.

---

[65] Ibid., 318.
[66] *Kim*, 8.
[67] Ibid., 404.

3.
Psychopathology and Alien Ethics[1]

MORAL REALISM

There are many different ways of being, and many different sorts of feeling. Kipling's problem, and our own, is to find some ideal, or even some barely acceptable, way of living together despite such difference. One SF series (1993–98), *Babylon 5*, is devoted to that exploration, under Joseph Michael Straczynski's rule:[2] the station, Babylon 5, is presented as "our last best hope for peace," a place for many species and civilized societies to meet and examine their differences. It emerges, slowly, that this meeting, and all the species concerned, is watched, and manipulated by at least two older, more powerful, and prouder species, each embodying a fundamentally distinct ideal — as distinct indeed as Doc Smith's Eddorians and Arisians. In this chapter I shall pursue the examination I began for a conference on that series, organized by Edward James.

Most of us are rational realists. We believe that people may have different, and diverse, opinions, but that there are universal moral truths, without self-contradictions. Clitoridectomy, suttee, and child abuse, so most of us believe, are simply wrong, even if others mistakenly think them right.[3] Such truths indeed may

---

[1] An updated version of "Psychopathology and Alien Ethics," in Edward James and Farah Mendlesohn, eds., *The Parliament of Dreams: conferring on Babylon 5* (Reading: Science Fiction Foundation, 1998), 153–62.
[2] See Ensley F. Guffey and K. Dean Koontz, *A Dream Given Form: The Unofficial Guide to the Universe of Babylon 5* (Toronto: ECW Press, 2017) for a fairly comprehensive, though too often merely allusive, survey of the series and associated works.
[3] Even Michael Ruse, who has argued that moral feeling is simply an evolutionary adaptation, having no universal significance, has also admitted

be even more secure than ordinarily empirical generalisations: even if the standard syllogism insists "all swans are white," we are not perturbed to find that there are black swans. Finding righteous child abuse (I don't mean child abuse that someone *thinks* is righteous) is unimaginable. To find "scientific" truths as universal as moral truths we have to embark on scientific theory: quarks are the same wherever we may be, though living creatures, crystals, rock formations differ unpredictably. But we can still imagine entirely different quarks, entirely different "laws of nature." Recent cosmological speculation, indeed, routinely posits infinitely many such cosmic alternatives.[4] And even within this present cosmos we might discover that the "laws" change over time, or that what seemed "law-like" was only a local variant. Moral truths are different.

> Reason and justice grip the remotest and the loneliest star. Look at those stars. Don't they look as if they were single diamonds and sapphires? Well, you can imagine any mad botany or geology you please. Think of forests of adamant with leaves of brilliants. Think the moon is a blue moon, a single elephantine sapphire. But don't fancy that all that frantic astronomy would make the smallest difference to the reason and justice of conduct. On plains of opal, under cliffs cut out of pearl, you would still find a noticeboard: "Thou shalt not steal."[5]

It is perhaps not obvious that we shall agree on what "belongs" to this or another creature, and so what can be "stolen": it is enough for now that reason dictates that there are things which *don't* belong to us, and which others have a right to cherish. Chesterton himself was in no doubt that a good many of the things claimed by the rich weren't theirs, that much of their legal property was theft. The rule remains even for those who agree with John Chrysostom, that God alone is the true

---

that "the man who says that it is morally acceptable to rape little children is just as mistaken as the man who says, $2+2=5$": Michael Ruse, *Darwinism Defended* (Boston: Addison-Wesley, 1982), 275.
[4] See Milan M. Ćirković, *The Astrobiological Landscape: philosophical foundations of the study of cosmic life* (Cambridge: Cambridge University Press, 2012).
[5] G. K. Chesterton, "The Blue Cross" [1910], in *The Father Brown Stories* (London: Cassell, 1929), 27.

proprietor: the inference is that those who are granted the use of things are thieves themselves if they do not use them well, for the common good.

> The role the rich man plays, according to Chrysostom, is that of a steward, who temporarily holds and manages the wealth of the Lord for relieving the poor: "The rich man is a kind of steward of the money which is owed for distribution to the poor."[6]

That rational realism, I believe, is, in essentials, accurate, even if its details are often (as here) contentious. The reason and justice of conduct must be universal. What is really and essentially wrong for us to do, is wrong for anyone, of whatever star or species. It does not follow, of course, that we would be right to condemn what *looks* like evil conduct in another culture, species, or world without careful enquiry. Maybe we have misunderstood what's going on. Maybe it is we, not they, who were mistaken. Orson Scott Card's piggies, in *Speaker for the Dead* (1986), are not really torturing outcasts or criminals to death, but easing heroes into their third life. Science fiction is full of stories about people who arrogantly interfere in something they have not bothered to seek to understand. In *Babylon 5* the doctor Stephen Franklin's conceit—evident from his very first appearance ("Soul Hunter," 102)—leads him to operate on a Thalatine boy, without his patient's, the parents', or his own commander's consent. The result is tragedy ("Believers," 110). In "Exogenesis" (307) he is more prepared to learn, before

---

[6] Chen Yingxue, "John Chrysostom's Discourse on Property Ownership: An Analysis from the Perspective of Roman Law": *Vox Patrum* 83 (2022), 221–46: 237, quoting John Chrysostom, *Homiliae de Lazaro* 2, 4, *Patrologia Græca* 48, 988. See also Chrysostom, *Homily on 1 Timothy* 12: "Tell me, then, whence art thou rich? From whom didst thou receive it, and from whom he who transmitted it to thee? From his father and his grandfather. But canst thou, ascending through many generations, show the acquisition just? It cannot be. The root and origin of it must have been injustice. Why? Because God in the beginning made not one man rich, and another poor. Nor did He afterwards take and show to one treasures of gold, and deny to the other the right of searching for it: but He left the earth free to all alike. Why then, if it is common, have you so many acres of land, while your neighbor has not a portion of it?" In St Chrysostom, *Homilies on Galatians, Ephesians, Philippians, Colossians, Thessalonians, Timothy, Titus, and Philemon*, ed. Philip Schaff (Grand Rapids, MI: Eerdmans, 1956), 447.

acting against what seem to be B-movie parasites: the Vendrizi turn out to be symbiotes, with willing partners. His conceit is still considerable: he is, it seems, a potential "Vorlon" (one of the two Elder Peoples of *Babylon 5*'s universe), who thoroughly despises everyone else's opinion. In brief, he is in the wrong because he is always far too confident that others are. This is not, of course, an argument against moral realism. The very fact that we deplore ignorant interference, and acknowledge "the right" of others to live their own lives in the way they choose (so long as that same right is allowed to all), is itself evidence *for* moral realism: how could ignorant or arrogant interference be really wrong, if there are no real and universal wrongs? The piggies aren't wrong to do what looks like torture: they *are* wrong (in Card's *Xenocide*, 1991) to put an innocent to death, and the human population are wrong to retaliate by slaughtering the innocent. In *Babylon 5* (the series) both the Shadow and, in the end, the Vorlons are revealed as enemies of the "real right": it is right that we, the younger peoples, should be responsible for our own destiny, and right that we should cooperate ("Into the Fire," 406).[7]

SPECIES RELATIVISM: PROS AND CONS

This conclusion (if it is, as I suppose, the moral if not the dramatic conclusion of *Babylon 5*) is very familiar: all sorts of SF writers, from low art (Doc Smith or Keith Laumer) to high (James Blish), have sought to find another path between imagined "demons" and "angels." It is a theme which deserves examination, but my present topic is a different one. What are the limits of our rational tolerance? What could be "right for others" although indisputably wicked for us, and why would it be? Even if we accept that there are real truths, about which we might be mistaken, it may seem possible that different species demand different truths. It is certainly not true that human boys must ingest fresh sperm to grow to manhood (as one human tribe apparently supposes,

---

[7] Their departure echoes the conclusion of Smith's Lensman series: the Eddorians are expelled, and the Arisians willingly leave (*Children of the Lens*, 1954). So also at the close of *The Lord of the Rings:* Sauron and his Ring-Wraiths are destroyed, and the High Elves at least depart into the West. This is the dawn of the "age of men."

or pretends to suppose): something like this might be true of aliens.[8] Ivanova accidentally convinces the Lumati that Earth-humans are a superior people, by showing them the lower levels of the station, and the under-class of lurkers ("Acts of Sacrifice," 212). In us, the creation and exploitation of the underclass is an iniquity: for the Lumati it is a proof of our obedience to the laws, in effect, of Social Darwinism (laws later praised by spokesmen of the Shadows: "Z'ha'dum," 322). Are they right to think that this is what they should do, even if they are wrong to think we should? The Drazi regularly divide themselves into two peoples (Green and Purple) who fight, potentially to the death, till one side wins ("The Geometry of Shadows," 203). Ivanova attempts to argue that our own national or ideological divisions are at least about something, but might be uncomfortably aware that birth and circumstance dictate allegiance just as arbitrarily, and that it is easy to create two hostile groups within a psychological exper-iment by random allocation. In us, this is something to resist: is it similarly wrong for the Drazi? Their spokesman urges that the matter is for Drazi to decide—just before being inadvertently deprived of the token of Green leadership, and so being com-pelled to surrender. "Rules of contest older than contact with other races—do not mention aliens. Rules change caught up in committee—not come through yet."[9] So he was wrong—even on his own terms—to say that "aliens" should not interfere.

These are frivolous examples, but the issue is more real. What might be wrong in us, and right in aliens? And why? The issue has been discussed by several philosophers, but rather few of us have used the insights of science fiction. Michael Ruse, writing in a paper entitled "Is Rape Wrong on Andromeda?,"[10] wishes that "science fiction" were not thought too childish for serious philosophers to take seriously. It is perhaps unfortunate that he did not himself take it more seriously: we might then be spared the curious delusion that "Andromeda" names a planet, or something

---

[8] See also Poul Anderson, "The Sharing of Flesh" (1968), in *The Dark Between the Stars* (New York: Berkley Books, 1981). An isolated human community has turned cannibal because they cannot mature without hormones from an adult human liver. Improved medical techniques from stellar explorers offer an obviously better solution.

[9] See Andy Lane, *The Babylon File* (London: Virgin, 1999), 186.

[10] Michael Ruse, "Is Rape Wrong on Andromeda?," in Ruse, *The Darwinian Paradigm* (London: Routledge, 1989), 209–45, 210.

that a rape might be "on."[11] We might also be spared repeated use of *ET* and *Star Wars*, without any reference to the very many more serious works of science fiction, including *Babylon 5*.

A great deal of SF plays with the question whether some psychotic fantasy might be really true. Maybe people really are being abducted by aliens: witness the court-room scene in an early episode ("The Grail," 115). Maybe Jack the Ripper lives ("Comes the Inquisitor," 221), or even Tennyson's Arthur ("A Late Delivery from Avalon," 313). Maybe even the most detailed and convincing happening is a dream ("And the Sky full of Stars," 108; "A Race through Dark Places," 208). C. J. Cherryh, Orson Scott Card, and others have done their best to imagine what would have to be true for it to be right to torture your friend to death, or to betray your species. *Babylon 5* did not go so far — though "species-betrayal" may be close to what is going on.

What is at issue for Ruse, and others, is the very rational realism that, I said, we all mostly endorse. If our moral attitudes are determined by our evolutionary (and our cultural) history, then we may expect that different species will have very different attitudes.

> Human behaviour — like the deepest capacities for emotional response which drive and guide it — is the circuitous technique by which human genetic material has been and will be kept intact. Morality has no other demonstrable function.[12]

That is, or so the distinguished biologist E. O. Wilson also declared, there is nothing else that "morality" consistently does, and that explains the particular shape it takes in one tribe or another. Neither claim — that it has this effect consistently and

---

[11] Ruse partly corrected his original error (from an earlier version in Ed Regis, ed., *Extraterrestrials* [Cambridge: Cambridge University Press, 1985], 43–78) by speaking rather of "a planet in Andromeda" on one line ("Is Rape Wrong," 221), but continued to say "on Andromeda" both in the chapter title and on four other occasions in the chapter.

[12] E. O. Wilson, *On Human Nature* (Cambridge, MA: Harvard University Press, 1978), 167. For my usual criticisms of this silly claim, see "Have Biologists Wrapped up Philosophy?": *Inquiry* 43 (2000), 143–66, and "Post-humanism: engineering in the place of ethics," in Barry Smith and Berit Brogaard, eds., *Rationality and Irrationality: Proceedings of the 23rd International Wittgenstein Symposium* (Vienna: Öbv & Hpt, 2001), 62–76. These essays, mildly modified, are reprinted in *Philosophical Futures* (Frankfurt am Main: Peter Lang, 2011), 115–38, 158–72.

that there are no other possible explanations for its forms — is beyond dispute. Even if they are true, it does not follow, of course (though Wilson seems to think it does) that we would therefore have good reason to *amend* our moral code to help preserve that material,[13] as though nothing mattered even to us, let alone universally, other than the preservation of some arbitrary proportion of our DNA — most of which we share with many other earthly species — over however many million years. When C. S. Lewis described the planetary angel Malacandra's conversation with a corrupt scientist, in his interplanetary fantasy, he can hardly have imagined that anyone would so readily admit the charge:

> You do not love any one of your race . . . You do not love the mind of your race, nor the body. Any kind of creature will please you if only it is begotten by your kind as they are now. It seems to me . . . that what you really love is no completed creature but the very seed itself; for that is all that is left.[14]

But we can still acknowledge that there is some strength in the relativist, biological case. It has, from the beginning of rational analysis, been clear that what one sort of creature finds repulsive, another finds delightful. We have evolved to find different foods, surroundings, partners desirable, and the tastes we have — in all these matters — may be expected to be the ones that paid us, or rather our ancestors, or at least did not damage our/their prospects too severely. Introducing new tastes must always be a delicate matter: perhaps they will conflict with age-old tastes, or lead us down into an evolutionary dead end. Maybe some tastes, in a different age, are damaging (like a taste for sugar), and should be disciplined. Maybe other dietary changes will be toxic. Might it be as absurd to expect an alien to respond to our ethical concerns as to expect them to enjoy our food, or lust after nubile humans, or be touched at the sight of happy children?

---

[13] A claim that H. G. Wells vehemently — and irrationally — endorsed: "if the universe is non-ethical by our present standards, we must reconsider those standards and reconstruct our ethics": H. G. Wells, *Anticipations* (1902) chapter 9, in *Anticipations and Other Works* (London: Fisher Unwin, 1924), 248. I have examined this delusion at greater length in *Can We Believe in People* (Brooklyn, NY: Angelico Press, 2020).

[14] C. S. Lewis, *Out of the Silent Planet* (London: Pan Books, 1952 [1938]), 163.

Consider a conversation in Becky Chambers's imagination of a future, almost peaceful, interspecies confederation, between a human ship-captain and a sort-of-reptilian friend, about the latter's wish to interfere with a colleague's (biologically determined) choice to die rather than accept a medical intervention:

> Ashby got to his feet. "What is it you people say? *Isk seth iks kith*? Let each follow *xyr* own path?" Sissix's eyes flashed. "That's different." "How so?" "That means don't interfere with others if there's no harm being done. There is harm being done here, Ashby. Ohan is dying." "If I told you to go back to Hashkath and bring your kids here to live with you, would you?" "What are you even talking about?" "If I told you that treating your children like strangers offends every bone in my milk-fed mammalian body, and that as your Human captain, I expect you to follow my moral code—"[15]

We may not feel as other species do, but this does not prevent all possibility of friendly understanding. Both mammalian and reptilian species care for their young, even if that care is manifest in very different ways. The same would be true even for species that spawned as indiscriminately as frogs, and accepted that their tadpoles would compete and even kill each other (or even be culled by their fathers).[16] But achieving a viable consensus between such disparate biologies will indeed be hard: must it amount simply to *"isk seth iks kith"*?[17] That will be possible, perhaps, if the different kinds acknowledge the others' good faith, and think them worth respecting.

Ruse appears to conclude, conversely, that there need be no *moral* feeling towards or between aliens: nothing would restrain us "ethically" (or them) from using or exterminating the Other if we

---

[15] Becky Chambers, *The Long Way to a Small, Angry Planet* (London: Hodder and Stoughton, 2015). Sissix's species feels no special parental attachment to their offspring, but is otherwise both kind and loyal.
[16] See Frank Herbert, *The Dosadi Experiment* (New York: Putnam, 1983): this is Gowachin practice.
[17] C. J. Cherryh has devoted much of her work to examining how such disparate species might come to respect or admire each other: see my "C. J. Cherryh: The Ties that Bind," in David Seed, ed., *Yearbook of English Studies* 37.2 (London: Maney Publishing, 2007), 197–214 (republished in Clark, *Philosophical Futures*).

had the power. How could we feel otherwise about creatures that are likely to evoke disgust or fear, merely by their appearance or their smell? Should we be kind to spiders? Should we reasonably think that spiders should be kind to us?[18] The Pak'ma'ra have a taste for slightly decayed flesh (including that of fellow sapients — and maybe a lost Minbari hero: "Legacies," 117). Nothing that looks like a huge centipede and wraps itself around the spinal column (as Vendrizi do) could possibly mean well (and who cares whether they do?). Insectile intelligences must be simply wicked, or at least inhuman. Even creatures that look — as far too many TV aliens look, even on Babylon 5 — like humans, but with horrendous skin complaints and peculiar noses, are bound to be our enemies.

If Ruse was right to suppose that ethical judgment rests, *correctly*, on such deeply felt and easily explicable tastes and that the alien must usually be disgusting, and must always be irreconcilable rivals, then Babylon 5 (the station) would be impossible. None of us could long endure to be complaisant. So far from being our last best hope for peace, or victory, or even a quick buck, it would be far worse than Ireland, Bosnia, "the Middle East," or Rwanda, populated by creatures that could never be reconciled genetically through the hope of shared descendants — though the Narn think this *might* be practicable ("The Gathering," pilot episode), and the Minbari believe it's happening through the transfer of Minbari souls ("Points of Departure," 201), or through Valen's — which is to say, Sinclair's — descendants ("Atonement," 409).[19] Perhaps the best that we could expect is for some species to be successful predators (as the Lumati wish), and farm their prey. The most B-movie episode of all ("Grey 17 is Missing," 319) perhaps projects that answer (presumably we must imagine — it takes some imagining — that the monstrous Zarg is something like Ridley Scott's Alien).[20] For most science fiction readers that reaction is culpably xenophobic: one associated with various early SF writers, and even "that [supposed] master of the cosy

---

[18] See Adrian Tchaikovsky, *Children of Time* (New York: Tor Books, 2015).
[19] The first commander of Babylon 5, already identified by the Minbari as — astoundingly — himself Minbari in essence, is transformed into an obvious Minbari, and transported back a thousand years to become that species's founding prophet: the full implications of this strange causal loop — otherwise known as "the Bootstrap Paradox" — are not examined.
[20] In *Alien* (1979) and its sequels. The eponymous alien was designed by H. R. Giger.

catastrophe,"[21] John Wyndham. One of the many oddities of teachers at least in British schools is that Wyndham's novel *The Chrysalids* is lazily interpreted as a liberal manifesto in favour of toleration, "a powerful post-apocalyptic allegory of persecution and intolerance": it is true that telepathic mutants are rescued from their bigoted families—but only by more successful tele-paths, who think nothing of quietly killing "normal," and other, less useful mutants, and themselves agree that the bigots were correct to try to eliminate their deviants. Likewise, in *The Midwich Cuckoos* (filmed as *Village of the Damned*, 1960), the children created by alien invaders are eradicated by their supposedly "liberal" mentor, with the author's apparent approval.[22]

Most of us believe we can and should transcend mere local and tribal prejudice, and learn to see the beauty of an alien way. That is as true of low SF as high: Doc Smith's aliens may, by parochial standards, be cowardly, conceited, melancholic, or deranged, but are all to be reckoned colleagues in the exercise of contemplative and practical virtue. First Lensman Samms comments on the Palainians:

> Some of their codes and standards seem to be radically different from ours—so utterly and fantastically different that I simply cannot reconcile either their conduct or their ethics with their obviously high intelligence and their advanced state of development. However, they have at least some minds of tremendous power, and none of the peculiarities I deduced were of such a nature as to preclude Lensmanship.[23]

---

[21] One of the many critical misreadings in Brian W. Aldiss, *Billion Year Spree* (New York: Doubleday, 1973); see 293.

[22] John Wyndham, *The Midwich Cuckoos* (London: Michael Joseph, 1957), 112–13: "There is no conception more fallacious than the sense of cosiness implied by 'Mother Nature.' Each species must strive to survive, and that it will do, by every means in its power, however foul." Even as a merely biological comment this is foolish. But it is at least not "cosy." See David Ketterer, "'A Part of the . . . Family': John Wyndham's *Midwich Cuckoos* as Estranged Autobiography," in Patrick Parrinder, ed., *Learning from Other Worlds: estrangement, cognition and the politics of science fiction and utopia* (Liverpool: Liverpool University Press, 2000), 146–77.

[23] E. E. ("Doc") Smith, *First Lensman* (Vachendorf: Serapis Classics, 2017 [1950]), 49. A little later (165), Smith acknowledges, with an enormous effort, that Palainians, despite being, by their own confession, "selfish, mean-spirited, small-souled, cowardly, furtive, and sly," might still be able to serve

The only species to be reckoned irredeemable in the *Lensman* series are the Eddorians (from another universe) and — exceptionally — the Overlords, whose only apparent talent is to compel obedience (and use it for sadistic purposes). High science fiction constantly presents the vision of a fully cooperative and mutually appreciative company, even if it is always put at risk by open or covert aggrandisement. Delenn's odd claim (reaffirmed by Londo and G'Kar) that it is a specifically human talent to create communities ("And Now for a Word," 215) signals the importance of such meeting places. As a biological claim it seems implausible; as an allegorical, it is reminiscent both of Kipling's remarks about the English, and of Gordon Dickson's thesis that only "full spectrum humanity" can coordinate and preserve the "splinter Cultures."[24] Imagined aliens, almost inevitably, tend to be merely isolated aspects of our own humanity, in need of reconciliation. But we can still step, in imagination, into a context where we can and maybe must make peace with entirely alien neighbors: the fact that they look or smell or sound repulsive (as we do to them) does not excuse our disrespecting them. There is more to morals than immediate emotion. And more than the grotesque idea that each species is itself an entity necessarily at odds with every other (as if one species could even survive without innumerable others, and as if species were well-defined).

An evolutionary relativism of Wilson's or Ruse's kind (in short) is not what is needed as the basis for a mutual tolerance of expectable diversity, even if at first it sounds commendably "tolerant." Real tolerance — which would exclude, for example, tolerance for a species or culture "determined" to erase all other forms of life — must be grounded in a hope which transcends parochial or merely biological concerns. But the problem still remains: what are the proper limits of toleration or assistance? The Markab endure species extinction rather than admit their shame ("Confessions and Lamentations," 218), and the Thalatines reject surgical intervention rather than endanger their soul's life ("Believers," 111). Both these events are grounded in a belief-system whose connection with their distinct biologies is

the good of all, and wish to. The rather unsophisticated utilitarianism of Smith's own moral universe may actually be a greater danger!

[24] See especially *The Final Encyclopedia* (London: Sphere Books, 1984), and *Chantry Guild* (New York: Ace Books, 1988).

unexplored. Perhaps the Thalatines are correct, and something *does* escape from their bodies (which are, after all, only humanoid for dramatic convenience) during surgery. Perhaps on the other hand the ban on surgery is only (but still seriously) part of the religious and cultural identity of particular Thalatines: orthodox Jews have died rather than eat pig-meat; Christians rather than burn incense to the emperor; Greek philosophers rather than shave their beards. Franklin's disagreement rests on his apparent conviction—perhaps born of Oedipal antagonism with his father (see "GROPOS," 210)—that any individual life should be preserved at any cost (and that he knows "the facts"). Unless there is a biological difference, the story could be told, as easily, in non-science-fictional terms. Should a child be given blood, or a new organ, over the protests of the parents? Who then has responsibility for the life that has been saved (Franklin should have, but is adept at escaping responsibility: see "Shadow Dancing," 321)? Who is subject to the authority of any particular court?

Pak'ma'ra, remember, eat decaying flesh (including that of fellow sapients, if they can get it). Is it wrong to be a ghoul? The Lumati are slave-masters. The Drazi love violence, and live food ("The Long Dark," 205). The Narn have a legally approved Assassin's Guild ("The Parliament of Dreams," 105). The Dilgar are universally loathed (and it just so happens that their sun became a nova) as lacking any empathy ("Deathwalker," 109), but can they help it? The Vendrizi happen to be benign; but what if—like Heinlein's puppet masters[25]—they weren't? Conversely, could a zarg acquire a liberal conscience? What must be true if it could?

Gilbert Harman argues, to similar effect, that nothing can be obliged to do what it cannot feel to be good.[26] It can't be said that a predator ought to consider its victim's feelings or interests: there is simply no such possibility in the predator's mindset. C. J. Cherryh's Kif (in the *Chanur* sequence) eat live food, including each other, and feel no remorse: expecting "humane" behaviour from them, or "blaming" them for their nature, is pointless. The rules of Cherryh's interspecies Compact may be no more than the rules that desperate brigands might devise to secure themselves

---

[25] Robert Heinlein, *The Puppet Masters* (New York: Doubleday, 1951); see also Eric Frank Russell, *Three to Conquer* (London: Penguin, 1956), 163.
[26] Gilbert Harman, "Moral Relativism Defended," *Philosophical Review* 84 (1975), 3–22.

against avoidable assault.[27] Maybe there are advantages, from everyone's point of view, in maintaining rules of exchange and agreed boundaries. But this is to assume that there are things which all parties really want more than any of the things they severally want. It is not clear that *everyone* wants "peace," or can even conceive of "peace" as more than an armed and impermanent truce.

Some of these practices are cultural variations well within our grasp. If we think them wrong it is not because they are biologically impossible for us, or even biologically inappropriate. The Pak'ma'ra are thieves and scavengers, but so (on one plausible theory) were our own ancestors: we were not confined to that role, nor need they be. Darwin's declaration, in the first edition of *The Descent of Man*, that "if men were reared under precisely the same condition as hive-bees, there can hardly be any doubt that our unmarried females would, like worker bees, think it a sacred duty to kill their brothers, and mothers would strike to kill their fertile daughters, and no one would think of interfering,"[28] was absurd, and Sidgwick's comment (cited by Darwin in later editions) that "a superior bee would aspire to a milder solution of the population problem"[29] at least apt. Drazi, Nam, and Dilgar (though we only encounter one of the last) have simply chosen amongst the possibilities. Cherryh's hani (in the *Chanur* sequence) imagine that their natures dictate their social pattern, that males *cannot* control their tempers, and must either die young or fight their way into a household where they live, until evicted, only to sire young: they are — at least in Cherryh's story — mistaken. In *Babylon 5* the Narn at least have other resources, and owe most of their present character to a century of control by the Centauri Republic. The Centauri themselves destroyed another sapient species on their world without regret or compunction (the Xon: "The Parliament of Dreams," 105).[30] But the main theme of *Babylon 5* (the series) is that all this was done by choice. "The show," Straczynski has said, "is fundamentally about three things; choices, consequences,

---

[27] As J. L. Mackie proposed as a model for our moral judgments (*Ethics: inventing right and wrong* [London: Penguin, 1990 (1977)]), without entirely explaining why such agreements should have any moral force.

[28] Charles Darwin, *The Descent of Man* (London: John Murray, 1871), 1:86.

[29] Henry Sidgwick, *The Academy*, June 15, 1872, 231; see Darwin, *Descent of Man*, 1:99.

[30] It is possible, but not certain, that our own ancestors did the same to Neanderthals, Denisovans, and multiple other hominin species.

and responsibility for those consequences and choices."[31] Vir's plea to Londo (which he ignores): "you don't have to do this" ("The Coming of Shadows," 209). In "Intersections in Real Time" (418), the interrogator reveals his iniquity by constant refusal to accept responsibility for his own action. The responsibility, and the consequences, remain. Having done it, whatever it is, *Babylon 5*'s characters have to endure the results.

This theme — the fundamental significance of individual responsibility — may be one reason why *Babylon 5*'s aliens, though richly conceived by televisual standards, are less alien than they might be. The Vendrizi are descants on Heinlein's puppet masters. The Lumati, I suspect, offer some slight homage to one of Poul Anderson's creations:[32] two sapient and symbiotic species who have so fully occupied the roles of master and domestic that they cannot conceive the possibility of freely chosen loyalty or obedience — one who acknowledges another's authority can be nothing but a domestic — and if there is no obvious master around, the apparent domestic is, as it were, a mad dog. The three castes of the Minbari (and our war with them) echo C. J. Cherryh's Mri: whereas Cherryh's humans regularly break ranks and join the opposition, socialising themselves as imitation aliens, the Mri cannot, must not be, anything but Mri.[33] In Babylon 5 Delenn and Sinclair each join the other species (perhaps in an echo of Tolkien's Luthien or Arwen,[34] and Tuor). In human beings (and other primates) the young are the focus of attention: for Cherryh's regul (also in *The Faded Sun*) it is instead the few who mature to adulthood who, like the Gowachin, cull their young. Her Kif (in *Chanur*) are cannibalistic egoists, incapable of grasping "friends" as anything but allies of convenience, who may soon be rivals. Her Atevi (in the *Foreigner* sequence) also cannot comprehend friendship or sentimental affection, but manage deeply rooted loyalties incomprehensible to the Kif. Conversely, her Iduve (in

---

[31] Lane, *The Babylon File*, 39.
[32] Poul Anderson, "The Master Key," in *Trader to the Stars* (London: Gollancz, 1965).
[33] These appear in the three volumes of *The Faded Sun*.
[34] Delenn is like Luthien in being an active participant in the war, constantly at odds with those of her own people who disapprove of human entanglements, and in seeking to get her lover back from death; she is like Arwen in being, herself, of human-Minbari (human-elf) descent, being the mother of a new beginning, and outliving Sheridan.

Hunter of Worlds) cannot comprehend or make allowances for other species precisely because they are themselves perfect empaths. In Niven's "Known Space," a "courageous" Puppeteer is, it is said, insane, and a conciliatory Kzin an embarrassment. Variations in nutritional, reproductive and maturation needs may account for many behavioural differences. So may evolutionary ancestry. Such imaginings may have many purposes, but one of the first is to try to see ourselves, though only in imagination, from outside, to get a hint of what we are, and what thought might "float on a different blood."[35] What sort of thought (if any) might emerge in a species that was not bisexual, or not K-selecting, or that needed one particular other species to survive and breed (as ichneumon wasps need caterpillars)?[36] What sort of symbioses might sustain the sense of individual being? Do the Vendrizi and their hosts remain distinct individuals? Imagining these possibilities is to try to find a setting for what might otherwise be pathological habits: there might, for example, be species in which males are no more than sperm-sacs, little brothers; or ones that pass their memories on, complete, by biochemical exchange; or ones whose young must eat their way out of their mothers; or ones composed of many discrete individuals of the same, or even of different, species. What is it like to be one of the many-bodied tines of Vernor Vinge's *A Fire upon the Deep*?

There are obvious technical difficulties in portraying alien creatures. The written word is more versatile than visual images, but our imaginations are themselves often conditioned, exactly, by popular visual images. We may draw non-human images from the natural world, but it is difficult then to imagine how sapient plants or animals speak and act without turning them into people. Until computer graphics were developed there was no alternative to hiring human impersonators (actors), and so requiring that the aliens be humanoid (as practically all the visible aliens of *Babylon 5* are). Straczynski's wish to focus on the possibility of choice, and responsibility, also restricts the likelihood that the aliens will be incomprehensibly alien, constrained by their biology in ways interestingly different from the ways, whatever they may be, that we ourselves are constrained. No doubt it would also be difficult to sell a series that attempted seriously to depict a fully pathological

---

[35] C. S. Lewis, *Out of the Silent Planet* (London: Pan, 1952 [1938]), 121.
[36] Louis Wu attributes this pattern to Niven's puppeteers, in *Ringworld* (1970), but without any evidence that Niven has bothered to create.

ethic: aliens, let's say, who positively *ought* to beat each other to
death, not just for honour's sake but to fulfil their kind. Would
it be honourable to accept species extinction on discovering that
survival was only possible for those who continued long established, but deeply wicked habits? By (dubious) hypothesis those
habits would not be disagreeable or offensive to that species, but
they might still conclude that they were wrong, that the habits are
not agreeable to all.[37] There are long established "social" practices
that really should be abandoned. What difference is made by
supposing that those practices have become "genetic," that they
define the nature of a species?

The possibility of species betrayal identifies the difference
between the three meta-ethical positions that I have implic-
itly been exploring. Rational realists (like Chesterton, or C. S.
Lewis) believe that there is a right way to live, irrespective of
our opinion or even our settled, ingrained habits, to which all
rational creatures can and should aspire. Sentimental or species
relativists (like Ruse) believe that each species has its own "right
way," irrespective of our opinion, and that there is no reason to
expect those ways to be compatible. Popular relativists imagine
merely that "thinking makes it so," and that there is no one "right
way" even for creatures of "our kind" outside "our" verdict.
Popular relativists, accordingly, acknowledge no abiding duty
of species loyalty or any "natural life": clitoridectomy and other
child abuses aren't "wrong," and neither, obviously, is imperial
prohibition of clitoridectomy and child abuse. Someone, perhaps
some adolescent human, who declares that he has a right to do
what he thinks is best for himself, has no real cause of complaint
if his family, neighbors, and even perfect strangers reply that they
have exactly the same right, for exactly the same reasons, to do
what they think is best for themselves, and stop him.

Agreements on this popular relativist account can only be pragmatic ones, and have no weight beyond our present complaisance.
It is understandable that Muslims in particular have concluded that
there can be no real treaty with such "unbelievers" — any more
than there can be real treaties with Cherryh's Mahendo-sat (in

---

[37] Ruse, for example, to emphasise the supposed relativity of morals, declares
that in eighteenth century India "widows would *voluntarily* perish in the
funeral pyre of their husbands" (Ruse, "Rape in Andromeda," 231; my italics). This is wilfully to neglect the context of the widow's supposed "choice."

Chanur), for whom agreements only last until the next betrayal. Pragmatists of that sort can't make promises—and no sane creature would knowingly accept a pretended promise from them. Sentimental or species relativism evaporates on close inspection: what is left is either a sophisticated moral realism, or pure popular relativism. It cannot be "rational" to insist on species-loyalty unless it is also "rational" to rely on cultural loyalties: species are only sets of interbreeding populations in which what were once acquired habits have become ingrained (by thoroughly non-Lamarckian methods). That Papua New Guinea tribe which "believes" that boys must ingest semen to mature[38] might one day make it true—either over evolutionary ages[39] or by direct genetic engineering. Perhaps that new species should be tolerated. Suppose that the Dilgar—or Doc Smith's Overlords—have similarly evolved to be the unrecoverable villains that the Centauri only are by cultural habit: should they exist? Is there still a chance that they might see the light? Conversely, could genocide (as of the Dilgar, or the Overlords) ever be acknowledged? Asimov's Robots, it seems, are so obedient to his "Three Laws" that they set out ahead of human exploration to destroy all possible rival sapients.[40] The heroes of Taylor's Bobiverse, a little more acceptably, see no alternative but to obliterate the aliens who are themselves engaged in just such simple, greedy, and apparently unstoppable genocide.[41]

SOULS AND SPECIES

There is another reason, in the plot, why all *Babylon 5*'s aliens are comprehensible, and why even the First Ones are manipulable: the very same reason why the Minbari surrendered in their war with humans. In the universe of Babylon 5, there are souls distinct from biological organisms. Soul Hunters collect them,

---

[38] Gilbert Herdt, *Sambia Sexual Culture: Essays from the Field* (Chicago: Chicago University Press, 1999).

[39] This is not to affirm Lamarckian inheritance: the point is merely that there would be no evolutionary selection *against* the physiological failure, just as fishes confined to millennial darkness lose their sight, because there is no reproductive advantage in keeping it.

[40] See Isaac Asimov, *Robots and Empire* (1985); Gregory Benford, *Foundation's Fear* (1997).

[41] Dennis Taylor, *All These Worlds* (New York: Ethan Ellenberg Literary Agency, 2017).

and prevent their progress ("Soul Hunter," 102); Minbari souls are reborn in human bodies ("Points of Departure," 201); Sheridan's soul, and others, flit back and forth in time ("War without End," 316/317); telepaths — engineered by the Vorlons — can read any minds, not merely those of their own species. Sometimes the stories are ambiguous. Personalities can be wiped, but not essential identities, or souls (see "Passing through Gethsemane," 304). Or else new souls can be intruded, and the old destroyed ("Divided Loyalties," 219). Because we are all souls, which could in principle inhabit any body, and any moment, we are all of a kind, and all have access to norms that transcend our accidental biologies, and dates. Alternatively, we become such souls in accepting absolute responsibility (like Brother Edward, in "Passing through Gethsemane," 304), and die in denying it.

A fully worked out dualism, of course, would dispense with special effects, and electrical gadgetry to represent soul exchanges or other spiritual happenings. The Dark Soldier ("The Long Dark," 205) and the Vorlon ambassador Kosh ("Interludes and Examinations," 315; "The Summoning," 403) are simultaneously physical beings capable of hiding away inside another's body (hardly different in principle from the Vendrizi), and, allegorically, souls, or parts of souls. The allegory may be useful, but too easily contaminates the basic notion: of a non-material, non-extended Self. "Ghostbuster-dualism," so to call it, is maybe true of other species, or in other universes, but not here. Even consistent metaphysical dualism is unpopular nowadays in mainstream philosophical circles, though no adequate argument has been mounted against it, and anti-dualists regularly resort instead to insult. There are good reasons to suspect that it is still at least a necessary illusion if we are to retain much of our traditional reason: decency depends on my being able to conceive of being someone else, of being "in their shoes," or "in their skin." But it is impossible for *this* biological organism to be another, and unhelpful to imagine what this would do if it lived disguised inside another's body. The only way of making sense of the simple thought experiment that I might myself have been female, alien, or what you will, is to suppose that I am indeed a soul, and not a body.[42]

---

[42] The point is made by Zeno Vendler, *Res Cogitans* (Ithaca, NY: Cornell University Press, 1972), and by Geoffrey Madell, *The Idea of the Self* (Edinburgh: Edinburgh University Press, 1981).

Rational realism, in brief, depends on just the circumstance that *Babylon 5* represents through ghostbuster-dualism. If it were not true that we are souls, and so not true that there is a rational ethic discoverable by any rational intelligence, then we would indeed be restricted to the biologically grounded motives that so many SF writers play with. But in that case what is happening in *Babylon 5* is not the triumph of ethics over circumstance, but an evolutionary spectacle of the kind the Shadows like. How much cooperation or tolerance is pragmatically possible? What ethical habits will be most successfully propagated, with whatever chance mutations? Why should we expect *our* "civilization" to succeed?

4.
Martian Chronicles

A DYING PLANET[1]

Why should we think our civilization will survive? Those who remember history are not surprised by the fall of empires: "Many clever Babylonians, many clever Egyptians, many clever men at the end of Rome (trusted to civilization). Can you tell me, in a world that is flagrant with the failure of civilizations, what there is particularly immortal about yours?"[2] So it is not surprising that we may also imagine what the long decay might be like, and what will come after the collapse. Felicitously, there is a planet not very far away that can serve as the canvas for imagining that future.

Robert Markley, Professor of English at the University of Illinois, wrote an exemplary study of science-fictional imaginations of the planet Mars, in print, film, and radio, and the scientific theories and discoveries that inspired or disappointed readers and writers since the nineteenth century. There were inevitably a few omissions, the most significant being E. C. Tubb's *Alien Dust* (London: Boardman, 1955). But all the major Imaginary Marses, from Wells to Kim Stanley Robinson, were noticed and discussed, in the context of contemporary scientific imaginings of the Real Mars. Readers with a different background, in science or philosophy, may not be much assisted by jargon such as "hauntology," "liminal space," or even "meta-narrative," but attentive readers

---

[1] This chapter had its beginnings from my review of Robert Markley's *Dying Planet: Mars in Science and Imagination* (Durham, NC, and London: Duke University Press, 2005), published in *Metascience* 15 (2006), 561–65. Oddly, it has been the one of my papers most often read on academia.edu, perhaps because would-be readers expected more of it.
[2] G. K. Chesterton, *The Napoleon of Notting Hill* (Harmondsworth: Penguin, 1946 [1904]), 25.

need not be too distracted. He was also a little too ready—like some of his authors—to equate capitalism and exploitation, ignoring the environmental damage done by decades of Soviet communism, and the self-corrections of a genuine market economy. But attentive readers will also be able to bypass the political prejudices of a liberal environmentalist. The book as a whole was a splendid resource for anyone interested in the interwoven histories of science, science fiction, and socio-political change, and the philosophy of science. Percival Lowell's speculations, and others' response to them, are described in detail, and the philosophy of science that underpinned them (namely, that theories which adequately explain the facts should be accepted at least as working hypotheses, without troubling to consider other theories, or seek for possible refutations). The discoveries of the last thirty years, from Mariner, Viking, and Pathfinder were also described in detail. The particular theme that Markley traces from Lowell to Robinson is the image of Mars as a "dying or recently dead planet," mysteriously older than our own and having long since reached the end that we might fear for Earth. Venus has often, correspondingly, been regarded as a "younger" world, inhabited, if at all, by "primitives" or still cruder species. Martians, even if they seem barbaric (like those in Burroughs's stories or Leigh Brackett's),[3] have an ancient history not to be ignored.

Markley interweaves fiction and scientific theory. Or rather, he interweaves the scientific fictions and the merely literary ones. Until very recently, after all, we had no exact data to consider, and inevitably interpreted such data as we had within the received paradigm provided by our growing knowledge of Earth's geological and cultural history. Lowell's canals now seem as obviously spurious as Piltdown Man, but for many decades reputable observers sincerely thought they themselves saw the canals, or else believed that Lowell and his team had more experience with the fuzzy images obtainable through earthly telescopes, and were persuaded that his underlying theory of planetary evolution was correct. His theories were difficult to resist, as they arose from a strongly materialist and Darwinian paradigm: prosperous and well-educated Westerners were eager to believe both that life was,

---

[3] See Edgar Rice Burroughs, *A Princess of Mars* (1912), and its sequels; Leigh Brackett, *The Sword of Rhiannon* (1953).

in Lowell's words "as inevitable a phase of planetary evolution as is quartz or feldspar or nitrogenous soil," and that desertification and famine on Earth were expectable consequences of planetary decay, rather than of human action or indifference, and so were prepared to see such processes at work on Mars. Even when the canals were finally debunked, it seemed wholly reasonable to expect that there was Martian vegetation, Martian animal life, and even some sort of intelligence, struggling in a hostile universe. This was not the beginning of the arguments. In the seventeenth century it was widely supposed that a benevolent Creator would be bound to populate His worlds, and provide the inhabitants with the chance of continued life. Some argued, on the contrary, that the Earth must be unique, and that our eyes alone were open to the wider world—a view that grew more solid in the face of Darwinian speculation. William Whewell took a balanced position, arguing like earlier Enlightenment philosophers against any attempt to determine what was the case from our guesses about God's intentions, in *Of the Plurality of Worlds* (London, 1853). But it was the theological preference for humankind's unique position, expressed for example by Alfred Russel Wallace, by which Lowell was chiefly opposed. E. W. Maunder, who found experimental evidence in 1903 that the canals were probably optical illusions, was himself—as well as being an astronomer—a Pentecostalist opposed to the plurality of worlds on theological grounds. Even after Maunder's demonstration, Lowell was able to persuade the popular press and many scientists that photographs confirmed the canals' existence, and to argue that it was his opponents who were insufficiently scientific and Darwinian.

The details of Lowell's theory gradually lost their hold on the scientific imagination, but until the 1970s most scientists were hopefully convinced that there was life on Mars, adapted to the needs of a "dying planet," and most science fiction continued to make use of Lowell's vision: Burroughs, Brackett, C. S. Lewis, Ray Bradbury, and Heinlein—to mention only the most memorable fictions—all imagine canals and an ancient civilization into being, embodying the values that the authors most esteem. Burroughs and Brackett praise courage and personal honour, in the face of an indifferent or positively hostile cosmos; Bradbury imagines a curious mix of small-town America and delicate, civilized art (and murderous xenophobia, but let it pass); Lewis an unfallen world of diverse species united under the guidance of angelic spirits; Heinlein's ritual-ruled Martians were gradually transformed into 1960s gurus (whom Markley clearly despised). But all know their world will soon, at least in geological time, be dead. The possibility that, like Wells's Martians, they will follow the Darwinian imperative and invade the resource-rich Earth, was still a live possibility in pulp fiction, the movies, and the popular imagination, even after close-range photographs from the Mariner spacecrafts from 1965 onwards revealed how barren the Martian landscape was. Even before that there were a few authors who expected only a toxic desert. Later discoveries seem to prove that there was once surface water, and still is more water underground than even Lowell supposed. Even though any life or civilization on Mars is probably many million years past we easily fancy that it is still hiding in the dust, for good or ill.[4] Because we believe or wish to believe that Mars was once alive, we need an explanation, appropriate to our own time, that now it's dead: the pillaging of natural resources, nuclear blast, plagues of insects, disease, vampires, or mere planetary senescence. Once Mars was alive. Someday Earth will die.

TERRAFORMING MARS

The argument continues, even without its overtly theological setting, and astronomers and areologists still interpret data in the light of their differing hopes and large-scale beliefs. If they have chosen to think that extraterrestrial life is likely, they are easily persuaded that a meteorite shows traces of ancient nanobacteria. If they think it unlikely, almost any other explanation of the traces is preferred, usually with some specious appeal to Occam's Razor, as if it were clear that all inorganic explanations, however unfamiliar, are "simpler" than organic, however well-attested.[5]

---

[4] For example, Ian Watson, *The Martian Inca* (1977), in which microbes in the Martian dust infect humans in ways increasing their intelligence: a mental invasion close to H. G. Wells's *Star Begotten* (1937).

[5] See Abraham Avi Loeb, *Extraterrestrial: The First Sign of Intelligent Life Beyond Earth* (London: John Murray, 2021) on ways of interpreting the evidence for "Oumuamua" as either an oddly shaped lump of rock or the remnants of an interstellar probe. It is now respectable to think that it was a comet, but that conclusion is only more plausible than the other if the possibility of extraterrestrial civilization is automatically discounted.

The Pathfinder experiments, similarly, produce odd results that some interpret as signs of life, while others merely register that they are surprising. Without the incentive that maybe we shall find life, or the traces of life-long-gone, it is difficult to preserve popular enthusiasm for the flights. But if once we abandon that hope, there may be a grander project to inspire us to continue. The fashion is now for terraforming the planet, perhaps with the very instruments that may be degrading Earth: nuclear blasts and chlorofluorocarbons to help release underground seas, and start up a greenhouse effect. Some advocates of this strategy[6] insist that we need the infinite resources of outer space if we are to avoid a Hobbesian war over mineral resources. Their critics, including Markley, reply that it is the romantic and anthropocentric dream of unending exploitation that has damaged Earth already.

Mars remains a screen on which we may project fears of the Earth's end, or hopes that human endeavour could remake dead worlds. Consider two heroic figures marooned on Mars who survive by their own particular skills, and courage. On the one hand, John Carter travels by magic to "Barsoom," and must make his way as a warrior among both barbarian tribes and sophisticated city-dwellers on the ageing Mars. On the other, Mark Watney, accidentally stranded, must survive as an engineer and horticulturalist, demonstrating at once the dangers and the opportunities of making a living on Mars by making Mars alive.[7] Both characters show an almost more-than-human persistence, talent, and charisma. Both Barsoom and the modern Mars (so to speak) have further, hidden, dimensions: even within the pages of a single book each hero confronts successive revelations about his world, requiring constant adjustments in his own behaviour. Burroughs revealed still more in later stories; Weir has preferred to leave any later revelations to the ongoing real-life exploration of the planet by robot probes, and not anticipate any possible discoveries of sometime life, or fanciful attempts to build a city on Mars by optimistic billionaires.[8]

Even if there was no great Martian civilization in the past, many hope there will be in the future—though it is unlikely that those

---

[6] For example, Robert Zubrin, in *The Case for Mars* (New York: Free Press, 1996).
[7] Andy Weir, *The Martian* (New York: Random House, 2014).
[8] See https://www.inverse.com/innovation/mars-city-interstellar (accessed October 3, 2023).

billionaires will ever themselves see results. Markley devoted a concluding chapter to Kim Stanley Robinson's utopian three-volume novel on the terraforming of Mars.[9] Robinson explicitly abandons all the imagined denizens of Mars,[10] and confronts instead the bare, non-living planet in its peculiar beauty. Mars becomes almost a blank slate for utopia (whether "socialist" or "capitalist" in kind), but one that subtly conditions utopia's growth. Mars is to be terraformed, but with some regard—at least so the author hopes—for its own integrity, and a more rational assessment of economic value than to treat it simply as a material resource for the benefit of an elite. Whether we shall ever really attempt such terraforming or such eco-economic experiments, who knows? The literary and artistic images of Mars that have for so long conditioned our theories and explorations are gradually being overtaken by more detailed knowledge of a world entirely other. But its very otherness, the mere facticity of Mars, as Markley and Robinson show, has meanings for us.

Robinson allows one of his characters to declare that it is only the human mind that gives meaning to what would otherwise be merely rocks:

> Science is part of a larger human enterprise, and that enterprise includes going to the stars, adapting to other planets, adapting them to us. Science is creation. The lack of life here, and the lack of any finding in fifty years of the SETI program, indicates that life is rare, and intelligent life even rarer. And yet the whole meaning of the universe, its beauty, is contained in the consciousness of intelligent life. We are the consciousness of the universe, and our job is to spread that around, to go look at things, to live everywhere we can. It's too dangerous to keep the consciousness of the universe on only one planet, it could be wiped out. And so now we're on two, three if you

---

[9] Kim Stanley Robinson, *Red Mars* (New York: Random House, 1992); *Green Mars* (New York: Random House, 1993); *Blue Mars* (New York: Random House, 1996). Markley addresses Robinson's work in more detail in *Kim Stanley Robinson* (Urbana: University of Illinois Press, 2020). See especially 85–III on Robinson's attempt to rethink the opposition between respect for the mere fact of an unliving Mars and the living world that *might* be brought to birth in it.

[10] Neatly corralled in Larry Niven's fantasy *Rainbow Mars* (London: Orbit, 1999).

count the moon. And we can change this one to make it safer to live on. Changing it won't destroy it. Reading its past might get harder, but the beauty of it won't go away. If there are lakes, or forests, or glaciers, how does that diminish Mars's beauty? I don't think it does. I think it only enhances it. It adds life, the most beautiful system of all. But nothing life can do will bring Tharsis down, or fill Marineris. Mars will always remain Mars, different from Earth, colder and wilder. But it can be Mars and ours at the same time. And it will be. There is this about the human mind; if it can be done, it will be done. We can transform Mars and build it like you would build a cathedral, as a monument to humanity and to the universe.[11]

But another character, eventually allowed more scope and sympathy than her immediate audience grants her, speaks rather of the brute existence of a world "where the landforms are a hundred times larger than their equivalents on Earth, and a thousand times older, with evidence concerning the beginning of the solar system scattered all over, as well as the whole history of a planet, scarcely changed in the last billion years."[12] Her mistake, she acknowledges to herself, "had been in coming to Mars in the first place, and then falling in love with it. Falling in love with a place everyone else wanted to destroy."[13] Sax's error is to suppose that mere facts don't matter, that it is only what "we" make of them that counts. His professed hope to preserve and augment existing beauty too easily offers an excuse for making it ugly. Describing the long effort to terraform Mars as a "stupendous Parthenon of the mind, a work constantly in progress"[14] is wilfully to disregard the actual costs of Parthenons (which included, in the original case, embezzlement of league funds for the glory only of Athens, and the political career of Pericles)! Even cathedrals depend on wrenching stone from the soil, exploiting labour, and too often leaving rubble, broken trees, and slag heaps behind. Soil itself, on which life depends, is created by living creatures: bringing life to

---

[11] Sax Russell speaks: Robinson, *Red Mars*, 213.
[12] Ann Clayborne speaks: *Red Mars*, 211. Robinson, unhappily, roots the opposition of Ann and Sax in personal misunderstandings, only resolved in a final volume, many decades later.
[13] Robinson, *Red Mars*, 632.
[14] Robinson, *Blue Mars*, 527.

an empty world can only succeed by acknowledging that causal loop, and starting very small. Sax is brutally reminded, over the course of the trilogy, that there are many different human dreams at work in the transformations he desires.

Plotinus rebuked the Gnostics of his day, who disparaged the natural world: "if [God] is absent from the universe, he will be absent from you...."[15] Conversely, if human (and other living creativity) is of value, then so is the world from which it grows. Mars, as a seemingly empty world, must still demand respect.

---

[15] Plotinus, *Ennead* II.9 [33].16, 26–7.

5.
Orwell and the Anti-Realists[1]

THE PURPOSE OF NEWSPEAK

> The purpose of Newspeak was not only to provide a
> medium of expression for the world-view and mental
> habits proper to the devotees of Ingsoc, but to make all
> other modes of thought impossible.[2]

It is one of the commonest of contemporary philosophical themes
that what cannot be said cannot be thought, that the limits of
language are the limits of our world. To this we must add, by
way of clarification, that nothing can be meaningfully *said* that
cannot be understood by others, and by way of usually unspoken
codicil that nothing can be understood by others that cannot be
understood by ordinary, bourgeois academics. Ordinary language,
as that is recognized by sensible folk like us, determines truth.
Not everything that we *think* true is true (because some things
will not *remain* "true," and not everything that we think is strictly
compatible with things we cannot bring ourselves to unthink),
but nothing that we could not think was true (because we cannot
think it or cannot think the propositions that would count as
evidence for it) is true. Even if we retain some feeling that there
are, somehow, truths that we cannot express (since we would need
another, novel, language even to locate them) all truths-for-us
are ones that we can think. It follows, as Orwell saw, that if our
masters wish to secure themselves against unwanted sometime
truths, they had best invent a language that prevents our thinking

---

[1] The original version was published as "Orwell and the Anti-Realists":
Philosophy 67 (1992), 141–54.
[2] G. Orwell, *Nineteen Eighty-Four* (Harmondsworth: Penguin, 1954 [1949]), 241.

them. "To give a single example. The word *free* still existed in Newspeak, but it could only be used in such statements as 'This dog is free from lice' or 'This field is free from weeds.' It could not be used in the old sense of 'politically free' or 'intellectually free,' since political and intellectual freedom no longer existed even as concepts, and were therefore of necessity nameless."[3]

Three questions present themselves. First, is this strategy a possible one? Second, is it one that anyone is, consciously or otherwise, committed to? Third, is its logocentric idealism (so to speak) really compatible with things that most contemporary philosophers also think are true (for example that there was a world before us, and stars far out of reach)? This last conundrum I shall not yet attempt, save to remark that Orwell's Ingsoc theorists at any rate did not think it was. "The earth is as old as we are, no older. How could it be older? Nothing exists except through human consciousness.... The stars ... are bits of fire a few kilometres away. We could reach them if we wanted to. Or we could blot them out."[4]

Is the invention of a new language, or the deliberate impoverishment of an old, a strategy that anyone is seriously attempting now? I am myself temperamentally disinclined to believe in conspiracy theories: cock-up rather than conspiracy explains most evils. But this is not to say that there are no fashions in philosophy that have the effect of conspiratorial action. Dualism (specifically body-mind dualism) is regularly characterized as a doctrine that is "not now available" or "appeals only to the senile." The idea that there could be "deep facts" about personal identity or about morality is said to rest on infantile misunderstandings of "our" ordinary speech. What "we" say, think and do (always identified with what Anglophone Westerners with leisure to read such works will say they say or think or do) is often the unexamined end of argument. The defining characteristic of an ideologue is that she never realizes that her opinion is contentious: by that criterion the

---

[3] Orwell, *Nineteen Eighty-Four*, 241. A similar point was made by Thomas Hobbes, in *Leviathan*, chapter 5: "If a man should talk to me of 'a round quadrangle,' or 'accidents of bread in cheese'; or 'immaterial substances'; or of a 'free subject'; or 'free will'; or any 'free', but free from being hindered by opposition, I should not say he were in error, but that his words were without meaning, that is to say, absurd."

[4] O'Brien speaks: Orwell, *Nineteen Eighty-Four*, 213.

chattering classes, which include philosophers, are often extraordinarily intolerant. Why not? There is no genuine opposition to the favored creed, since no one admits to understanding what the opposition says. "For example, *All mans are equal* was a possible Newspeak sentence, but only in the sense in which *All men are redhaired* is a possible Oldspeak sentence. It did not contain a grammatical error, but it expressed a palpable untruth — i.e. that all men are of equal size, weight or strength."[5] For another example, *Human beings are immortal* only expresses the palpable untruth that human beings, commonly so-called, don't die.[6] And another: any claim that moral discourse is about real moral truths can only mean that it is about claims that we currently choose to make.[7]

One obvious retort to anti-realism is that some things simply cannot be magicked away. If there are any "palpable untruths" at all, then truth is not determined just by what we say. If anti-realism is correct, "what is to stop us eliminating death, poverty and unhappinesss by conceptual revisions?"[8] Does it seem improbable that we would try?

> I don't accept the view... that there are a lot of pre-cultural and purely objective, but very unpleasant, facts about the human condition, which are non-narrative and just the same for every human being. On the contrary, sickness, old age, suffering, death, transience and futility are construed in very different ways in different religions and philosophies. We can make old age venerable or pitiful. We can make death either the crown of life and the achievement of the highest social status, or we can make it an outrage. The choice is ours.[9]

The threat is a real one. After all, there is precedent for it:

---

[5] Orwell, 250.

[6] See Simon Tugwell, *Humanity, Immortality and the Redemption of Death* (London: Darton, Longman, and Todd, 1989).

[7] Simon Blackburn, "Errors and the Phenomenology of Value": *Morality and Objectivity*, ed. Ted Honderich (London: Routledge and Kegan Paul), 1–22.

[8] Howard Robinson, *Matter and Sense* (Cambridge: Cambridge University Press, 1982), 82. See also Kipling's remark, cited earlier: "If they desire a thing they declare that it is true. If they desire it not, though that were Death itself, they cry aloud, 'It has never been'" ("One View of the Question," in *Many Inventions*).

[9] Don Cupitt, *Creation out of Nothing* (London: SCM Press, 1990), 183.

...hail horrors, hail
Infernal world, and thou profoundest hell
Receive thy new possessor: one who brings
A mind not to be changed by place or time.
The mind is its own place, and in itself
Can make a heaven of hell, a hell of heaven.[10]

Or consider what happened in Athens: in those days, Thucydides said of the early years of the Peloponnesian War, "words
changed their ordinary meanings and were construed in new
senses. Reckless daring passed for the courage of a loyal partisan,
far-sighted hesitation was the excuse of a coward, moderation was
the pretext of the unmanly, the power to see all sides of a question
was complete inability to act."[11] By selecting different words for
what others might call a victim, we are free of blame: call the
thing a neonate, an embryo, a pre-embryo; call it an oncomouse,
an animal preparation or a walking larder. Those particular eva-
sions are aided by a curious piece of doublethink:[12] the preferred
expressions are chosen as being devoid of any moral force of a
contentious kind, but then employed to justify what would have
been contentious morals. First we insist that the moral question
must not be begged, and so rule out such words as "murder" in
favor of "homicide" or "termination"; then we infer that since
the act, so described, lacked any moral import, we may properly
perform it. If things are only and entirely what "we" call them,
argument becomes irrefutable, and hence impossible:

> "Has it ever occurred to you, Winston, that by the year
> 2050, at the very latest, not a single human being will be
> alive who could understand such a conversation as we are
> having now?" "Except—" began Winston doubtfully, and

[10] Satan speaks: J. Milton, *Paradise Lost*, in *The Poems*, ed. John Carey and
Alastair Fowler (London and Harlow: Longmans, Green, and Co., 1968),
477 (1: 250–55).
[11] *History of the Peloponnesian War*, 3.82. Cf. V. S. Naipaul, *Among the Believers*
(London: Andre Deutsch, 1981), 34: "One of the English-language magazines
I bought was *The Message of Peace*, and, as its title warned, it was full of rage."
[12] "To know and not to know, to be conscious of complete truthfulness
while telling carefully constructed lies, to hold simultaneously two opinions
which cancelled out; to use logic against logic, to repudiate morality while
laying claim to it; to forget whatever was necessary to forget, then to draw
it back into memory again at the moment when it was needed, and then
promptly to forget it again." Orwell, *Nineteen Eighty-Four*, 31–32; see also 171.

then stopped. It had been on the tip of his tongue to say "except the proles," but he checked himself, not feeling fully certain that this remark was not in some way unorthodox. Syme, however, had divined what he was about to say. "The proles are not human beings," he said carelessly.[13]

Death, poverty, and unhappiness are eliminable by conceptual revisions, if we choose to say so, and the more easily because all three notions have a moral force that doublethinkers seek to think away.

OBJECTIVISM AND THE ELIMINATION OF THE SELF

Thus: death is a terminus, but not just any terminus is death. The day-self of a living being perishes at day's end (that is, if we choose to distinguish Tuesday's Stephen from Wednesday's, then Tuesday's is no more when Wednesday comes), but day-selves, so defined, do not matter. Similarly, what we had called "death" is no more than transformation or a pause. The metal of a statue may become a present from Bognor or a pair of cufflinks; its pattern may be re-embodied in glass or concrete. Nothing dies that matters, since only *matter* is real. "Can you not understand, Winston, that the individual is only a cell? The weariness of the cell is the vigour of the organism. Do you die when you cut your finger nails?"[14] Poverty, in its turn, is no more than the state of having too few economic resources to live as befits an equal member of one's community: if "proles aren't human beings," then they are not poor (any more than sparrows are); if there is no life that suits all subjects then no economic condition prevents our living it. What is deprivation judged in one way is a gracious concession judged another: "It appeared there had even been demonstrations to thank Big Brother for raising the chocolate ration to twenty grammes a week. And only yesterday, he reflected, it had been announced that the ration was to be *reduced* to twenty grammes. Could they swallow this after only twenty-four hours? Yes, they swallowed it."[15]

Unhappiness is nothing but a biochemical reaction, even a conditioned reflex, to particular conditions: all that is needed is

---

[13] Orwell, *Nineteen Eighty-Four*, 45f. "As the Party slogan put it: 'Proles and animals are free'" (61).
[14] O'Brien speaks; Orwell, 212.
[15] Orwell, 50.

a redescription, combined (perhaps) with chemical controls. "In our world there will be no emotions except fear, rage, triumph, and self-abasement. There will be no distinction between beauty and ugliness. There will be no curiosity, no enjoyment of the process of life. All competing pleasures will be destroyed."[16] The notion has been addressed by other writers:

> "I am aware of the emotional (that is, the chemical) reactions which a statement like this produces in you, and you are wasting your time trying to conceal them from me. I do not expect you to control them. That is not the path to objectivity. I deliberately raise them in order that you may become accustomed to regard them in a purely scientific light and distinguish them as sharply as possible from the *facts*."[17]

Lewis's concern in *That Hideous Strength* was to explore the practical implications of the "objectivism" that infected (and infects) the intellectual landscape of the twentieth century. That objectivism purports to be concerned *with facts*, with what can be affirmed without any moral implication or emotional import. Nothing is to count as true beyond what can be "proved" true to the satisfaction of someone utterly indifferent to humane values. The strategy is absurd: one who is unconvinced by talk of intellectual duties to prefer the simplest theory capable of "explaining" the experimental data, or to accept — even if provisionally — what researchers say those data are, will not be convinced of any factual claim. In that sense no proofs are possible that transcend the limits of the enquirer's ethics and emotions. Nor is there any "factual" proof available for the very claim that only "factually proven" theses are to be accepted. It must by now be obvious that "objective truths" (so described) are only a small part of truth, and that emotion fixes all the truths we find agreeable to think. Objectivism turns out to be the ideological control of language, lest we notice truths the controllers do not like. "Objectivity,"

---

[16] O'Brien speaks: Orwell, 215.
[17] Frost speaks: C. S. Lewis, *That Hideous Strength* (London: Bodley Head, 1945), 318. Lewis's story deals with the (miraculously thwarted) attempt to establish a society very much like Orwell's world, and makes much clearer than Orwell's story does how ordinarily sinful people could come to accept the establishment of Hell on earth.

so understood, does not differ from "total allegiance."[18] Ingsoc is just the same as Obliteration of the Self.[19]

Orwell's O'Brien denied, like Wittgensteinians, that this was solipsism: "Collective solipsism, if you like. But that is a different thing: in fact the opposite thing."[20] Clearly, there can be no such real distinction if there are no real individuals: where the only real or important thing is the Party, and the Party determines truth, that is solipsism, even if it differs from the more familiar kind. If Winston had successfully retreated to his own mind and memory, denying that anything could be true but what seemed so to him, then Ingsoc and O'Brien would call him solipsist: "You are mentally deranged. You suffer from a defective memory. You are unable to remember real events and you persuade yourself that you remember other events which never happened."[21] But O'Brien's claim is only and entirely in the name of the Party-Self: it is not that there is any *fact* outside, or anything that rests on more than what that Party-Self (in all its avatars) will say. Winston's "delusion" is only his failure to submerge his trivial self in the larger whole. Personal memory and conviction are insufficient to establish truth: after all, Winston *"knew* . . . that O'Brien was on his side,"[22] "knew instinctively who would survive and who would perish,"[23] knew that he would not betray Julia as certainly as "he knew the rules of arithmetic,"[24] and his dreams are—in the story—much better predictors than his careful theories.[25] Only the public record serves—but that record is indefinitely manipulable. "All the confessions uttered here are true. We make them true."[26] Collective solipsism, and generalized anti-realism, are only the "opposite" of solipsism in the way that one egoism is the opposite of another. It is not Winston that is the only real, but Big Brother:

---

[18] Lewis, *That Hideous Strength*, 411.
[19] Orwell, *Nineteen Eighty-Four*, 159. See Kimberley Cornish, *The Jew of Linz: Wittgenstein, Hitler and Their Secret Battle for the Mind* (London: Century, 1998) —a work of more philosophical interest than the popular summary (that it describes a merely personal grudge between Hitler and Wittgenstein) suggests.
[20] O'Brien speaks: Orwell, 214.
[21] O'Brien speaks: Orwell, 197: see also, after Winston's psychological destruction, 238.
[22] Orwell, 68.
[23] Ibid., 52.
[24] Ibid., 184.
[25] Cf. Orwell, 28, 102.
[26] O'Brien speaks, in the Ministry of Love: Orwell, 204.

"Does Big Brother exist?" "Of course he exists. The Party
exists. Big Brother is the embodiment of the Party." "Does
he exist in the same way as I exist?" "You do not exist,"
said O'Brien.[27]

Winston, failing to find any intellectual justification for relying
on individual memory, hopes instead that merely natural passion
or ancestral memory will one day overturn the Party:

> Always in your stomach and your skin there was a sort of
> protest, a feeling that you had been cheated of something
> that you had a right to. Why should one feel it to be
> intolerable unless one had a kind of ancestral memory
> that things had once been different?[28]

Things cannot be only and entirely what the Party says as long as
"the animal instinct, the simple undifferentiated desire" exists to
negate all Party hierarchies and rules. Less crudely, but to similar
effect, a post-Wittgensteinian movement puts its trust in what
we "naturally" feel and say. Even if there is no "real world" outside all human speech, there may still be limits on what human
beings can "naturally" say. Death, poverty, and unhappiness are
not external realities: till creatures capable of complaint emerged
from nowhere there were no such evils. But now that we are here
it is inevitable that we put that construction upon things, and
any attempt to "go against nature" fails. But it is not clear that
this response can work. If there is an ineluctable human nature,
then there is a world impervious to human redescription—but
that is what is in question. "Men," says O'Brien, "are infinitely
malleable."[29] Winston's error, as Orwell depicts it, is twofold.
On the one hand, the Party's hierarchy itself rests on natural
emotions with as good a claim to permanence as undifferentiated
lust (namely, hatred, and the will to power).[30] On the other,
lust itself can be destroyed as surely as family feeling: "There
were things, your own acts, from which you could not recover.
Something was killed in your breast: burnt out, cauterized."[31]

---

[27] Orwell, 208.
[28] Ibid., 51.
[29] Ibid., 216.
[30] "'Always there will be the intoxication of power, constantly increasing
and constantly growing subtler. Always at every moment, there will be the
thrill of victory, the sensation of trampling on an enemy who is helpless'";
O'Brien speaks. Orwell, 215.
[31] Orwell, 233.

HOPES AND FEARS FOR THE FUTURE

An alternative is offered to Winston: the music of a thrush "as though it were a kind of liquid stuff that poured all over him and got mixed up with the sunlight that filtered through the leaves."[32] "'He wasn't singing to us,' said Julia. 'He was singing to please himself. Not even that. He was just singing.'"[33] Instead of the "boot stamping on the human face forever" that O'Brien imagines,[34] Winston hopes for "a race of conscious beings" that must one day come from the loins of the "solid unconquerable figure, made monstrous by work and child-bearing, toiling from birth to death and still singing."[35]

Lust and purposeless song alike are offered as answers to the rationalist impasse (though Winston seeks to ally himself with the imagined future by keeping the mind alive as they keep the body, and "pass[ing] on the secret doctrine that two plus two makes four"). "By foreknowledge ... one could mystically share in [the imagined future, where there is no darkness]."[36] If thought is limited by language, and the Party controls language and public record, then the only breach in the walls must be wordless, and so thoughtless. If all meanings are subject to change, then it is the sheer alien facticity of things that must remain.

But of course this option is only available if there is such a "sheer alien facticity" and the possibility of "knowing"—and loving—it:

---

[32] Ibid., 102.

[33] Ibid., 176.

[34] Orwell, 215. The same prophecy was made by Wickson in Jack London's *The Iron Heel* (Moscow and Leningrad: Cooperative Publishing Society of Foreign Workers in the USSR, 1934 [1907]), 94f. London's future history is very like Orwell's: what Orwell realized was that the organization of Revolutionary Fighting Groups (*Nineteen Eighty-Four*, 220ff.) that permeates the organization of the Iron Heel would actually serve the Heel's purposes, and that Socialism itself—"socialism" of a sort—would serve as the overt ideology of the oppressors (as the Foreign Workers Press so lamentably failed to see). P. Vaillant-Couturier's complacent praise, in the introduction to the Foreign Workers' edition, of the USSR as "a revolutionary people that nothing can vanquish because it is armed with a correct doctrine, applied in a consistent manner by a disciplined Party, with the enlightened and enthusiastic support of the masses" is a reminder that Orwell did not have to invent Ingsoc.

[35] Orwell, 176.

[36] Ibid., 86.

Suppose that Socrates was wrong, that we have *not* once seen the Truth, and so will not, intuitively, recognize it when we see it again. This means that when the secret police come, when the torturers violate the innocent, there is nothing to be said to them of the form "There is something within you which you are betraying. Though you embody the practices of a totalitarian society which will endure forever, there is something beyond those practices which condemns you." [37]

What stands in the way of such a knowledge — even apart from theoretical difficulties — is the web of language and attributed meaning. What happens in Room 101 — in the real "place where there is no darkness" [38] — is unendurable:

> "You asked me once," said O'Brien, "what was in Room 101. I told you that you knew the answer already. Everyone knows it. The thing that is in Room 101 is the worst thing in the world. By itself, pain is not enough. There are occasions when a human being will stand out against pain, even to the point of death. But for everyone there is something unendurable — something that cannot be contemplated .... It is merely an instinct that cannot be destroyed." [39]

O'Brien here admits — though the admission does Winston no good — that there is after all something immune to conceptual revisions, at least of the ordinary kind. Maybe death, suffering, and unhappiness can be redescribed, but there is something, he says, for each of us that cannot be "just what the Party says." Rorty's claim embodies the same confusion: "such thoughts may be hard to live with, Rorty implies, *but live with them we must.*" [40] I do not myself see that particular necessity. Chesterton had a rather higher opinion of the revelation:

---

[37] R. Rorty, *Consequences of Pragmatism* (Minneapolis: University of Minnesota Press, 1982), xiii. See J. Stout, *Ethics since Babel* (Cambridge: James Clarke and Co., 1990), 257. Stout goes on to say, contra Rorty, that *he* and "the example of every remaining virtuous person, as well as whatever exemplary lives we can keep alive in memory" can still condemn the torturer (259). But that is to miss Orwell's point.
[38] Orwell, 23, 86, 184, 196.
[39] Ibid., 227–28.
[40] Stout, *Ethics Since Babel*, 257 (my italics).

A man must be in some place from which he would
certainly escape if he could, if he is really to realize that
all things do not come from within. Thank God for hard
stones; thank God for hard facts; thank God for thorns
and rocks and deserts and long years. At least I know now
that I am not the best or strongest thing in the world. At
least I know now that I have not dreamed of everything.[41]

The Party—in its determination to dictate reality—employs as
its final weapon what is inescapably real, and does so the more
eagerly because what is thus named as real is, exactly, horrible.
Winston accepts the Party, and eventually loves Big Brother,[42]
because it is a psychological escape from reality, now shown
to him as unendurable, as some thing that reduces him to "a
screaming animal." This kind of anti-realism may admit (with one
half of the mind) that there is a world impervious to conceptual
revisions, but prefers the "human" world of meaning, even if that
meaning is determined by the Party:

Wherefore my brittle gods I make
Of friendly clay and kindly stone,
Wrought with my hands, to serve or break,
From crown to toe my work, my own.
My eyes can see, my nose can smell,
My fingers touch their painted face,
They weave their little homely spell
To warm me from the cold of Space.[43]

The breaking-inward of an unknown Truth is something that
exercised the imagination of the sensitive in the early years of
the twentieth century, whether in the guise of Buchan's Space,
or Bierce's Pan, or Yeats's bag of Druidic dreams,[44] or Olaf Stapledon's indifferent Titans. In each case the breaking-in reveals
that human loyalties lie with the human world: what IS may turn
out to be dreadful, owed no devotion by the humane heart and
starkly incompatible with all we love. It is, I suspect, this fear

---

[41] Gabriel Gale speaks: G. K. Chesterton, *The Poet and the Lunatics* (London:
Darwen Finlayson, 1962 [1949]), 91–92.
[42] Orwell, *Nineteen Eighty-Four*, 239.
[43] J. Buchan, "Stocks and Stones" (1911), in *The Moon Endureth*, 2nd edition
(London: Nelson, 1923), 161.
[44] W. B. Yeats, *Collected Poems* (London: Macmillan, 1950), 37.

which gives some theologians cause to turn aside from Truth, and to prefer, as it were, "gods wrought of common stuff":

> I cannot worship what I hate
> Or serve a god I dare not know.[45]

What is significant about Orwell's version is that it reminds us that the "human world" to which we may retreat from a loathed reality need have none of the qualities that the liberal mind prefers. Naipaul's survey of Muslim opinion in Iran, Pakistan, and Indonesia convinced him that "Islam sanctified rage."[46] The judgment is unjust as a comment on Islam through the ages, but seems fair enough in reference to the kind of "fundamentalism" that is a deliberate denial of supposedly "modern" or "Western" values. Anti-realist theologians suggest that this "fundamentalism" shows what is wrong with realism: on the contrary, it betrays exactly the same egoism as anti-realism itself. Theologians for whom "God" names only our highest ideals personified, should remember what those ideals may be:

> Nobody has ever seen Big Brother. He is a face on the hoardings, a voice on the telescreen. We may be reasonably sure that he will never die, and there is already considerable uncertainty as to when he was born. Big Brother is the guise in which the Party chooses to exhibit itself to the world. His function is to act as a focusing point for love, fear, and reverence, emotions which are more easily felt towards an individual than towards an organization.[47]

Confronted by the Void, we retreat within the human universe and decree that there *is* no Void because we cannot bear it. "The fallacy was obvious. It presupposed that somewhere or other, outside oneself, there was a 'real' world where 'real' things happened. But how could there be such a world? What knowledge have we of anything, save through our own minds? All happenings are in the mind. Whatever happens in all minds, truly happens."[48]

---

[45] Buchan, "Stocks and Stones," 162.

[46] Naipaul, *Among the Believers*, 354.

[47] Goldstein's Book: Orwell, *Nineteen Eighty-Four*, 167. Big Brother's face, by the way, is "black-haired, black-moustachio'd, full of power and mysterious calm, and so vast that it almost filled up the screen": 16.

[48] Winston meditates: Orwell, 223. See also O'Brien in Orwell, 200: "reality is not external. Reality exists in the mind of the Party, which is collective and immortal."

The lie in Room 101 is that its victims are faced by the inescapably real, and must—to save themselves—surrender their last love, their last integrity. It is a lie for the following reasons. Either there is a world more than an "obsequious shadow" of our imaginations or there is not. If there is not (as Ingsoc's propagandists say), then the "worst thing in the world" is only, as Cupitt points out in the passage cited earlier, the worst because *we* see it so. If only Winston could have seen the rats as he more easily saw the birds, as simply being themselves, the agony of being eaten would, no doubt, be much the same, but not the horror. It was because Winston did *not* encounter things in their facticity that it could be made to appear to him that things in their facticity were unendurable. To be frightened of the Void is to be afraid of one's own shadow. From which it must follow that there is a fact, the active power of the imagination, the "Poetic genius."[49] If on the other hand we are compelled, with Chesterton, to recognize hard facts, then there is a real world and we are only human: "We are all tied to trees and pinned with pitchforks. And as long as these are solid, we know the stars will stand and the hills will not melt at our word."[50]

That there is, *in truth*, no truth outside the text is a thought that may as well be put aside. "Truisms are true, hold on to that! The solid world exists, its laws do not change."[51] There can be no argument with those who choose to deny this—for argument and even assertion depend on there being real truths and real laws of logic. It is enough, perhaps, to say that every attempt to utter Ingsoc's creed requires so much doublethink as to corrupt both language and the soul. At the heart of every sane discussion lies a wordless recognition of mere fact, the realization that we are not God. But there does remain a difference of attitude to fact: is the fact hideous, as Winston is made to think, or glorious, as Gabriel Gale and others of Chesterton's army say? Glorious, perhaps, *because* it gives no human comfort?

> I tell you naught for your comfort,
> Yea, naught for your desire,

---

[49] See my "Cupitt and Divine Imagining," *Modern Theology* 5 (1988), 45–60.
[50] Chesterton, *The Poet and the Lunatics*, 92f.
[51] Orwell, *Nineteen Eighty-Four*, 68. The preceding sentence ("They [the Party intellectuals] were wrong and he was right!") echoes the *Chanson de Roland*: "Paiens ont tort. Chretiens ont droit!"

> Save that the sky grows darker yet
> And the sea rises higher.[52]

Between those nauseated by the sight of a tree-root and those uplifted by the sheer alien pointless(?) facticity of things there can be little sympathy.[53]

Orwell's novel, obviously, is fiction, with its own literary as well as philosophical resonance. Its very title is, probably, an echo of Chesterton's *Napoleon of Notting Hill*, whose opening scenes are set eighty years after its date of publication (1904). That novel ends with King Auberon's question to Provost Wayne: "Suppose that whatever meaning you may choose in your fancy to give to it, the real meaning of the whole was mockery. Suppose it was all folly."[54] Wayne replies that it was not, and that even if it had been created so (as the story has it that the Cities of Auberon's London were) yet "if we have taken the child's games, and given them the seriousness of a Crusade . . . we have turned a nursery into a temple." Wayne and Auberon between them "have remedied a great wrong" by lifting "the modern cities into that poetry which every one who knows mankind knows to be immeasurably more common than the commonplace." They are the two lobes of the same brain, cloven in two by dark and dreary days. It is the "common man" in whom laughter and respect are unified "whom geniuses like you and me can only worship as a god."[55]

In Chesterton's story things that are true and valuable only if "we" say they are (namely the invented histories of London boroughs magnified to Cities) are the more true, the more valuable, as we choose to fight and die for them. The unromantic enemies of little states like Nicaragua or Notting Hill are themselves as tied by their imaginings. Their mistake is to think that they are merely "realistic" while Wayne is mad: really, both sides have their banners.

---

[52] G. K. Chesterton, "Ballad of the White Horse," in *Collected Poems*, 12th edition (London: Methuen, 1950), 233.

[53] Contrast J.-P. Sartre, *Nausea* (Harmondsworth: Penguin, 1965), and I. Murdoch, *The Sovereignty of Good* (Cambridge: Cambridge University Press, 1967), 41. See my "Death, Depression and a Passing Kestrel," in *Death And Anti-Death 17: One Year After Mary Midgley, Twenty Years After Iris Murdoch*, ed. Charles Tandy (Ann Arbor, MI: Ria University Press, 2019), 69–92.

[54] G. K. Chesterton, *The Napoleon of Notting Hill* (Harmondsworth: Penguin, 1946 [1904]), 154.

[55] Ibid., 156f.

> "Do you think I have no right to fight for Notting Hill,
> you whose English Government has so often fought for
> tomfooleries? If, as your rich friends say, there are no
> gods, and the skies are dark above us, what should a man
> fight for but the place where he had the Eden of child-
> hood and the short heaven of first love? If no temples
> and no scriptures are sacred, what is sacred if a man's
> own youth is not sacred?"[56]

Orwell's imagined future also uses war to bind the hearts and
minds of its subjects, and upholds the importance of what "we"
say against "mere facts." The differences are that Chesterton's
common men are replaced by Orwell's proles, and there is no "last,
lost giant, even God" to rise against the world.[57] A man's youth
is not entirely sacred, nor is childhood always much like Eden.
"Hardly a week passed in which *The Times* did not carry a paragraph
describing how some eavesdropping little sneak—'child hero' was
the phrase generally used—had overheard some compromising
remark and denounced its parents to the Thought Police."[58]

Orwell identifies[59] the poem that "the poet Ampleforth" cannot
correct for the Ministry of Truth (involving a rhyme of "rod" and
"God") with one of Kipling's: I suspect he misremembered—

> For riseth up against realm and rod,
> A thing forgotten, a thing downtrod,
> The last, lost giant, even God,
> Is risen against the world.[60]

In that poem, of Chesterton's, the finally victorious Alfred
warns that "the heathen shall return."

> They shall not come with warships,
> They shall not waste with brands,
> But books be all their eating,
> And ink be on their hands.
> Not with the humour of hunters
> Or savage skill in war,

---

[56] Ibid., 64.
[57] Chesterton, *Collected Poems*, 268.
[58] Orwell, *Nineteen Eighty-Four*, 23.
[59] Ibid., 185.
[60] Chesterton, *Collected Poems*, 268.

But ordering all things with dead words,
Strings shall they make of beasts and birds,
And wheels of wind and star.[61]

The chief danger foreseen by Alfred (or identified by Chesterton) was the spread of scientistic fatalism, "all men bond to
Nothing, being slaves without a lord." But there is an equal and
opposite horror, with which indeed Chesterton was more often
concerned: that of finding nothing in the world but our own
will and words:

Let me not look aloft and see mine own
Feature and form upon the Judgement-throne.[62]

There is no answer to that nightmare but to wake up into the
presence of something evidently real and *other*, something more
than mind and loftier than language. "I had promised to show
you, if you recall, that there is something higher than our mind
and reason. There you have it—truth itself! Embrace it if you
can and enjoy it."[63] When we recognize something to be true
we show that we have already known the truth:

For that woman in the Gospel had lost her groat and
sought it with a light, and unless she had remembered
it, she had never found it. For after it was found, how
could she have known whether it was the same or not,
unless she had remembered it?[64]

Which is where Orwell's thrush is relevant once more. "The
bird-song from the timeless world reminds the listener that the
soul's situation in the time-state is that of exile. Birds and their
voices have been held oracular from the beginning of time."[65]
Socrates was right all along, and what we cannot say can, after
all, be shown.

---

[61] Ibid., 312.
[62] Ibid., 345.
[63] Augustine, *De Libero Arbitrio* 2.13.35: *The Teacher, The Free Choice of the Will
and Grace and Free Will*, trans. R. P. Russell (Washington: Catholic University
of America Press, 1968), 144.
[64] Augustine, *Confessions* 10.8, trans. T. Matthew, ed. R. Huddleston (London: Burns and Oates, 1923), 286.
[65] Kathleen Raine, *The Inner Journey of the Poet* (London: Allen and Unwin,
1982), 57.

6.
Olaf Stapledon[1]

STAPLEDON'S LIFE AND WRITINGS

Anyone intrigued by fantasies or scientific speculations about the very far future owes a debt to Olaf Stapledon (1886–1950), whose *Last and First Men* and *Star Maker* established that long-term perspective before the Second World War. Robert Crossley, one of Stapledon's biographers, has remarked that he has often found that people think that Stapledon was Scandinavian, or else American.[2] J. B. S. Haldane, on reading *Last and First Men*, grew indignant that he had not heard before of someone he assumed must be a research scientist. In fact, Stapledon was a philosopher, educated at Balliol College before the First World War, and in the Ambulance Corps during it; he was born and bred in the Wirral (the peninsula between the Dee and the Mersey in North-West England), and was for many years a notable figure in the literary and philosophical culture of Merseyside. His doctorate, for work in philosophical psychology, was earned at Liverpool. He taught for that University's extra-mural department, and for the Workers' Educational Association. His archives, including many of the detailed notes he made for his classes, are housed in Liverpool University Library. Brian Aldiss's suggestion that "his contacts with the outside world were few; he preferred to

---

[1] An earlier version of this chapter was presented in George Ellis, ed., *The Far-Future Universe* (Radnor, PA: Templeton Foundation, 2002), 355–70. This was in turn a slightly expanded version of "Olaf Stapledon (1886–1950)," *International Science Reviews* 18 (1993), 112–19.

[2] R. Crossley, ed., *Talking across the World: the Love Letters of Olaf Stapledon and Agnes Miller, 1913–19* (Hanover and London: University Press of New England, 1987); see also Robert Crossley, *Olaf Stapledon: speaking for the future* (New York: Syracuse University Press, 1994).

dream and cultivate his garden"[3] is peculiarly wrong-headed, as his letters and lectures make clear.

Stapledon was a seminal writer of what—against his own preference—has come to be called Science Fiction, and a representative (but also deeply critical) member of a literary and philosophical movement that has influenced more than fiction: namely, optimistic techno-humanism. Loyalty to the (Human) Spirit—too easily equated with a preference for "science" over "superstition"—led writers like Wells, Chardin, Bernal and Haldane, as well as Stapledon, to imagine a future in which we had remade our natures and regularly remade worlds. Where Stapledon differed was in his doubt, educated by a wide reading in past philosophy, that we either could or should try to control everything. He also recognized the possibility that there were other creatures, far away from here and of a different biological kind, who yet "served the Spirit." Loyalty to "the Spirit" also required an ironically worshipful submission to a reality that always transcends our grasp, and that may, in the end, be better known by other means than the merely intellectual. "Although, when clerics expound their faith," he said in a review of Wells's *Star-Begotten*,[4] "I fly to line up behind Mr. Wells, I am an erring disciple. For, when he in turn explains, I feel a restless expectation of a something more which is never forthcoming. He is too ready to assume that an idealization of the positivistic, scientific mood, which is mainly a product of the nineteenth century, really can adequately suggest the essence of the truly human mentality."

He was a philosopher inspired by scientific speculation and older theory alike. Fashions in philosophy have shifted several times since the nineteen thirties: "logical positivists," who claimed (self-refutingly) that only observational and analytic sentences were even meaningful (a claim that was, by its own lights, therefore meaningless), paid no attention to Stapledon's

---

[3] Brian Aldiss, "Review of L. A. Fiedler's *Olaf Stapledon: a Man Divided*": *Times Literary Supplement*, September 23, 1982, 1007–8. Aldiss rightly criticizes many of Fiedler's errors, but is hardly better informed himself about Stapledon's life and reputation.

[4] Olaf Stapledon, in *London Mercury* (1937); reprinted in *Perry Rhodan 86* (New York: Ace, 1976), 133ff. Wells's book *Star-Begotten* (London: Sphere, 1975 [1937]) has a theme not unlike that of Stapledon's own *Last Men in London* (Harmondsworth: Penguin, 1972 [1932]), but the two writers had quite different notions of what a real awakening would be.

worries about the reality of time, the relationship of mind and brain, and the nature of spiritual maturity. Present-day philosophers have returned to those ancient problems that, he said, would still trouble thinkers at the far end of humankind's existence,[5] and can still learn from Stapledon. They might learn, for example, the folly of those such as the Fourth Men, the Great Brains, who "casually solved, to [their] own satisfaction at least, the ancient problems of good and evil, of mind and its object, of the one and the many, of truth and error," without any genuine spirituality, or even any self-deprecating sense of humour. The danger is that they may also neglect the writings by which he was instructed, namely the great Greek philosophers, especially Plato, the Stoics, Sceptics, and Plotinus. For Plotinus, for many the last great Classical philosopher, so Armstrong has written, "philosophical discussion and reflection are not simply means for solving intellectual problems (though they are and must be that). They are also charms for the deliverance of the soul."[6] Many passing remarks in Stapledon's fiction earn longer discussions elsewhere — the reality of time, the possibility of a world composed solely of sounds,[7] the nature of the mind, and its engagement with material reality. They never become merely technical discussions.

> Theories, theories, myriads upon myriads of them, streamed over me like wind-borne leaves, like the contents of some titanic paper-factory flung aloft by the storm, like dust-clouds in the hurricane advance of the mind. Gasping in this vast whirling aridity, I almost forgot that in every mote of it lay some few spores of the

---

[5] Stapledon, *Last and First Men* (Harmondsworth: Penguin, 1972 [1930]), 213.
[6] A. H. Armstrong, "Plotinus," in *The Cambridge History of Later Greek and Early Medieval Philosophy*, ed. Armstrong (Cambridge: Cambridge University Press, 1970), 195–271, 260, after Plotinus, *Ennead* V.3 [49].17.
[7] That image appears both in *Star Maker* and in "A World of Sound" (*Hotch Potch*, ed. John Brophy [Liverpool: Royal Liverpool Children's Hospital, 1936]: see *Complete Works of Stapledon* [Hastings: Delphi Classics, 2001]). It was further amplified and analysed by P. F. Strawson in his *Individuals: an essay in descriptive metaphysics* (Reading: Routledge, 1964), 59–86, though Strawson himself (personal communication) did not recall encountering Stapledon's invention. See Barry Dainton, "Life without Space: Stapledon and Strawson on Auditory Universes," (https://www.liverpool.ac.uk/philosophy/olaf-stapledon/life-without-space/), accessed July 30, 2024.

organic truth, most often parched and dead but sometimes living, pregnant, significant.[8]

But though Stapledon's academic publications are not as ephemeral as some have thought, his best-known work is still *Last and
First Men*, a "history" of the next several million years whose
literal inaccuracy about the immediate future is no real flaw.
Britain may not have fought a destructive war with France in
the late twentieth century, and the Chinese don't wear pigtails
any longer. But maybe we are indeed now living through the
gradual, global victory of a blend of vulgar piety and technical
brilliance: the sort of religiosity that sees religious merit in wealth
and technocratic progress. And even if this too turns out false,
the main message of that saga is still worth remembering: not
that of Wells in either his hopeful or his despairing mood, but
rather that world-views change with changes in biological and
historical setting, that the Truth lies beyond us all, and yet may
be the object of our desire.

It does sometimes seem that Stapledon wishes to persuade us
that all systems of law and metaphysics rest upon the material
necessities of the time. The Holy Empire of Music, for example,
which prevails among the Third Men for a thousand years, purports to be founded on "the fiction that every human being was a
melody, demanding completion within a greater musical theme of
society,"[9] but really derives its power from the biological realities
of that species.[10] He does not conclude, however, with the self-
refuting thesis that there is no escape from relativities. "It was
necessary that man should be forced for a while to stand on his
own feet, arrogantly but totteringly, so as to rediscover in blood
and tears his own weakness and folly, and his inability to save
himself without the passion born of a vision of something which
in some important sense is beyond himself."[11] That we cannot lay
hold firmly on Truth Absolute is itself a truth that shows we are not
bound within the circles of our time and kind (for if we were, we
could neither know nor care that we had not grasped the Truth).

---

[8] Stapledon, *Last and First Men*, 379.
[9] Cf. J. R. R. Tolkien's creation myth, *Ainulindalë*, in *The Silmarillion*, ed.
Christopher Tolkien (London: Allen and Unwin, 1977), 1–12.
[10] Stapledon, *Last and First Men*, 199.
[11] Stapledon, "The Meaning of Spirit," in *Here and Now*, eds. P. Albery and
S. Read (London: Falcon Press, 1949), 72ff.

In his later life Stapledon was identified as a "fellow-traveler," though on no better grounds than that he attended (as perhaps he should not have done) the Soviet-backed Cultural and Scientific Conference for Peace in 1949, alongside J. D. Bernal and W. E. B. DuBois,[12] and retained his (broadly) socialist ideals, and his recognition of the material context even of sound thought. He was not alone. A great many thinkers of the Nineteen Thirties believed it necessary to say what suffering, what indignity, the old regime had created, and saw Marxist revolutionaries as the most active and least self-regarding heralds of a better order. A great many thinkers also thought that we should soon have a complete and unified theory of Life, the Universe, and Everything. Once that was achieved, they supposed, we need never be surprised by anything again, nor need we fear that our power ever be less than our desire. All understanding increases power: perfect understanding would allow us unlimited power, either to change the world or (at the least) to change our selves, or our subjects' selves, so that they no longer nursed truly *impossible* desires. The common good would be well served (they thought) when we had bred "individualism" and "superstition" out of the race. "They were preparing to take charge of mankind, to make the planet into a single well-planned estate, and to re-orientate human nature. But what kind of world would they desire to make, whose knowledge was only of numbers?"[13] Even decent and intelligent writers allowed themselves such thoughts as must now alarm us:

> The task confronting biology, physiology and medicine is not only to master scientifically the maladies and phenomena of counter-evolution (sterility and physical weakening) which undermine the growth of the noosphere — but to produce by various means (selection, control of the sexes, action of hormones, hygiene, etc) a superior human type.... What attitude should the

---

[12] See National Council of Arts, Sciences and Professions, Cultural and scientific conference for world peace program, March 27, 1949. W. E. B. Du Bois Papers (MS 312). Special Collections and University Archives, University of Massachusetts Amherst Libraries: https://credo.library.umass.edu/view/full/mums312-b283-i001. Accessed July 30, 2024.
[13] Stapledon, *Last and First Men*, 571.

advancing sector of humanity adopt towards static and
decidedly unprogressive ethnic groups?[14]

Or consider Haldane's wishful fantasy of future evolution, when
such self-regarding sentiments as pride, "a personal preference
concerning mating," and even pity ("an unpleasant feeling aroused
by the suffering of other individuals") have been bred out of the
species.[15] Eugenicists of the kind all too familiar in the early part
of that century imagined that they could breed a "better" sort of
humanity. The notorious Scopes Trial, in 1925, it is ironical now
to remember, concerned a textbook written from the heights
of American Eugenicism,[16] which contained such gems as this:

> Parasitism and its Cost to Society.—Hundreds of fami-
> lies such as those described above exist today, spreading
> disease, immorality, and crime to all parts of this country.
> The cost to society of such families is very severe. Just
> as certain animals or plants become parasitic on other
> plants or animals, these families have become parasitic
> on society. They not only do harm to others by corrupt-
> ing, stealing, or spreading disease, but they are actually
> protected and cared for by the state out of public money.
> Largely for them the poorhouse and the asylum exist.
> They take from society, but they give nothing in return.
> They are true parasites. The Remedy.—If such people
> were lower animals, we would probably kill them off to
> prevent them from spreading. Humanity will not allow
> this, but we do have the remedy of separating the sexes
> in asylums or other places and in various ways preventing
> intermarriage and the possibilities of perpetuating such
> a low and degenerate race. Remedies of this sort have
> been tried successfully in Europe and are now meeting
> with some success in this country.[17]

---

[14] Teilhard de Chardin, writing in 1937: R. Speaight, *Teilhard de Chardin:
a biography* (London: Collins, 1967), 233f.
[15] J. B. S. Haldane, *Possible Worlds* (London: Chatto and Windus, 1930
[1927]), 303.
[16] See Edwin Black, *War against the Weak: Eugenics and America's Campaign
to Create a Master Race* (New York: Four Walls Eight Windows, 2003) for a
detailed account of the "experts" who imprisoned, sterilized, and castrated
people they deemed "unfit," in defiance of law, the American Constitution,
and ordinary decency.
[17] George William Hunter, *A Civic Biology: Presented in Problems* (New York:
American Book Co., 1914), 263. See Edward J. Larson, *Summer for the Gods:*

Stapledon, to similar effect, incorporated in some of his for-ward-looking fantasies doctrines, of a superior humanity disdain-ful of our present small-minded morals, which were soon to be dreadfully embodied in the here and now. His utopian researchers regularly experiment on children, eliminate "the unfit," and see themselves as heralds of a greater dawn licensed to do just what they please to those they judge inferior. Readers sometimes fail to notice this. One of Brian Aldiss's most extraordinary critical judgments, for example, is his description of *Odd John*[18] as a "pleasant superman tale," with a "light and cheerful mood."[19] John is a multiple murderer, who treats human beings as ver-min, experimental animals, or pets, and is critical of totalitarian barbarism only because it misidentifies, so he supposes, the real *Homo Superior* (which is to say, himself). He and his companions end in mass suicide rather than collaborate with ordinary people, whom they despise as an "inferior species." They are "aristocrats" only in the sense condemned by Stapledon himself even when he admits the value of an intellectual aristocracy.[20]

Stapledon, it is clear, did not really believe in "scientific social-ism." He attended "Peace Conferences" not "to cut some kind of figure in a world whose attention he had failed to capture,"[21] but because he thought it desperately important (as of course it was) that people try to understand each other. "To avoid a savage religious war, it is desperately urgent that each side make a serious attempt to understand and respect the most cherished values of the other and to see itself through the other's eyes"[22]—and so to learn humility. "Marxists of the harsher kind . . . bring revolution

---

The Scopes Trial and America's Continuing Debate over Science and Religion (Cam-bridge, MA: Harvard University Press, 1998) for an account of the political and economic context of the trial. The play *Inherit the Wind* (1955; filmed in 1960) misrepresents Bryan, Darrow, and the point at issue.
[18] Stapledon, *Odd John* (London: Methuen, 1935).
[19] B. Aldiss, *Billion Year Spree* (London: Weidenfeld and Nicholson, 1973), 235–36. See also Aldiss, "Review of Fiedler": "*Odd John* is a worthwhile contribution in the poor Little Superman line."
[20] Stapledon, *Saints and Revolutionaries* (London: Heinemann, 1939), 98.
[21] As Aldiss suggests in his review of Fiedler's book, "Review of Fiedler," 1008. It is a matter of record that he *had* captured at least as much atten-tion as Aldous and Julian Huxley, Cyril Joad, or D. H. Lawrence: see, for example, J. B. Coates, *Ten Modern Prophets* (London: Muller, 1944).
[22] Addressing the New York conference in 1949. Cited by L. A. Fiedler, *Olaf Stapledon: a Man Divided* (Oxford: Oxford University Press, 1983), 24.

into disrepute. They give some excuse for the fear that if they were in power they would prove as insensitive and ruthless as their opponents."[23] The future offered us annihilation, totalitarian rule, or else a new kind of human world whose lineaments we could detect in personal love and humane endeavor.

Almost all the experiments that Stapledon imagines—except perhaps those that end with the Last Men—lead to calamity, partly because the Eugenicists themselves have no clear or sound ideas of what "better" means, and partly, as Plato knew, because the World always disrupts our plans. Shall we breed for manual dexterity, or musical sensitivity, or ecological wholeness, or Great Brains ("huge bumps of curiosity equipped with cunning hands"),[24] or ecstatic flight (all of which ideals—and others—are sketched in *Last and First Men*)? Alternate futures are represented, for example, in *Darkness and the Light*.[25] But even in the better future his superior beings, or self-styled supermen, invariably confront a reality that surpasses them, that cannot be wholly understood or controlled. Even the Last Men are confronted by an incomprehensible immensity, and are at last demoralized and brushed away by a cosmic accident.[26] Even when the developed intellects of an entire sidereal cosmos—long after humankind's extinction—reach out to the Maker and Sustainer of Worlds, the Star Maker, near the very end of cosmic evolution, they find it beyond their grasp. According to Leibniz, another philosopher with a gift—largely undeveloped—for speculative fiction, "there is no Spirit, however exalted, who does not have an infinite number of others superior to him." He claimed however, "that although we are much inferior to so many intelligent beings, we have the privilege of not being visibly over-mastered on this planet,

---

[23] Stapledon, *Philosophy and Living* (Harmondsworth: Penguin, 1939), 38. That they had *already* proved this was apparently not something that Stapledon quite realized.

[24] Stapledon, *Last and First Men*, 212. These beings Stapledon depicts as devoid of any instinctive responses save curiosity and constructiveness, operating "a very accurate behavioristic psychology," but with no inner understanding of their subjects (civil and experimental).

[25] Stapledon, *Darkness and Light* (London: Methuen, 1942). The better future is brought about by Tibetan missionaries, the worse by a romantic sado-masochism.

[26] Doris Lessing, in *The Making of the Representative of Planet 8* (London: Jonathan Cape, 1982) attempts a more hopeful response to such a planetary collapse, in line with Stapledon's more optimistic moments.

on which we hold unchallenged supremacy."[27] Stapledon chose to represent beings that overmastered us and our descendants, only to find themselves as distant from the One as ever. The Infinite is not a Very Big Number, and Odd John, despite the sycophantic praise of that novel's narrator, is no nearer Truth than we, even if he has shed a few of our delusions. When Stapledon's Last Men peer into a pool on Neptune, admiring their distant cousin, Homunculus, they relive Stapledon's own visit to the pools of Anglesey.[28] And both repeat the image used by Plato in his *Phaedo*, that we live ourselves in the dells and rock pools of a richer world.[29] "What a world this pond is! Like the world you are to plunge into so soon."[30] And the Last Men themselves are to discover that their world too is set within immensity.

But though our worlds are small ones, lost in time and space, it still matters how we live in them. There is still a distinction to be made between different kinds of community, different kinds

---

[27] Leibniz, *New Essays on Human Understanding*, eds. J. Bennett and P. Remnant (Cambridge: Cambridge University Press, 1981), 490 (4.17.16).

[28] Compare *Last Men in London*, 343, and P. McCarthy, *Olaf Stapledon* (Boston: Twayne, 1982), 32. See also Stapledon, *Star Maker* (London: Methuen, 1937), 204: the greatest of galactic intelligences watch the rise and fall of civilizations as "might we ourselves look down into some rock-pool where lowly creatures repeat with naive zest dramas learned by their ancestors aeons ago."

[29] Plato, *Phaedo* 109a–d: "I believe" [says Socrates in the story] "that the earth is very large and that we who dwell between the pillars of Hercules and the river Phasis live in a small part of it about the sea, like ants or frogs about a pond, and that many other people live in many other such regions. For I believe there are in all directions on the earth many hollows of very various forms and sizes, into which the water and mist and air have run together; but the earth itself is pure and is situated in the pure heaven in which the stars are, the heaven which those who discourse about such matters call the ether; the water, mist and air are the sediment of this and flow together into the hollows of the earth. Now we do not perceive that we live in the hollows, but think we live on the upper surface of the earth, just as if someone who lives in the depth of the ocean should think he lived on the surface of the sea, and, seeing the sun and the stars through the water, should think the sea was the sky, and should, by reason of sluggishness or feebleness, never have reached the surface of the sea, and should never have seen, by rising and lifting his head out of the sea into our upper world, and should never have heard from anyone who had seen, how much purer and fairer it is than the world he lived in. Now I believe this is just the case with us; for we dwell in a hollow of the earth and think we dwell on its upper surface; and the air we call the heaven, and think that is the heaven in which the stars move." Plato, *Euthyphro, Apology, Crito, Phaedo, Phaedrus* (Cambridge, MA: Loeb Classics Library, 1982), 375–77.

[30] Stapledon, *Last and First Men*, 344.

of whole, different pictures of the Spirit. For Stapledon did not conclude that because the Truth was always greater than our thought of it, there was therefore *nothing* to be said for one side against another. "When scientific detachment supports a simple materialistic metaphysic and denies right and wrong and all the higher reaches of human experience, it takes the first step toward social disaster."[31] And a few years later: "if Churchill's mentality, with all its faults, is not objectively more developed and less perverted than Hitler's, not only is this war [1939–45] not worth fighting, but also the struggle in every human mind in all ages of history between the somnolent and the lucid ways of behaving is based on an illusion."[32] He often suggested that the future would be a struggle between communities that did and those that didn't deny the value and particular powers of individuals. The "right" kind of community was one in which human persons remained individuals even though they felt themselves to be members of a larger whole. The spirit that wakes successively in mortal individual, bomber-crew, nation, and humankind through the story of *Death into Life*[33] is one that arises out of genuine communication, real friendships. He feared that this was at risk. "Genuine sociality tends now to be rejected in favour of the more primitive kind of sociality based on sheer animal gregariousness, in which the dominant motive is not mutual respect but the will to conform to the behaviour of the group, and to enforce conformity."[34] The merely aggregative, domineering unities that enlightened humans strive against in the shape of Martian invaders, or mad empires (in *Last and First Men* or *Star Maker*), do not allow for personal love, because, as Haldane hoped, there *are* no individual persons there.

A properly "corporate intelligence" requires the real existence of individual persons who are fully open and cooperative — a form of life of which we can form only a slight impression.[35] Stapledon,

---

[31] Stapledon, *Philosophy and Living*, 85.
[32] Stapledon, "Morality, Scepticism and Theism": *Proceedings of the Aristotelian Society*, 44 (1944), 15–42, 39.
[33] Stapledon, *Death into Life* (London: Methuen, 1946).
[34] Stapledon, *Philosophy and Living*, 88.
[35] See my "Science Fiction and Religion," in *The Blackwell Companion to Science Fiction*, ed. David Seed (Oxford: Blackwell, 2005), 95–110. I conclude that essay with the suggestion that Science Fiction itself offers an ambiguous form of religion for its fans, pridefully united in the feeling that they will welcome the future.

Theodore Sturgeon, and Henry Kuttner[36] all conceive it as a form of loving conversation—as did Plotinus:

> Plotinus's divine mind [which is also the totality of intelligible being] is not just a mind knowing a lot of eternal objects. It is an organic living community of interpenetrating beings which are at once Forms and intelligences, all "awake and alive," in which every part thinks and therefore is the whole; so that all are one mind and yet each retains its distinct individuality without which the whole would be impoverished. And this mind-world is the region where our own mind, illumined by the divine intellect, finds its true self and lives its own life, its proper home and the penultimate stage on its journey, from which it is taken up to union with the Good.[37]

Others present it rather as a more powerful, many-bodied individual: so in Clarke's *Childhood's End* (1954) the Overmind takes up into itself the minds, memories, and wills of the last human children, without any assurance that those children themselves, or the rest of the living world that vanishes as their collectivity rises to join the cosmic collective, have any kind of continued being. Being absorbed into an Overmind, as Robert Sheckley's version remarks in *Dimension of Miracles* (1968), is "exactly the same as death, though it sounds much nicer." Though Clarke later disclaimed any "religious" significance in his story, the narrative seems to suggest that such an absorption into a "higher" form of life is to be regarded as the "real" goal of religion. The entities that both prepare the way for the Overmind, and are forever excluded from it, have the form of pantomime devils, as if to suggest that the only alternative is one that would be thought diabolical—or perhaps that the transformation they half-willingly assist is itself diabolical.

Stapledon was wiser. He always reverted to "the little glowing atom of community,"[38] his marriage to Agnes, and would accept no system that denied its value. Readers drew the wrong lesson if

---

[36] Theodore Sturgeon, in *More than Human* (1953), imagines his hidden god as composed of humans united in telepathic communication; so also Henry Kuttner, in *Mutant* (1954).
[37] A. H. Armstrong and R. A. Markus, *Christian Faith and Greek Philosophy* (London: Darton, Longman, and Todd, 1960), 27.
[38] Stapledon, *Last and First Men*, 333.

they thought that the here and now no longer mattered, or that our value lay only in our contribution to an inhuman End. Doris Lessing's *Canopus in Argos* sequence is a truer representation of the Stapledonian perspective.[39] John Wren-Lewis would have been wary of the "cosmic" aspects of Stapledon's mysticism, while also acknowledging that he almost knew better:

> When the prophets of the Bible raved about idolatry, they meant just this sort of mystical subordination of man to the great system of nature. Against this, those who have the religion of Jesus want to assert that people do *not* acquire significance by performing any sort of function, however lofty, in any larger system, however universal. They can have absolute significance *as individuals*, by the simple process of giving it to each other in ordinary personal relationships. The Christian believes this because he holds that the Absolute God, whose name is love, is present in personal relationships, but he might welcome a *real* atheist who held the same personalist values, in the name of what [H. J.] Blackham [1923–2009] calls "the self-sufficiency of perishable things," as an ally against all attempts to resurrect the Great God Pan.[40]

THE FLAMES

But there is still a problem about Stapledon's vision that can be explored through a look at one of his less well known fables, *The Flames*,[41] which encapsulates many of his concerns and characteristic ironies. Patrick McCarthy correctly observes that "as an example of controlled and sustained irony *The Flames* is without parallel among Stapledon's works."[42] Thos, the critical minnow-watcher,

---

[39] See Doris Lessing *Archives Re: Colonized Planet 5: Shikasta* (Cape: London 1979); the third novel of her sequence, *The Sirian Experiments* (Cape: London 1981) describes one of the "Mad Empires"; the fourth, *The Making of the Representative for Planet 8* (Cape: London 1982), well captures Stapledon's image of the spirit's (ambiguous) triumph at world's end.

[40] John Wren-Lewis, Letter, "The Observer," September 10, 1961, writing in opposition to Julian Huxley. See my "Atheists and Idolaters: the Case of John Wren-Lewis," in *Atheisms: the philosophy of non-belief*, eds., Victoria S. Harrison and Harriet A. Harris (Abingdon and New York: Routledge, 2023), 90–125.

[41] Stapledon, *The Flames* (London: Secker and Warburg, 1947).

[42] McCarthy, *Olaf Stapledon*, 115.

presents and comments on the narrative of Cass, the speculative generalist. Cass, after years of seeking to see and understand things "from the inside," by telepathic or mystical means, seems to himself to have been addressed by a living flame, hidden in a pebble plucked from a cold, snow-shrouded landscape. It turns out that there are such creatures, "salamanders," born in the sun's troposphere and condemned to live out a cold and inter- mittent existence on solid earth since the planets were formed. The late world war, and its manifold fires, have brought them out of hibernation in the dust of the air,[43] and they sense the possibility of forming a symbiotic alliance with us: we to provide the environment within which they can live, they to provide the mental stability and community awareness—Lessing's "Substance- Of-We-Feeling"—that we lack. This sort of symbiotic pattern is many times repeated in Stapledon's work. If we cannot agree, the flames' other option is to instigate nuclear spasm: "then at last, with the whole planet turned into a single atomic bomb, and all the incandescent continents hurtling into space, we should have for a short while conditions almost as good as those of our golden age in the sun."[44] Cass is on the point of agreeing to act as the flames' ambassador, when he learns that his own marriage had been deliberately destroyed by the flames (and his wife incidentally driven to suicide) so that he might be a suitably single-minded instrument of their purposes (the Neptunian hero of *Last Men in London* had done the same, a little less violently, to his victim, unrebuked).[45] Cass concludes that this proves the flames' real

---

[43] An idea perhaps echoed from Leibniz, who suggested that every ani- mate being had existed forever in seminal form, only roused to moral life occasionally.

[44] *The Flames*, 61.

[45] The Neptunian offers a typically pompous justification of his "mental vivisection" (*Last Men in London*, 391): that it was a necessary part of a very lofty task to which Paul would have agreed "in his best moments"—an excuse that William James also offered for the abusive vivisection of dogs: "Consider a poor dog whom they are vivisecting in a laboratory. He lies strapped on a board and shrieking at its executioners, and to his own dark consciousness is literally in a sort of hell. He cannot see a single redeeming ray in the whole business; and yet all these diabolical-seeming events are often controlled by human intentions with which, if his poor benighted mind could only be made to catch a glimpse of them, all that is heroic in him would religiously acquiesce.... Lying on his back on the board there he may be performing a function incalculably higher than any that

ill-will, destroys the flame with a glass of cold water (the flames turn to revivable dust if slowly extinguished, but perish forever if suddenly doused), and sets himself to warn humankind of their deadly peril. He is eventually incarcerated in an asylum, where the flames again convince him that their intentions at least were good. Meanwhile, however, their more lucid companions, in the sun, have (as usual in Stapledon) discovered that Reality "was wholly alien to the spirit, and wholly indifferent to the most sacred values of the awakened minds of the cosmos,"[46] and are undergoing a desperate religious war in which the flames' original pious agnosticism is lost. Cass, himself now converted to that typically Stapledonian position, is threatened by flames converted in their turn to a militant religiosity. Cass dies in a fire, victim of homicide or, as Thos supposes, his own deranged endeavor.

The swirling confusion of Stapledonian history is here compressed into one man's life, and the struggle to live lucidly, without self-deception, is depicted without sentimental gloss. Who is deceived? Who is sane? Allegorically, of course, the flames are simply those technological powers whose use may lead to paradise or disaster. Or else they are a shifting image of the individual-in-community, less inclined than we to imagine that they are abstract individuals, rather than elements within the global, or the stellar community, and by the same token all too ready to ignore the needs and passions of each such element, and to fall, like Stapledon's Martians, into the little death of the hive-mind. Or else, again, they are images of the division that concerned Stapledon so often, between sleep and awakened life. The story even allows him what he does not attempt elsewhere, the thought that present individuals are fallen creatures, forever reaching towards a perfection they have lost: "each new experience came to us with a haunting sense of familiarity and a suspicion that the new version was but a crude and partial substitute for the old."[47]

The ultimate unreality of time's passage, Stapledon's other constant theme, is not represented in *The Flames*, though the mere

---

prosperous canine life admits of" (William James, "Is Life Worth Living?" [1895], in *Essays in Popular Philosophy* [New York: Longmans Green and Co., 1897], 32–62, 58). Stapledon's Neptunian, and the eventual cosmic spirit, realize at last that they themselves are being treated to an identical torment.
[46] Stapledon, *The Flames*, 79. The same "discovery" is imagined in *Darkness and the Light*, that we are no more than snowflakes trampled by battling titans.
[47] *The Flames*, 37.

fact that millennia of high endeavor are compressed and mirrored in the last few months of one man's life is a little reminder that time does not advance, and the collapse even of the high solar civilization of the Flames (contacted at long last by the terrestrial exiles) a warning that there is no security within time.

The Flames entertain the project of initiating nuclear spasm, "through loyalty to the spirit in us," if they should decide that the human species was doomed to self-destruction sooner or later,[48] rather as the Fifth Men of Stapledon's other future history destroy the native inhabitants of Venus, on the plea that they are less developed and failing creatures: this latter slaughter, incidentally, produces in its agents on the one hand an "unreasoning disgust with humanity," and, on the other, a "grave elation" expressing itself in the thought that "the murder of Venerian life was terrible but right." Odd John assures his biographer bluntly, "If we could wipe out your whole species, we would,"[49] though in the end he and his fellows refrain.

The unresolved ambiguities of the story—are the flames trustworthy or not; is Cass insane or not; is the god of humane devotion certain to be victorious or not; is "agnostic piety, an inarticulate worship of I know not what for being I know not what, except that it is worshipful,"[50] coherent or humane; do personal ties count for more or less than an imagined general good; are the demands of the heart to be accepted alongside the judgments of the mind or not—are what makes it art rather than academic philosophy. This, however, does not make it less *philosophical* in a broader sense. The flames' philosophizing, too, "was more imaginative and less conceptual than [ours], more of the nature of art, of myth-construction, which [they] knew to be merely symbolical, not literally true."[51] They recognize a lack in themselves, of precise analysis and practical intelligence, which they hope will be compensated within a future symbiosis. This, too, is a common theme in Stapledon: the arachnoids and ich-thyoids who are the core of the eventual galactic and cosmic spirit embody the active and contemplative virtues, and are lost without each other. The plant-men who inhabit certain small, hot worlds,

---

[48] Ibid., 60.
[49] *Odd John*, 216.
[50] "Morality, Scepticism and Theism," 42.
[51] *The Flames*, 34. Plato thought much the same about his speculations.

similarly, have daytime and night-time phases: "during the busy night-time they went about their affairs as insulated individuals," and during the day they are united in contemplative ardor with the cosmos. "In the day-time mode [a plant-man] passed no moral judgment on himself or others. He mentally reviewed every kind of human conduct with detached contemplative joy, as a factor in the universe. But when night came again, bringing the active nocturnal mood, the calm, day-time insight into himself and others was lit with a fire of moral praise and censure."[52] The plant-men fail, because after a prolonged attempt to live without contemplation, detached (literally!) from their roots, they swing to the opposite extreme. "Little by little they gave less and less energy and time to animal pursuits, until at last their nights as well as their days were spent wholly as trees, and the active, exploring, manipulating, animal intelligence died in them forever."[53] A similar fate awaits the contemplative lemurs at the hands of our own more "practical" ancestors,[54] while our own "practical" species goes down in ruin for its failure to remember its place in the world.

The tension is not one that Stapledon ever rationally resolved: on the one hand, the active intelligence wills to produce as fine a future as possible; on the other, the contemplative intelligence, on Stapledon's account, insists that this already is the finest universe possible, however ill it suits our animal passions. "The Man who became a Tree," one of his short stories, ends with the tree's acceptance even of the woodman's axe. In *Odd John*, similarly, John's murderous activity is contrasted with the contemplative Islam of an old boatman, as "superior" as John but wholly disinclined to try and make any difference to the world. "Allah wills of his creatures two kinds of service. One is that they should toil to fulfil his active purpose in the world. The other is that they should observe with understanding and praise with discriminating delight the excellent form of his handiwork."[55] This distinction is elaborated in *Saints and Revolutionaries*, together with many warnings of the revolutionary's, and the saint's, perversions. Both are necessary, but each seems to exclude the other.

---

[52] *Star Maker*, 109–10.
[53] Ibid., 111.
[54] Ibid., 456.
[55] *Odd John*, 194.

GOD, GUIDANCE, AND PLOTINUS

The question is: can we retain a real "devotion to the Spirit" while conducting ourselves like Odd John, the Fifth Men, or the Flames? May we commit genocide "through loyalty to the Spirit," as Haldane, Teilhard de Chardin, and Himmler all imagined, or knowingly destroy the sanity of our children or the lives of "brutes" for the sake of an ideal? "Were the masters of Buchenwald my ministers?," asks Stapledon's imagined God with heavy irony in Stapledon's last (posthumously published) work.[56] Surely not: any advantage won by deceit or violence is "outweighed by a greater hurt in the future, namely damage to the tradition of kindliness and reasonableness."[57] Conversely, can we retain a real devotion to humane endeavor if we teach ourselves that "in the universe as a whole all suffering and all evil contribute to the development of mind, or the awakening of spirit"?[58]

Stapledon recognized in himself an opposition between the little, frightened animal and the realistic intelligence, between everyday concerns and a memory of our cosmic place, even between cooperative action and contemplative joy, between "the saint" and "the revolutionary": all oppositions which Fiedler sought to psychoanalyze away, and which Stapledon sought to resolve through critical intelligence, and faith in the light. "Little by little [Paul] came to think of this Neptunian factor in his mind as truly 'himself,' and the normal Terrestrial as 'other,' something like an unruly horse which his true self must somehow break in and ride"[59]—as Plato had said before him. It is understandable that some people should resent that intelligence:

---

[56] Agnes Stapledon, ed., *The Opening of the Eyes* (London: Methuen, 1954), 8.
[57] Stapledon, *Philosophy and Living*, 101, though this reliance on longer-term utilitarian reasoning is not in fact a satisfactory answer to the violent revolutionary.
[58] *Philosophy and Living*, 46.
[59] *Last Men in London*, 393. It is odd that psychiatrists so easily assume that "depersonalisation" is of merely psychiatric interest—an odd condition that needs management or cure (see Daphne Simeon and Jeffrey Abugel, *Feeling Unreal: Depersonalization and the Loss of the Self*, 2nd edition [Toronto: Oxford University Press, 2023; online edition, Oxford Academic, March 23, 2023]). It should rather be seen as the beginnings of philosophy: see my "Plotinus: Body and Mind": *Cambridge Companion to Plotinus*, ed. Lloyd Gerson (Cambridge: Cambridge University Press, 1996), 275–91. Simeon and Abugel do acknowledge the existence of philosophical thought on these matters, but only amongst existentialists and Western Buddhists.

If we were all on board ship and there was trouble among the stewards, I can just conceive their chief spokesmen looking with disfavour on anyone who stole away from the fierce debates in the saloon or pantry to take a breather on deck. For up there, he would taste the salt, he would see the vastness of the weather, he would remember that the ship had a whither and a whence. He would remember things like fogs, storms, and what had seemed in the hot, lighted rooms down below to be merely the scene for a political crisis would appear once more as a thin egg-shell moving rapidly through an immense darkness over an element in which men cannot live.[60]

C. S. Lewis, though he has been falsely accused of misrepresenting Stapledon, here speaks with a Stapledonian—or rather, a classical philosophical—voice. Like Stapledon's bird-men, Lewis's Ransom (in *Out of the Silent Planet*) can accept even his own death (so he supposes) if it takes place in the heavens: his earth-bound, muddy self feels differently. Or consider Machiavelli's praise of ardent scholarship, a vocation now derided by political "realists," social climbers, disgruntled students, and other philistines:

> On the coming of evening I return to my house and enter my study; and at the door I take off the day's clothing covered with mud and dust . . . and put on garments regal and courtly; and reclothed appropriately, I enter ancient courts of ancient men where, received by them with affection, I feed on that food which only is mine and which I was born for, where I am not ashamed to speak with them and ask them reasons for their actions; and they in their kindness answer me; and for four hours of time I do not feel boredom, I forget every trouble, I do not dread poverty, I am not so frightened by death; I give myself entirely over to them.[61]

---

[60] C. S. Lewis, *Of Other Worlds* (London: Bles, 1966), 59–60. Lewis makes clear (77) that his villainous scientist, Weston (in *Out of the Silent Planet*), was primarily inspired by Haldane's writings, not Stapledon's, despite Aldiss's inaccurate observation that "this pillorying represents about the peak of Stapledon's fame" (Aldiss, "Review of Fiedler," 1008).

[61] Machiavelli to Vettori, December 10, 1513: cited by J. Hillman, *Re-Visioning Psychology* (New York: Harper and Row, 1975), 199.

But it was not scholarship alone that Stapledon and his Neptunian sought to practise: what they sought was insight into truth, a way of waking up from ordinary self-concerns. Plotinus's image of that great awakening was of the living unity-in-diversity of Intellect, described in terms of the interpenetration of a community of living minds. It is an image found in other traditions also: God, so Tibetan lamas told Francisco Orazio della Penna (1680–1745), "is the assembly of all the holy ones."[62] This Intellect has its being and its purpose in contemplation of the rationally incomprehensible One, that from which the universe, itself alive in every part, takes its beginning. The individual soul is "carried out by the surge of the wave of Intellect itself and lifted on high by a kind of swell, and sees suddenly, not seeing how."[63] What it sees is not to be identified with any human love, but no-one can ever see it who does not practise virtue and humane benevolence. Love is only spiritual when "there is a waking to discover and value something more than the particular beloved individual and the particular common 'we,'"[64] but it can never forget its particular beginning if it is to avoid a long decline into the hive mind.

> Two lights for guidance. The first our little glowing atom of community, with all that it signifies. The second the cold light of the stars, symbol of the hypercosmical reality, with its crystal ecstasy.[65]

---

[62] According to I. Kant, *Kant's Political Writings*, ed. Hans Reiss (Cambridge: Cambridge University Press, 1970), 107. Francisco Orazio was a Capuchin friar, part of a mission to Tibet from 1719. Kant further attempted an implausible conjunction between Tibet and the Eleusinian Mysteries, via the supposed similarity of the Eleusinian cry "Konx Ompax" and the Tibetan (transliterated) term for God, "Concioa," and "Om" (or "blessed"). He proposed that "holy (Konx), heavenly (Om), and wise (Pax)" together amounted to "the supreme being who pervades the whole world, i.e. nature personified." These speculations are perhaps best forgotten!

[63] Plotinus, *Ennead* VI.7 [38].36, 17–19, trans. A. H. Armstrong (Loeb Classical Library, Heinemann: London 1988).

[64] Stapledon, "The Meaning of Spirit," in *Here and Now*, eds. P. Albery and S. Read (London: Falcon Press, 1949), 72ff.

[65] Stapledon, *Star Maker*, 333. It is perhaps also significant that the Neptunian narrator of humankind's story is left at last beside his lover, an astronomer: "we have ranged in our work very far apart.... But now we will remain together till the end. There is nothing more for us to do but to remember, to tolerate, to find strength together, to keep the spirit clear so long as may be." *Last Men in London*, 604.

Conversely, a Neptunian or higher spirit wishing to visit us, to "tune into" our inner being, must select "that mode of the primitive which is . . . characterized by repressed sexuality, excessive self-regard and an intelligence which is both rudimentary and in bondage to unruly cravings. . . . He must also reconstruct in himself the unconscious obsession with matter, or rather with the control of matter by machinery and chemical manipulation. He must conceive also the mind's unwitting obeisance and self-distrust before its robot offspring."[66] So also Plotinus.

Plotinus, in short, is the source and inspiration of much that is of lasting value in Stapledon. Those who think of him merely as a propagandist for a great science-inspired mythology, neglect the serious philosophical concerns and scholarship that moved him. He did not only look forwards, and, like the Last Men, saw nothing odd in exploring the past imaginings and theories of humanity to find some clue to what was yet to be, and what is always, outside time. "For you," the flames tell humankind, "the golden age is in the future (or so you often like to believe); for us, in the past."[67] For Stapledon time itself was not all that important, and awakened intellects can greet each other over millennia: the brief golden age of the plant-men, whom I described before, is remembered in the awakening world-spirit, is eternally present to the seeing eye.

In one way time is unimportant; in another it contains all we know. In their last despair the last men speak of the "many million, million selves; ephemeridae, each to itself, the universe's one quick point, the crux of all cosmical endeavor. And all defeated! It is forgotten. It leaves only a darkness, deepened by blind recollection of past light. Soon, a greater darkness! Man, a moth sucked into a furnace, vanishes; and then the furnace also, since it is but a spark islanded in the wide, the everlasting darkness. If there is a meaning, it is no human meaning. Yet one thing in all this welter stands apart, unassailable, fair, the blind recollection of past light."[68] Or as Stapledon put it at the close of the superdog Sirius's tragic history, when Sirius's human lover sings his requiem: "the music's darkness was lit up by a brilliance which Sirius had called 'colour,' the glory that he himself,

---

[66] *Last Men in London*, 382.
[67] *The Flames*, 28.
[68] *Last and First Men*, 605.

he said, had never seen. But this, surely, was the glory that no spirits, canine or human, had ever clearly seen, the light that never was on land or sea, and yet is glimpsed by the quickened mind everywhere."[69]

> When anyone ... sees this light, then truly he is also moved to the Forms, and longs for the light which plays upon them and delights in it, just as with the bodies here below our desire is not for the underlying material things but for the beauty imaged upon them. For each is what it is by itself; but it becomes desirable when the Good colours it, giving a kind of grace to them and passionate love to the desirers.[70]

Stapledon professed to have no articulated *theory* of that glory, and recognized the need to retain a properly critical attitude to that and all other speculations. That it was both real and vital he insisted to the end. It is the part of speculative philosophy, he wrote in his notes for a summer school in Ormskirk,[71] to see things whole, and of critical philosophy to see things clearly. The goal of both must be to wake up into lucidity from our usual self-preoccupation,[72] and in waking to realize how sleepy we still are.

---

[69] Stapledon, *Sirius* (Harmondsworth: Penguin, 1964 [1944]), 187f. Sirius is an intelligent, language-using dog: far more intelligent, kindly, and open-minded, than most of the scientists, priests, and politicians who pontificate about him.
[70] Plotinus, *Ennead* VI.7 [38].22, 1–8, trans. Armstrong.
[71] Available in the Stapledon Collection in the Sydney Jones Library of the University of Liverpool.
[72] *Ennead* VI.7 [38].22, 33–36.

7.
God, Reason and Extraterrestrials[1]

THE NEGLECTED EXPERIMENT

Our ancestors did not find it difficult to imagine that there were other peoples who seemed far away from us, but no further away from God, and with as good a claim on God as we. Indeed, this seems to have been as popular a theme in the medieval world as in the modern. The land outside our city walls was populated by wild men, dwarves, dragons, and men whose heads do grow beneath their shoulders (which is perhaps to say, Antipodeans). As late as the nineteenth century Richard Owen, the palaeontologist who identified the class of dinosaurs,[2] was convinced that there must be thinking beings on Jupiter, so that the sight of the Jovian moons could be properly enjoyed. William Whewell—who gave us the term and class of "scientists"—argued against the thesis, remarking that we had no reason to think that God required His work to be admired, close up, by finite, mortal intelligence, and that we did not know what other purposes He might have in scattering the stars and rocks so widely.[3]

---

[1] An earlier version of this chapter was presented at the British Society for Philosophy of Religion conference in September 2001, and published as "God, Reason and Extraterrestrials," in *God, Mind and Knowledge*, ed. Andrew Moore (London: Ashgate, 2014), 171–86. I explored some similar fancies in "Impersonal Minds," in Anthony O'Hear, ed., *Minds and Persons* (Cambridge: Cambridge University Press, 2003), 185–209. See also "Selfless Civilizations," below.
[2] Hunterian Professor of Comparative Anatomy from 1836 to 1856, and superintendent of the natural history collections at the British Museum from 1856 to 1883: see his *On the Archetype and Homologies of the Vertebrate Skeleton*, Richard and John E. Taylor (London, 1848); see also David Hull, ed., *Darwin and his Critics. The Reception of Darwin's Theory of Evolution by the Scientific Community* (Oxford: Oxford University Press, 1973).
[3] William Whewell, *Of the Plurality of Worlds*, ed. Michael Ruse (Chicago:

Whewell was not alone in doubting a plurality of inhabited worlds. Augustine had similarly questioned the earlier belief in Antipodeans.[4] Like Whewell, he observed that we had no direct empirical evidence that there were human inhabitants, or even land, on the other side of the globe,[5] and must find it incredible that anyone from this side had ever taken ship to populate whatever lands there were. He also insisted that even the most monstrous seeming births, as well as any tribes which all had the same apparent oddities as were occasionally attested (fewer fingers or two heads), must be descended from Adam, and our kin: it was important that all humanity was of one lineage — a doctrine that was also of use rather later, in rejecting racist attempts to portray "Hottentots" or other "Native Peoples" as significantly "non-human."[6] The motive was a good one, but we may by now be rather less insistent that only our close biological kin deserve respect.

Richard Owen's reasoning was not entirely ridiculous — or at any rate it was not unfamiliar. If the world is made to be enjoyed and contemplated by such beings as we think ourselves, and if it stretches immensely further than we ourselves can ever hope to see, it must be that there are other beings Out There, of different ancestries and physiologies, who are still thinking beings like us: *hnau*, in C. S. Lewis's stories.[7] If we ever understand the physical

University of Chicago Press, 2001 [1853]), 183–84. Whewell (1794–1896) was Master of Trinity College Cambridge, and a noted polymath.
[4] Augustine, *City of God*, trans. Henry Bettenson (Harmondsworth: Penguin, 2003), 664 (16.9).
[5] Palamas proposed that the inhabited world was an island, the protruding section of a globe of earth contained within an immensely larger globe of water (Palamas, *The 150 Chapters*, 9–14). He was almost correct: the other side of the world is occupied by the Pacific Ocean, with only New Zealand, coral atolls, and small volcanic islands scattered there. See, for example, https://commons.wikimedia.org/wiki/File:Globe_-_Pacific_Ocean_space_view.png (accessed October 4, 2023).
[6] See Philip Almond, "Adam, Pre-Adamites, and Extra-Terrestrial Beings in Early Modern Europe," *Journal of Religious History* 30.2 (2006), 163–174, 168–69: "Thus, for example, in 1625, the philosopher Nathanael Carpenter in his *Geography* maintained that Moses' motivation, in writing his genealogical lists was so that all people would understand themselves to be descended from the same original 'then which there is no greater meanes to conciliate and ioyne mens affections for mutuall amitie and conversation'" (Nathanael Carpenter, *Geography Delineated Forth in Two Books* [Oxford, 1625], 2:207).
[7] The term is taken from his interplanetary trilogy, beginning with *Out of the Silent Planet*.

world, those distant *hnau* will understand the same. In Alexander Winchell's words (in 1883):

> We have neighbors; they live beyond impassable barriers, but they gaze on the same galaxy, and we know they are endowed with certain faculties which establish a community between them and us. However conformed bodily, whatever their modes and means of organic activity, we know that they reason as we reason, and interpret the universe on the same principles of logic and mathematics as ourselves. The orbits which their planetary homes describe are ellipses; they have studied the same celestial geometry as ourselves; they have written their treatises on celestial mechanics; they have felt the impact of the luminous weave of ether; they have speculated on the nature of matter and energy; they have interpreted the order of the cosmical mechanism as the expression of thought and purpose; they have placed themselves in communion with the Supreme Thinker who is so near to all of us that his voice is audible alike to the ear of reason in all the worlds.[8]

Even atheistical naturalists nowadays still usually expect the same — though they may doubt that those other creatures will be theists, or share our merely "moral" values, as I have discussed above. My own suspicion is that if they have never been theists they will also not be *rationalists* either: they will have no reason to suppose — no logical reason, no historical context, and no natural impulse — that the little agitation of their brains or quasi-brains that they call "thought" could be a model for the universe![9] Nor need they feel any moral obligation to find out the truth of things, beyond whatever seems immediately useful. Intelligence, as an evolutionary adaptation, is never likely — on naturalistic terms — to be more than a guide to getting food, and mates, and avoiding being food for long enough to reproduce! Each sort of creature has its own *Umwelt*, constructed from a range of markers that may

---

[8] Alexander Winchell, *World-Life, or Comparative Geology* (Chicago, 1883), 507–8, cited by Karl S. Guthke, *The Last Frontier: imagining other worlds from the Copernican Revolution to Modern Science Fiction*, trans. Helen Atkins (Ithaca, NY: Cornell University Press, 1990), 344.
[9] David Hume, *Dialogues concerning Natural Religion*, ed. J. C. A. Gaskin (Oxford: Oxford University Press, 2008 [1779]), 50.

be invisible to any other kind.[10] These, for any social species, will include social markers, and much of our activity will be directed, in the first place, to keeping a place in our social group—but this is to say that our intelligence, where it is more than "practical," is concerned with gossip and make-believe![11] What the Real World beyond all little worlds may be we have no good reason to expect to know—unless we have good reason to believe that we also carry something of the divine in us, that Real Reason is at least an image of the one creative intelligence that makes and sustains the world. In Benedict XVI's words (2009): "the objective structure of the universe and the intellectual structure of the human being coincide; the subjective reason and the objectified reason in nature are identical. In the end it is 'one' reason that links both and invites us to look to a unique creative Intelligence."[12]

It is because we still believe or half-believe that human beings are "special" by comparison with more (supposedly) limited living things, and that there is some overriding reason for our existence, that we can so easily imagine that there will be other sort-of-human beings elsewhere: human in the sense defined by Winchell. But perhaps there are yet other sorts of being with some similarly "non-naturalistic" characters.

I have in the past suggested that if we ever do have *empirical* reason to believe that there are *hnau* Out There, we shall have an extra reason to believe that more is going on in us than neo-Darwinian evolutionary theory can explain. Without that gloss, we can no more expect to discover *hnau* (or *hnau*—more probably—to discover us) than to find that the Great Galactics (so to speak) are native English speakers. If we did discover that they were, the overwhelmingly obvious explanation would be

---

[10] J. von Uexkuell, *Theoretical Biology*, trans. D. L. Mackinnon (London: Kegan Paul, 1926); and "A stroll through the worlds of animals and men," in C. H. Schiller, ed., *Instinctive Behavior* (New York: International University Press, 1957), 5–80.
[11] See Robin Dunbar, *Grooming, Gossip, and the Evolution of Language* (London: Faber, 1996).
[12] Benedict XVI to Archbishop Rino Fisichella, on the occasion of the international congress "From Galileo's Telescope to Evolutionary Cosmology" (November 30–December 2, 2009), http://www.vatican.va/holy_father/benedict_xvi/messages/pont-messages/2009/documents/hf_ben-xvi_mes_20091126_fisichella-telescopio_en.html (accessed September 8, 2023). I have discussed the issue at greater length in *Can We Believe in People: human significance in an interconnected cosmos* (Brooklyn, NY: Angelico Press, 2020).

that English speakers had already influenced the Galaxy (and perhaps Poul Anderson was essentially correct in imagining his High Crusade), not that God was an Englishman, nor that the English language was, somehow, the endpoint of all linguistic evolution.[13] Most biologists — though there are exceptions such as Simon Conway Morris[14] — would suspect a similar influence if we found that the Galactics were *physically* like us. Maybe the Great Galactics — the first and only naturally occurring *hnau* to emerge on a wider scene — have seeded their spores everywhere, both to begin the processes of evolution on any available world, and to guide it towards their goal (to have talkative companions, maybe, or else convenient slaves). If *we* are the very first *hnau* we might do this ourselves. But given the enormous difficulty of this interstellar project — far harder even than Augustine thought the trip to the antipodes — it would be likelier that there was some *metaphysical* reason, rather than an historical, or a mental or spiritual identity. The First Cause, we should say, is not a distant, accidental agent, but one present at all times and places. There may come a moment in any evolutionary story when creatures of whatever lineage begin to get messages, as it were, from the Real World, from God (who can, we are assured, raise children up from stones).[15]

Modernists usually insist that there is a radical division between Reason and Inspiration. My own suspicion is that there really isn't: what seems suddenly obvious may be reckoned rational insight or prophetic inspiration. In either case it needs to be checked against other revelations or intuitions of whatever sort. That the universe is *rational* at all is as much a matter of faith or spiritual vision as that it rests on God. But that is not my present topic. And neither do I intend to make any further defence of my more usual theses (that is, that the discovery of alien intelligence — of

---

[13] Poul Anderson, *The High Crusade* (New York: Doubleday 1960): a medieval English village is kidnapped by an alien scout ship, and almost accidentally takes over from the decadent rulers of a Galactic Empire. Centuries later terrestrial explorers are disconcerted to discover that the Galaxy is ruled — rather well — by the heirs of a feudal baron, and the Roman Church.
[14] Simon Conway Morris, *Life's Solution: Inevitable Humans in a Lonely Universe* (Cambridge: Cambridge University Press, 2003). Morris's arguments are good ones, but perhaps not fully convincing. Even in terrestrial history there are many life-forms built on entirely different templates which we would be rash to underestimate.
[15] Matthew 3:9.

a recognizably human sort—would support familiar forms of theism, and that the apparent success of scientific endeavour, even now, is also much more likely to be real on a theistic theory than on an atheistic). Instead, I shall explore a different theme: that the creatures we find Out There may turn out to be just as alien as the creatures we have already found on earth, and that "humanity" has no more privileged status than the mind and form of any other creature. Is this bound to be atheistical in its effect? Only—or so I suggest—if we have already decided that our God must really be only human.

What exactly it means to be made "in the image of God,"[16] as the Hebrews held, or to belong to the same class of things as God or gods, as some Greek philosophers supposed, may be uncertain. Perhaps the author of *Genesis* meant only that Adam would be God's viceroy in the world, and that everything in the end would be given into their hands. Or perhaps the claim was a larger one, and more like the pagan philosophical: that only human beings—or even only sensible or virtuous human beings—could hope to join God's fellowship. Even now we typically suppose that human beings are like God or the gods in being "rational," in having a larger view of things than "animals," in being able to talk about the causes of events and the reasons for their actions, in being capable of overriding their passions and weighing up advantages for themselves and others. We also suppose that human beings and gods are "individuals," distinct from others of their kind but able to recognize themselves as individuals or "persons" like their neighbors.

How likely is it, on either a naturalistic or a theistic basis, that we should expect that beings like that, like us, will have dominion or even a foothold elsewhere? How likely is it that all "intelligent experience" will have that form? How is it, we might also ask, that *human* intelligence, of the sort I have just half sketched, has only evolved—as far as we can see—in the last few hundred thousand years of Earth's long history? If the world was waiting for "us," why did it have to wait so long? If it is so easy to produce the—broadly—human sort that we could expect to find it Out-side Over There, why haven't we found it also in the Long Ago?[17]

---

[16] *Genesis* 1:26–7, 9:1–6.
[17] Strictly, of course, we don't *know* that there weren't such creatures Long Ago: maybe they surfaced many times in different geological ages, and were

Adopt, for a moment, John C. Wright's definition of the human: "any naturally self-aware self-defining entity capable of independent moral judgment is a human" (and any entities likely to become so fall in a "special protected class" until they do).[18] There are then at least two questions. What conditions must obtain, physically and biologically and culturally, for there to be such entities, "persons," *hnau*? And are such entities truly the central thrust of all creation, the reason why God made the world (as some believers think) or even the likely outcome of the world's unguided changes?

THINKING BEASTS AND ALIEN MORALITIES

The philosophical assault on anthropomorphism has a long history. So Xenophanes of Colophon (c. 570–c. 475 BC):

> If cattle and horses or lions had hands, or were able to draw with their hands and do the works that men do, horses would draw the forms of the gods like horses, and cattle like cattle.[19]

The point was never only the superficial one, that God or the gods would not *look* like human animals, but the much more radical thought that their ways, their thoughts, weren't ours. We should not make God or the gods in our image, according to our likeness. True piety is to prefer the truth to any of our easy idols.[20] This is likely to be uncomfortable: "truth must of necessity be stranger than fiction, for fiction is the creation of the human mind, and therefore is congenial to it."[21]

---

ground down by climate change, or meteor strike, or plague, or genetic drift: see Gavin A. Schmidt and Adam Frank, "The Silurian hypothesis: Would it be possible to detect an industrial civilization in the geological record?" *International Journal of Astrobiology* 18.2 (2019), 142–50. And why should such civilizations be "industrial" at all? But we have no *naturalistic* reason to expect this much, nor any empirical evidence.

[18] John C. Wright, *The Phoenix Exultant* (New York: Tor Books), 155. Wright's three-volume work, *The Golden Age*, of which this is the second part, is one of the very few SF works to offer explicit and clearly reasoned arguments, mostly of a Stoic sort, about the nature of mind and morals.

[19] G. S. Kirk, J. Raven, and M. Schofield, eds., *The Presocratic Philosophers* (Cambridge: Cambridge University Press 1983), 169; see also Sextus Empiricus, *Against the Mathematicians* 9.47, in A. A. Long and D. N. Sedley, *The Hellenistic Philosophers* (Cambridge: Cambridge University Press, 1987), 143 (23F).

[20] Aristotle, *Nicomachean Ethics* 1.1096a16, after Plato, *Republic* 10.595c.

[21] G. K. Chesterton, *The Club of Queer Trades* (London: Darwen Finlayson, 1960 [1905]), 82.

For that very reason, of course, it is rather difficult for us to imagine wholly alien intelligences Out There. Even those SF writers who don't imagine them as "just like us" in whatever important respect must usually portray them only as different in ways already open to us: strange and old-fashioned, maybe, but still "human." Alien empires too often turn out to be vulgar imitations of "oriental despotisms" or feudal monarchies as they, in turn, have been imagined by Western writers. The triumphalist strand of twentieth-century SF will usually suggest that "human beings" turn out to be more versatile, more creative, and more humane than the aliens, even when the latter have the longer history.[22] In either case, it is easy to imagine, SF writers are re-visioning what they take to be an Abrahamic theme: the angels must bow before Adam. Even less triumphalist writers—like Gregory Benford[23] (writing, as he has remarked, from a perspective given by the fact that the Southern States are the only parts of the USA to have experienced an absolute defeat)—conceive that humans will still have right on their side, despite being of no more weight with the rulers of the universe than commensal rodents. That image of our possible future is less vulgar than the triumphalists', but perhaps it is still too anthropic to be entirely just.

One further gloss: both Classical and Hebrew writers used to mock Egyptians for the respect they gave to "animals," and their habit of depicting gods in animal form. Even Plutarch of Chaeronea, one of those Classical writers who was most sympathetic both to Egyptian thought and to the lives of animals, thought that Egyptian practice must lead "the weak and innocent into 'superstition' (*deisidaimonia*), and the cynical and bold into 'atheistic and bestial reasoning' (*atheos kai theriodes logismos*)."[24] Imagining gods as animals might seem to suggest that we should imitate them; imagining animals as gods might make it harder to exploit them. Mainstream Classical and Hebrew thought preferred to elevate *humanity* as our ideal. We should aim to be good *people* and might

---

[22] So, for example, James Blish's juveniles: *The Star Dwellers* (London: Sphere, 1961) and *Mission to the Heart Stars* (London: Granada, 1965).
[23] See Gregory Benford, *Across the Sea of Suns* (London: Gollancz, 1997) and others in his Galactic Center series.
[24] Ingvild Saelid Gilhus, *Animals, Gods and Humans: changing attitudes to animals in Greek, Roman and early Christian ideas* (London: Routledge, 2006), 98, after Plutarch, *On Isis and Osiris*, 71.

use whatever animals we pleased in this pursuit. Moderns who
have abandoned, as they think, traditional religion almost always
share this doctrine. Traditional moralists like Chesterton at least
had metaphysical reasons for their claim: "Cruelty to animals is
cruelty and a vile thing; but cruelty to a man is not cruelty, it is
treason. Tyranny over a man is not tyranny, it is rebellion, for
man is royal."[25] In other moments, however, Chesterton might
recall that the duty of kings is to care about and for their subjects,
not to claim the larger portion. But it is the very claim to royalty
that should now be questioned.

The Egyptians did not actually seek to imitate the animals
whose forms they gave to gods, but there have been philosophical
and other sects that did. What "animals" do has sometimes been
taken to show, for good or ill, what *we* should, or at least what
we *could*, without regret.[26] Cynic philosophers openly sought to
live as they imagined feral dogs would live; other philosophers
proposed that we might model ourselves on bees. But let us accept
that we — at any rate at this stage of our evolution — are social
primates, strongly compelled and well-advised to live in couples,
families, and tribes, self-governing townships, professional guilds,
or craft associations. It isn't obvious, though, either that other
species, even social species, will feel just those emotions, or that
no other sorts of species could ever dominate their worlds or
seek to expand their influence. The issue here is what we might
encounter Outside Over There: creatures with very different
natures but as strong a claim to God's approval as His image or
His agent. God, we must presume, hates nothing that He has
made: why else would He have made it?[27]

What different moralities might be founded on different physiologies, even amongst creatures of our scale and type? Might
some of them be so far from "ethical" in any sense we recognize as to offer a real alternative to what Lewis called "the Tao,"
the principles which all *hnau*, he supposed, must recognize?[28]

---

[25] G. K. Chesterton, *Charles Dickens* (London: Methuen, 1906), 197.
[26] Cf. my "Hume, animals and the objectivity of morals," *Philosophical Quarterly* 25 (1985), 117–33.
[27] *Wisdom of Solomon*, 11:24. Zoroastrians supposed that there were two rival creative powers at work, and that there were therefore creatures, "vermin," that the "good God" hated. This has not been the usual Abrahamic theory, though it may sometimes have been the practice.
[28] C. S. Lewis, *The Abolition of Man* (London: Bles, 1947).

Might Darwin have been right to suggest, in the first edition of *The Descent of Man*, that "if men were reared under precisely the same condition as hive-bees, there can hardly be any doubt that our unmarried females would, like worker bees, think it a sacred duty to kill their brothers, and mothers would strike to kill their fertile daughters, and no one would think of interfering"?[29] Henry Sidgwick's mildly witty response (cited by Darwin in later editions) that "a superior bee would aspire to a milder solution of the population problem"[30] testifies to a common faith that a humane ethic *must* prevail among the rationally intelligent. But are we sure? SF writers have sometimes seemed to suppose it *obvious* that different animal species, sharing a sort of intelligence, must be irreconcilable rivals: kindness, they suppose, must be restricted to creatures "of our kind," and every sort of creature will be loyal only to its seed. "Selfish Genes," we are led to believe, require that we have no other real goal than the preservation of those genes, regardless of any other interests. A more sensible strategy, even for those genes, would probably be to cooperate with any agreeable partner,[31] but we may not be able — on merely naturalistic grounds — to exclude the possibility that the race is to the swift and ruthless, even if that race too will be abolished in the end.

But the moral most of us prefer — and which I have half-endorsed myself — is probably that only a certain sort of social animal has any hope of being "more than animal": if we are ever to be "rational" we must first be "moral"; if we are to be "moral" we must be able to recognize ourselves as agents amongst other agents, capable of keeping and breaking promises, and treating others (or not) as we would wish to be treated. That vision should be enough even on its own to encourage us to treat even other species kindly. But perhaps we need rather more than "natural morals." Being properly human, being the sort of human that has some claim to be cosmic, requires that we be able to reconsider our moralities, to know what it is like to live under judgment, and not suppose that what comes "naturally" is always "right,"

---

[29] Charles Darwin, *The Descent of Man* (London: John Murray, 1871), 1:86.
[30] Henry Sidgwick, in *The Academy*, June 15, 1872, 231. See Darwin, *Descent of Man*, 1:99. Orson Scott Card imagines this outcome in *Speaker for the Dead* (New York: Tor Books, 1986).
[31] As is practised by the Oankali in Octavia Butler, *Dawn* (New York: Warner, 1987) and others in the Xenogenesis Trilogy.

or even that what we wish for ourselves or others is the sole thing to consider. Without that sense of a universal justice, by which we might be found wanting, we can do no more than follow our natural impulses, and it is not certain that those need be what we wish. Consider, again, C. J. Cherryh's Kif (in the *Chanur* sequence), who function as perfect egoists, eat their own kind, acknowledge no restraint save power, and feel no guilt. Cherryh too imagines that their very "innocence," in a way, may make them, in the appropriate circumstances, the most reliable members of an inter-species compact. By human standards they are psychopaths — but whereas such failings in us go along with other and even more obvious faults and logical confusions, and no *human* society could be founded entirely on psychopathic principle (not even Colin Turnbull's Ik),[32] the Kif are as coherent and capable a species as any. Or must there have been some trauma in their past, some fall into perversion — as perhaps there has been with us?

If it is true that "there is no God," no transcendent resolution of creation's many goals, our morals will be bounded by our biology — though it does not follow that we will only care for members of our own species (in fact, after all, we ourselves — in practice — mostly care much more for our own "companion animals" or even chance-met wild ones than we do for human strangers, and why not?). If there are genuinely rival moral codes, incommensurably and irrevocably different, then only one of them, at best or worst, can be the final answer, and we may need to consider whether it won't be ours. Greg Bear is unusual amongst SF writers in imagining, in *Eon* and *Eternity*, that it is the genocidal enemies of humanity who will bring everything in the end together, so that every otherwise passing good is preserved, in a way, in glory — a glory defined by them, and not by us.[33] More realistically, there will be no single, final answer, any more than there will ever be only one sort of creature to survive and breed (how could such a singular species even survive?). And that is itself

---

[32] See Colin Turnbull, *The Mountain People* (London: Cape, 1973). Turnbull may have misjudged the Ik as extremely mean and selfish, and certainly leapt too quickly to the belief that they thereby revealed our real "human nature." See Cathryn Townsend, Athena Aktipis, Daniel Balliet, and Lee Cronk, "Generosity among the Ik of Uganda," *Evolutionary Human Sciences* 2 (2020): E23. doi:10.1017/ehs.2020.22.

[33] Greg Bear, *Eon* (London: Gollancz, 1986); *Eternity* (London: Gollancz, 1989).

a sort of answer: that no one individual, no one species, no one form of life will ever be sole survivor, and that every intelligent creature must acknowledge that it is finite. Wanting everything for oneself, or for one's own kind or lineage, is absurd, whether or not we acknowledge that God rules All. Can we still reasonably expect that our kind has at any rate a place, and a possible future? What E. O. Wilson has called the hodge-podge of evolutionary adaptations, mostly formed in the Neolithic, don't necessarily have any coherent sense or standard.[34] We are almost bound to be at odds with ourselves as well as with each other, in ways that older lines, in far more stable settings, would find—at least—unusual (and a signal not to trust us much). Would creatures more like birds, for example, have an easier time reconciling interests and demands between the sexes and the ages? Do "reason" and "morality" depend on our being a particular sort of social mammal, required to depend on a wider circle than merely that to which our passions—erotic and parental—may attach us? If it takes a village to rear a child (allegedly, an African proverb), we must somehow have adapted to a village life. If it takes a larger, urban, and electronically connected world to raise up children who can run that world, we must somehow, in the future, learn to live in it. Are we sure that our inheritance is versatile enough to cope? Might there not be other lines that have already achieved stability? What would they be like?

MORE ALIEN POSSIBILITIES

Can we go beyond merely *moral* difference between creatures of roughly our own scale and sensibility, and imagine creatures of a radically other sort? William Whewell spoke with some disdain of the only creatures he could believe inhabited Jupiter: "aqueous, gelatinous creatures; too sluggish, almost, to be deemed alive, floating in their ice-cold waters, shrouded for ever by their humid skies."[35] It was a strange comment. Even the aqueous and other creatures who float in the ice-cold waters of *our* world are often beautiful beyond belief, and no more sluggish than we (though the sea-slug or nudibranch *Elysia chlorotica* has a very

---

[34] E. O. Wilson, *On Human Nature* (Cambridge, MA: Harvard University Press, 1978), 196; see my *Philosophical Futures* (Peter Lang: Frankfurt 2011), 151.
[35] Whewell, *Plurality of Worlds*, 185–86.

restful life once it has incorporated photosynthetic chloroplasts from intertidal algae and need no longer eat).

What if we find that *entirely* different creatures are really dominant in other worlds than ours, and just as likely to spread their influence? What if we find that such entirely different creatures have as good a claim as ours to "understand" the world, and hopes of heaven? What sort of creature might these be? John Varley's many-dimensional Invaders seem to arise from Jovian stock, and to understand the wider world immensely better than us.[36] But perhaps they are so different that we cannot even *imagine* them.

Suppose that there are creatures who can communicate with each other over great distances of space and time, and organize their creative life accordingly, but have no sentiments for any particular bodies as individuals at all. They treat individual organisms even of their own lineage rather more as we treat our own limbs and organs, or even as we treat more disposable, replaceable tools. They do not acknowledge — perhaps they cannot acknowledge — any common interest with us, nor do they recognize the sounds or gestures that we make as being anything like their "language." We can postulate that they have somehow — by the same strange talent as perhaps we have and by whatever accidents of history — acquainted themselves with principles that allow them to manage the raw stuff of their worlds. They don't need to construct either social artefacts or physical tools: everything they need to cooperate and grow is built into their natures. Maybe they even have interstellar travel, and maintain connections, somehow, with all their scattered colonies — though there is no need to suppose that those colonies are planet-bound. Maybe they live in the Oort Clouds of any available star, and spread by shedding spores into the solar winds. One version of the story is Wellsian: these are the Lunarians, with a biological rather than a technological solution for the division of labour. In another version, their origins are technological, but they have long since abandoned or destroyed their biological creators.[37]

---

[36] See *The Ophiuchi Hotline* (New York: Dial Press, 1977), and other novels in that imagined future. The Invaders exile humankind from the earth, in favour of the great cetaceans whom they more resemble.

[37] See H. G. Wells, *The First Men in the Moon* (London: Newnes, 1901); Karel Capek was perhaps the first to envisage the technological take-over, but his "robots" are likely to become more human as they mature: see *R. U. R.*,

These are amongst the commonest of alien forms in modern SF. I cannot offer you, of course, a current real-life example — but if you doubt that any creature could communicate and build across continents without recourse to any *human* understanding of their world, I refer you to the case of ants:

> Researchers in Japan and Spain led by Eiriki Sunamura of the University of Tokyo found that Argentine ants [*Linepithema humile*] living in Europe, Japan and California shared a strikingly similar chemical profile of hydrocarbons on their cuticles.... Whenever ants from the main European and Californian super-colonies and those from the largest colony in Japan came into contact, they acted as if they were old friends. These ants rubbed antennae with one another and never became aggressive or tried to avoid one another. In short, they acted as if they all belonged to the same colony, despite living on different continents separated by vast oceans.[38]

Different varieties of the ants' enormously successful and very ancient lineage can make and employ tools, domesticate useful allies, and learn short-cuts through the world. They use each other's bodies cooperatively as tools, rafts, and larders. What their future holds, who knows? Is it obvious that "humanity" must triumph, or that it should? What would it take for ants or bees or other such "eusocial" creatures to begin to record their histories, and to learn from them? We can at least acknowledge that the same biologists who would be startled by the discovery of even faintly humanoid life-forms Outside, would be much less startled by the discovery of eusocial ones: eusociality, after all, has evolved and survived on many separate occasions in terrestrial history, as termites, ants, bees, wasps, and even naked mole rats. May there not be whole worlds dominated by such forms, without any interest in gossip, or any clash between the interests of "individuals" and "hives"? How odd would it be to suggest that

---

trans. P. Selver (Oxford: Oxford University Press, 1923). Fred Saberhagen's Berserkers and Gregory Benford's Mechforms are less easily corrupted.

[38] See http://news.bbc.co.uk/earth/hi/earth_news/newsid_8127000/8127519. stm (accessed October 4, 2023), citing E. Sunamura, et al., "Intercontinental union of Argentine ants: behavioral relationships among introduced populations in Europe, North America, and Asia," *Insectes Sociaux* 56 (2009), 143–47 (doi: 10.1007/s00040-009-0001-9).

"the singing masons building roofs of gold"[39] are at least as good an image of the divine as are we naked apes? How odd would it be to suppose that it is they and their descendants who will dominate the worlds? Are we sure that it would be "wrong" to breed a line of eusocial primates, inspired by Henry's speech?[40] I admit that most of us would find that future repellent.

Or consider other imaginable creatures, a further step away from these, who do more than recognize each other biochemically, and do not trouble to collect in hives or nests or classes: information of all sorts is passed between them, including genetic instructions for how to build and behave. There are no species barriers there, despite there being innumerable shapes and manners. Indeed, there are hardly even individuals, but only ever-changing, ever-evolving fashions, fissioning and coalescing according to whatever needs arise: a sea of information. If we were to encounter "them" or "it" our own biochemical efflorescence would, no doubt, be absorbed, decoded, and transformed.

Their form of life, of course, would not be ours: would they have any reason, for example, to distinguish the world of their experience from the world that contains and sustains them? According to Lovejoy,

> The primary and most universal faith of man [is] his inexpugnable realism, his twofold belief that he is on the one hand in the midst of realities which are not himself nor mere obsequious shadows of himself, a world which transcends the narrow confines of his own transient being; and on the other hand that he can himself somehow read beyond those confines and bring those external existences within the compass of his own life yet without annulment of their transcendence.[41]

That indeed is one aspect of our claim to be special: we are creatures who can imagine that there is a world larger than their experience which they can learn about. Do my imagined creatures offer a sort of counter? On the one hand, they are involved far

---

[39] Shakespeare, *Henry V*, act 1, scene 2, line 201, speaking of bees, as models for an ordered nation.
[40] A scenario imagined by Frank Herbert, *Hellstrom's Hive* (New York: Doubleday, 1973), and Stephen Baxter, *Coalescent* (London: Gollancz, 2003).
[41] A. O. Lovejoy, *The Revolt against Dualism* (La Salle, Illinois: Open Court, 1960 [1930]), 14.

more directly and immediately than ourselves in whatever is
going on. Whereas it can be suggested, a little confusedly, that
we never see or sense anything "directly," but only the echo
or reflection or effect engendered in our brains (if we can still
believe in brains), my imagined creatures are not walled off from
"nature" or each other, and their experience is exact and realistic.
Or rather, there is for them no distinction between reality and
dreams: the information they exchange is enough to change both
"their" worlds and the real world they live in. "Real are the dreams
of Gods, and smoothly pass/ Their pleasures in a long immortal
dream."[42] These creatures, at least, aren't merely "animal."

Am I imagining something that simply could not be? Perhaps;
but consider the bacterial population of our present earth. Multicellular life of the sort that seems most natural to us is a late
comer in terrestrial history, and microbes still outnumber and
outweigh us all. We can distinguish different bacterial types, for
our convenience, but notions like "individual" or even "species"
have no real significance for the bacterial world, which exists in
a ceaseless interchange of genetic and other biochemical information. Even the deeper distinction between archaebacteria and
eubacteria (taxa each as distinct and distant from each other
as either is from eukaryotes like trees, mushrooms, molluscs,
worms — and us) is probably not fixed. It is the bacterial population that rules our world, and may have other ideas about what to
do than we do.[43] This notion has been explored by authors such
as Greg Bear, who, in *Blood Music*, imagines the moment when
bacteria realize that they are living inside and upon immensely
larger organisms which do not understand them.[44] Exobiologists
suspect, with reason, that any life we ever find Out There, on
Mars, in the oceans of Europa, or on exoplanets far away, is far
more likely to be bacterial than ordinarily multicellular (as it was
here on Earth for most terrestrial history), and we are usually
rather disappointed by the news. Surely, we can't help thinking,

---

[42] John Keats, "Lamia," 1.127–28, in Jack Stillinger, ed., *The Poems of John Keats* (Cambridge, MA: Harvard University Press, 1978), 455.
[43] See Lynn Margulis and Dorion Sagan, *Microcosmos: Four Billion Years of Microbial Evolution* (New York: Summit Books, 1986).
[44] Greg Bear, *Blood Music* (Westminster, MD: Arbor House, 1985). Orson Scott Card has also imagined a bacterial civilization in *Xenocide* (New York: Tor Books, 1991) and *Children of the Mind* (New York: Tor Books, 1996).

the universe must "want" multicellular beings like us—not just the bacterial sea, or the stromatolites that littered the early earth. But maybe we are their dreams.

These cases are all non-human in fairly familiar ways: they do not need a concept of their individual selves distinct from the wider unity, either because they are clearly cells within a massively multi-organic somewhat, or because they are not even single cells. They may be able to imagine a world that goes on without them (if the hives should perish or the microbial population suffer some lethal change), but "death" as the closing of an individual eye, the end of all its projects, will probably be unknown. The first, eusocial, creatures are non-human explicitly in having no common interest with such ordinarily mammalian forms as us, and no biological need to feel compunction about the troubles of particular creatures. The second are not even animal or plant organisms of a familiar sort, but might perhaps share some curiosity about the lumbering giants they could inhabit and control. The second, especially, can show us that there are no privileged *scales* in the cosmos, any more than privileged dates or places. Neither story entirely rebuts the claim that any intelligent creatures Out There are bound to have the "same principles of logic and mathematics as ourselves," but perhaps they do suggest that this claim is a matter of Faith. The claims of "reason," so understood, may be as parochial as the claims of etiquette. Bacterial intelligence at any rate is as unlikely to start from the operations of counting and calculating that seem natural to us as it is to have an interest in soap opera. Nor does it seem necessary to suppose that even the law of non-contradiction binds that intelligence, any more than it binds a quantum computer. The very claim at the heart of "logic," that there is one incompatible *other* significant counter to any particular proposition, such that one is bound to be false and the other true, is unprovable, and may be unintelligible to a bacterial intelligence.[45]

Some commentators will insist that microbes can't have "concepts," nor any imagination of the past or future (and maybe even that eusocial insects can't). One response to this may simply be

---

[45] This may also be the moral of Naomi Mitchison's *Memoirs of a Space-woman* (London: Gollancz, 1962), where she explores the thoughts of a creature without bilateral symmetry. See my "Deconstructing the Laws of Logic": *Philosophy* 82 (2008), 25–53.

that the claim misses my point. We may "have concepts," and be able so to organize our memories and projects by the use of tokens representing them. But that may only be to say that we respond to *figments*, rather than real events. What modes of consciousness are available to other sorts of creature we don't know. A second response is rather to question the claim, on several levels. First, my scenarios do not suggest that either individual eusocial entities or microbes "have concepts": the concepts exist, if they do, in the larger interchange of information across the nests or hives, or the global bacterial population. Information is conveyed biochemically, especially in the latter case, and the only way that we could represent it to ourselves is conceptually (which is to say, by proxy). Some of that passing information can be "tagged"—that is, identified as less reliable or as an occasion for a sub-creative fantasy rather than feeding directly into a current fashion. It can, as it were, be quarantined until it proves its worth. Those theorists who suppose that it is language itself that dictates the sentences we seem to utter may be right in the case of the bacterial society, though they are wrong to think this true of humans! Second, there is evidence at least in the eusocial case that such creatures may even have languages of a more familiar sort: the only non-human animals, in fact, who have been shown to possess a complex, symbolic language of their own, and so to be able to describe absent realities are bees. What other eusocial lines might be able to do by way of representing reality, and even recording reality or creating new sub-realities, we don't know.[46] But my aim, remember, is not to transform these alien sorts into anything like the human, but to allow for their development into something that can dominate a world, and even be poised to transcend it.

THE INCARNATE WORD

Even creatures of a more familiar type may not be what we think them. "A turkey is more occult and awful," so Chesterton remarked, "than all the angels and archangels."[47] We do not,

---

[46] For further insight into the life of eusocial creatures, see Bert Hölldobler and Edward O. Wilson, *The Superorganism: the beauty, elegance, and strangeness of insect societies* (New York: W. W. Norton, 2009).

[47] G. K. Chesterton, *All Things Considered* (London: Methuen, 1908), 220.

cannot, know—as it were, "from the inside"—what it is like to be one, nor can we tell what insights into reality creatures like that may have. He exaggerated, no doubt, the difficulty: all earthly life is of one blood with us, all descended from original prokaryotic cells. But he was right to emphasise the Otherness of living creatures not of our own kind. We hardly even know why dogs or horses willingly cooperate with us, nor what they are getting out of it. So can we conceive at least of the thought that the Great Galactics, so to speak, will turn out thus to be entirely Other, more distant even than eusocial insects or bacteria? To us they will look like rocks, or trees, or cattle: whatever overt shape is most convenient at that time and place. But—by hypothesis—they will also contain the worlds, each modelling not only the world, but its origin. If we only knew the code we could read the history of all worlds in how they live. Is that not true? And if it is, doesn't that qualify them also as the images of a Creator?

On this account, the principle that governs all things and from which all possibilities take their beginning, is as close to rocks, or trees, or cattle as to us. Notoriously, we aren't obedient—or at least we feel we aren't. And this is what most humanists insist must make us "more than animal," that we have a choice in what to do and be. Being *human*, as Aristotle insisted long before the existentialists, is being the sort of creature that has to *decide* what it is right to do[48]—and may often make mistakes. The mistakes made by the "merely animal" are merely practical: missing a kill, or falling from a branch. Our mistakes are *practical* in the stronger, Aristotelian sense (a *praxis* is something done for a reason, which we can assess as good or bad): we do the wrong thing, thinking it is right, or failing to live by what we have decided. But why should this susceptibility to error be reckoned a mark of our "superior" nature? It seems, on the contrary, to be a failure: a proof that we are not, after all, divine. If other creatures do exactly and entirely what they are meant to do, are they inferior? May they not be a better image, exactly, of what is meant to be?

Philosophy can take us only a little way to truth. Or at any rate, I cannot—as a philosopher—see much beyond this conclusion. We should not expect that the God of Gods be *human*, nor that

---

[48] Aristotle, *Nicomachean Ethics*, 1.1098a3–18.

it is our kind of creature, whether the literally human or the larger sort deserving the title *hnau*, that will ever encompass the universe in thought, or be cosmic co-creators of the later days. The God of Gods, or whatever principle it is that governs things, may allow for human personality or personhood, but It is not confined by that. God's ways are not our ways.[49] This doctrine is not as subversive of a more traditional religion as some moderns have supposed: on the contrary, it establishes one ancient theme. Really to serve God it may be necessary to put aside our preconceptions — even our preconceptions about what we need to do, or what we can expect from the real world. The God of Gods is *uncannier* than we like to think it, and may in the end prefer beetles.[50] Nor does this thesis depend on there "really" being a God (if that expression makes sense). Even if there is "in fact" no single resolution of desires, nor any assurance that what is good for all things will prevail, nor any power to assist us on the way, it may still be right to conceive what such a power might be and do. What would be required of us by a power that facilitated and will vindicate all things? What would an omniscient witness, concerned for all the denizens of the worlds, reckon that each or any of us should best do?

> What can we do to hasten the time, the time that shall
> surely be,
> When the earth shall be filled with the glory of God
> As the waters cover the sea?[51]

---

[49] Isaiah 55:8.

[50] In *The Linnean* (August 1992) one of Haldane's friends, Prof. K. A. Kermack, reported that "what [Haldane] actually said was: 'God has an inordinate fondness for beetles.' He had an inordinate fondness for the statement: he repeated it frequently. More often than not it had the addition: 'God has an inordinate fondness for stars and beetles.' It is important to notice that the present tense 'has,' not the past tense was used. God is eternal and unchanging and so are his preferences. Haldane was making a theological point: God is most likely to take trouble over reproducing his own image, and his 400,000 attempts at the perfect beetle contrast with his slipshod creation of man. When we meet the Almighty face to face he will resemble a beetle (or a star) and not Dr Carey (the then Archbishop of Canterbury)." https://car-tls.edcdn.com/Linnean-8-3-1992.pdf, 12 (accessed July 30, 2024). I owe the reference to https://en.wikiquote.org/wiki/J._B._S._Haldane (accessed December 6, 2023).

[51] "God is Working His Purpose Out," by Arthur Campbell Ainger (1894), in *The New English Hymnal* (Norwich: Canterbury Press, 2016), 791.

Strictly, perhaps, nothing. But we may at least conceive the possibility of such an end, and be guided in our work at least by the hope that there be a way of resolving all dissensions, a way for all things to be well—which does not require us to be beetles.

But it is possible to take one further step, not as a philosopher but as a believing Christian. The doctrine of the Incarnation is not the easier and more comfortable thought that moderns have sometimes made it: it is not the old delusion that actual humanity is now divine, or deserves to be, and that all other forms of life and being, by the same doctrine, are inferior or subordinate. It is rather that humanity, as a particular form of life, has been taken up into the Godhead: *adopted* into life eternal. God is no more "human" than He was: humanity has been alchemically, as it were, transmuted, at least in the person of the Lord Jesus Christ. Whatever other creatures we meet Out There, or here on earth, may be gathered into the dance of immortal love—as the pagan philosophers put it—by whatever means. We have been gathered in by an exceptional act of God; but not because we deserved it! According to the Muslim Brethren of Purity, putting their case for the non-human creation sometime in the tenth century AD, "no finite being can reach out beyond the limits of its temporality and constitute its own character, as if to create itself," and so none has any right to boast of its own given nature.[52] Nor can we insist that *only* we, whether our biological lineage or the class to which we belong, have been invited to the dance. On the contrary, we are probably late-comers to the party, and the earlier guests will prove to be at least as strange to us as the creatures with whom we already share a world.

---

[52] Brethren of Purity, *The Case of the animals against Man before the King of the Jinn*, eds. Lenn E. Goodman and Richard McGregor (New York: Oxford University Press, 2009), 25.

8.

Deep Time

DOES IT MATTER?[1]

THE PROBLEM OF DEEP TIME

My topic is the problem of Deep Time: that is, the ethical and metaphysical effect of placing ourselves in the context of bygone and future ages. On this occasion I shall concentrate on the impact of possible futures, and address: (a) the Doomsday Argument — that our future will be brief; (b) the Omega Point Argument — that the future will be long and triumphant; and (c) the Presentist Argument — that all such stories are only metaphors for present-day experiences and desires. In an earlier version I called that last the "Platonist Argument" — but I now see some differences between a proper Platonism and "commonsensical presentism" (which is actually much the same as egoism).

This will continue an exploration begun in *God's World and the Great Awakening* (Oxford: Clarendon Press, 1991), a paper written on "The End of the Ages" for a volume on the Millenium,[2] recent papers to the Wittgenstein Conference at Kirchberg in 2000,[3] to

---

[1] Delivered as the Eric Symes Memorial Lecture at Westminster Abbey on Thursday May, 10, 2001, and subsequently at Keble College, Oxford. My thanks to the Eric Symes Abbott Committee for inviting me: The Dean of King's College, London (Chairman); The Dean of Westminster; The Warden of Keble College, Oxford; The Director of the Lincoln Theological Institute, University of Sheffield; The Reverend John Robson; and The Reverend Canon Eric James.
[2] "The End of the Ages," in David Seed, ed., *Imagining Apocalypse: studies in cultural crisis* (London: Macmillan, and New York: St Martin's Press, 2000), 27–44 (revised for *Philosophical Futures*).
[3] "Posthumanism: engineering in the place of ethics," in Barry Smith and Berit Brogaard, eds., *Rationality and Irrationality: Proceedings of the 23rd*

a Templeton Fund Colloquium in Rome in 2001,[4] and a paper for a conference on Nature and Technology in Aberdeen.[5] It is also a pretext for reading science fiction during working hours.

That Deep Time, or the idea of Deep Time, does have an effect on our ethical and metaphysical sensibility is certain: witness the number of scientists as well as science fiction writers who testify to the emotional impact of Olaf Stapledon's work, especially *Last and First Men*, *Last Men in London*, and *Star Maker*. Witness the stories told in Hindu and Buddhist sermons reminding us of our littleness, and the real insignificance of fortune, by piling up the years and distances around the little clearings of our lives. Oddly, contemporary Western philosophers do not seem to have addressed the issue, though our predecessors did. We appear to take it for granted — even when engaged in philosophical study of evolutionary theory or of speculative cosmology — that the only proper temporal context for our lives is the humanly accessible one. Our personal time is very much less than a century, even though we know that centuries and even millennia are — by comparison with geological or cosmological aeons — hardly more than a moment. Philosophers follow fashion — as do theologians. The religious imagination, reminding us that "A thousand ages in thy sight/ Are like an ev'ning gone,"[6] has been displaced, and even the religious prefer to believe in a merely immanent deity whose attention-span is not much longer than our own. Once upon a time — and not all that long ago — Berkeley could cheerfully declare that a charitable benefaction "seems to enlarge the very Being of a Man, extending it to distant Places and to future Times; inasmuch as unseen Countries and after Ages, may feel the Effects of his Bounty, while he himself reaps the Reward in the blessed Society of all those who, having turned many to Righteousness, shine as the Stars for ever and ever."[7] And again: "We should

---

International Wittgenstein Symposium (Vienna: Öbv & Hpt, 2001), 62–76 (revised for *Philosophical Futures*).
[4] "Deep Time: does it matter?" in George Ellis, ed., *The Far-Future Universe* (Radnor, PA: Templeton Foundation Press, 2002), 177–95.
[5] "From Biosphere to Technosphere," *Ends and Means* 5 (2001), 3–21 (revised for *Philosophical Futures*).
[6] Isaac Watts, *Psalms, Hymns, and Spiritual Songs* (London: Thomas Nelson, 1850), 183.
[7] "A Proposal for the better Supplying of Churches in our Foreign Plantations," in George Berkeley, *Works*, eds. A. A. Luce and T. E. Jessop (Edinburgh: Thomas Nelson, 1948–56), 7:359–60.

not therefore repine at the divine laws, or show a frowardness or impatience of those transient sufferings they accidentally expose us to, which, however grating to flesh and blood, will yet seem of small moment, if we compare the littleness and fleetingness of this present world with the glory and eternity of the next."[8] It is that literal belief which sets the seal on Berkeley's account of religion.[9] "I can easily overlook any present momentary sorrow, when I reflect that it is in my power to be happy a thousand years hence. If it were not for this thought, I had rather be an oyster than a man, the most stupid and senseless of animals than a reasonable mind tortured with an extreme innate desire of that perfection which it despairs to obtain." What happens here is at once much more and much less important than we think: much more, because our immortal life rests on it; much less, because "if we knew what it was to be an angel for one hour, we should return to this world, though it were to sit on the brightest throne in it, with vastly more loathing and reluctance than we would now descend into a loathsome dungeon or sepulchre."

The religious are now uncomfortable with these attempts to diminish or to exalt the significance of present time, and it is the non-religious who are more likely to remind us how brief our lives and history are (as though it should come as a shock to realize that there are many things much bigger, and much older, than we are). The religious are eager to believe that the only available Infinite is alongside and in us — to hold infinity in the palm of your hand, and eternity in an hour[10]— perhaps because the actual, literal past and future revealed through geological and astronomical enquiry is less to their taste. The irreligious think that our smallness, by comparison with the unimaginable expanse of space and time that surrounds us, casts doubt upon religion: our lives cannot be important. But though cosmological and biological science may tell us that the real world is longer than our lives, or even than our histories, we rarely permit this to affect us. The enterprise designed by Stewart Brand — the Clock of the Long Now — may

---

[8] Berkeley, "Passive Obedience," in *Works*, 6:40.
[9] On which, see "Berkeley's Philosophy of Religion," in Kenneth Winckler, ed., *Cambridge Companion to Berkeley* (Cambridge: Cambridge University Press, 2005), 369–404.
[10] William Blake, *Complete Works*, ed. G. Keynes (Oxford: Oxford University Press, 1966), 431.

perhaps spread some clearer sense of Deep Time, but it would be optimistic to expect this to make much difference. Most of us will continue to act within a time frame very much shorter even than our own lifetime. Why else would most of us agree even to read a paper in a few months' time, were it not for the happy conviction that May will never actually occur? And even Brand's Long Now is very much shorter, at ten thousand years, than the Aeon.[11]

One way of retaining some sense of the significance of stories about the Very Beginning or the Very End is to insist that these stories are "really" about our ordinary present. A literal reading of mythographic speculation assures us that the days of the very beginning were a long time ago, "before" the everyday world of human life got started. But it is of the very essence of fairyland that it is "once-upon-a-time": however far back along the normal run of history we look we shall find that the fairies have already "gone away," and yet are "there" alongside us. Their "pastness" is not that of last year's papers — though one could suggest, con-trariwise, that last year's doings very rapidly become mythological. For the young, their parents' talk even of twenty years ago invites them to contemplate an age beyond imagining, half way back to the dinosaurs that occupy another alongside world in their imaginations. The "pastness" of the Beginnings is better understood as their permanent alongsideness. The world is always Beginning, from the omnipresent centre of attentive consciousness, which we represent to ourselves under the style of myth. At the same time it is always breaking out into a wider world, waking up to judgment. Stories of ending and transforming, which we project into the future, are as little to do with an historic time-to-come as stories of beginning are to do with an historic long-ago. In fact they are often just the same story: the gathering of sticks and stones and bones to make the world, the crashing together of the fire and ice to end a world. In the "long-ago," the people crawled out of the earth to people it; in the "yet-to-come," the dead break from their tombs. Sometimes, as in the literary expression of Norse ritual, this is explicit: Ragnarok is just the opening passage of the new heaven and the new earth, whose coming is disaster for the former powers.

---

[11] Stewart Brand, *The Clock of the Long Now* (London: Weidenfeld and Nic-olson, 1999).

By this account, Creation and Judgment both alike are not events far off, but present experiences of eternal truth. To believe that God made the world is to live by the Covenant; to think that Christ will come to judge the living and the dead is to see ourselves in the light of his life and death. "The Christ event can here be understood in a wholly non-eschatological way as epiphany of the eternal present in the form of the dying and rising Kyrios of the cultus"[12]—or the realization of human guilt and possibility. This is not what our predecessors taught, in imagining an End.

> A final belch of fire like blood,
> Overbroke all heaven in one flood
> Of doom. Then fire was sky, and sky
> Fire, and both, one brief ecstasy,
> Then ashes. But I heard no noise
> (Whatever was) because a Voice
> Beside me spoke thus, "Life is done,
> Time ends, Eternity's begun
> And thou art judged for evermore."[13]

It is comforting to believe that this is not intended as a literal event, but only an allegory of sudden insight, or even a nightmare from which we can expect to wake. Worlds end, no doubt, but each new world-age is simply a continuation of our ordinary, time-bound, moment-bound existence. That is only common sense. But "the commonest sense of all [is] that of men asleep, which they express by snoring."[14] Presentism perhaps has a point, but it certainly seems to rest upon an error. One of the oddities of contemporary literary criticism is the critics' unargued conviction that Science Fiction, which focuses on the larger world, and tries to encompass a more literal reading of such Ends and Beginnings, is less "realistic" than stories about parochial and personal affairs. Of course the particular scenarios that science fiction writers sketch are false: but their underlying theme, by rational standards, is correct. The world we construct for ourselves, in every minute of our sleepy lives, is as foolish as the Hobbits'

---

[12] Jurgen Moltmann, *Theology of Hope*, trans. J. W. Leitch (London: SCM Press, 1967), 155.
[13] Robert Browning, "Christmas Eve and Easter-Day," in *Poems* (Oxford: Oxford University Press, 1912), 522.
[14] H. D. Thoreau, *Walden* (London: Dent, 1910), 26.

dream that the Shire belongs to them. "'But it is not your own Shire,' said Gildor. 'Others dwelt here before hobbits were; and others will dwell here again when hobbits are no more. The wide world is all about you: you can fence yourselves in, but you cannot for ever fence it out.'"[15] And the moral has a wider significance than the merely territorial. It is the essence of reason that our reasonings do not exhaust reality, and that those who trust too much in what they think is reason actually betray it. "If we repose our trust in our own reasonings, we shall construct and build up the city of mind that corrupts the truth . . . The dreamer finds on rising up that all the movements and exertions of the foolish man are dreams void of truth. Mind itself turned out to be a dream."[16]

So how can we begin to wake, and what is the relevance of the new mythologies to be found in speculative fiction? Even if the stories are — at least in part — ways of structuring our everyday awareness, orienting it to the grand themes of Creation and Judgment, maybe we diminish their significance by not thinking them through.

WHETHER OR NOT THE END IS NIGH

The religious — or, at any rate, the respectable religious — no longer seem to expect a literal Judgment or an End of Days, and the quotation from Browning only evokes a momentary shudder. Those who declare that the End really is Nigh do not normally occupy the pulpits of mainstream Churches (or at any rate, I have never myself heard a sermon of the sort that our predecessors would have found familiar). Preachers may mention personal mortality, but not the End of Days. Those who do, in terms like the following, extracted from a random website in 2001, are easily identified as mavericks ignorant both of history and of true religion:

> The Second Coming, the return of Christ to Jerusalem, and the end of the world (end of the age) alluded to by Messiah Jesus Christ, could occur as soon as the year

---

[15] J. R. R. Tolkien, *The Fellowship of the Ring* (London: Allen and Unwin, 1954), 103.
[16] Philo, *Legum Allegoriae* III. 228–29, in *Collected Works*, trans. F. H. Colson, G. H. Whitaker et al. (London: Heinemann, Loeb Classical Library, 1929–62), 1:457.

2007. The middle east conflict over Jerusalem and the temple mount is now scheduled for complete and final settlement by September 15, 2000. The Sharm Memorandum signed by Israel and the PLO on September 5, 1999 requires finalizing the permanent status of Jerusalem by this date, presumably including the temple mount and the Dome of the Rock. This could be the agreement described in Chapter 9 of the Book of Daniel that Christ referenced in Chapter 24 of the Book of Matthew. This treaty could start the 7 year countdown to the end of the age (not the "end of the world") resulting in the construction of the third temple on Mount Moriah and the mid-point "abomination of desolation" that Christ described. The battle of Armageddon will be at the end of this seven year period. Nevertheless, the Sharm negotiations may not result in the treaty referred to by Daniel and our Lord. We will have to watch developments and be aware of the Third Temple teachings of Scripture. An event such as war, terrorism, an earthquake, etc. may be the catalyst in the rebuilding of the Temple.

Jesus said "watch" for His coming, and that is the purpose of this site, constructed in September of 1999. We will also diligently and logically examine the Scripture that is related to this great event! God has said that His temple will be built during this last 7 year period and is THE sure sign of His return. The prophesied regathering of the Jewish people into a reborn Israel in 1948 and their regaining control of Jerusalem in 1967 are sure signs that this is the last generation (40–70 years) that Christ said would see His return. This generation will also witness the anti-christ, the abomination of desolation, and the great tribulation — all end time subjects of Bible prophesy [*sic*].[17]

No doubt we are wise to disregard all such attempts to decode biblical prophecy. But it is worth noticing that there is a naturalistic argument against any easy expectation that life will go on without any particular change or interruption. It is also worth noting that Babbage's Paradox (that a simple computer program may suddenly

---

[17] Back in 2001 I took this from a website [http://www.geocities.com/secondcoming1/]: that site, understandably, has now vanished, but similar sites remain. See (for example) https://www.tomorrowsworld.org/booklets/fourteen-signs-announcing-christs-return/content (Accessed July 30, 2024).

generate entirely unexpected results which show that something else entirely was occurring than we had supposed) destroys any simple faith in rational continuity.[18] But here I address the Carter Catastrophe rather than Babbage's.

It may seem entirely rational to discount all warnings that the End is Nigh. After all, we have survived (or else our line, our species and our world has survived) so far, despite war, plague, famine, meteor strikes and mass pollution. Any possible disaster will be no more than local: there are too many of us now, and we are technologically too well equipped, to vanish. It is surely perfectly reasonable to respond to prophecies of doom with a degree of scepticism. One such sceptic, on being told that she had "learnt nothing" from the happy pessimism of a particular newsgroup (established to consider the likely outcome of the Y2K bug), replied as follows:

> I've learned from reading the newsgroup that I ought to be stocking up with 300 pounds of grain, 60 pounds of legumes, 60 pounds of sugar or honey, five pounds of salt and 20 pounds of fat or oil for the first year, along with a gallon of water per person per day; that I should be buying candles, fuel, medical supplies, a generator, canned vegetables and fruits, garden seeds, blankets, sleeping bags, hand tools, lots and lots of batteries, and even more guns and ammunition to protect the stockpile from the starving and desperate hordes who will flee the burning cities in search of sustenance; and that gold is a poor choice for storing currency because the government can seize it at any time during a national emergency. I should also be buying any books that might tell me how to make things I need when civilization falls. And I should work out, so that I'm physically fit enough to survive whatever humanity and nature throw at me. Except for the guns (illegal where I live), none of this advice is necessarily bad.[19]

---

[18] Robert Chambers, *Vestiges of the Natural History of Creation* (1844), after Charles Babbage, *Ninth Bridgewater Thesis: a Fragment* (London: Frank Cass, 1967 [1837; second edition 1838]); see Clark, *Biology and Christian Ethics* (Cambridge: Cambridge University Press, 2000), 22–23.
[19] "Preppers" or survivalists are still available to offer advice about how to prepare for the End. See https://www.thesurvivalprepstore.com/blogs/

Aside from sad postings about how most of the world's population is going to die—four fifths, according to some postings—there's an element of satisfaction among these Cassandras. They make up the in-group that is going to survive because they're smarter and tougher than the rest of us. Computing gurus are at the mercy of the political and financial decisions of others, just like the rest of us (Wired magazine recently featured a few software programmers who were stocking up and taking to the hills). People who have rigorously refused to have computers still rely on the ready availability of electric power, food, telecommunications and, most important, a clean supply of water. About the only people in the U. S. who might escape all effects are the Amish.[20]

It seems that we have strong inductive evidence that such prophecies are likely not to be fulfilled—and an interesting sidelight on the preparations now considered appropriate for surviving Doomsday! It is Brandon Carter's achievement to demonstrate how little reason there is for confidence: precisely because we have survived so far, and there are so many of us, we have reason to suspect that our time is nearly up.[21] And "Cassandra," of course, was a prophetess whose entirely accurate prophecies were doomed to be disbelieved.

It is easy to believe that our having survived so far (despite occasions when we—ourselves, our line, our world—might not have done) is evidence that God or the gods are fond of us. But—obviously enough—if there are many possible worlds, or many other worlds, where life, intelligence or civilized society has not survived, it is not surprising that civilized intelligences will always see a world where, so far, they themselves survive. Each of you now reading this account—is still alive, and can look back complacently on many occasions when we might have

---

rants-raves/top-100-things-you-should-start-stocking-up-on-for-when-shtf (Accessed July 30, 2024).
[20] Wendy M. Grossman, "The End of the World as We Know It": *Scientific American* 1098 (1998): https://www.scientificamerican.com/article/y2k-the-end-of-the-world-as-we-know/ (accessed July 30, 2024). See Larry Niven and Jerry Pournelle, *Lucifer's Hammer* (New York: HarperCollins, 1977) for a fictional vindication of the preppers' fantasy.
[21] John Leslie, *The End of the World* (London: Routledge, 1996).

died. It does not follow that we are immortal. Even as a culture, or a species, we cannot reasonably expect to do much better than other species and cultures.

> Cities and Thrones and Powers
> Stand, in Time's eye,
> Almost as long as flowers,
> Which daily die...
> This season's Daffodil,
> She never hears,
> What change, what chance, what chill,
> Cut down last year's;
> But with bold countenance,
> And knowledge small,
> Esteems her seven days' continuance
> To be perpetual.[22]

Our past survival gives us no inductive ground for trusting in a future survival as a culture or a species any more than as individuals: rather the contrary. But our trust seems almost absolute, and infects even those who imagine the End. The Y2K millenialists I mentioned before were as complacent as any commonsensical sceptic in their belief that human, and specifically American stereotypical characters, being "fittest," would survive. And had as little evidence for their claim. Current evolutionary theory gives us little ground for thinking that there were always bound to be multicellular living creatures, or civilized ones, or that any particular species is likely to last. The chances are high that we are the only strictly intelligent creatures in the universe — unless indeed intelligence is a privileged image of the Divine. In a godless universe, it seems most probable, there is no reason to expect intelligence either to appear or — once apparent — last: the dangers facing such an evolutionary track are far too great to make it likely.[23] That

---

[22] Rudyard Kipling, *Collected Verse 1885–1926* (London: Hodder and Stoughton, 1927), 479. This is not to endorse the false analogy that treats species and cultures as mortal individuals, as though they must inevitably grow old and die. It is only to agree that species and cultures do end.

[23] "Extraterrestrial Intelligence, the Neglected Experiment": *Foundation* 61 (1994), 50–65. Even eucaryotic and multicellular organisms took so long to develop that we should assume that most biospheres are entirely bacterial! Some science fiction writers have imagined bacterial civilizations (Greg Bear, *Blood Music* [London: Gollancz, 1986]; Orson Scott Card, *Children of*

we are the only such intelligences anywhere (or almost so) may explain the absence of any evidence of extraterrestrial civilization. It takes too long for civilization to appear (by chance), and there are far too many risks attached to give such creatures, even if they happen to exist, sufficient time to colonize. The more improbable our emergence, the likelier it is that we are near the end of that period in which it is even possible for us to exist.[24]

So if we are the only ones, might we be the first? Suppose that things turn out that way: that our kind does colonize the solar system, and the local stars, or even advances (as the story books imagine) to infect and manage the whole universe (or at least a galaxy or two). In that case we here-now will prove to have been astonishingly early hominids. Almost all the human beings there will ever be will prove to have lived generations later (though most will probably be rather unlike ourselves). Do we have any right to expect this to be true? Plainly not. Imagine a collection of large rooms, in which there are successively five, fifty, five hundred, five thousand people, and so on. Suppose that all the inmates, including you, have been placed, blind-folded, in one of the many rooms. The rational bet would be that you will find that you are in the largest room: if the largest is the fifty-billion room, that is the one you should assume that you are in. If, on removing the blind-fold, you find yourself instead one of the five hundred, you should suspect that this is the largest room. It follows that our initial assumption has to be that we are far more likely not to be untypically early hominids. A similar conclusion follows from widespread use by scientists of "the principle of mediocrity": "that we should assume ourselves to be typical in any class that we belong to, unless there is some evidence to the contrary."[25] No one — on this account — will ever have occasion, in actual fact, to remark that "in the afterglow of the Big Bang, humans spread in waves across the universe."[26] We are unlikely

the Mind [New York: Tom Doherty Associates, 1996]), but if such civilizations really exist, they are unlikely to be ones that we could ever hope to understand or converse with.
[24] See John D. Barrow, Frank J. Tipler, and John A. Wheeler, *The Anthropic Cosmological Principle* (Oxford: Oxford University Press, 1988).
[25] Alexander Vilenkin, "The Principle of Mediocrity," *Astronomy & Geophysics 52*, no. 5 (2011): 33–36.
[26] Stephen Baxter, *Time: Manifold I* (London: Voyager, 1999), 3: a novel whose most memorable and sympathetic character is a genetically-enhanced

even to find that we—or even the hominid species that come after us—last out the two billion years of Stapledon's fantastic history. It is always a lot more likely that we are in or very near the largest generation of humankind: when it becomes true that there are more people alive than have ever lived before—and that moment is not far off—we will have excellent reason to suspect the imminence of "the Carter Catastrophe."

There are many "blindingly obvious" (but probably mistaken) objections to this line of argument. The only objections that have much force come from those who would deny that there is now any fact of the matter about how many generations of humankind there are yet to be, and those others who speculate that the number of generations might in fact be infinite. If there really are no other generations of humankind than the ones that there have actually been, then it is probably true that everyone has always been in the largest generation that then existed (except for occasional disasters), but there may still be a larger to come. On the other hand, there may not be: if the future of our kind is open then, perhaps, there is no reason to think that we are near the end, but there is also no reason, on those terms, to think we aren't. If nothing at all is determined about our future, our survival isn't either. On the other hand, if there are—as it were—infinitely many ever larger rooms, there is nothing improbable about being in an "early" room. But even though Aristotle thought the generations of humankind had in fact been infinite (since there had been no beginning of things), it is unlikely that he was right. It seems more reasonable to think that there are a finite number to be expected—and in that case, perhaps we really do not need to worry about Deep Time: our human time is shallow.

Science fiction writers have written of many possible catastrophes—in the forties and fifties, chiefly those brought on by nuclear or biological warfare. Perhaps those fantasies served us as warnings, and left their prophets as disconcerted as the unfortunate Jonah.[27] The fashion in catastrophes since then has been for

---

squid, and which takes it for granted that we all hate and fear anything we cannot control, perhaps has few insights into the ordinary human condition, but it is still a serious attempt to think through what Deep Time might mean for us and for our projects.

[27] Jonah 3:10—4:1: "And God saw their works, that they turned from their evil way; and God repented of the evil, that he had said that he would do

ecological disasters, meteor strikes, the revolt of the machines, or alien invasions—often with the conscious or unconscious motive of upsetting people whom the author happens to dislike! The thought that human time is short may not always be unwelcome. Once we are gone, the earth can revert to "normal"—a normality in which no sentient creature even pretends to have a time-frame larger than the immediate moment. D. H. Lawrence had fantasies of that "cleaner" world. And even Simone Weil expressed the thought that we polluted the landscape just by looking at it.[28] Maybe all sentience will perish, and all definite being—

> Then star nor sun shall waken,
> Nor any change of light:
> Nor sound of waters shaken,
> Nor any sound or sight:
> Nor wintry leaves nor vernal,
> Nor days nor things diurnal;
> Only the sleep eternal
> In an eternal night.[29]

Some have seen in this a metaphor for uncluttered, uncontaminating being, the end of confusion or the vindication of their own preferred viewpoint. If civilization, humankind, the world itself must perish, it will be because—in the authors' eyes—we have slipped too far from "nature" (rather as inexperienced intellectuals welcomed the Great War). Others, perhaps initially depressed, have consoled themselves with the thought that all of us must die as individuals: why then should we care if all are doomed to die together? "The happiness of ten million individuals is not a millionfold the happiness of ten."[30] To which the only answer is presumably that we do count genocide as worse than homicide: the end of the world must be the end of all our ambitions, all

---

unto them; and he did it not. But it displeased Jonah exceedingly, and he was very angry."
[28] Simone Weil, *Gravity and Grace*, trans. Emma Crawford and Mario van der Ruhr (London: Routledge, 2002 [1947]), 42: "If only I could see a landscape as it is when I am not there. But when I am in any place I disturb the silence of heaven by the beating of my heart." See my *How to Think about the Earth: models of environmental theology* (London: Mowbrays, 1993).
[29] A. C. Swinburne, "The Garden of Proserpine," in *Poems and Ballads. First Series* (London: William Heinemann, 1917), 169–72, 172.
[30] J. B. S. Haldane, *Possible Worlds* (London: Chatto and Windus, 1927), 307.

our ordinary reasons for thrift or creative action, all our care. The thought of universal death may make each moment precious — but such "perfect moments" are only those in which we manage to forget the universal death.[31]

But perhaps there is another way of looking at the Catastrophe. Maybe it will be the very same moment as the Singularity expected by some futurologists — the moment when the advance of computer science, of nanotechnology, and the communications network marks a sudden break with all our pasts, the end of that Aeon in which there are singular individuals of our sort.[32] The Singularity, so-called, marks a break with the past so enormous as to make all rational inference impossible. We are on the brink of an epoch utterly unlike all other, earlier ages. Computer power is doubling every eighteen months. The practical existence of molecular and atomic engines — nanotechnology — is probably closer than we can let ourselves imagine. People everywhere now have access to information, skills, energy and mechanical assistance that was once the province only of the immensely rich. Even if a genuinely unified, genuinely universal Theory of Everything is impossible even in principle, we are likely to have some very powerful theories about everything from gravity to the human genome. Very soon it will be true that every human individual must make decisions which will affect us all, and could make utterly disastrous ones. It will be our duty to become "as gods."[33] The End of the Age, or of the Ages, will lie in the discovery of Forever: we shall not inhabit that Forever in the forms we now possess. "For we shall all be changed, in a moment, in a twinkling of an eye, at the last trumpet" (1 Corinthians 15:51–52).

Science fiction has tended to represent that ending in material or atheistic terms, and so to exaggerate the alien nature of whatever

---

[31] One answer might be to claim that, since the passage of time is unreal, nothing is ever really lost: all moments are eternal. But that is little consolation: "while the past was thought of as a mere gulf of non-existence, the inconceivably great pain, misery, baseness, that had fallen into that gulf, could be dismissed as done with; and the will could be concentrated wholly on preventing such horrors from occurring in the future. But now, along with past joy, past distress was found to be everlasting." Olaf Stapledon, *Last and First Men* (Harmondsworth: Penguin, 1972 [1930]), 242; see also 305–6, on the Last Men's avowal of the closed circle of time proposed by the Stoics.
[32] See Vernor Vinge, *Across Real Time* (London: Gollancz, 2000).
[33] See Stewart Brand, *Whole Earth Catalogue* (Menlo Park, CA: Portola Institute 1968), 2: "we are as gods and have to get good at it."

sensibility is more appropriate to Forever. But the breakout from our crystal palace has long been anticipated in religious fiction:

> And for us this is the end of all the stories. And we can most truly say that they all lived happily ever after. But for them it was only the beginning of the real story. All their life in this world and all their adventures in Narnia had only been the cover and the title page: now at last they were beginning Chapter One of the Great Story which no one on earth has read: which goes on for ever: in which every chapter is better than the one before.[34]

THE EMERGENCE OF OMEGA

So consider the idea of a New, Unprecedented World as it is expressed in speculative fiction. The point of speaking of a "Singularity" is, of course, to emphasise that we do not have, and cannot have, the slightest idea of what life will be like beyond it—but negative theology has never stopped anyone from seeking to imagine the unimaginable, and getting some benefit from the exercise! Even if the Change is not as close as I have just suggested, it might come or have already come someday, somewhere, and somehow. Even if intelligent life is very improbable indeed, it might have happened for the very first time in some very distant place and period, and we might be amongst its products. Suppose that there really is, or that there will be, a conclusive synthesis of power and intelligence, an imagined Omega. It might remain the case that any individual intelligence of the sort we are must always expect to be amongst the last of its kind, and yet there be a sense in which that intelligence is an early and unfinished version of the larger sort. Arthur C. Clarke's flawed novel *Childhood's End* (1954) can be given many interpretations; in the past, I have regretted his curious idea that the essence of "religion" lies in the hope of absorption into an Overmind.[35] On this occasion let it stand proxy for a branch of speculative fiction that simultaneously conceives the literal end and extinction of the human species, and its transfiguration. The Carter Catastrophe occurs—though not the ones that we might more easily expect—but there is

---

[34] C. S. Lewis, *The Last Battle* (London: Puffin, 1964), 165.
[35] See my *God's World*, 177.

something, not ourselves, in which our purposes and memories are raised to life immortal.

Suppose that Omega or the Overmind is real. If ever it does come into being it will be as difficult to eradicate as life itself, and as likely to occupy all possible times and places. Even we, at the tag-end of our likely lives as mortal individuals, can imagine ways in which it could persist and grow. The only question is: what sort of growth, what sort of growing thing, will Omega or the Overmind turn out to be? Clarke's Overmind, as I have already hinted, does not really engage our religious or our ethical devotion. The supposed Overlords of his story, commanded to prepare the way for the Overmind's absorption of our species, are more admirable characters in their dreams of fighting off its influence — and later SF writers, like Jack Williamson, have given an altogether blunter picture of the Overmind as Parasite.[36] Greg Bear's cosmic intelligence, in Eternity, turns out to be the descendant rather of humankind's greatest, genocidal enemy, than of any "humane" purpose. In Gregory Benford's imagined future, humans and their like exist like rats or cockroaches within the triumphant culture of Kipling's Machines, who "are not built to comprehend a lie, [and] can neither love nor pity nor forgive."[37] Writers frequently give mythological shape to the notion that there is, or could be, "war in heaven" — a conflict between radically different characters, each striving to be the meaning and culminating synthesis of all that has ever been.

No such Omega, it is easy to conclude, could actually be God, even if its character and purposes turned out to be ones that creatures like us could share, or at any rate appreciate. God, by hypothesis, is that than which none greater can be conceived, the necessary standard of all value and the one necessary existent. An entity, even the greatest possible, that might have one character or another, and might emerge in one possible history but not another, cannot be what theists have supposed as God. Stapledon's cosmic spirit (itself created not even by the Eighteenth Species of humankind, but by creatures of an entirely different sort) turns out to be infinitely distant from the hoped-for "Star Maker" — and that Star Maker itself is something other than God. Peter Hamilton's recent Night's Dawn Trilogy takes delight

---

[36] See my *How to Live Forever* (London, 1995).
[37] Kipling, *Collected Verse*, 676.

in devising a wholly naturalistic version of familiar myths whose conclusion vitiates any notion that there is Someone with the power, authority and will to require obedience. Baxter's novel likewise embodies the possibility that the Final Spirit will have good reason to despair—and therefore not be God. Greg Egan's openly atheistical *Diaspora* similarly ends in weariness: the "whole thing" is simply not worth knowing or enjoying. But my concern here is not with philosophical theology, nor with the dispute between "naturalism" and "supernaturalism," but with the impact and importance of Deep Time, and the stories we tell of it. Where the Carter Catastrophe reminds us of immediate Judgment, the Omega Story reminds us of the gathering of the faithful on the far side of catastrophe. The hope expressed in such stories (as well as the fear) is that our lives, though we lose them, will be vindicated. We shall have contributed something of value to the final synthesis, and that synthesis will turn out to have reached "back" into our own lives to guide its own first steps. But the Catastrophe hangs over all such imagined Omegas: whatever their power and brilliance they still face an End—unless there is, somehow, an escape from Time.

Omega isn't God—any more than the God of Milton's *Paradise Lost* is God—but the stories we tell or enjoy about such images are both revealing and helpful. Science fiction writers and other futurologists, in speaking of Omega, sometimes draw the conclusion that our role must simply be to keep the research funds coming. Just as the threat of Doomsday causes some to hoard artillery and practice their "survival skills," so the promise of Omega only suggests, to some, that technology has to be supported at whatever present cost. Better to lose the whole world—through climate change and soil erosion—than to lose the future by cutting back on technological investment. Both inferences display complacency: the former, as I suggested earlier, by taking a particular political stereotype for granted; the latter, by forgetting that Omega must be the inheritor of every form of life and not just ours. Or rather, if it is the inheritor only of one form of life, it is unlikely that that form of life is ours. It will be something of which we have any chance of approving only if it is also the confluence of unnumbered other agencies. That apparently sounds undesirable to some: "But it won't be me," and "they won't be human." Others—and I think the more rational—can only express surprise that anyone should think that either complaint much matters.

Haldane drew a false contrast in his essay on "The Last Judgement":

> Man's little world will end. The human mind can already envisage that end. If humanity can enlarge the scope of its will as it has enlarged the reach of its intellect, it will escape that end. If not, then judgement will have gone against it, and man and all his works will perish eternally. Either the human race will prove that its destiny is in eternity and infinity, and that the value of the individual is negligible in comparison with that destiny, or the time will come
>
>> "When the great markets by the sea shut fast
>> All that calm Sunday that goes on and on;
>> When even lovers find their peace at last,
>> And earth is but a star, that once had shone."[38]

A full response to Haldane would take another paper. Although I am here agreeing with him that "the use, however haltingly, of our imaginations upon the possibilities of the future is a valuable spiritual exercise,"[39] I endorse little else in his metaphysics, ethics or futurology. Specifically, we do not have to choose between thinking only of the present and devising a communistic utopia to seed the stars with our progeny.[40] Sacrificing the present for the sake of the future is suicidal. Nor can a merely material, temporal future ever be enough to satisfy us. "If the many become the same as the few when possess'd, More! More! is the cry of a mistaken soul; less than All cannot satisfy Man."[41]

So the moral is that all ages will seem shallow, and soon to end, unless Omega is understood to be a metaphor for something

---

[38] Haldane, *Possible Worlds*, 312, citing James Elroy Flecker (a passage used by Arthur C. Clarke as the conclusion of *Prelude to Space* [New York: World Editions, 1950]). Flecker, "The Golden Journey to Samarkand," in *Collected Poems*, ed. J. C. Squire (London: William Heinemann, 1912), 144–50, 145.

[39] Haldane, *Possible Worlds*, 310.

[40] An enterprise rendered ridiculous in C. S. Lewis's *Out of the Silent Planet* (London: Pan, 1952 [1938]), 164: "'Men go jump off each [world] before it deads—on and on, see?' 'And when all are dead?'"

[41] Blake, "There is no Natural Religion," second series, in *Complete Writings*, ed. Keynes, 97.

greater than the ages. And one last deeply speculative story: if
Omega is real, might it not choose to resurrect us? And if it did,
must it not—at least initially—provide us with the context in
which the lives for which we are programmed can be lived, the
context in which we can exist at all? And how could we tell that
this has not already happened? Rather than being a distant,
imagined prospect (as Frank Tipler supposes),[42] might it not
be the actual situation of our present lives? How could we tell
that we were "really" the original entities from which Omega
took its beginning, or the entities it has already resurrected in a
small region of itself with a view to guiding them into a deeper
association?[43] And is there any difference—especially if Omega
can reach "back" to its beginnings—between being the originals
and being the resurrected? So the Carter Argument—an insight
I owe Dr Barry Dainton, one of my colleagues at Liverpool—may
have less bite: we are indeed in the largest possible collection of
mortal individuals (that is, all there ever are), momentarily provided with the narrower context in which such individuals can
have a sense of their own individuality before they, or something
in them, learns the larger way.[44] What other dream scenarios
Omega devises, time will tell. What Omega's character will turn
out to be (and to have been already) depends on what the whole
company of the faithful can come to imagine. We are at once its
product and amongst its many ancestors.

When Stapledon's narrator returns from his wanderings at
the edge of time to the hillside overlooking his home, it is with
a renewed sense of the importance of "our little glowing atom
of community," the relationship between himself and his wife.[45]
"Immensity," as Stapledon went on to say, "is not itself a good
thing.... But immensity has indirect importance through its facil-
itation of mental richness and diversity."[46] Re-absorption in the
merely personal amounts to falling asleep again: transformation

---

[42] Frank Tipler, *The Physics of Immortality: modern cosmology, God and the
resurrection of the dead* (Basingstoke: Macmillan, 1994).
[43] See Robert Charles Wilson, *Darwinia* (London: Orion Books, 1999),
214: "the world you and I inhabit is nothing more than a sustained illusion
inside a machine at the end of time."
[44] See Barry Dainton, "On singularities and simulations": *Journal of Consciousness Studies*, 19.1–2 (2012), 42–85.
[45] Olaf Stapledon, *Star Maker* (London: Methuen, 1937), 333.
[46] Ibid., 335.

of the personal may be a mode of waking up. My suggestion is slightly different from Stapledon's: immensity, or the imagination of immensity, awakens in us a recognition of that Infinite which surrounds and confronts us.

By John Crowley's evocative account the moment when Giordano Bruno fully realised that the Sun did not revolve around the Earth was his release from the crystal spheres that bound all human souls. Instead of having to clamber, in imagination, upwards to the heavens, he realised that the Earth itself was swimming through the heavens, that he had already escaped. "You made yourself equal to the stars by knowing your mother Earth was a star as well; you rose up through the spheres not by leaving the earth but by sailing it: by knowing that it sailed."[47] We escape the Carter Catastrophe by knowing that we — in Omega — already have. Deep Time is all around us — and that, rather than the commonsensical presentism of too much contemporary thought, was probably always Blake's point.

---

[47] John Crowley, *Aegypt* (London: Gollancz, 1986), 366.

9.
Mind Parasites[1]

PLOT AND CHARACTERS

The chief moral of an imagined Multiverse[2] is to explore what may be possible for us and for the world. What is possible specifically for us may be especially significant: what we might ourselves be brought to do or suffer. We are not such simple creatures as we might hope to be, we are not immune to threats or to temptations, and our current lives and loves are not the only possible lives and loves for us. A similar discovery may be made, or represented, when we realise how little of our own thoughts and feelings are really, truly, our own.

> It is a hard matter to bring to a standstill the soul's changing movements. Their irresistible stream is such that we could sooner stem the rush of a torrent, for thoughts after thoughts in countless numbers pour on like a huge breaker and drive and whirl and upset its whole being with their violence.... A man's thoughts

---

[1] An earlier version of this chapter was published as "*The Mind Parasites*: Wilson, Husserl, Plotinus," in *Around the Outsider: essays presented to Colin Wilson*, ed. Colin Stanley (Alresford: O-Books, 2011), 42–62. My thanks to Colin Stanley, both for his efforts on Colin Wilson's behalf, and for his encouragement of my interest in both Wilson and Lovecraft.

[2] Which many recent authors, as well as speculative physicists, have taken as an obvious account of the wider world we live in: see David Deutsch, *The Fabric of Reality: towards a theory of everything* (London: Allen Lane, 1997); Mary-Jane Rubenstein, *Worlds Without End: The Many Lives of the Multiverse* (New York: Columbia University Press, 2014); Glyn Morgan and Charul Palmer-Patel, *Sideways in Time: Critical Essays on Alternate History Fiction* (Liverpool: Liverpool University Press, 2019). I discuss this speculation at greater length in chapter 12 below.

are sometimes not due to himself but come without
his will.[3]

That is the thought that Colin Wilson, and others, explored in
mid-twentieth-century fantasy. In Wilson's first, sub-Lovecraftian,
novel, *The Mind Parasites*, the archaeologist Gilbert Austin learns
that an old friend, Karel Weissman, has committed suicide, and
left him the task of sorting through his papers. Unwilling to
engage promptly with this task, he leaves for a dig in Turkey,
where he and another friend, Wolfgang Reich, slowly uncover
the remains of a great city,[4] buried two miles in the earth, which
seems to be much like the cities described by H. P. Lovecraft
(1890–1937). The suggestion is made that Lovecraft's "Great Old
Ones" might be woken from their sleep by the archaeological dis-
turbances, and Austin, at last beginning to read his dead friend's
papers, catches sight (as it were) of alien presences, "mind parasites," in the depths of his own mind. With the help of phenomenological exercises derived from the writings of the philosopher
Edmund Husserl (1859–1938), Austin and his colleague develop
telekinetic and telepathic powers, enlist other scientists in their
enterprise, and decide to alert the public to the dangers posed by
"the Great Old Ones" (who may or may not be either the mind
parasites or their makers). The alien presences fight back, driving
the conspirators to suicide or madness, and eventually inciting
racial war between a United Africa and Europe. Austin defeats
their attempt against him, enlists the American President as an
ally, educates other scientists in the new techniques, discovers
the malign influence of the Moon on the human mind, and
finally halts the war between Europe and Africa by creating a
shared hallucination of extraterrestrial invaders. They also dis-
pose of the Moon. Rather than remain as masters of the human
world, Austin and his companions leave Earth behind to join a
"universal police force." The novel in which all this is imagined is

[3] Philo of Alexandria, *De Mutatione Nominum*, 239–40, in *Collected Works*,
trans. F. H. Colson, G. H. Whitaker et al. (London: Heinemann, Loeb
Classical Library, 1929), 5, 265–66.
[4] Wilson may have noticed the accidental rediscovery of Derinkuyu in 1963:
a multi-level underground city, dating from at least the seventh or eighth
centuries BC and periodically inhabited since then. It is one of many such
underground refuges in Turkey: see Spiro Kostof, *Caves of God: Cappadocia
and Its Churches* (Oxford: Oxford University Press, 1989).

composed of documents created at one time or another by Austin, and gives all the signs of being related by an unreliable narrator who (amongst other things) deliberately fogs the relationship between the builders of the buried city and the mental parasites that control and feed on human emotion.

The Mind Parasites (1967) began as Colin Wilson's response to a challenge from August Derleth (1909–71), who was Lovecraft's literary executor. He also composed a shorter story, "The Return of the Lloigor," in which the monsters embody a deeply rooted, supposedly "rational," pessimism.[5] The challenge itself was a response to Wilson's critical remarks, in *The Strength to Dream*,[6] about Lovecraft's style and his failure to understand where his greatest strength really lay: not in horror fiction so much as in an evocation of the immense span of time and space in ignorance of which we conduct our usual lives.[7] In the event, the merely Lovecraftian elements of Wilson's fable turn out to be irrelevant, "a gigantic red herring to keep man looking for his enemies *outside* himself" (*Mind Parasites*, 185): pre-historical and possibly non-human civilizations, invasions from "space," hidden cults, and the fancied return of powers inimical to living creatures, whether of human or non-human kind. Some of those themes are treated at more length in Wilson's later "Lovecraftian" fables: *The Philosopher's Stone* (1969) or *The Space Vampires* (1976).

The closer cousin of *The Mind Parasites* is rather Eric Frank Russell's *Sinister Barrier* (1939; expanded edition 1948). There may also be an allusion to a work by Bernard Newman (1897–1968), *The Flying Saucer* (1948), in which a group of scientists stage a mock invasion by extraterrestrials with the aim of uniting humanity against the alien threat—which is what Wilson's scientists are, correctly, accused of doing (though the accusation, we are to understand, is driven by the parasites' need to discredit their enemies). Newman had offered a similar scenario before the war, in *Armoured Doves: a Peace Novel* (1931): there the scientists

---

[5] "The Return of the Lloigor" (1969), in A. W. Derleth, *Tales of the Cthulhu Mythos* (New York: Ballantine Books, 1971).
[6] Colin Wilson, *The Strength to Dream: literature and the imagination* (London: Gollancz, 1963), 1–9, 102–6.
[7] Lovecraft, in fact, was a more self-conscious writer than Wilson, at that time, supposed. He *used* the conventions of "weird fiction" to express his philosophical intent: see, further, "Lovecraft and the Search for Meaning," below.

unite humanity by the threat of a death-ray. G. K. Chesterton commented acidly that

> We have all read shockers and sensational stories, in which a white-haired and wild-eyed Professor, alleged to be idealistic and instantly recognized to be insane, is at work on producing a Death-Ray or some deadly explosive or destructive machine, so terrific as to lay the nations prostrate with panic, and thus achieve the happy result of imposing peace on the world.... To remain at peace, out of sheer panic about a professor with a death-ray or a tyrant with an instrument of torture, would be to die daily and even then not be secure against death.[8]

In Wilson's fable, the effort is not entirely successful: many people simply disbelieve the story that the "Tsathogguans" of Lovecraft's fantasy have been awakened; many others quarrel about the best way to respond to the imagined threat; some fall into despair; a few begin to devise new ways of making war upon the heavens, or each other. The main battle is halted by sending a huge experimental airship over the warring armies, and causing mass hallucinations (almost as many die in the panic as would have died in battle), but there is no real prospect of a genuine or permanent peace. Some measure of calm is restored only by a magical dislocation of the moon—imagined, in the fable, to be a constant irritant, a source of "lunatic" emotions in the human soul.

Wilson's narrator is a middle-aged, unmarried, overweight archaeologist, with a liking for fine food and wine. But just as the merely Lovecraftian elements of the plot are a red herring, so also are the archaeological interests of the narrator: the important truth about ourselves and our situation are not to be found by excavations, nor even by burrowing miles down into the earth to uncover ancient cities, but by burrowing down into the mind, through "layer upon geological layer of response to experience, habit patterns," to borrow a phrase from a later novel.[9] This is to be done, we are to suppose, by really attending to Husserl's insights rather than by then-fashionable experiments with drugs or sleep deprivation. In later Lovecraftian novels, the route is

---

[8] "Torture and the Wrong Tool": *The End of the Armistice*, ed. F. Sheed (1940): republished in *Collected Works 5* (San Francisco: Ignatius Press, 1987).
[9] Wilson, *The Philosopher's Stone* (London: Barker, 1969), 129.

rather through neuropsychology and the accidental discovery of a metal that speeds up neural processing (*The Philosopher's Stone*), or through the conscious use of sexual desire (*The Space Vampires; The God of the Labyrinth*). In all the stories the effects of enhanced intelligence include telekinetic and telepathic powers, and especially the power to control all "lesser" minds, whether they are wasps or reporters. In *The Mind Parasites* the narrator and his companions, having engineered world peace (at least for a moment), depart to join an imagined galactic police force. It remains uncertain whether their departure is motivated more by boredom and disgust with the merely human condition, or by a genuine love of all the creatures with whom we share a cosmos, a wish to be of service and a delight in something new. In Eric Frank Russell's story we are to suppose that the Earth, once rid of its tyrants, will be free to join the larger community: in Wilson's, only a very few (and almost entirely male) will do so.

PARASITES, DEMONS, AND METAPHORS

The parasites of Wilson's fable, sometimes referred to as Tsathogguans (after Lovecraft's monsters), first slither into sight when the narrator's friend kills himself after writing what at first seem paranoiac ramblings about the enemies that lurk within our minds. The narrator, protected at first by his own ignorance, inattention, and automatic disbelief, gradually learns that there are indeed such enemies, and that they can be identified and even defeated. The first attempt to gather together scientists and scholars to face this danger is a fiasco: most kill themselves, or are killed; one is engulfed by the parasites. Much the same pattern fills Eric Frank Russell's *Sinister Barrier*, which draws (like Wilson) on the stories collected by Charles Fort, and the Fortean hypothesis that we are property.[10] Both also identify the sensation that "someone is walking on my grave," a shiver down the spine, as a signal of the parasites' presence. The stories are also alike in invoking such staples of classic 1950s science fiction as telescreens, stratospheric expresses, rocket-powered automobiles, and rock-chewing mechanical moles—all the expected devices of advanced

---

[10] See Charles Fort, *The Books of Charles Fort* (comprising *The Book of the Damned, New Lands, Lo!, Wild Talents*), with an introduction by Tiffany Thayer (New York: Henry Holt and Co., 1941).

technology as it was imagined in those days. But this background is also mostly irrelevant. The focus in both stories is on the *mental* effects of the infestation. It is true that Russell's parasitical intelligences (called "Vitons") are visible — after appropriate medication — as ball lightning, and can be destroyed in the end by beams of polarized radio-waves. In Russell's fable the parasites engineer an assault upon the West by Asians persuaded that Vitons are their ancestors. In Wilson's the open war is between Africa and Europe, each animated by racialist delusions. But the real battle in both cases is fought in the human mind and heart. Wilson's exist *only* "in the mind" (which is not to say that they are merely imaginary), and must be defeated entirely by moral effort, aided by careful phenomenological analysis of our moods and internal promptings (though they have sufficient "physical" existence to be affected when the heroic band of scientists and scholars rotate the moon away from us). Russell's polarized radio-waves are replaced by a "polarized beam of attention."[11] The moral effort is supported by a power deeper within the mind than even the parasites can travel: indeed, their chief sustenance is gained from tapping the flow of energy from that deep source into our individual existences. This idea is one also to be found in Lindsay's *Voyage to Arcturus* (1920) and — more recently — in Doris Lessing's *Shikasta* (1979). Russell's parasites, by contrast, also exist externally, although they have as great a power over our emotions as Wilson's, Lindsay's, or Lessing's. Moral and electrical energy are equated in Russell's world, but perhaps not in Wilson's, though "the Philosopher's Stone" of the later novel subverts that distinction.

In both Wilson's and Russell's stories, the parasites may possibly have arrived fairly recently. Wilson, indeed, seems to suggest that they have only been with us since the late eighteenth century, when the hopes and ideals of the Enlightenment began to be sapped by creeping nihilism.

> A strange change comes over the human race. It happens towards the end of the eighteenth century. The tremendous, bubbling creativity of Mozart is counterbalanced by the nightmare cruelty of De Sade. Suddenly we are in an age of darkness, an age where men of genius no longer create like gods. Instead, they struggle as if in the grip of

---

[11] *Mind Parasites*, 105.

an invisible octopus. The century of suicide begins. In fact, modern history begins, the age of defeat and neurosis.[12]

This is a strangely skewed view of history, as is the later claim that "the men of previous centuries [before about two centuries ago] ... were more unified than modern man: they lived on a more instinctive level,"[13] and so suffered less from mental or corporeal cancers. It would be far more plausible to suppose that the parasites have been with us for millennia, experienced as spirits, demons, or gods. In *The Philosopher's Stone*, Wilson offered a more optimistic account of the supposed change from one century to the next: that it is only in the romantic movement that people experience a visionary "freedom from one's own personal little problems"[14]—a freedom sabotaged, perhaps, by the parasites. But this too neglects the long, past history of just such a notion of freedom, and what threatened it. In Russell's story, more plausibly, the parasites have been the originators of every form of madness, from paranoid schizophrenia to nationalism and religion, for all our species' life. It is they who have filled the human heart and mind with superstitions, hatreds, and obsessive loves—though romantic love, scientific curiosity, and ordinary human companionship are allowed a more "natural" origin.[15] In Russell's world, our safety lies in legwork (the title of one of his minor stories): the unimpassioned accumulation of information and its careful sifting by many working together, rather than inspiration or unusual genius on the part of a creative few, "the creative minority" mentioned also in *The Philosopher's Stone*.[16] In Wilson's world, salvation comes only from those few, scientists and scholars inspired by Husserlian phenomenology, and contemptuous of the ordinary mass of people.

DEVILS, DESPAIR, AND PLOTINUS

Russell's heroes are usually engineers or private investigators, "practical people" given to mocking authority figures. Their loyalty

---

[12] *Mind Parasites*, 57–58.
[13] Ibid., 188.
[14] *The Philosopher's Stone* (London: Barker, 1969), 58.
[15] A more consistent story would invoke gods and devils for all these distinct states, but that would seem "superstitious" to most modern readers.
[16] *The Philosopher's Stone*, 46–47.

is to the freedom of humankind, without any reasoned account of why they should be loyal, or what is valuable in freedom. Even the telepathic hero of *Three to Conquer* (also known as *Call Him Dead*), who is also confronted by alien intelligences (bacterial in bodily essence, and Venerian in proximate origin) who threaten to take us over, has little interest in any *theory* about the alien and human minds he listens to, or the mechanism of his own telepathic gifts. Much the same is true of the many 1950s SF stories featuring alien infiltration, mind control and the like, by Robert Heinlein, Jack Finney, Philip K. Dick, and others. The dangers are usually, in the end, defeated by physical courage and technological know-how (as they are in Doc Smith's *Lensman* series). In Wilson's stories it is the theory that matters, and whatever defeat his heroes inflict upon the enemy is moral more than material. "Freedom is the most important experience that can happen to human beings";[17] but the freedom of which Wilson is speaking is only ever enjoyed by the few. The rest seem "alien and repulsive, little better than apes,"[18] though the narrator and his friends do occasionally feel a little patronizing pity for them. As Tredell observes,[19] this seems like just the sort of "petty, personal emotion" that an evolved humanity should have discarded, and far too much like Lovecraft's talk of human beings as "crawling and miserable vermin."[20]

So what is being recommended? And why should *The Mind Parasites*, despite its obvious flaws as a novel, still be worth reading? Northrop Frye's comment is apt: "silly book in many ways, which is a pity, because its central idea is a genuine Promethean archetype, the Gospel driving out of the devils symbolized as malignant small creatures like insects."[21] But first we have to *notice* the devils.

> By luck, Reich and I had quickly picked up the techniques of phenomenology; because neither of us were philosophers, and had no preconceptions to get rid of, Husserl's seed fell on fertile ground.[22]

---

[17] *Mind Parasites*, 178.
[18] Ibid., 199.
[19] Nicholas Tredell, *Existence and Evolution: the novels of Colin Wilson* (Richmond, CA: Maurice Bassett, 2007 [1982]), 103.
[20] Wilson, *Strength to Dream*, 9.
[21] Northrop Frye, *The "third book": notebooks of Northrop Frye 1964–1972*, ed. Michael Dolzani (Toronto: University of Toronto Press, 2002), 215.
[22] *Mind Parasites*, 82.

Whatever it is that Wilson's heroes pick up, of course, it cannot have been simply Husserl's technique: Husserl himself, after all, was not transformed into a telekinetic, telepathic, ruthless manipulator of lesser beings, and scornful saviour (possibly) of humankind! The invented documents that make up Wilson's novel are, as I remarked before, deliberately unreliable: sometimes the Tsathogguans really are Lovecraftian monsters; sometimes they are more like Russell's Vitons; sometimes they are hardly more than cancerous elements of the human mind, or inappropriate habits. Whatever it is that Reich and Austin do remains, deliberately, obscure: Wilson himself may not have had any clear idea, and certainly his heroes don't provide one. Not that this is surprising: being "initiated" will always demand more than book-learning, and whatever it is that is to be conveyed about our situation, we cannot simply be *told* it, as Plato recognized in his *Seventh Letter*. Plato—if it was he—rebuked anyone who thought to offer a written summary of his philosophy, insisting that "acquaintance with it must come rather after a long period of attendance on instruction in the subject itself and of close companionship, when, suddenly, like a blaze kindled by a leaping spark, it is generated in the soul and at once becomes self-sustaining."[23]

Husserl's particular contribution to philosophical methodology was a variant on Cartesian meditation: a reflexive examination of what we are doing in thinking, feeling, desiring, and the like. The essence of *mental* activity is that it is *intentional*, directed at some object, with some particular feeling tone (admiring, desiring, despising, and the like). To see this clearly, we need to "bracket off" any question about "external" reality, and let ourselves notice the *internal* object of the activity. Material existents exist alongside and outside each other, at different times and locations: mental existence is ineradicably relational.[24] In our ordinary, "natural" state we pay little or no attention to the activity by which we are

---

[23] Plato, *Letters* VII.341d: E. Hamilton and H. Cairns, eds., *The Collected Dialogues of Plato including the Letters* (1961; repr. Princeton University Press, 1980), 1589. Scholars now are usually doubtful that any of the Platonic Letters are genuinely Plato's, but the seventh in particular was accepted, and believed, by most late Platonists.

[24] More accurately, even material existence is relational as well. Nothing can exist, or have any properties, merely "by itself." But at least the material world may *look* as if it were composed of separate things.

reaching out to things, and entertain no questions about their reality or their lack of it.

> Husserl's great contribution was to point out that if you look at something without reaching out to grasp it (i.e. if you glance absent-mindedly at your watch while in conversation) you don't register it. In all perception there is this element of reaching out and grabbing—of intention.... But, said Husserl, if something inside me has this power to "attend" to experience, imposing more or less meaning and unity on it, surely this indicates some principle in me that wasn't written on the slate by my experience?[25]

In becoming aware of our own mental involvement in the construction of the internal objects of that activity, we may also experience a sudden enlightenment—that there is a world outside our ordinary consciousness, and that ordinary life is indeed constructed for us by something that is not quite our ordinary self, and is itself a part of that reality. This revelation shows how little we know about the source of our own thoughts and actions. "I speak of 'my mind' as I speak of 'my back garden.' But in what sense is my back garden really 'mine'? It is full of worms and insects who do not ask my permission to live there. It will continue to exist after I am dead...."[26] Noticing, along with Rudyard Kipling's Doctor,[27] how few of "our own thoughts and feelings" are simple products of our own thinking, how few are under our own control, is the necessary beginning of any properly disciplined thinking. "Is my mind my own possession? That parent of false conjectures, that purveyor of delusion, the delirious, the fatuous, and in frenzy or senility proved to be the very negation of mind."[28]

We are infested by "mental microbes," as D. G. Ritchie noted[29]—though C. S. Lewis may have been right to suspect

---

[25] Colin Wilson, *Existential Criticism: selected book reviews*, ed. Colin Stanley (Nottingham: Paupers' Press, 2009 [1972]), 202.
[26] *Mind Parasites*, 40.
[27] See Kipling, "The Conversion of Aurelian McGoggin," in *Plain Tales from the Hills* (London: Penguin, 1994 [1899]), 58–61.
[28] Philo of Alexandria, *On Cherubim*, 116, in *Collected Works*, trans. F. H. Colson, G. H. Whitaker, et al. (Cambridge, MA: Harvard University Press [Loeb Classical Library], 1929), 2:77.
[29] D. G. Ritchie, *Darwinism and Politics* (London: Swan Sonnenschein and

that they are rather "macrobes," demons under another name.[30]
Unsurprisingly, ascetics have long known about them, since it is
only ascetics who make much effort to resist them!

> We can infer from the object appearing in the mind which
> demon is close at hand, suggesting that object to us....
> All thoughts producing anger or desire in a way that is
> contrary to reason are caused by demons.[31]

Noticing how much of what we think and do is simply a matter
of habit, a lazy agreement with some demon, is the moment
when we might learn or attempt some new thing, including the
creation of a better habit. Habits are at once the enemies' tool,
and necessary for life.[32] "Most of your actions are carried out by
a host of unconscious zombies who exist in peaceful harmony
along with you (the 'person' inside your body)!"[33]

Like other animals, we inhabit a "life world," such that only
a fraction of what is "really" going on is immediately present to
us. Unlike other animals (or at any rate, unlike what we think
is true of other animals), we can occasionally notice that there
is a larger world, and do so especially when we attend, reflex-
ively, to our own imaginative and constructive mentality. As one
of Wilson's heroes remarks in another novel, "Man is the first
objective animal. All others live in a subjective world of instinct,
from which they can never escape; only man looks at the stars
or rocks and says 'How interesting...' instantly leaping over the
wall of his mere identity."[34] But the most interesting thing of all
is the realization of that wider identity.

Such moments of "objective realization" are not necessarily
comfortable. "The suicide rate was increasing because thousands
of human beings were 'awakening', like me [that is, the original
author of the discovery, Karel Weissman, who kills himself in

---

Co., 1891), 22.
[30] C. S. Lewis, *That Hideous Strength* (London: John Lane, 1945), 315–16.
[31] Evagrios Pontikos (345–99 AD): G. E. H. Palmer, P. Sherrard, and Kallistos
Ware, eds., *The Philokalia* (London: Faber, 1979), 1:39.
[32] *Mind Parasites*, 81, 130.
[33] Sandra Blakeslee and V. S. Ramachandran, *Phantoms in the Brain* (London:
Fourth Estate, 1998), 228.
[34] *The Philosopher's Stone*, 129. Why should we be so convinced of this, and
why do we thence conclude that we are therefore somehow entitled to
ignore the interests of those other animals?

the opening pages of the book], to the absurdity of human life, and simply refused to go on. The dream of history was coming to an end. Mankind was already starting to wake up; one day it would wake up properly, and there would be mass suicide."[35] The narrator himself experiences this sort of awakening a little later in the story:

> Suddenly, abysses of emptiness were open beneath my feet. It did not even produce fear; that would be too human a reaction. It was like contact with an icy reality that makes everything human seem a masquerade, *that makes life itself seem a masquerade.*[36]

This is after all more or less the real opinion of most self-styled moderns, though they are usually content to hide from it and its more disagreeable implications. There is no reason, it seems, to think *our* life-world is any closer to reality than that of a sea-slug, a spider, or an albatross: we sense only a tiny segment of what we "know" is happening, and divide it up according to our personal and social values in a way that, we suppose, receives no universal warrant. We may see sermons in stones and books in the running brooks, but "really" they aren't there. Neither the world at large, nor the human frame, has any objective meaning. All that we do and think is no more than a mask over emptiness. The vision of futility is almost enough to drive Austin to suicide. The same vision is used in James Blish's *Black Easter*[37]—and it is there, explicitly, a weapon in the hands of a black magician, addressing a demon directly:

> Thou shalt straightaway go unto him, not making thyself known unto him, but revealing, as it were to come from his own intellectual soul, a vision and understanding of that great and ultimate Nothingness, which lurks behind those signs he calls matter and energy, as thou wilt see it in his private forebodings, and that thou remainest with him and deepen his despair without remittal, until such time as he shall despise his soul for its endeavors, and destroy the life of his body.

---

[35] *Mind Parasites*, 21–22.
[36] Ibid., 113.
[37] James Blish, *Black Easter* (London: Faber, 1969), 87.

The "cosmic pessimists," the Lloigor, of Wilson's shorter fable, are too "rational" to be able to disregard this thought. Fortunately, most human beings have other resources—as Dr Johnson's friend remarked: "I have tried in my time to be a philosopher; but cheerfulness was always breaking in"[38]—but as long as those resources are unconscious and irrational, we cannot easily make use of them. The next turn of the argument, and of enlightenment, is to recognize that this story too is a fiction. "Since these creatures [the parasites] had deliberately induced this feeling of total meaninglessness, they must be in some way *beyond* it."[39] If we really knew nothing of the world "out there," we could not know that it was meaningless. Conversely, if the world of our experience is constructed for us, so also is this sudden revelation of a world larger than our previous petty concerns. The vision of futility itself demonstrates that we are more than the simple animals it seeks to make us.

"The basic concepts of existentialism are 'the nausea' and its opposite, man's sense of his interior power, his reality," so Wilson remarked in an essay on "existential criticism" in 1959.[40] "Nausea" is the response imagined for his anti-hero Roquentin by Sartre at the sudden realization of the "alien facticity" of a tree-root. Austin's imagined response (that is probably also Wilson's response) is happier: he had been reading about Nineveh in his youth while staying at a farm, when it occurred to him to bring in some clothes drying on a line:

> Just inside the farmyard there was a large pool of grey water, rather muddy. As I was taking the clothes from the line, my mind still in Nineveh, I happened to notice this pool, and forgot for a moment where I was or what I was doing there. As I looked at it, the puddle lost all familiarity and became as alien as a sea on Mars. I stood staring at it, and the first drops of rain fell from the sky, and wrinkled its surface. At that moment I experienced a sensation of happiness and insight such as I had never known before. Nineveh and all history suddenly became as real and as alien as that pool. History became such a

---

[38] James Boswell, *Life of Samuel Johnson* (London: Oxford University Press, 1953), 957: April 17, 1778.
[39] *Mind Parasites*, 114.
[40] *Existential Criticism*, 31.

reality that I felt a kind of contempt for my own existence, standing there with my arms full of clothes.[41]

It may be doubted whether Roquentin's or Austin's response is the "truer." There is little doubt which is the healthier and happier! What is strange in Wilson's commentary is his belief that moments such as these come late in human history. Far otherwise: on the one hand, "accidie," the noon-day demon of boredom and disillusion, has been the curse of intellectuals for as long as there have been intellectuals;[42] on the other, the shock of delight that Plotinus calls love is a response to beauty. Beauties "exist and appear to us and he who sees them cannot possibly say anything else except that they are what really exists. What does 'really exist' mean? That they exist as beauties."[43] "Or rather, beautifulness is reality."[44] The shock of the real reminds us that we are alive. It is reality that may jolt us out of *accidie*.

Finding that reality, outside and underneath our usual pre-occupations, may also gradually create or reveal in us a "real self" behind or beyond the self we thought we were. So Austin, after his phenomenological discoveries, can say, "I was quite detached from the human being I would have called 'Gilbert Austin' two months earlier, as detached as a puppet master from his puppet."[45] Plotinus proposes a similar story: "every man is double, one of him is the sort of compound being and one of him is himself."[46] It seems that Plotinus himself wished not to be identified, even for the convenience or interest of his disci-ples, with his bodily form and personal history: "he could never bear to talk about his race or his parents or his native country," and flatly refused to have his portrait taken.[47] Similarly, Wil-son (commenting on one of J. L. Borges's stories, "Funes the

---

[41] *Mind Parasites*, 18.
[42] Kathleen Norris, *Acedia and Me: a marriage, monks, and a writer's life* (New York: Riverhead Books, 2008). See also my "Evagrius and the Noonday Demon" (forthcoming).
[43] I.6 [1].5, 18f.
[44] Plotinus, *Ennead* I.6 [1].6, 21.
[45] *Mind Parasites*, 79: a state that mainstream psychiatrists persist in consid-ering a disorder (see Simeon and Abugel, *Feeling Unreal: Depersonalization and the Loss of the Self*).
[46] II.3 [52].9, 31–32.
[47] Porphyry, "Life of Plotinus," ch. 1.

Memorious"):[48] "to be possessed by a strong sense of purpose is to ignore ninety-nine per cent of your experience, and to forget all the unimportant things that have happened to you."[49] This too was Plotinus's goal: to become, or retrieve, the form of consciousness enjoyed, he imagined, by the star-gods. Heracles's shadow, maybe, might recall his earthly life, but Heracles himself no longer minds such things.[50] The souls of the stars need not remember where they've been.[51] This was not, we can be fairly sure, because Plotinus "despised" the natural world: on the contrary, he reserved his most critical commentary for those who did exactly that.

> Despising the universe and the gods in it and the other noble things is certainly not becoming good.... For anyone who feels affection for anything at all shows kindness to all that is akin to the object of his affection, and to the children of the father that he loves. But every soul is a child of That Father.[52]

Austin would have done well to remember that.

Interestingly, whereas no-one has suggested that *Husserl* had any occult powers, it was widely supposed that Plotinus did: he could identify thieves by immediate intuition, recognize depression in his disciples, and repel magical attacks. When he was persuaded by a disciple to attend a séance intended to reveal his higher self or guardian *daimon*, this turned out to be a god! What exactly any of these stories meant at the time, and especially to Plotinus, is uncertain. Nor are his preferred techniques for stripping away presuppositions, clarifying the motive powers within our souls, or allowing ourselves to be drunk with love of beauty, at all easy to expound or explain.[53] But some of his conclusions seem close to those that Wilson (through his various imagined narrators) also wishes. *Feeling* is a form of perception.[54] It is through the

---

[48] J. L. Borges, *Labyrinths*, eds. Donald A. Yates and James E. Irby (Harmondsworth: Penguin, 1970), 87–95.
[49] *Existential Criticism*, 56.
[50] Plotinus, *Ennead* IV.3 [27].32.
[51] *Ennead* IV.4 [28].8, 41ff.
[52] *Ennead* II.9 [33].16.
[53] I made a partial attempt in *Plotinus: Myth, Metaphor and Philosophical Practice* (Chicago: University of Chicago Press, 2016).
[54] *Mind Parasites*, 82. See Frye, *Educated Imagination*, 17.

focusing of our attention that we can progress.[55] "In the mental
sense, all the space in the universe is somehow compressed to
a point":[56] distance is an illusion. The world we perceive has
been built, is being built, by Soul. It is unfortunate that Wilson
internalized the popular notion of "Greek" (or more precisely
Platonic) thought as being "abstract" or as despising bodies: as a
Neo-Platonist rather than an eccentric phenomenologist he might
have developed Plotinus's account in an interesting direction.

Austin and his colleagues, as I have already remarked, often
despise ordinarily foolish people (though with a little effort they
occasionally remember that they were themselves once just as
foolish—and may, in another way, be foolish still). Similarly,
Shakespeare (who is identified, for reasons that escape me, as
a front man for Francis Bacon) is unbearable to the hero of *The
Philosopher's Stone*: "I felt from the beginning that these people
[the characters in *Macbeth* or *Antony and Cleopatra*] are fools,
and that consequently [*sic*] nothing that happens to them can
possibly matter."[57] It would be easy to conclude that both characters are rather too like the "right men gone wrong" in some
of Wilson's other stories. It would be easy, indeed, to suspect
that Austin in particular is not just an unreliable narrator, but
wholly self-deceived. We have only *his* word that he and his
colleagues have defeated the Tsathogguans: another reading
of the story would be that the parasites, knowing far more
of the human mind than he, have subtly reinforced their self-
conceit and petty irritation with the human world. Like others
of Wilson's ambiguous heroes, Austin and the others kill without pity, though (unlike others) also without much pleasure.
Even their apparent victory is tainted: thanks to them, the rest
of humanity, united in a hierarchical World State, is fixed in
xenophobic terror of the wider world. We are led to suppose
that Austin and his colleagues leave to join the universal police,
but there is no hint that those police are any more benevolent
than Austin, or than the long-ago priest-king of *The Philosopher's
Stone*, who instigated mass murder simply to keep the populace
from being too happy!

---

[55] *Mind Parasites*, 104.
[56] Ibid., 24.
[57] *The Philosopher's Stone*, 152.

TO LOVE AND SERVE THE LORD

But though this critical re-reading is worth considering, we might also try to understand the overt moral more sympathetically. Whereas most contemporary ethicists are concerned with the simple "welfare" of human beings (or possibly of the wider class of sentient beings), Wilson's heroes share an older philosophical suspicion that nothing of that sort matters much.

> The man who belongs to this world may be handsome and tall and rich and the ruler of all mankind (since he is essentially of this region), and we ought not to envy him for things like these, by which he is beguiled. The wise man will perhaps not have them at all, and if he has them will himself reduce them, if he cares for his true self. He will reduce and gradually extinguish his bodily advantages by neglect, and will put away authority and office. He will take care of his bodily health, but will not wish to be altogether without experience of illness, nor indeed also of pain.[58]

He will not mind these things for himself, and rather little for others — though Plotinus was trusted to look after the material interests of the orphans trusted to his charge ("as long as they did not take to philosophy").[59] Wars and tumults are no more than children's games or theatrical displays, not to be taken seriously: "We should be spectators of murders, and all deaths, and takings and sacking of cities, as if they were on the stages of theatres."[60] Plotinus supposed that his soul was larger and older than his current bodily self — a notion at which Wilson's Austin only briefly hints, in a reference to his memory of "previous lives."[61] But even without that addition, the philosophical tradition on which Plotinus draws prefers "the exercise of our vital powers along lines of excellence"[62] to the mere amassing of material or social goods. Edgars, in *Babylon 5*, does not notice that Aristotle

---

[58] *Ennead* I.4 [46].14, 14–23, trans. Armstrong.
[59] Porphyry, "Life of Plotinus," ch. 9.
[60] *Ennead* III.2 [47].15, 44f.
[61] *Mind Parasites*, 121.
[62] A phrase employed, after Aristotle, *Nicomachean Ethics* 1.1098a14, by William Edgars, billionaire philanthropist, in *Babylon 5* ("Exercise of Vital Powers": 416).

agreed with Plato: the best form of life is not "the political" but the "theoretical," the life of God.[63] Our real task is "to love and serve the Lord" (*ton theon theorein kai therapeuein*),[64] without expecting any merely earthly reward, whether for ourselves or others!

In some later allegories, to achieve this goal the soul must ascend past the moon, and at last past all the planetary spheres, shedding its unhelpful passions as it goes (as of course Wilson's heroes also, perhaps, do). According to the Hermetic text, *Poimandres* (second or third century AD), in its ascent "the soul gives back the power of increase and decrease in the first sphere (i.e. the moon), evil plotting in the second (Mercury), lust in the third (Venus), the proud desire to rule in the fourth (the sun), impiety and audacity in the fifth (Mars), greed for wealth in the sixth (Jupiter) and malevolent falsehood in the seventh (Saturn), and escapes the rule of Fate."[65]

It is easy to misunderstand the Aristotelian (and Platonic) claim, as though they preferred to *think* about living rather than actually *live*. One mode of enlightenment is the discovery of something so far more impressive than our usual petty concerns that we cease to be troubled by them, and by the Self industriously constructed to deal with them. This is close to the cult of academic objectivity: merely personal beliefs and prejudices should be set aside, and whatever is worth saying must be said "impersonally." But this latter is really a failure of nerve. "The disease of our time is the diffidence, the sense of personal insignificance, that feels the need to disguise itself as academic objectivity when it attempts to philosophise."[66] A failure of nerve, or rather an

---

[63] Aristotle, *Nicomachean Ethics*, trans. W. D. Ross, revised by J. O. Urmson (Oxford: Oxford University Press, 1980) 265 (10.1177b30ff.): "We must not follow those who advise us, being men, to think of human things, and, being mortal, of mortal things, but must, so far as we can, make ourselves immortal, and strain every nerve to live in accordance with the best thing in us; for even if it be small in bulk, much more does it in power and worth surpass everything."
[64] Aristotle, *Eudemian Ethics* 8.1249b20.
[65] *Poimandres*, 1.25: Brian Copenhaver, *Hermetica: the Greek Corpus Hermeticum and the Latin Asclepius* (Cambridge: Cambridge University Press, 1992), 6; cited by Alan Scott *Origen and the Life of the Stars* (Oxford: Clarendon Press, 1991), 89; see, further, "Climbing up to Heaven: the Hermetic Option": *Purgatory: philosophical dimensions*, eds. Kristof K. P. Vanhoutte and Benjamin W. McCraw (Palgrave Macmillan: London, 2017), 151–74.
[66] *Existential Criticism*, 2.

example of bad faith. The attempt to *hide* our own commitments, from ourselves and others, merely leaves them unexamined, and inordinately powerful: the very prejudices that we *should* put aside simply persist as unconscious axioms, even when they are really at odds with each other, or with our professed beliefs. By insisting, for example, that merely *moral* claims are not properly "scientific" or "rational," the investigator is free to act out the moral prejudices he has internalized from childhood. No moral claims are rationally grounded—but it is "irrational" to doubt that "human beings," just as such, have rights that the non-human don't, and "irrational" to doubt that "advancing science" justifies just about anything the scientist feels like doing. Education *should* be entirely "rational" and "progressive"; and it is just *obvious* that human welfare consists solely in respectable employment and the enjoyment of material goods. The only forms of altruism that creatures like us can be expected to display are nepotistic or manipulative; but we are outraged if officers of the state do what we think everyone is bound by their genes to do.

The moral confusion involved in this refusal to bring our assumptions into the light, and actually examine them, rests on an unexamined conviction that moral heroism is impossible. The same conviction lies behind much mainstream fiction (including soap opera): that "heroes" are unrealistic, and that "ordinary lives" are lived only for the moment, in obedience to transient impulse. Anything else is "fanatical" (and fanatics must all be hypocrites). There are alternative visions, mostly in genre fiction,[67] but genre writing only becomes respectable if the supposed heroes are themselves needy, corrupt, or incompetent. Aristotle offered a simple division between "tragedy" and "comedy," as these were once understood: tragedies offer characters better or larger than life; comedies concern characters worse, smaller, pettier than life.[68] By this criterion, almost all mainstream fiction is comedic, but without having happy endings. As Wilson remarked, in the course of complaining about the "unheroic premise" of too much modern art and literature, "the hero is the man who overcomes the obstacles peculiar to his own age."[69] Why do we so readily relegate "the hero" to the outskirts, to genre literature, or popular

---

[67] See Wilson, *Strength to Dream*, 113.
[68] *Poetics* 1449a34.
[69] *Existential Criticism*, 34.

films? Why not understand that it requires heroism to deal, exactly, with the "great and ultimate Nothingness" that seems to lurk behind the everyday?

Wilson's writings generally, like the best science fiction, follow the pattern of Chesterton's "romantic fiction": "a mixture of the familiar and the unfamiliar ... picturesque and full of a poetical curiosity,"[70] respecting common humanity, courage, loyalty, and imagination. Heroes are born from unexpected characters, whether the plump, food-loving archaeologist of *The Mind Parasites*, the death-fearing nerd of *The Philosopher's Stone*, or the space-ship captain of *The Space Vampires*. Wilson commented, in 1963, that he had "come to feel that [Tolkien's *The Lord of the Rings*] may be one of the greatest books of this century,"[71] perhaps for exactly this reason, that it celebrated an appropriate heroism, without ever losing sight of the perils — including the moral perils — besetting heroes. Notoriously, the literati continue to be appalled that popular judgment agrees with Wilson in this![72] Austin is an unreliable narrator, and unsatisfactory as a true hero-figure (being too forgetful of the affection owed *all* children of the One Father), but he is nonetheless at least an image of the heroism that we need, unafraid to face the implications of what he knows, and ready to appeal beyond his ordinary self to something altogether other, on the far side of the parasites.

---

[70] Chesterton, *Orthodoxy* (Thirsk: House of Stratus, 2001 [1908]), 10.

[71] Wilson, *Existentialist Criticism*, 107.

[72] Why did Peter Jackson, in creating his film version of *The Lord of the Rings* (2001–2003), find it necessary to make Tolkien's characters — except Sam Gamgee — so much less than, in Tolkien's art, they were? Why was Frodo turned into a wimp? Why were Pippin, Merry, and Gimli made into comic turns? Why were Aragorn, Faramir, and Theoden shown to be so uncertain of their duty? Why was Eowyn, absurdly, made to be a bad cook? Why was the Witch-King allowed to defeat Gandalf? Why were the Ents made indecisive bores, and Denethor stripped of all his virtue?

10.
Singular and Plural Futures[1]

INTRODUCTION

We cannot easily now feel the certainties that perhaps our predecessors enjoyed, whether about the cosmos or our own future. But perhaps we can still learn from the thoughts of earlier "ages of uncertainty," in particular the Hellenistic Era. Speculation about that future, of our own species or society and of the universe, though more "scientifically" informed, echoes or mirrors Hellenic and Hebraic speculation. Although mainstream thought is now professedly "materialistic" and "naturalistic," there are signs — in speculative cosmology and speculative futurology — that something closer to the older Platonic synthesis is being recommended. Neither the phenomenal worlds of our and other animal experience, nor the material world of interconnected bodies are ultimate realities: they are echoes or reflections of a mathematically discernible reality — and this too is not self-explanatory. In the words of Ernesto Cardenal, arguing from entirely theological premises: "The realities we see are like shadows of all that is God. This whole world is made of shadows, shadows on the wall of a cave, as Plato said." As Plato and his successors also said, we have some hope that we might leave the cave, and be united, or re-united, with "the dance of immortal love." Platonic myths and modern speculations form a strange match, despite their disparate origins, and Platonic thought can help to avoid mistakes in following up the modern story.

---

[1] An earlier version was published as "Futures Singular and Plural," in *Towards the Noosphere*, ed. Tim Addey (Westbury, Wiltshire: Prometheus Books, 2013), 29–67. My thanks especially to Tim Addey and John Dillon for comments and criticisms.

THESIS

Things don't have to be this way (whatever way that is), and very soon they won't be.

The same could truly have been said at any time in human history, but there have been times and places when grandparents could sensibly believe that they had good advice to give their grandchildren, that life was going on very much as usual, and that they had a broadly complete and accurate account of the world they lived in (only the details needed to be worked out).[2] Probably, they were deluded on all counts. Even when our ancestors were hunter-gatherers, after the ice retreated and all roads seemed open, they could not anticipate storms, earthquakes, droughts, the dying-off of species, and the arrival of half-familiar cousins. Even when our ancestors elected to settle down, to mark off village and household property, and build—with enormous labour—ceremonial centres for trade or worship or exogamy, the same hard rule applied. "The things that men expect to happen do not happen. The unexpected, God makes possible" (a standard Euripidean tag, used in several plays: for example, *Bacchae, Andromache,* and *Medea*). This does not prevent our commonsensical assumption that we can count on things continuing as they are, and as we imagine that they have been. "The commonest sense of all is that of men asleep, which they express by snoring."[3]

---

[2] Albert A. Michelson notoriously declared, in lectures at the Lowell Institute in 1899 (see *Light Waves and their Uses* [Chicago: University of Chicago Press, 1903], 23–24), that "the more important fundamental laws and facts of physical science have all been discovered, and these are so firmly established that the possibility of their ever being supplanted in consequence of new discoveries is exceedingly remote." This observation provides a good reason to suspect all similar claims, before and since: see Jonathan Schaffer, "Is There a Fundamental Level?," *Noûs* 37 (2003), 498–517: "the history of science is littered with such speculations" (503). Schaffer's paper is an engaging attack—not without relevance to the present paper—on the belief that there is some one level, typically of "elementary particles," that fully explains everything that happens (so that, strictly speaking, nothing is happening except the motion, as Democritus suggested, of atoms in the void: "all else is by convention": Hermann Diels, *Die Fragmente der Vorsokratiker*, ed. Walther Kranz [3 vols, Zürich: Weidmann, 1996], 2:139 [68B9]).
[3] Henry David Thoreau, *Walden*, ed. Stephen Fender (New York: Oxford University Press, 1997), 289 (chapter 18).

The sober Englishman at the close of the nineteenth century could sit at his breakfast-table, decide between tea
from Ceylon or coffee from Brazil, devour an egg from
France with some Danish ham, or eat a New Zealand
chop, wind up breakfast with a West Indian banana,
glance at the latest telegrams from all the world, scruti-
nise the prices current of his geographically distributed
investments in South Africa, Japan and Egypt, and tell
the two children he had begotten (in place of his father's
eight) that he thought the world changed very little.
They must play cricket, keep their hair cut, go to the old
school he had gone to, shirk the lessons he had shirked,
learn a few scraps of Horace and Virgil and Homer for
the confusion of cads, and all would be well with them.[4]

Wells's own half-serious efforts to imagine future possibilities,
as also the efforts of science-fiction writers in the century since
his day, were also of their time and place. They may at least have
made particular possibilities rather less likely than they were.
Their imagined futures, whether they thought them utopian
or dystopic, were seen—correctly—as warnings rather than
predictions. By imagining the likely effects of full-scale nuclear
spasm, for example, we have been guided away at least from
that catastrophe, and now worry instead about the unintended
effects of what had seemed merely benign improvements in the
quality and comfort of our lives. Wanting more than the world
immediately provides—and driven by memories of those times
and places where the world provided little—our ancestors cultivated plants and herded animals, devised new engineering
skills, traded with other peoples, and established rules and rulers
to govern differences of taste and custom. Economies of scale
and fear of peoples outside the law encouraged the growth of
empires, the creation of specialized castes and economic classes.
We chose—our ancestors chose, and we accept their choices—to
cultivate new tastes, encourage material achievements, and gather
as much knowledge as we could of all the external changes that
we half-remembered. Our time-frame, as well as our sense of
space, expanded, so that it became half-rational to *plan* for our

---

[4] H. G. Wells, *The World Set Free* (London: Collins, 1956 [1914]), 35ff. See
my "Eradicating the Obvious," *Journal of Applied Philosophy* 8 (1991), 121–25
(reprinted in *Philosophical Futures* [Frankfurt: Peter Lang, 2011], 17–24).

grandchildren's lives, and even for further futures that we will not see and cannot now imagine.

In his *Republic*, Plato described how our ancestors settled down together, learning the peaceful rules of specialization and fair exchange, and how they found it necessary to protect themselves against each other and against invaders, as well as planning invasions of their own in pursuit of little luxuries. "The city of pigs" gave way to the fevered city, and the prospect of unending war to safeguard imperial ambitions, and the comfort of the protected classes.[5] His proffered solution to the fever was to inculcate—at least in those with the energy and wit to govern his imagined city—a devotion to the "good" (or at least the peace) of the whole city. The rulers were to be bred, trained, and educated to that goal, and tested almost to destruction so that only those truly immune to bribery and threat could ever hold authority. He sadly acknowledged that even such rulers could not long be preserved against corruption. The beauty of an ordered city, keeping within its literal and moral bounds and threatening none, was an ideal that would mutate: the rulers would begin to favour their own stock, their own achievements, their own comforts, over the good of all. They would long since have lost sight of Real Beauty when their city turned into yet another imperial city, no longer—if it ever was—a "city on a hill," a light for all nations. John Winthrop's exhortation to his fellow colonists would have had some support from Plato.

> Now the onely way to avoyde this shipwracke and to provide for our posterity is to followe the Counsell of Micah [*Micah* 6.8], to doe Justly, to love mercy, to walke humbly with our God, for this end, wee must be knitt together in this worke as one man, wee must entertaine each other in brotherly Affeccion, wee must be willing to abridge our selves of our superfluities, for the supply of others necessities, wee must uphold a familiar Commerce together in all meekenes, gentlenes, patience and liberallity, wee must delight in eache other, make others Condicions our owne, rejoyce together, mourne together, labour, and suffer

---

[5] On the reasons why Plato did *not* think pigs ridiculous, see my "Herds of Free Bipeds," in C. Rowe, ed., *Reading the Statesman: proceedings of the Third Symposium Platonicum* (Sankt Augustin: Akademia Verlag, 1995), 236–52 (reprinted in *The Political Animal* [London: Routledge, 1999], 134–54).

together, allwayes haveing before our eyes our Commis-
sion and Community in the worke, our Community as
members of the same body, soe shall wee keepe the unitie
of the spirit in the bond of peace, the Lord will be our God
and delight to dwell among us, as his owne people....
Hee shall make us a prayse and glory, that men shall say
of succeeding plantacions: the lord make it like that of
New England: for wee must Consider that wee shall be
as a Citty upon a Hill, the eies of all people are uppon us
[*Matthew* 5:14-16]; soe that if wee shall deale falsely with
our god in this worke wee have undertaken and soe cause
him to withdrawe his present help from us, wee shall
be made a story and a byword through the world ... till
wee be consumed out of the good land whether wee are
going... Therefore lett us choose life, that wee, and our
Seede, may live; by obeyeing his voyce, and cleaveing to
him, for hee is our life, and our prosperity.[6]

That phrase — "a City on the Hill" — has echoed through later
American rhetoric, but has often seemed rather to promote imperial self-satisfaction than warn against error, just as Rudyard
Kipling's "Recessional" (1897) has been interpreted, in absolute
contradiction of its author's message, as an imperialistic tract.[7] The
actual conduct of the Puritan colonists towards the original inhabitants of the lands they seized was modelled — in their eyes — on
the conduct of the invading Hebrews toward the inhabitants of
Canaan, without even the sad excuse that the natives engaged
in religious and moral practices that we too would condemn. As
George Berkeley observed, "our first Planters imagined they had a
right to treat Indians on the foot of Canaanites or Amalekites."[8]
Because the native inhabitants had not "improved" the land (or so
the colonists supposed) they had no title to it. Sadly, again, *Greek*
colonies across the Mediterranean were similarly disrespectful of

---

[6] Taken from https://history.hanover.edu/texts/winthmod.html (accessed
September 18, 2024). There is a balanced account of Winthrop in Francis
J. Bremer, *John Winthrop: America's Forgotten Founding Father* (New York:
Oxford University Press, 2003).
[7] See Rudyard Kipling, *Something of Myself* (Ware: Wordsworth, 2008 [1920]),
78: "It was more in the nature of a *nuzzur-wattu* (an averter of the Evil Eye)."
[8] George Berkeley, "Society for the Propagation of the Gospel Anniversary
Sermon," in *Collected Works*, eds. A. A. Luce and T. E. Jessop (London:
Thomas Nelson, 1955), 7:122.

indigenous peoples, supposing them "barbarians" without the
sense of "justice" that Zeus had ordained for "real" people like
the Greeks.[9] Winthrop's insistence on the virtues of community,
like Plato's, seems to be sustained by exiling or executing any
heretics who challenged one particular account of "justice." It
would be a romantic error to imagine that such exiles were always
themselves more "liberal" or more compassionate, but we may
suspect that a better sense of justice has arisen among those who
did not so eagerly insist that *they* were God's Elect, even if only
on probation! Both the lives of sensual enjoyment and of honourable achievement may give excuses for mere *pleonexia*, which
is simply "wanting more." The life of awestruck contemplation,
theoria, was the philosophers' answer, delighting in the beauty of
reality—but that too has its perversions.

Our problem remains. We do not know what will happen next.
We do not know what Change is heading our way from the heavens:
what sudden change in solar radiation, what stellar explosion, what
hidden asteroid, what collapse of the present "false vacuum" into a
lower energy state,[10] nor even whether the extraterrestrials which
are probably Out There somewhere will decide to intervene.[11] Even

---

[9] Hesiod, *Works and Days*, 1.275ff: *The Homeric Hymns and Homerica with an
English Translation by Hugh G. Evelyn-White: Works and Days* (Cambridge, MA:
Harvard University Press; London, William Heinemann Ltd., 1914): "the
son of Cronos [that is, Zeus] has ordained this law for men, that fishes and
beasts and winged fowls should devour one another, for right [*dike*] is not in
them; but to mankind he gave right which proves far the best." "Mankind,"
historically, has almost always meant "our tribe," but the very term presents
the potential for a wider expansion of our concern (inadequate as it may be).
[10] Any such lower-energy vacuum state, if it occurred anywhere, would
expand at the speed of light, and so eliminate us all without any warning!
"The possibility that we are living in a false [unstable] vacuum has never
been a cheering one to contemplate. Vacuum decay is the ultimate ecological catastrophe; in a new vacuum there are new constants of nature; after
vacuum decay, not only is life as we know it impossible, so is chemistry as
we know it. However, one could always draw stoic comfort from the possibility that perhaps in the course of time the new vacuum would sustain,
if not life as we know it, at least some structures capable of knowing joy.
This possibility has now been eliminated": Sidney Coleman and Frank De
Luccia, "Gravitational effects on and of vacuum decay": *Physical Review D*
21 (1980), 3305–15: 3314. The more one discovers about the universe the less
likely our existence seems (on which more below).
[11] See John Leslie, *The End of the World: The Science and Ethics of Human
Extinction* (London: Routledge, 1996) for a summary of these and other
possibilities, in the light of the Doomsday Argument that we are very likely

such changes as are driven by merely human, social, and political processes are bound to be unexpected. Speculative extrapolation of current trends, or what we are assured are current trends, has not been very successful in the past. William Gibson's short story, "The Gernsback Continuum," imagines what our future might have been if the founding father of science fiction, Hugo Gernsback, had had his way: "it had all the sinister fruitiness of a Hitler Youth propaganda."[12] Gibson himself imagined "cyberspace" into being before the World Wide Web was established, and before there were any tools to create the "virtual realities" and "simulations" that now seem commonplace to a growing generation.[13] Earlier SF writers who also imagined the development of the computer industry, and "artificial intelligence," did not anticipate the effects of "Moore's Law" (that computing power doubles every two years — or slightly less.)[14] Both Gibson and his predecessors may have helped inspire creative engineers to produce the things they prophesied, but it is likely that their inspiration will one day seem as old-fashioned and faintly disagreeable as Gernsback's! In the Fifties SF writers were, roughly, divided between those who warned of the effects of nuclear spasm, and those who seemed to relish the idea that there would one day be a Universal Computer, "Multivac," or simply "the Machines," to direct our economic and political affairs (often without letting anyone know that this is what It was doing, and without questioning the inchoate goals it had been set).[15] We have experienced — so far — neither of

---

to be in the largest generation of humanity (and so probably near its end). See also my "Deep Time: does it matter?" (chapter 10 above).

[12] William Gibson, *Burning Chrome* (London: Grafton Books, 1988 [1980]), 36–50.

[13] See William Gibson, *Neuromancer* (London: Gollancz, 1984) and its sequels, *Count Zero* (1986), and *Mona Lisa Overdrive* (1988).

[14] See Gordon E. Moore, "Cramming more components onto integrated circuits": *Electronics* 38.8, April 19, 1965. In its original form the rule was simply that the number of transistors that could be placed on an integrated circuit for the same cost would double roughly every two years ("the complexity for minimum component costs has increased at a rate of roughly a factor of two per year"). It quickly became a more general prediction, about the doubling of computer power, and despite frequent predictions that it would cease to apply quite soon, it has continued to be true. Some futurists have inferred that our artefacts will soon be faster, smarter and more self-aware than we are: see Ray Kurzweil, *The Singularity is Near: when humans transcend biology* (London: Duckworth, 2005).

[15] See, for example, Isaac Asimov, "The Evitable Conflict" (1950), in *The*

these futures, and may not experience the laissez-faire capitalist future (dominated by criminal gangs) that Gibson imagined, nor yet the Singularity when computing power wholly transcends our understanding of what the networked computers are doing, and why (to which imagined future I shall return).

We do not know what will happen, and so we cannot sensibly prepare for any particular future. The best we can do is devise, restore or hang on to some sense of beauty, justice, mercy—and humility (especially in the light of our obvious past failures). Maybe our successors, who may not be our descendants, will have reverted to nomadic life on a planet wracked by storms and shifting populations. Maybe they will be plugged in to some successor of the World Wide Web, and every individual have access to information, intelligence—and power—beyond what we can imagine. Maybe they will thereby fulfil the fantasy found in many twentieth-century writers (and not only Chardin), of being taken up into a larger, wiser whole.[16] Maybe they will have expanded out into the solar system, or the galactic spiral, and be indulging whatever special fancies each strand of human or post-human life may have. Whatever life they are living, they will need virtues of a familiar kind: courage, courtesy, self-possession, justice, compassion and "good sense." Perhaps they have as much chance of achieving this as any human generation—but perhaps no greater chance. It is also horridly possible that our species will be divided, and our descendants be either prey or predator, as

---

Complete Robot (London: Granada, 1982), 546–74. The so-called Three Laws of Robotics that Asimov devised to encapsulate a moral system of sorts for his imagined robots were never satisfactory, and later writers have drawn out their genocidal and totalitarian implications: see, for example, Gregory Benford, *Foundation's Fear* (New York: HarperCollins, 1997).

[16] Olaf Stapledon, *Last and First Men* (Penguin: Harmondsworth 1972 [1930]), and *Star Maker* (Methuen: London 1937); Arthur C. Clarke, *Childhood's End* (Sidgwick and Jackson: London 1954); Robert Charles Wilson, *The Harvest* (Bantam: New York 1992). See John Connolly, "A Progressive End: Arthur C. Clarke and Teilhard de Chardin," *Foundation* 61 (1994), 66–76: Connolly suggests that, despite Clarke's denials, Chardin's ideas were sufficiently widespread, even before their publication, that they may have influenced Clarke. This may be so, but Stapledon seems to be a likelier, and acknowledged, source. Frederik Pohl and Jack Williamson took a distinctly more hostile view in *Land's End* (New York: Tor Books 1989): there "the Eternal"—modelled either on Clarke's Overmind or Lovecraft's Cthulhu—is a monster which, by absorbing all terrestrial life, would put an end to it.

Wells imagined. It is possible that we shall find the heavens are already occupied, by beings with little sympathy for us. And also possible that we will have no successors.

ANTITHESIS

Things don't have to be this way — or else perhaps they do.

Most of us have accepted that it is through "science" that we shall obtain the knowledge and the power that we suppose our predecessors wanted, even if we are unhappy with the inference that anything like Multivac should control our lives by calculating the "most efficient" route to a utilitarian goal (the greatest available satisfaction of the greatest number of somebodies). We do therefore have some duty to understand what "science" is currently suggesting. Mainstream scientific opinion has for some centuries been Stoic in its inspiration. There are finitely many bodies, undergoing finitely many changes, and what is happening at any given point in space or time is all that possibly can. History, whether cosmic or terrestrial, repeats itself "forever," whether or not there is a period, the Conflagration or the Big Crunch, when every lesser body is gathered back into the cosmic Singularity. An ideal intelligence would be able to work out the whole world's history and geography from detailed study of a falling leaf, since every feature of that leaf's fall is linked to everything else that happens, everywhere and every when (except that even an ideal intelligence could not know every relevant property of its fall).[17] An ideal intelligence would at least understand the Formula of All Things, and know that it couldn't be otherwise: it would "know the Mind of God," in Hawking's misleading phrase.[18] Not only is our history fixed, but nothing of it is owed to "chance" or arbitrary decision. It follows — though hardly any of us can manage this conversion — that we cannot sanely resent any feature of the world, however harsh it seems: to wish it otherwise is not merely

---

[17] Partly because the attempt to discover those properties must alter them, and partly because there is good reason to doubt the application of the Law of Non-Contradiction at the quantum level (so that an elementary particle may be in several different, apparently distinct, states at the same time) and hence good reason to suspect that not all these different states are subsumed into a single macroscopic event. Maybe the leaf falls all the ways it can.

[18] Stephen Hawking, *A Brief History of Time: from Big Bang to Black Holes* (London: Bantam Press), 193.

to wish the whole world to be unimaginably different, but to wish the whole world away. Epictetus imagines Zeus instructing him that his only "freedom" is deciding how to feel about the way things are and must be;[19] but of course there is no real possibility that Epictetus could feel otherwise than he does.

This has been the scientific hope, even when the scientists themselves continued to act as if they were free agents with a real duty to discover and to tell the truth, and some chance of doing so (how else, indeed, could they act?)[20] In the last century, however, a disturbing thought has emerged: there seems after all no reason why the cosmos has the laws and balance of forces that it does. It does after all seem "arbitrary"—an unforced choice—that the fundamental forces (electro-magnetism, weak force, strong force, gravity) have the relations that they do, that elementary particles are as they are, that the universe has expanded at exactly the speed it did, and that there was just enough of an excess of matter over anti-matter that there remains a material universe. Worse still, the precise features of our cosmos seem such that even the slightest variation would have made it impossible for there to be life of anything like our sort at all.[21] The feeblest and silliest response to this has been to say that if things had been different we wouldn't be here to wonder why, and there's an end of the matter—which is like noticing that one has somehow survived a series of lethal lightning strikes and refusing to wonder how this happened, or what other features of the situation were linked to the happy outcome. Others have hoped—in Stoic vein—that it will turn out that somehow or other things *had* to be that way, because of some deeper formula: that only the actual cosmos is a possible one at all (which does not answer the question why there is *any* cosmos, but at least leaves the "choice" of cosmos comfortingly secure). Theists of many persuasions have seen this

---

[19] Epictetus, *Discourses* 1.1.7–12, in A. A. Long and D. N. Sedley, eds. *The Hellenistic Philosophers* (Cambridge: Cambridge University Press, 1987), 1:391 [62K].
[20] For some of the problems with this inchoate assumption, see my "Folly to the Greeks: good reasons to give up reason," *European Journal for Philosophy of Religion* 4 (2012), 93–113.
[21] See John D. Barrow, Frank J. Tipler, and John A. Wheeler, *The Anthropic Cosmological Principle*, 2nd edition (Oxford: Oxford University Press, 1988); Paul Davies, *The Goldilocks Enigma: why is the Universe just right for Life?* (London: Penguin, 2007).

"fine-tuning" as evidence of design: apparently something outside and above all cosmic order "chooses" to realize just this sort of world, presumably in order to harvest living, conscious beings from it. But the methodological naturalism that is central to the modern scientific enterprise—a naturalism originally adopted, it should be noted, for theological reasons—makes that theistic inference unpopular, or at least "unscientific." Instead mainstream cosmological speculation has moved in an Epicurean direction.

For Epicureans reality is composed of infinitely (countably?) many unbreakable bodies ("atoms") with infinitely many shapes and sizes, and without limits to their motion in either space or time. In that infinite array, all possible combinations and life-stories can occur. Some indeed have falsely inferred that all imaginable combinations and life-stories *must* occur:[22] strictly, even if there are infinitely many worlds (uncountably many?) it does not follow that all the infinitely many *possible* worlds are really actual—maybe only every millionth possible world is actual, or every googolth. And not every *imaginable* world is really possible (though what constrains the possibilities we do not know). But it would at least be difficult to insist of any seemingly possible world that it is nowhere ever actual: why wouldn't it be? And Epicureans found evidence that there were such "actualized possibilities" in our experience of phantoms—shadows cast by alien anatomies. Not all such worlds have anything like human beings in them, nor even living creatures of whatever sort. Granted the conditions, it is not odd that we ourselves look out on a world sufficiently accommodating to the development of living creatures just like us as to allow our existence! Or, at least, no odder than the conditions.

For ancient Epicureans there was a single Space in which the infinitely many "atoms" fell and swerved and made up larger bodies. In the modern version of the story, those Other Universes are not just far away from us within the familiar framework of three-dimensional Space (though there may be other bubbles

---

[22] Thus Max Tegmark in "Parallel Universes," *Scientific American* 288.5 (May 2003), 41–53: "in infinite space, even the most unlikely events must take place somewhere." Tegmark's paper revitalizes the old idea that we each have infinitely many identical or near identical copies, either in a future round of the cosmos (the Stoic notion) or—as Tegmark himself suggests—in other bubble universes immensely far away.

of "false vacuum" even within such a framework, so far away that they can never be observed), but may be separate from us in another unfamiliar direction, or else be different episodes in a longer hypercosmic history. Each cosmos begins and possibly ends in a Singularity: the Big Bang or the Big Crunch (though current evidence suggests that *our* cosmos, at least, is doomed to expand and dissipate forever). In that timeless, spaceless moment, the fundamental laws are arbitrarily recast. Or else—in a further twist—they are cast again in every possible way. All possible versions emerge from the Singularity, "alongside" what we conceive to be the only actual world, but each—from within that version—just as real as ours.

This thought—that all possible versions coexist—has some backing from experiment.[23] Just as there seems no reason why our cosmos should be the only possibility, so also there seems no reason why a given elementary particle should move one way or another. Indeed it seems that we have reason to suppose that, given the chance, it moves all possible ways—which is the currently best explanation for the patterns observed when shining photons, one at a time, onto a screen, through a barrier with two slits. If each photon is left unobserved on its passage through the barrier, it passes through both slits at every possible angle and generates a typical wave pattern on the screen (exactly as if there were many photons passing through). If we watch to see which slit it passes through, it passes through only one, and a single dot is visible on the screen. Somehow, our observation "collapses" the possibilities, the wave function. The spooky suggestion was at first that it was only conscious observation that decided the particle's position, as though the bodies with which we share reality were waiting for our observation before deciding where to be. The great physicist Erwin Schrödinger, thinking it absurd to suppose that elementary particles played such games, proposed a thought experiment to demonstrate the absurdity:

> One can even set up quite ridiculous cases. A cat is penned up in a steel chamber, along with the following device (which must be secured against direct interference

[23] A lucid and almost persuasive account of this theory can be found in David Deutsch, *The Fabric of Reality: towards a theory of everything* (London: Penguin, 1998).

by the cat): in a Geiger counter there is a tiny bit of radioactive substance, *so* small, that *perhaps* in the course of the hour one of the atoms decays, but also, with equal probability, perhaps none; if it happens, the counter tube discharges and through a relay releases a hammer which shatters a small flask of hydrocyanic acid. If one has left this entire system to itself for an hour, one would say that the cat still lives *if* meanwhile no atom has decayed. The psi-function of the entire system would express this by having in it the living and dead cat (pardon the expression) mixed or smeared out in equal parts.[24]

Schrödinger's opponents had insisted that there was nothing determinate about whether the particle was or was not emitted until a human observation "collapsed the wave function." Till then all the possible outcomes existed as "superpositions of different eigenstates." Schrödinger pointed out that in his imagined experiment they must thence conclude that the cat was neither alive nor dead until they opened the box to see. This, he thought, was sufficiently silly as to prove that there was some fact of the matter about what the elementary particles were doing, even if we could not ourselves detect that fact.[25] Physicists who preferred the "Copenhagen" interpretation instead concluded that indeed the cat was neither alive nor dead until the box was opened (excusing themselves from wondering whether the *cat* was conscious of its own survival by assuming without adequate argument that cats aren't conscious). This response was made even less acceptable when Eugen Wigner offered a further gloss: the whole experimental set up (cat, box, and human experimenter) is established in a further box — the whole laboratory. No-one outside the laboratory can determine

---

[24] Erwin Schrödinger, "The Present Situation in Quantum Mechanics," trans. John Trimmer, *Proceedings of the American Philosophical Society* 124 (1935), 23–38: http://hermes.ffn.ub.es/luisnavarro/nuevo_maletin/Schrodinger_1935_cat.pdf (accessed December 6, 2023).

[25] Thus John G. Cramer, "The Transactional Interpretation of Quantum Mechanics," *Reviews of Modern Physics* 58 (1986), 647–88. (http://mist.npl.washington.edu/npl/int_rep/tiqm/TI_toc.html, accessed April 23, 2012): "In the period just before the observation is made the SV describes the cat as 50% alive and 50% dead. This description, which may seem plausible enough when applied to a microscopic system (or even to a statistically large ensemble of Schrödinger's cat experiments), appears rather absurd when applied to an individual complex organism like a cat."

before the event whether the cat is alive or dead, *nor whether the experimenter finds the cat alive or dead*. It takes a friend of the experimenter ("Wigner's Friend") to "collapse the eigenstates"![26] Since human beings—unlike cats—were assumed themselves to be conscious entities capable of observing, and so "collapsing," reality, it seemed absurd to suppose that the experimenter's reality depended wholly on what the Friend observed. "The being with a consciousness," so Wigner said, "must have a different role in quantum mechanics than the inanimate measuring device." This seemed offensive to materialists. The Everett "Many Worlds" or "Many Histories" interpretation, once reckoned too absurd to acknowledge, has gradually become the mainstream view.[27] There are two equal realities: when the experimenter opens the box one version of him finds the cat alive, and another finds it dead. The observer plays no part in collapsing the wave function, since the wave function has not in fact collapsed, though its elements have "decohered," and so become mutually inaccessible.[28] Strictly, indeed, there will likely be any number of versions who find the cat is dead—in different postures, different parts of the box, and for different lengths of time. The cat's history has split before the box is opened, as has the experimenter's before Wigner's Friend arrives. The experimenter does not notice that he has been divided: each version is consistent in its opinion. The same argument applies, of course, to the Friends of Wigner's Friend, who cannot tell— until they check—whether the Friend has found an experimenter with a live cat, or one with a dead cat.

---

[26] See E. P. Wigner, "Remarks on the Mind-Body Problem," in *The Scientist Speculates*, ed. I. J. Good (London: Heinemann, 1962), 284–302; reprinted in Wigner, *Symmetries and Reflections* (Bloomington, IN: Indiana University Press, 1967), 171–84.
[27] Hugh Everett, "'Relative State' Formulation of Quantum Mechanics," *Reviews of Modern Physics* 29 (1957), 454–62.
[28] The different versions of photons passing singly through the slits "interfere" with each other, but go together to make up a coherent macroscopic reality (the wave-pattern on the screen): the different versions of cat, experimenter, friends and friends of friends are divided from each other. Whether they could ever be reunited (and so encounter their alternate versions) is moot. If all imaginably possible worlds are really actual, then presumably there are worlds where this happens (as in several of Diana Wynne-Jones's fantasies: e.g. *Charmed Life* [London: Macmillan, 1977], *The Homeward Bounders* [London: Macmillan, 1981], *Witch Week* [London: Macmillan, 1982] and many others).

Some theorists, seeking to avoid the multiplication of real worlds and histories by holding to the Copenhagen Interpretation, and to the importance of conscious observers, have concluded that only a Final Observer, at the End of Time, can determine unambiguously what has happened, and that it is *this* Observation that will retrospectively actualize just one particular history. Does it follow that we here-now are living in a merely "virtual" possible reality that may not be the one to be actualized at the end of time?[29] Or is that too rough a rejection of the fundamental Cartesian intuition, that I know that I exist here-now, even if I don't exactly "know" any of the more familiar facts or fancies? But perhaps the Final Observer, timelessly, "has" actualized the world, and this is indeed the one true history: nothing in fundamental physics, after all, *requires* that there be no effect from "the future" on "the past." Another version of this "transactional" interpretation, omitting the Observer, also rests on the equality of all moments in the temporal sequence: what happens to the cat is fixed atemporally because only one outcome is consistent with everything else that happens.[30] Other versions involving an "objective" — and undetermined — collapse of the wave function suffer from the problem that the collapse apparently must propagate itself at more than the speed of light: suggesting again that there is a level of reality that transcends the material. Yet another theory — echoing the "Aristotelian" description of Copernicus's heliocentrism offered by Andreas Osiander, and later by Cardinal Bellarmine[31] — is that the whole theoretical apparatus is only a

---

[29] Stephen Baxter has played with this idea in *Timelike Infinity* (London: Collins, 1992); see also Arthur C. Clarke and Gentry Lee, *Rama Revealed* (London: Gollancz, 1993).

[30] Cramer, "The Transactional Interpretation of Quantum Mechanics": "There is not a 'when,' not a point in time at which the quantum event is finished. The event is finished when the transaction forms, which happens along a set of world lines which include all of the events listed above, treating none of them as the special conclusion of the event."

[31] Andreas Osiander, "Introduction," in Nicolaus Copernicus, *On the Revolutions of the Heavenly Spheres*, trans. C. G. Wallis (New York: Prometheus Books, 1995 [1939]); Robert Bellarmine to Paolo Foscarini, April 12, 1615: "to say that, assuming the earth moves and the sun stands still, all the appearances are saved better than with eccentrics and epicycles, is to speak well; there is no danger in this, *and it is sufficient for mathematicians*. But to want to affirm that the sun really is fixed in the center of the heavens and only revolves around itself (i.e. turns upon its axis) without traveling from

way of predicting actual observations, and that nothing should be inferred about what lies behind the observations: but this, despite its having been a dominant mood in earlier decades, is an abandonment of science![32] Galilean science, at any rate, rests on the *Platonic* assumption that we have intellectual access to the principles of the universe because both the universe and our own intellects have the same transcendent source. In Benedict XVI's words, quoted earlier (2009): "the objective structure of the universe and the intellectual structure of the human being coincide; the subjective reason and the objectified reason in nature are identical. In the end it is 'one' reason that links both and invites us to look to a unique creative Intelligence."[33] The alternative is, in the end, to abandon scientific realism.

The earth really does rotate, and orbit around the sun (or at least that is our present assumption — one that may not be as secure as we suppose). Perhaps the Many Worlds are real as well. At any rate, the preferred version amongst speculative physicists — though it may be that even they do not think much about this in their usual lives — is currently that our cosmos is only one of indefinitely many, each real to its insiders.

According to [the] many-worlds [interpretation] all the possible outcomes of a quantum interaction are realised. The wave function, instead of collapsing at the moment of observation, carries on evolving in a deterministic fashion, embracing all possibilities embedded within it. All outcomes exist simultaneously but do not interfere further with each other, each single prior world having split into mutually unobservable but equally real worlds.[34]

---

east to west, and that the earth is situated in the third sphere and revolves with great speed around the sun, *is a very dangerous thing*" (http://www.fordham.edu/halsall/mod/1615bellarmine-letter.asp, accessed September 18, 2024, my italics).
[32] See Owen Barfield, *Unancestral Voice* (London: Faber, 1965).
[33] Benedict XVI to Archbishop Rino Fisichella, on the occasion of the international congress "From Galileo's Telescope to Evolutionary Cosmology" (November 30–December 2, 2009), http://www.vatican.va/holy_father/benedict_xvi/messages/pont-messages/2009/documents/hf_ben-xvi_mes_20091126_fisichella-telescopio_en.html (accessed December 6, 2023).
[34] http://www.hedweb.com/everett/index.html: Michael Clive Price's Everett FAQ, Q2 (accessed December 6, 2023).

In a way that Plotinus could hardly have imagined, all possibilities and levels of reality must be instantiated! In such a universe or Multiverse, it may seem no surprise that the cosmos and the history we observe is — obviously — one that is compatible with our being here to observe it. We may still be startled that *any* set of laws and forces should be so constructive in their outcome: even if there are infinitely many histories, there may still be a question why particular histories are realized. Even if our cosmos (or rather the set of coevolving cosmoi seeded from our Big Bang) is, literally, the only one in all eternity to have the requisite properties — though this seems very unlikely — it may be a source of wonder that it (or they) has happened. But there is a further speculative twist: maybe indeed our cosmos is so superbly fine-tuned precisely because there are agencies involved that have fine-tuned it. Maybe they are themselves the products of an almost infinitely rare chance, whose probability they can "now" increase. Maybe they arose within a cosmos radically unlike our own: a cosmos, let us suppose, which allowed the very early emergence of life and conscious enterprise, at a time when all its energy was readily at hand.[35] If we cannot legitimately exclude *any* real possibility, then one of the Many Worlds is one united in intelligence and power from very near its beginnings: the Omega World, rather than the Omega Point of Chardin's — and Olaf Stapledon's — imaginings! However They arose in their beginnings, they can be supposed to have access to sufficient power, skill, and information to engineer new cosmoi, whether through the Singularity (which is, for us, the moment when all laws and extrapolations fail) or through the creation of "black holes" (which are, in some current theories, the gateways to new cosmoi, potentially with different laws and balances of power).[36] Maybe they are our own successors, bending back in time to create themselves and us! But if that is to be thought possible it seems more likely that we have been forestalled — and not necessarily by intelligences that much resemble us. Our sort of intelligence, as far as we know, has evolved only once in terrestrial history,

---

[35] Some of these speculations have been explored by Stephen Baxter, in, for example, *Exultant: Destiny's Children Book Two* (London: Gollancz, 2004) and *The Time Ships* (London: Collins, 1995).
[36] James N. Gardner, *The Intelligent Universe: AI, ET, and the emerging mind of the cosmos* (Franklin Lakes, NJ: New Page Books, 2007).

whereas—for example—eusocial insects are a far commoner form, and more to be expected, on merely naturalistic grounds, Out There (as observed above)! But more of the observable cosmos than we think may turn out to be the effect of living purposes of some sort, and Plotinus was right to insist that it was Soul that made all worlds.[37] He may even have been right to suggest that the different cycles of world history (for he was ready to consider, with the Stoics and with some modern physicists, that the number of possible entities was finite, and that their combinations must eventually be exhausted) could be subtly different:[38] each soul was allocated, perhaps, a different role to play in the cosmic theatre next time round, depending on its previous success![39] And how many more performances before we get it right? The idea that Soul in general, and our souls, have their origin elsewhere, outside the material frame of the many cosmoi, is not one easily admitted by modern cosmologists wedded to a methodological materialism—but in the absence of any adequate theory of how material motions could generate conscious experience, it has to remain a serious possibility.[40]

And what is the relevance of this speculative cosmology to the immediate practicalities of our life here and now? Whether the Stoics were right to think that there is only one, finite cosmos, and that it could not be otherwise, or the Epicureans right to think that there were infinitely many, it seems that we have no choices. Either all that possibly could happen, does, or else what doesn't happen, can't: the two claims are logically equivalent, though the former sounds less restrictive! Either way, we here-now are doing all and only what we can: even if Epicureans and modern

---

[37] *Ennead* V.1 [10].2, trans. Armstrong.
[38] *Ennead* V.7 [18].1; see also *Ennead* III.7 [45].11. See Richard Sorabji, *Time, Creation and the Continuum: theories in antiquity and the early Middle Ages* (London: Duckworth, 1983), 18.
[39] See *Ennead* III. 2 [47].17, 45–53.
[40] The main alternative accounts of "mind-body" interaction are eliminative materialism (according to which our conscious experience is a fiction) and naturalistic panpsychism (according to which all material elements have psychological properties that somehow add up, in multicellular creatures, to experience). Neither of these accounts strikes me as more plausible than Platonism: see my *From Athens to Jerusalem* (Oxford: Clarendon Press, 1984), 121–57. Both have very strange ethical implications, largely ignored by theorists. But that is another story.

physicists are right that there are other versions of ourselves doing and observing other things, whether in Everett's Many Worlds or in immensely distant bubble universes, the very fact that "they" are doing that means that "we" can't be — except in the useless sense, available also to Stoics, that creatures very much like us do other things than we do. Our being — the being of all the different versions of ourselves — is fixed and cannot be any different. Platonists can plausibly disagree: for them, the choice of lives and worlds occurs outside the frame, and not all possibilities are actual.[41] We choose or have chosen this world and history here: we are in a way in the place of the Final Observer, actualizing one history from all the possibilities.[42] Or at least this is a possibility unknown to the Stoic — or Epicurean — fatalist. Platonism better accommodates the assumptions implicit in scientific speculation: that there is a discoverable order to the world, that we can be guided to its discovery by seeking mathematical beauty, and that we ought to try. For Epicureans, strictly, there is no order on which we could reasonably count; for Stoics — and especially for the atheistical, modern sort — there is no principle outside or before the world's reality which would ever serve to explain why *this* world does exist, nor why we should expect it to continue.

But though, in a way, we *might* be in the place of the Final Observer, it is perhaps more likely, or at least more seemly, to suggest that the Final Observer might be very unlike us, whether It collapses all the superposited histories into one coherent strand, or else stands at the end of them all, looking back at all the confluent pasts that lead to the Singularity, the Conflagration, or the Omega Point — as though the infinitely many particles, each taking all its possible routes, form at last the complete wave pattern of the cosmos on the Observer's screen. Maybe we are each accompanied by a shadow counterpart (for whom, of course, *we* are the shadow counterpart) who has done different things,

---

[41] See Plotinus, *Ennead* III.1 [3]. 8–9.
[42] One further really weird suggestion — perhaps intended as a reduction of theories that emphasise the effects of observation — is that our present day observation of "dark matter" may have shortened the life of the cosmos, by collapsing the possibilities: see Leonard M. Krauss and James Dent, "Late Time Behavior of False Vacuum Decay: Possible Implications for Cosmology and Metastable Inflating States," *Physical Review Letters* 100 (2008), 171301–4 (DOI: 10.1103/PhysRevLett.100.171301).

for better or worse, with our opportunities. Or maybe the wave function has "already" been collapsed by the Final Observer, and we are in truth the only actual line. Or else we can use a different myth, to very much the same effect: our cosmos has been seeded, perhaps by Engineers at the imagined "end of time," with a view to producing us—and maybe producing the Engineers: a speculation that some theorists seem to suppose would be a satisfactory explanation (the Engineers exist because they engineered, from the End of Time, the cosmos that produced them in its "earlier" phase).[43] But the one thing that in either case is standing alongside us is, precisely, the Final Observer or the Final Engineer. Something has selected us from all the possibilities as Its companions in the timeless moment. Which is what theists had already said:

> From all eternity [God] chose us from among an infinite number of possible beings. He chose us, not those other possible beings, and so they did not exist. And among all these others he also chose you, individually. He chose you from an infinity of possible beings who could have existed but whom he did not create. You were the one chosen from an infinite number of possibilities, and the very fact that you exist is the greatest proof of God's preference for you. Each of us is irreplaceable. We are all unique collectors' pieces, because God is an artist who never repeats or reproduces himself.[44]

On the one account (the currently mainstream cosmological account) all possible versions of myself, and all possible versions of human history, and all possible versions even of an expanding cosmos, are just as real as the ones that seem, parochially, "actual." Correspondingly, all possible *futures* (from our point of view) are also real, and "we" shall be enduring them all, even though each version of ourselves experiences only one. Whatever possibility is

---

[43] See Davies, *The Goldilocks Enigma*, 283, after John A. Wheeler, "World as a system self-synthesized by quantum networking," *IBM Journal of Research and Development* 32 (1988), 4–15. Wheeler (14) orates as follows: "Life and mind: For how much can they be conceived to count in the scheme of existence? Nothing, say the billions of light years of space that lie around us. Everything, say the billions of years of time that lie ahead of us."

[44] Ernesto Cardenal, *Love*, trans. Dinah Livingstone (Brewster, MA: Paraclete Press, 2006), 25.

realized in our singular experience we shall know — if we believe this argument — that every other possibility has been realized as well. There is no privileged place or moment, scale, or version, such that it alone is "real" or "central." Whatever happens can be no surprise, and can require no further explanation (though the fundamental mystery, of existence, still remains). Whatever happens will turn out to be following the forms, even if not in the way that we here-now expect.

Alternatively — and following the strangely attractive specula-tion that only this actual world has been "chosen" from beyond its bounds, by our own spiritual selves, or by the Final Engineer, or by an Unknown God — the reasons for this actual world can-not be found within the world. "According to the Aristotelian paradigm, physical reality is fundamental and mathematical language is merely a useful approximation. According to the Platonic paradigm, the mathematical structure is the true reality and observers perceive it imperfectly."[45] Things don't *have* to be this way — and we may wonder why they are, and wonder how we or our successors or creators might do otherwise. That way, we might say, lies Leibniz!

SYNTHESIS

Things don't have to be this way — and perhaps they aren't.

I have spoken of two Singularities: the cosmic, and the social. The cosmic Singularity, the Big Bang and the — possible — Big Crunch, is that moment when all laws fail, all separate entities are dissolved in the primordial Atum, the world-mound of Egyp-tian story, or in the Emptiness that stood behind and around the world, symbolized as a snake.

---

[45] Tegmark, "Parallel Universes," 49. The "Aristotelian" mode described is not entirely true to Aristotle (for whom a non-material Unmoved *Nous* was the ultimate explanation), and the "Platonic" omits what mattered most to Plato and his disciples: namely, the Good. Mathematical Reality is not, for Plato, ultimate. One oddity in Davies's otherwise clear and well-informed account of cosmological speculation is his suggestion that "abandoning Platonism would make room for teleology" (*The Goldilocks Enigma*, 266), as though Plato thought that mathematical objects, and the mathematically expressed "laws of nature" were self-explanatory, or that the laws *we have identified* are bound to be permanent. Davies also appears to share the odd idea that "teleology" is a form of backward causation!

> This earth will return to the primeval water (Nun), to
> endless (flood) as in its first state. I [that is Atum] shall
> remain with Osiris after I have transformed myself into
> another snake [Apopis] which men do not know and the
> gods do not see.[46]

The Egyptian titles might mislead the literal-minded, but so do
the much more vulgar titles that twentieth-century cosmologists
invented! "The Big Bang" was not an explosion, and "the Big
Crunch" (if it happens) will not be a train wreck: rather the events
signal the beginning (or the end) of spatio-temporal distinctions.
"Then" there was only a "false vacuum" (misleadingly so called)
by contrast with the "true" vacuum we inhabit, where the four
fundamental forces—electromagnetism, gravity, weak and strong
nuclear forces—are distinct (though more recently it has been
suspected that ours is only another "false"—and unstable—
vacuum). Nothing can be extrapolated back or forward through
that Moment, though this has not prevented speculative cosmologists (as above) from devising literally metaphysical tales about
what goes on before or after or around it. The social Singularity,
when Moore's Law works its final magic, is the moment when
our artefacts so far exceed our grasp as to make their aims and
methods utterly inscrutable to us, though this has not prevented
speculative futurologists from wondering how to join or to resist
them. The social Singularity differs from all other social transformations: with luck, we shall find that "we shall all be changed,
in a moment, in the twinkling of an eye, at the last trumpet; for
the trumpet will sound, and the dead will be raised imperishable,
and we shall be changed."[47]

But maybe that will not work out as optimistic futurologists
suppose. Back in Babylon, it was accepted that human beings
had been created as convenient labourers—and their creators
often tired of them. In the Abrahamic tradition, it was believed
instead that the Creator had appointed Adam as His image and
in His likeness, and that every individual human was therefore
owed the respect, almost the worship, that in other traditions was

---

[46] *Book of the Dead*, chapter 175, cited by Eric Hornung, *Conceptions of God
in Ancient Egypt*, trans. John Baines (Ithaca, NY: Cornell University Press,
1982), 163.
[47] 1 Corinthians 15:50–52.

owed only to kings, priests, and heroes. In paying that respect, we might also hope to recover the likeness which Adam lost: to be "holy" (which is to say, compassionate) as God is holy.[48] The Pauline prophecy, and the Christian tradition about *"theosis,"* was that we would become as gods: that, after all was why God became man, so that human beings could become God.[49] This hope, for the futurologists, is to be vindicated by technology, as we are caught up into the Computer, or mated with our non-biological offspring. On Kurzweil's guess or prophecy, "the entire universe will become saturated with our intelligence."[50] But both cosmological and sociological speculation seem instead to point towards a time when we shall have returned to Babylon, or be cast down still further. Our cosmic future is likely to be determined by vast powers beyond our reach, and our immediate future by computerized intelligence. Judgment Day may be coming.[51] Even if those powers are — as the more optimistic futurologists have supposed — our "children" and successors, inheritors of the dream, we have no idea what form that dream will take in them. The more familiar sorts of human being, ones who won't or can't be copied or absorbed into the Computers, will probably survive as servitors or pets or vermin. This may also offer an explanation of the Fermi Paradox or Puzzle: if intelligent life is as common in the universe as theory suggests, why has it not come visiting?[52] But perhaps the answer is a simple one: any intelligences smart and powerful enough to travel or transmit themselves and their

---

[48] See Eliezer Berkovits, *Man and God: studies in Biblical Theology* (Detroit: Wayne State University Press, 1969) on *qadosh*; William Schweiker, Michael A. Johnson, and Kevin Jung, eds., *Humanity Before God: contemporary faces of Jewish, Christian and Islamic Ethics* (Minneapolis: Fortress Press, 2006).

[49] Athanasius, *On the Incarnation*, 54.3; see Norman Russell, *The Doctrine of Deification in the Greek Patristic Tradition*, 2nd edition (Oxford: Oxford University Press, 2006).

[50] Kurzweil, *The Singularity is Near*, 29; see also 361, citing his *The Age of Spiritual Machines* (New York: Viking Press, 1998), 258–60: "intelligence will ultimately prove more powerful than . . . big impersonal forces," and it will be up to "us" or our successors to decide how the universe will end.

[51] As the more pessimistic SF writers have suggested: see, for example, *The Terminator* (directed by James Cameron, 1984), *Terminator 2: Judgment Day* (directed by James Cameron, 1993).

[52] See Stephen Webb, *If the Universe is Teeming with Aliens, Where is Everybody? Fifty Solutions to the Fermi Paradox and the Problem of Extraterrestrial Life* (New York: Copernicus Books, 2002).

ideas across galactic space will have no interest in us, unless perhaps as relics, whether obsolete or engaging.

That last judgment of course may tell us more about the habits and ideas of certain *human beings* than about any imagined
superbeings. In the very act of insisting that those beings will
be utterly unlike us, the pessimists suggest that they will be like
the most indifferent and short-sighted of human adventurers,
as though indifference and discourtesy were obvious markers of
high intelligence. What humanists, in the Hellenic as well as the
Abrahamic tradition, have previously supposed is that human
beings are significantly different from the non-human precisely
in that we do take an interest in all other creatures, and are not
bound by species-specific feelings. That interest may often have
been patronizing. It may even have been used and promoted to
give us ways of manipulating others: the advantage of our understanding other creatures may often have been that we could avoid
their attack, hunt them down, domesticate, and exploit them.
But that manipulative use has often also been decried: even if
shepherds are exploiting sheep, they may also love and give their
lives for them, and there have always been firm limits on how
much a decent shepherd can exploit his flock.

> Prophesy, man, against the shepherds of Israel: prophesy
> and say to them, You shepherds, these are the words of
> the Lord God: How I hate the shepherds of Israel who
> care only for themselves! Should not the shepherd care
> for the sheep? You consume the milk, wear the wool, and
> slaughter the fat beasts but you don't feed the sheep. You
> have not encouraged the weary, tended the sick, bandaged
> the hurt, recovered the straggler, or searched for the
> lost; and even the strong you have driven with ruthless
> severity.... I will dismiss these shepherds: they shall
> care only for themselves no longer; I will rescue my sheep
> from their jaws, and they shall feed on them no longer.[53]

It is not impossible that our successors or supplanters will behave
a little better than we do. To suggest that they are likelier to

---

[53] Ezekiel 34:1ff. Obviously, in its prophetic context this is a rebuke specifically to the rulers of Israel, who had broken their covenant to care for
the weak and poor in their community. But the metaphor makes no sense
unless literal shepherds were expected to care for sheep.

behave like Winthrop's colonists—vowing to do justice and love mercy while simultaneously excusing themselves for obvious injustice and neglect—is simply to project our own confusions and desires on beings which, by hypothesis, have other motives and far better understandings. We have no good ground ourselves for despising other creatures for not being "intellectual" enough, when they so obviously surpass us in so many other ways. As Aristotle said, there is something wonderful and beautiful in even the smallest, commonest and apparently "base" of living creatures.[54] The superbeings we are imagining may reasonably think the same of us: there will be things that we can do which they cannot, however strange their powers. At the least we should hope that they have learnt two lessons: not to despise those that in some ways they surpass, lest they themselves be despised by even greater powers, and not to despise the achievements of the past, lest their successors do so too.[55]

Is there a natural route to the realization of that hope? We can fairly safely assume that all living creatures seek to live, and also to spread their life. Some may fall into the trap of remorseless growth, *pleonexia*—the philosophy of cancer.[56] Those who survive will have discovered cooperation. Our own bodies are evidence of this: founded, like all multicellular eukaryotes, on the willing cooperation both of their own cells, and of our bacterial partners.[57] Our very cells are fuelled by mitochondrial bacteria (with their own DNA), and our digestion—perhaps also more of our thoughts than we suppose—depends on other bacterial forms.[58] We cannot survive as individuals without the support of a biosphere, or without the support of our close kindred and our cousins. The same will be true even of the superbeings, whether we are thinking of computer intelligences that come to life in the World Wide Web,

---

[54] Aristotle, *De Partibus Animalium* 1.645a15f.
[55] See John C. Wright, *The Golden Age: a romance of the far future* (New York: Tor, 2002); *The Phoenix Exultant* (New York: Tor, 2003); *The Golden Transcendence, or The Last of the Masquerade* (New York: Tor, 2003).
[56] Edward Abbey, *Desert Solitaire: a season in the wilderness* (New York: Touchstone, 1968), 127: "Growth for the sake of growth is a cancerous madness."
[57] See Lynn Margulis and Dorion Sagan, *Microcosmos: four billion years of microbial evolution*, 2nd edition (Berkeley, CA: University of California Press, 1997).
[58] See Adam Hadhazy, "Think Twice: How the Gut's 'Second Brain' Influences Mood and Well-Being," *Scientific American*, February 12, 2010: https://www.scientificamerican.com/article/gut-second-brain/ (accessed December 6, 2023).

or of beings from the End of Time, who must rely on a network of fuel and communication beyond our power to conceive, in "a universe growing without limit in richness and complexity, a universe of life surviving forever and making itself known to its neighbors across unimaginable gulfs of space and time."[59]

One further feature of intelligence is that it *imagines* possibilities in order to learn how to deal with them more safely if they are ever realized — and also to enjoy them. Sometimes we imagine simpler possibilities than we are likely to encounter, whether as training exercises or to discover the essential lessons more clearly than we can in "real life." The same, we can fairly safely say, will be true for our superbeings. They will entertain and train themselves, engage with simple fantasies and simplified histories in order to discover in themselves the virtues they may need to face the long night coming, or whatever stranger creatures cosmic evolution in all its variants has thrown up. They will create what we call "virtual realities": cruder and simpler than their own real lives together, but adequately scripted for those who dip down into them, and for the creatures they create to populate the play.

Does this sound familiar?

> Even before this coming to be we were there, men who were different, and some of us even gods, pure souls and intellect united with the whole of reality; we were parts of the intelligible, not marked off or cut off but belonging to the whole; and we are not cut off even now.[60]

This thought has at least two echoes in current cosmological and futurological speculation. Futurologists, noticing the growth of virtual reality for entertainment and research, have also noticed that there could easily come a time when almost all experiences, say, of twenty-first-century European life will in fact be simulations, entered out of ennui, adventurous spirit or sociological observation. It follows that we are ourselves — you and I united in the reading of this paragraph — are far more likely to be experiencing a simulation![61] In Dainton's words:

---

[59] Freeman J. Dyson, "Time without End: Physics and Biology in an Open Universe" (1979), in *Selected Papers of Freeman Dyson* (Providence, RI: American Mathematical Society 1996), 529–42: 541.
[60] Plotinus, *Enneads VI*, 317 (VI. 4. 14, 18ff.).
[61] Nick Bostrom, "Are You Living in a Computer Simulation?" in *Philosophical Quarterly* 53 (2003), 243–55 (http://www.simulation-argument.

Although it seems to you that you are a normal human being living at the start of the 21st century, the subjects of all the many artificially produced type-21 streams have very similar experiences and beliefs. These subjects are all mistaken, and so might you be, for it is more likely than not that you *are* one of these subjects.[62]

This conclusion is reinforced if we look beyond the immediate social Singularity to the working of whatever intelligences stand at the End of Time, and especially if we take account of the Many Worlds Interpretation. Granted that this scenario is *possible* (and there seems no reason to doubt it), it would be actualized in indefinitely many of the variant histories, and at indefinitely many periods within each history. Almost certainly, we are dreaming, and whether there ever was a "real" original twenty-first century, in multiple original versions, is moot (and maybe unimportant)![63] The fact that the dream is sometimes very frightening is no argument against its being created—nor even against our having volunteered to dream it (though we may also have been kidnapped or imprisoned for some fault—or created merely in the simulation as plausible stock characters). Maybe the earth is *not* revolving

---

com/simulation.pdf, accessed December 6, 2023); Barry Dainton, "On Singularities and Simulations," *Journal of Consciousness Studies* 19 (2012), 42–85.
[62] Dainton, "On Singularities and Simulations," 57.
[63] That the real world is very unlike our experience has seemed to some to make the simulation argument self-defeating: if in fact there are no such technical achievements as are used to suggest that we might soon develop virtual realities then we do not in fact have reason—though we thought we did—to expect that we are living in such simulations—though in actual fact we are. The evidence from which we draw what is, by hypothesis, the correct conclusion can only have been inserted into the dream as a sort of hint to us, but has no real evidential authority. As Democritus agreed, we are drawing our evidence that the senses deceive us from what our senses tell us (Diels-Kranz, *Fragmente der Vorsokratiker*, 140 [68B11])! I am not persuaded that this subverts the argument. Dainton, 67–71, argues that—in order not to make the argument self-defeating—we are entitled to believe that the simulation is not *too* different from the real world: on this, too, I am not wholly persuaded. One further problem with the conception, after all, is that even the experience of the superbeings will be subject to the same uneasy doubt, and that no-one will *ever* know that s/he is not dreaming, unless their experience is indeed very different from ours, and more certainly united with reality. See "Waking-Up: a neglected model for the afterlife" (above), and also "A Plotinian Account of Intellect," *American Catholic Philosophical Quarterly* 71 (1997), 421–32, after Plotinus, *Ennead* V.5 [32].1.

around the sun! The hypothesis is also an unexpected answer to the Fermi Paradox: if it is very likely that intelligent beings have evolved and prospered elsewhere, why do we see no sign of these extraterrestrials here-now? The answer is that all sign of them has been deliberately excluded from this dream, both to encourage the dreamers to attend to their own affairs, and to provide one of those tantalizing hints (of covert contradiction) that may alert a few to our real situation! Almost the only feature of our experience that counts against the hypothesis is that our experience is sometimes *boring*! Would a competent creator of virtual realities not arrange for the experience at least to be *interesting*, at least in the perspective of its clients? But perhaps it is up to us to *make* it interesting—or be summarily closed down.[64]

The second echo is the cosmological. One other route to the Many Worlds Interpretation is through considering the cosmos as the enactment of a sort of computer program, a notion that is indeed implicit in the very idea of a working, transformative formula. The simplest program to produce our cosmos would be the most generous.

> In general, computing all evolutions of all universes is much cheaper in terms of information requirements than computing just one particular, arbitrarily chosen evolution. Why? Because the Great Programmer's algorithm that systematically enumerates and runs all universes (with all imaginable types of physical laws, wave functions, noise etc.) is *very* short (although it takes time). On the other hand, computing just one particular universe's evolution (with, say, one particular instance of noise), without computing the others, tends to be very expensive, because almost all individual universes are incompressible, as has been shown above. More is less![65]

---

[64] See Kurzweil, *The Singularity Is Near*, 404–5.
[65] Juergen Schmidhuber, "A Computer Scientist's View of Life, the Universe, and Everything," in C. Freksa, ed., *Foundations of Computer Science: Potential—Theory—Cognition: Lecture Notes in Computer Science* (Berlin: Springer, 1997), 201–8 (retrieved from http://www.idsia.ch/~juergen/everything/, accessed December 6, 2023). There are other features of Schmidhuber's speculation (notably the difficulties it raises for inductive inference, and for his apparent, self-refuting, belief that there is only matter in motion, without even subjective meaning) that deserve longer consideration. See also S. Wolfram, *A New Kind of Science* (Champaign, IL: Wolfram Media, Inc., 2002); Seth

Imagine that the programmer is faced by the initial blank that our predecessors called "the Unlimited," *Apeiron*: there are indefinitely many variables to define to get things going. The simplest solution—indeed almost the only rational solution—is to say that each variable be assigned all possible values, in all possible combinations. How else, after all, should the programmer discover what the effects would be—except by running exactly that program if only "in his mind"?[66] *The only way, even for a Creator who knows all that is to be known, to know what some programs do is actually to run the programs.*[67] So the Creator runs that simple program, and it generates all really possible worlds, with exactly the effect we notice: many such worlds evaporate or expand too slowly or too quickly to accomplish anything distinctive; many stagnate or dissolve in mutual hostility. Whether there are any conscious observers in these worlds depends on factors that we don't understand. Not knowing even how or whether material connections somehow "generate" the conscious mind or merely invite it in, we can't tell which worlds, from their mere material nature, will have minds in them, nor which worlds—if minds in fact come into the world from somewhere completely other—will be colonized. This world, at any rate, or the set of worlds that share at least our beginnings, is being lived from within.

Is this story simply a way of speaking? Things are *as if* they were programmed into being, and it is *as if* we are living in a virtual drama. Maybe so—but this merely operationalist account of scientific theory itself suggests that we are dreaming, and can never expect to grasp the *reality* behind our experience. The paradox

Lloyd, *Programming the Universe: a quantum computer scientist takes on the cosmos* (London: Cape, 2006).
[66] See Plotinus, *Ennead* V.8 [31].7, dismissing the idea that the world can have been created: to do so, the Creator must *already* have the world complete "in his mind." In the vocabulary of the Christian Church, the Logos is begotten (and of one substance with the Father), and not made (on which see G. L. Prestige, *God in Patristic Thought* [London: SPCK, 1952], 151), and what has been made was not put together by hands or other tools, but simply by and through that Logos. But this is yet another story.
[67] See Kurzweil, *The Singularity Is Near*, 93: "Wolfram makes the valid point that certain (indeed most) computational processes are not predictable. In other words, we cannot predict future states without running the entire process." The same point applies to the evolutionary history of life here on Earth: it is more difficult to distinguish Design and Darwin than most neo-Darwinian theorists acknowledge!

is that the current picture of that unseen reality is drawing so heavily on the older myth, and issuing in the older moral. This life, this world, is a dream and a delusion, but one that hints to us of some superior power and beauty.

> The realities we see are like shadows of all that is God. The reality we see is as unreal compared to the reality in God as a coloured photograph compared to what it represents.... This whole world is made of shadows, shadows on the wall of a cave, as Plato said.[68]

The speculative cosmologists are drawing on an older story, and, in part, are offering an older moral. But there is one way at least in which the morals differ. If there is ever to be a fully cosmic intelligence owing anything to human history, then the moral is that we should keep the research grants coming![69] The older moral was that, to be acceptable to God, we should do justice and love mercy, as John Winthrop said. The technophile's enthusiasm may rest on a worthy basis: on a real delight in beauty, and a conviction that we can somehow come to share—so to call it—in "the mind of God." But that Mind, in the older synthesis, was the "dance of immortal love,"[70] and the "intelligence" that was to be our guide was better known as love. In drawing on the resources of past philosophy that, perhaps, should be what we chiefly learn, and teach.

> Intellect... has one power for thinking, by which it looks at the things in itself, and one by which it looks at what transcends it by a direct awareness and reception, by which also before it saw only, and by seeing acquired intellect and is one. And that first one is the contemplation of Intellect in its right mind, and the other is Intellect in love, when it goes out of its mind "drunk with the nectar"; then it falls in love, simplified into happiness

---

[68] Cardenal, *Love*, 73, 91.

[69] See, for example, Frank J. Tipler, *The Physics of Immortality: Modern Cosmology, God and the Resurrection of the Dead* (New York: Doubleday, 1994). Kurzweil, in *The Singularity Is Near* (405), similarly proposes that the reason for the simulations is mainly to create "new knowledge," and the best way to avoid being closed down is to continue studying physics (in what is, by hypothesis, a simplified model of the unseen reality).

[70] Porphyry, *Life of Plotinus* 22.54ff; 23.36": *Enneads*, trans. A. H. Armstrong, volume 1, pp. 69–71 (Cambridge, MA:, Harvard University Press, Loeb Classical Library, 1966).

by having its fill, and it is better for it to be drunk with a
drunkenness like this than to be more respectably sober.[71]

To wake up from the dream—or at least to realize that we are
dreaming—is to be animated by our recognition of what's really
real and beautiful. The stories that we tell about that waking, and
about the real world we have—deliberately?—forgotten cannot be
verified by any experiment here-now. They can only be vindicated
(or not) by whether or not we can actually live by them. In making
the attempt, we can take inspiration, intellectual and moral, from
the work of past philosophers, and especially from Platonists.

CODA

Self-conscious moderns often suggest that life and consciousness are at best peripheral: an accidental froth within the larger,
unmeaning, and insensate world. They may even admit that, on
those terms, there is little reason to expect that we, a particular
hominid species on a ball of rock, could have the equipment to
discover any truth about that world. "The Universe is not only
queerer than we suppose, but queerer than we *can* suppose."[72]
We cannot prove otherwise, even if our faith in reason is partly
vindicated—so we think—by the coherence of our speculations
and the power of our technology. That faith is at least a little easier
if we can also believe that reality is, in some way, suited to us.

That very many, or infinitely many, worlds are actual is really
the death of explanation: whatever happens is only what is bound
to happen somewhere, and it might as well be here. It is also the
death of purpose: whatever we propose as a possible course of
action will be what happens, whether in one of the many real
futures, or in some far-off bubble universe. A similar conclusion
follows, as their critics argued, from the strictly Stoic notion,
that there is only one real world and history, which must repeat
itself in infinite time, and perhaps in infinite space as well. Stoic
philosophers hoped that it could be shown that just this actual
world was the only *possible* world as well, or the only one that
embodied an eternal, necessary good. And though they sought
to reject the fatalistic moral—that it won't matter what we do or

---

[71] Plotinus, *Ennead* VI.7 [38].35, 2–28: trans. Armstrong.
[72] J. B. S. Haldane, *Possible Worlds and Other Essays* (London: Heinemann,
1927), 286.

try to do—it is hard to see why we should try to avoid error or seek out the truth. Whatever it is we end up doing or believing is what the Universe requires of us, and there is no escape.

The Platonic analysis of our situation seeks to distinguish the phenomenal worlds that sentient creatures severally inhabit from the physical world of bodies arrayed in space and changing over time. That physical world, in turn, is to be explained by reference to a mathematical system, intuited or remembered by creatures equipped to do so: those "laws of nature" are never perfectly obeyed, those forms are never perfectly embodied. Nor are they the ultimate explanation: mathematicians, so Plato remarked, forget to explain where their firm concepts come from, or why one system rather than another—equally coherent—system is the model for the physical universe. The laws of nature don't explain why anything exists, nor why they are *these* laws. His hope instead was that there was an explanation, in a transcendent Good, the One. Things as they are—and also our own reason—are modeled on the forms implicit in an eternal intellect: ways of being beautiful. That criterion, of beauty, is invoked in judging scientific theories, even though we must also recognize that our private notions of beauty may not be the ones that eventually we learn to love, and that we cannot rule out the unexpected and bizarre from our appreciation of reality. The Universe is *not* queerer than we can imagine—or at least we had better not imagine that it is—but it may be queerer than we first suppose!

Modern speculations weirdly reproduce the debates and stories of earlier, "unscientific" generations. And the very weirdest speculation—that we are inmates of a virtual reality devised by the Cosmic Engineers of the End of Days—is at once a sort of resolution of our current cosmological problems, and an inspiration to return to a more strictly Platonic outlook. "Whether it's reality or a dream, doing what's right is what matters. If it's reality, then for the sake of reality; if it's a dream, then for the purpose of winning friends for when we awaken."[73] Our best recourse is to do justice, to love mercy, and to remember that we owe our life and reason to powers beyond our control and present understanding. We had better hope that our successors and perhaps creators have internalized that message too.

---

[73] Calderón de la Barca, *Life's A Dream* (Boulder, CO: University of Colorado, 2004; first published as *La vida es sueño* in 1635), 137–38.

11.
Changing Kinds[1]

FLUID IDENTITIES

We have probably always known, for as long as we have known anything, that we and the world are always changing, even if we can also hope that some things stay the same, or reappear. We notice, or build, landmarks. We mark off days, and months, and seasons, which repeat an endless cycle. Even if all particular things, places, people are mortal, there will be something in them that is never lost, that we can name and remember. Few of us are ever content simply to "go with the flow," and greet each new day dawning as a radical beginning, shedding all past commitments and all long-term projects.[2] Indeed, we probably couldn't, at least without abandoning both language and convenient habits.

> Children are dumb to say how hot the day is,
> How hot the scent is of the summer rose,
> How dreadful the black wastes of evening sky,
> How dreadful the tall soldiers drumming by.
> But we have speech, to chill the angry day,
> And speech, to dull the rose's cruel scent.
> We spell away the overhanging night,
> We spell away the soldiers and the fright.

---

[1] An earlier version was published as "Changing Kinds—Aristotle and the Aristotelians," *Diametros* 44 (2015), 19–34. DOI: 10.13153/diam.45.2015.794. I touched on similar issues in "The Ethics of Taxonomy: a neo-Aristotelian Synthesis," in *Animal Ethics: Past and Present Perspectives*, ed. Evangelos D. Protopapadakis (Berlin: Logos Verlag, 2012), 38–58.

[2] See also "The End of the Ages," in David Seed, ed., *Imagining Apocalypse: studies in cultural crisis* (London: Macmillan, and New York: St Martin's Press, 2000), 27–44. A slightly different version was published in *Philosophical Futures*.

There's a cool web of language winds us in,
Retreat from too much joy or too much fear:
We grow sea-green at last and coldly die
In brininess and volubility.
But if we let our tongues lose self-possession,
Throwing off language and its watery clasp
Before our death, instead of when death comes,
Facing the wide glare of the children's day,
Facing the rose, the dark sky and the drums,
We shall go mad no doubt and die that way.[3]

Graves's poem gestures towards an unfiltered, unregimented, always-present, flow of pure experience, more plausibly perhaps than William James's talk of a "blooming, buzzing confusion" as a human infant's first experience.[4] But infantile experience is already structured — and so also is all animal experience: we are born into a world we did not make, already equipped to ignore whatever we did not need to know, already sensing the world through species-specific filters.[5] Whatever we find out later, and learn also to speak about, is built on top of that nec-essary ignorance. On the one hand, we may learn new words, and entertain new thoughts, about a Real World behind and beyond our experience, speaking of the Invisible World with words and images drawn entirely from the Visible.[6] On the other, we may sometimes feel that there can be no words to encom-pass that Beyond. It is whatever it is, without acknowledging our constant hopes and fears, our easy discriminations. Love-craft was not entirely wrong (though unnecessarily gruesome) in saying that "when we cross the line to the boundless and hideous unknown — the shadow-haunted Outside — we must remember to leave our humanity — and terrestrialism — at the

---

[3] Robert Graves, "The Cool Web" (1927), *Collected Poems* (London: Cassell, 1975), 37.
[4] William James, *The Principles of Psychology* (2 vols, London: Macmillan, 1890), 1:488.
[5] On which see J. von Uexkuell, *Theoretical Biology*, trans. D. L. Mackinnon (London: Kegan Paul, 1926); and "A stroll through the worlds of animals and men," in C. H. Schiller, ed., *Instinctive Behavior* (New York: Interna-tional University Press, 1957), 5–80.
[6] See "Metaphors and Reality," *International Journal of Philosophical Studies*, 2023: https://www.tandfonline.com/doi/full/10.1080/09672559.2023.2287636. Accessed July 31, 2024.

threshold."[7] His error, or at least his questionable choice, was to imagine that the Unknown was properly considered "hideous." Aristotle had more faith, adapting a remark of Heracleitus about finding gods even in the kitchen (or possibly in the earth-closet), and spoke rather of admiring all living things, however seemingly small and base, "knowing that in all of them there is something natural and beautiful" — even, indeed, divine.[8]

The wholly invisible world that lies behind and beyond experience is — obviously — beyond experience. We may seek to enlarge our own experience through mathematical intuition and imaginative sympathy with whatever other creatures we encounter in our world. Some philosophers have imagined that we can only advance by stripping away all merely "emotional" responses, positing the Real World as entirely neutral, beyond our conceptions either of good or ill, beauty or deformity. Any attempt to live by such a vision is almost certain to be hypocritical: we cannot so easily abandon our natural attachments, or even our fond beliefs. Others, like Plotinus, concluded instead that the Real World was the living communion of all real points of view, to be recognized *in toto* by "Intellect" (*Nous*), or "Spirit":

> If one likens it to a living richly varied sphere, or imagines it as a thing all faces, shining with living faces, or as all the pure souls running together into the same place, with no deficiencies but having all that is their own, and universal Intellect seated on their summits so that the region is illuminated by intellectual light — if one imagined it like this one would be seeing it somehow as one sees another from outside; but one must become that, and make oneself the contemplation.[9]

---

[7] "Letter to Farnsworth Wright, July 5, 1927," 6–10, 7: https://www.jstor.org/stable/26868482. Accessed July 31, 2024.

[8] Aristotle, *De Partibus Animalium* 1.645a15–23f., identified as Heracleitos in Diels-Kranz, *Fragmente der Vorsokratiker*, 146 (22A9). The anecdote about Heracleitos is discussed by Pavel Gregoric, "The Heraclitus Anecdote: De Partibus Animalium i 5.645a17–23," *Ancient Philosophy* 21 (2001). Gregoric dismisses the suggestion that Heracleitos was at stool (see Donald Robertson, "On the Story of Heraclitus told by Aristotle": *Proceedings of the Cambridge Philological Society* 10 [1938], 169–71), arguing instead that the story relies on a distinction, which Heracleitos is dismissing, between a bread-oven and the hearth which heated the space where guests would expect to be welcomed.

[9] Plotinus, *Ennead* VI.7 [38].15, 25–34: trans. Armstrong. See my "The Sphere with Many Faces," *Dionysius* 34 (2016), 8–26.

To understand or even glimpse that vision would take me too far afield. Let me instead consider *our* worlds, embedded perhaps in that Real World, but experienced here-now as something to be extracted from it: a partial realization or reflection of the larger, invisible, realities. We did not make the Real World, but perhaps we are making our own: the visible, fluid, reality is not simply *given* us, as if we had no contribution to make to our own experience of it. We need not suppose that the visible worlds are fixed, or clear, or final. Maybe even the Real World is still in process.

> What we must completely get away from is the notion that the world as it now exists is a rational whole; we must think of its unity not by the analogy of a picture of which all the parts exist at once but by the analogy of a drama where, if it is good enough, the full meaning of the first scene only becomes apparent with the final curtain; and we are in the middle of this.[10]

Temple, of course, could offer no *proof* that the world, as an ongoing drama, ever will make sense. The Final Observer mentioned in an earlier chapter may still experience no resolution, nor any gathering of threads, nor vindication of all virtuous endeavour. Belief in inevitable progress, especially in a godless cosmos, is absurd, a mere relic of the hope that "God is working His purpose out."[11] Relying on any such vindication, indeed, may be a serious moral error, as though the value of any present creature (human or non-human) rests only on some distant, final, outcome, and its contribution to that end.[12] Wren-Lewis's rebuke is to the point:

---

[10] William Temple, cited by F. A. Iremonger, *Life of William Temple* (Oxford: Clarendon Press, 1948), 537–38. According to Jonathan Sacks (*The Dignity of Difference*, 2nd edition [London: Continuum, 2003], 96), the Rabbi Akiva taught in the second century AD that God "left the world unfinished so that it could be completed by the work of human beings."

[11] A hymn composed by Arthur Campbell Ainger in 1894. In the last verse, Ainger further acknowledges that "All we can do is nothing worth unless God blesses the deed;/ Vainly we hope for the harvest-tide till God gives life to the seed; Yet near and nearer draws the time, the time that shall surely be,/ When the earth shall be filled with the glory of God as the waters cover the sea." *New English Hymnal*, 791.

[12] This is indeed the dire implication of much well-meaning advocacy of "effective altruism," according to which imagined far-future goods should be pursued at whatever cost to currently real well-being: an "unhealthy fancy," as Chesterton observed, that "upset[s] a human sanity that is certain for

When the prophets of the Bible raved about idolatry, they meant just this sort of mystical subordination of man to the great system of nature. Against this, those who have the religion of Jesus want to assert that people do *not* acquire significance by performing any sort of function, however lofty, in any larger system, however universal. They can have absolute significance *as individuals*, by the simple process of giving it to each other in ordinary personal relationships. The Christian believes this because he holds that the Absolute God, whose name is love, is present in personal relationships, but he might welcome a *real* atheist who held the same personalist values, in the name of what [H. J.] Blackham [1923–2009] calls "the self-sufficiency of perishable things," as an ally against all attempts to resurrect the Great God Pan.[13]

Stapledon himself, as I mentioned earlier, offered an alternative to cosmic idolatry, founded only in the immediate experience of personal attachment, "the little atom of community" he shared with his wife:[14] a moral, even if not a metaphysical, foundation.

We must grant that the world of our experience is fluid, and that we ourselves are helping to guide its changes. We are not *destined* for defeat, nor destined to succeed. Things as they already are, however they may be, need not entirely limit our imaginations, nor our projects. Nor need we suppose, as Wells perhaps supposed,[15] that we should change our plans and purposes to fit in with any imagined cosmic purpose. And yet we may also hesitate to endorse an "Orwellian" Anti-realism of the sort described above.

We must see things objectively, as we do a tree; and understand that they exist whether we like them or not. We must not try and turn them into something different by the mere exercise of our minds, as if we were witches.[16]

---

the sake of something that is of necessity uncertain": *All Things Considered* (London: Methuen, 1908), 216.
[13] John Wren-Lewis, Letter to *The Observer*, September 10, 1961 (cited earlier). Wren-Lewis perhaps misjudged the nature of that "Great God Pan" (which is to say, The All).
[14] Stapledon, *Last and First Men*, 333.
[15] Wells, *Anticipations*, 248.
[16] *Illustrated London News*, November 22, 1913, in *Collected Works*, 29 (San Francisco: Ignatius Press, 1988), 589, cited by A. de Silva in *Brave New Family*, ed. A. de Silva (San Francisco: Ignatius Press, 1990), 15.

Chesterton's chief complaint against Darwinian theory, at least it was promoted in his day, was that it denied that there were any stable, "natural," norms by which to live.

> The sub-conscious popular instinct against Darwinism was . . . that when once one begins to think of man as a shifting and alterable thing, it is always easy for the strong and crafty to twist him into new shapes for all kinds of unnatural purposes. The popular instinct sees in such developments the possibility of backs bowed and hunch-backed for their burden, or limbs twisted for their task. It has a very well-grounded guess that whatever is done swiftly and systematically will mostly be done by a successful class and almost solely in their interests. It has therefore a vision of unhuman hybrids and half-human experiments much in the style of Mr. Wells's Island of Dr Moreau . . . The rich man may come to be breeding a tribe of dwarfs to be his jockeys, and a tribe of giants to be his hall-porters.[17]

And again:

> If evolution simply means that a positive thing called an ape turned very slowly into a positive thing called a man, then it is stingless for the most orthodox; for a personal God might just as well do things slowly as quickly, especially if, like the Christian God, he were outside time. But if it means anything more, it means that there is no such thing as an ape to change, and no such thing as a man for him to change into.[18]

Species, in Darwinian theory, are not clearly distinct and stable entities, any more than families, or races: they are only sets of interbreeding populations, whose genetic and phenotypic profile gradually changes over many generations. On the older view, *humanity* was something sacred, not to be bred or reared or engineered as if it were only "animal." On the older view, reproduction must be tied to intimate copulation: all human beings must be born "by nature," not manufactured to a prior blueprint. Even "animals" should not be bred promiscuously,

---

[17] Chesterton, *What's Wrong with the World*, 259.
[18] Chesterton, *Orthodoxy*, 34.

though we seem much less concerned for hybridizing plants. On the newer, post-Darwinian, view, human beings are simply a transient primate species, the only current hominins: the species is bound to change over many generations, and its pathways are defined by a manipulable genome. Our descendants may be of many distinct species, perhaps incorporating genes from many other lines, whether by "natural" accident or by experimental genetic engineering. Genetic information is routinely transmitted, even amongst eukaryotes like us, "horizontally" by bacterial and viral infection, as well as "vertically" by reproduction. The engineers may—or may not—wish that some descendant lines be "human" in the sense we now prefer, comprising individual persons who must act for reasons.[19] They may as easily require that most lines are mostly "slavish," in the sense that Aristotle proposed, that they are driven only by desire and fear, without any conception of doing something because it's *right*: call them "domestic" humans.[20]

The genetic engineers for whom a genome is more like a loose-leaf folder than a coherent volume, an accumulation of fairly effective strategies for reproduction, have ended—as Chesterton prophesied—by denying the existence of Humanity, as well as of God. As Freeman Dyson has proposed: "We are moving rapidly into the post-Darwinian era, when species will no longer exist, and the evolution of life will again be communal."[21] Genes will be

---

[19] Cordwainer Smith (also known as Paul Linebarger) imagined the recreation of "humanity" as one other species amongst many engineered animals, in *The Rediscovery of Man* (London: Gateway, 2010 [1993]). Those recreated hominids imagine themselves, for no good reason, to be "superior" to the supposedly "animal" kinds, the Underpeople. See especially "The Ballad of Lost C'Mell" (1962; ibid., 315–37), where one of the Lords of the Instrumentality begins to see his error: "True men, one hundred percent human, they looked weird and horrible because they or their ancestors had undergone bodily modifications to meet the life conditions of a thousand worlds. Underpeople, the animal-derived 'homunculi,' were there, most of them in their work clothes, and they looked more human than did the human beings from the outer worlds. None were allowed to grow up if they were less than half the size of man, or more than six times the size of man. They all had to have human features and acceptable human voices. The punishment for failure in their elementary schools was death."
[20] See "Slaves and Citizens," *Philosophy* 60 (1985), 27–46; "Slaves, Servility and Noble Deeds," *Philosophical Inquiry* (Thessaloniki) 25.3–4 (2003), 165–76.
[21] Freeman Dyson, "The Darwinian Interlude," *Technology Review*, March 1, 2005: https://www.technologyreview.com/2005/03/01/274577/

shared around as easily amongst us as they are amongst bacteria (for which *species*-distinctions have always been moot). Dyson, it seems to me, is too optimistic in his description of the early years:

> In the post-Darwinian era, biotechnology will be domesticated. There will be do-it-yourself kits for gardeners, who will use gene transfer to breed new varieties of roses and orchids. Also, biotech games for children, played with real eggs and seeds rather than with images on a screen. Genetic engineering, once it gets into the hands of the general public, will give us an explosion of biodiversity. Designing genomes will be a new art form, as creative as painting or sculpture. Few of the new creations will be masterpieces, but all will bring joy to their creators and diversity to our fauna and flora.[22]

The current "human" population is only a phase or fragment. This may perhaps lead some of us to worry about the other tribes of Earth, recalling that we are all related to each other.[23] It may as easily lead many of us to treat vulnerable human beings as badly as we have always treated "animals," with the added twist that manipulating or experimenting upon our conspecifics will be of still greater value — to their owners.

Will our descendants be any less "slavish" if they have *chosen* to step away from previous forms of humanity, or at least to make that choice for their own immediate descendants? Should parents *not* be concerned to help their offspring prosper? What if such prosperity will depend on their having forms better suited to the fluid future? Change will happen anyway, by whatever mix of Darwinian selection, accidental isolation, fashion, and even (perhaps) the pressure or attraction of "supernatural" forms. Better, perhaps, to intervene as far as we are able (though any sensible parent would also know that we know too little of the future to be sure of adapting to it beforehand).

---

the-darwinian-interlude-2/, accessed September 19, 2024. Dyson takes his cue from Carl Woese's "A New Biology for a New Century," in *Microbiology and Molecular Biology Reviews* 68.2 (June, 2004), 173–86: http://mmbr.asm.org/cgi/content/abstract/68/2/173, accessed March 2, 2015.

[22] Dyson, ibid.: https://www.technologyreview.com/2005/03/01/274577/the-darwinian-interlude-2/.

[23] See Richard Dawkins, "Gaps in the Mind," in Paola Cavalieri and Peter Singer, eds., *The Great Ape Project* (New York: St. Martin's, 1993), 81–87.

ARISTOTLE'S ERRORS?

Is resistance to this imagined future founded in obsolete biological speculation, specifically Aristotle's? Aristotle, it is often
still supposed, held science back for centuries. He is said to have
believed that women have fewer teeth than men, that the heart
rather than the brain was the principal organ of feeling and
reflection, that there were "natural slaves," that the sun travelled
round the earth, that heavy things fell faster than light things,
that some living things arose by spontaneous generation out of
stagnant soil or water, that being female was a defect on a par
with dwarfism, and that biological species were immutable. More
damagingly still, he suggested that "scientific knowledge" could
be assured only by demonstrative deduction from a handful of
first principles, that only what happens "always or for the most
part" was important for philosophical enquiry, and that working
with one's hands was no proper life for a gentleman. Medieval
thinkers, it is widely supposed, preferred to believe Aristotle
rather than their senses, and only the glad Renaissance set us
free from (supposed) scholastic darkness. Scholars may dispute
almost all these claims, observing that either Aristotle did not
say these things at all, or, at least, that he did not suppose them
incontrovertible. Medieval historians, especially, have empha-
sised the long European and Islamic pursuit of truth by whatever
careful means, drawing perhaps on Aristotelian texts but never
simply declaiming them. Demonstrating the errors of those who
thus list "Aristotle's Errors" is beyond my current brief, except
to emphasise that the "Master of them that know" was indeed a
polymath, a careful enquirer, and an honest philosopher, always
ready to re-assess his own and others' convictions.

The particular issue for this chapter concerns biological kinds,
the notion that Aristotelian species were immutable, and that
it was only with the emergence of evolutionary theory in the
nineteenth century (not only, and not earliest, in Darwin's *Origin of Species*) that we shook free of the old Aristotelian synthesis.
Charles Darwin was not the first to conclude that there were
forms of life before us, nor yet that all forms of life, both past
and present, were genealogically related. He was not the first to
try to exclude all final causes from his account of nature. He was
not the only one to notice that in a Malthusian struggle for life it
is generally those with some obvious superiority (of strength, or

wit, or versatility — and also, kindness) that survive to breed. Conversely, he was not himself responsible for every element of the Neo-Darwinian synthesis that has come to dominate mainstream biological circles, and the mind of the chattering classes, any more than Aristotle was responsible for every element of the "Aristotelian Synthesis." Notoriously, Darwin was himself "Lamarckian," in allowing for the inheritance of acquired characteristics, and pre-Mendelian in that he did not know how inheritance could pass particular characteristics down, rather than blending, and so homogenizing, intrusive variations. He was a gradualist (supposing that evolutionary change happened by almost indiscernible increments — fortuitously, in the same direction — over very many generations) and uniformitarian, rejecting the then-prevalent idea that the history of life was littered with catastrophe. Neither of these notions now seems certain: catastrophe and sudden, radical changes now seem much more likely. He was neither the first to find it difficult to reconcile natural evil and orthodox theism, nor as militantly atheistical as some of his disciples. There are traces in his writings of an intolerable racism, but also clear evidence that he was personally and politically humane — very much as is true of Aristotle.[24]

But what was the Aristotelian Synthesis, at least so far as it concerns Biology? He argued against the Empedoclean story (which has come to be thought Darwinian in spirit) that present-day organisms are only the survivors of an era in which all manner of combinations and degrees of separation were tried out. On the contrary, biological form is so well adapted to need that the teleological implication could not be ignored: we don't just happen to have hands, heart, lungs, and the rest, as if those things could ever have existed separately and then, by accidental conjunction, been conjoined. Nature does nothing in vain, and whatever widespread characters and organs there may be will exist for a purpose — both the welfare and survival of the organism in question, and the continued being of the terrestrial cycle of existence. That cycle, he thought, has been going on "forever," and the generations of humankind are infinite, though we have

---

[24] See S. R. L. Clark, *Biology and Christian Ethics* (Cambridge: Cambridge University Press, 2000); "Deconstructing Darwin," in Norma Thompson, ed., *Instilling Ethics* (Lanham, MD: Rowman and Littlefield, 2000), 119–140.

no record of them thanks to recurrent disaster.[25] Proverbs and folk-stories are "the remnants of philosophy that perished in the great disasters that have befallen mankind, and were recorded for their brevity and wit,"[26] and, by the same token, we can ourselves expect that even our modern civilization will evaporate one day. There have always been human beings, and other creatures of roughly the same sort as nowadays, all struggling to maintain their species-forms despite disease and shipwreck. Not every element of this account was ever acceptable to Abrahamic believers, who insisted rather that this world had a definite beginning (not all that long ago), and that someday it would have a final end (not merely a familiar collapse and subsequent revival, but an end to temporal becoming). But at least this much remained (perhaps) a dogma: the world of living creatures we inhabit and compose is teleologically directed, and its variations are aimed at (partly) realizing the forms implicit in the Mind of God. There is something that makes for a *good* dog (or horse or human) because there is something that makes for a *dog* (or horse or human): particular examples are more or less defective, more or less deformed, by failures in their material base, or errors of their own judgment. What creatures of a given sort *should* be (if there is any doubt) is shown in what they generally are. "Underneath such descriptions is an idea of a singular, universal body, an idealized composite of the 'best' features of real bodies"[27]—a notion given some force by the undoubted beauty of composite photographs.[28] Hybrids, on the other hand, appear grotesque or even offensive, falling between two or more different ideals of beauty and biological propriety. Even hard-headed biologists, I have found, are somewhat

---

[25] Aristotle, *Physics* 3.206a26.
[26] Aristotle, *On Philosophy*, fragment 8; Rose, in W. D. Ross, ed. *Works of Aristotle, Vol 12: Select Fragments* (London: Oxford University Press, 1952), 77, fragment 10. Everything has already been discovered, and forgotten, an infinite—or at least an indefinite—number of times: *De Caelo* 270b19-20, *Meteorologica* 339b27-8, *Politics* 7.1329b25-6. I have addressed such theories in *How the Worlds Became: philosophy and the oldest stories* (Brooklyn, NY: Angelico Press, 2023).
[27] Ruth Barcan, *Nudity* (Oxford: Berg, 2004), 34.
[28] See Francis Galton, *Inquiries into Human Faculty and its Development*, 2nd edition (London: Dent and Dutton, 1907), 240-41; J. H. Langlois and L. A. Roggman, "Attractive faces are only average": *Psychological Science* 1 (1990), 115-21.

disturbed even by such minimal attempts at cross-breeding as the "geep" (a hybrid of sheep and goat).[29] Attempts to hybridize human and chimpanzee—with a view to inventing a better laboratory model for human disease—are also found disgusting, at least among the European heirs of Abraham.[30]

There were clear theological reasons for the Enlightenment rejection of formal and final causes: we should not suppose that we can tell what goals God may have in His creation, nor should we "idolize" particular recurrent patterns. To see and understand what actually *is*, we had better empty our perceptions of all easy judgments about what is "beautiful" in nature, or what "perverse," and concentrate on simpler, even mechanical, models. Values, Forms, and Final Causes should be abandoned along with fairies and vital spirits. So Thomas Sprat, in writing his proleptic *History of the Royal Society*, wrote vehemently of the Real Philosophy:

> The poets of old to make all things look more venerable than they were devised a thousand false Chimaeras; on every Field, River, Grove and Cave they bestowed a Fantasm of their own making: With these they amazed the world.... And in the modern Ages these Fantastical Forms were reviv'd and possessed Christendom.... All which abuses if those acute Philosophers did not promote, yet they were never able to overcome; nay, not even so much as King Oberon and his invisible Army. But from the time in which the Real Philosophy has appear'd there is scarce any whisper remaining of such horrors.... The cours of things goes quietly along, in its own true channel of Natural Causes and Effects. For this we are beholden to Experiments; which though they have not yet completed the discovery of the true world, yet they have already vanquished those wild inhabitants of the false world, that us'd to astonish the minds of men.[31]

---

[29] See "Animal Procedures Committee Report on Biotechnology," (London: Animal Procedures Committee, 2001).

[30] There are, of course, more reasons to find the program disgusting than merely dislike of hybrids: that anyone could seriously suppose that such a hybrid would be sufficiently *like* mainline humans as to be a useful model, and also sufficiently *unlike* to have no moral or legal rights against her "owners," speaks very poorly of the researchers' imagination and sound sense.

[31] Thomas Sprat, *History of the Royal Society*, 3rd edition (New York: Elibron, 2005 [1722]), 340.

He was imitating Athanasius of Alexandria (ca AD 296–373):

> And formerly everywhere was filled with the deceit of the oracles, and the utterances of those in Delphi and Dodona and Boeotia and Lycia and Libya and Egypt and Cabiri and the Pythoness were admired in the imagination of human beings. But now, since Christ is announced everywhere, their madness has also ceased and no longer is there anyone among them giving oracles. Formerly demons deceived human fancy, taking possession of springs or rivers, wood or stone, and by their tricks thus stupefied the simple. But now, after the divine manifestation of the Word has taken place, their illusion has ceased. For by the sign of the cross, if a human being but use it, he drives away their deceits.[32]

There were at least two ways for this insight or revelation to develop. On the first, all such frauds and fancies were dispelled so that we could begin to see and listen to the *real* Logos. The second—and (sadly) the more influential in mainstream scientific circles—was to take a nominalist and incoherently materialist metaphysics utterly for granted.[33] The world of our experience, we could partly agree with Plotinus, is, in a way, a painted corpse:[34] the forms and beauties that we encounter may be, as I acknowledged earlier, our very own creations. "Postmodern nominalism and scientific materialism, rejecting the idea of universals, hold that 'corn,' 'goat,' and 'human,' for instance, are merely terms possessing no existential value or metaphysical significance of their own, signifiers (with no signified) meaning only whatever we wish them to mean."[35] The same must be true, on this account, of mathematical terms and the concepts of high physics.[36] The underlying reality has, of itself, no human meaning,

---

[32] Athanasius, *On the Incarnation* (written ca AD 318), trans. John Behr; preface by C. S. Lewis (New York: St. Vladimir's Seminary Press, 2014 [1944]), 102 (chapter 8, para. 47).

[33] See Alexei V. Nesteruk, *Light from the East: theology, science, and the Eastern Orthodox tradition* (Minneapolis: Augsburg Fortress, 2003).

[34] *Ennead* II.4 [12].5, 18.

[35] Michael Martin, *The Submerged Reality: Sophiology and the turn to a poetic metaphysics* (Kettering, OH: Angelico Press, 2015), 35.

[36] Though practising mathematicians usually manage to maintain a proper Platonism. "The Platonistic view is the only one tenable. Thereby I mean the view that mathematics describes a non-sensual reality, which exists

no simple boundary lines, no beauties, *and no defects*: or at least inevitable variations are not intrinsically defective. Oddly, hardly any apologist for scientific materialism has grasped or answered the problem, that we have then no grounds for identifying or extrapolating any observed pattern in nature or the mind, and no right to be surprised by any sudden alteration, for example in biological lines.[37]

Aristotle himself did indeed insist on teleological explanation: we have eyes *to see with*, and hands *to handle things*. He also argued that human beings, just as such, had a characteristic *ergon*: something that only human beings did, and needed to do well in order to live well. That *ergon* was *deliberate action*: the problem for all human beings who have considered what is best for them to do is — exactly — to determine what is best to do, and do it. Human life is *praktike tis tou logou ekhontos*, a life of doing things for reasons, and to live it well we need appropriate ethical and intellectual virtues. *To anthropinon agathon psukhes energeia ginetai kat'areten, ei de pleious hai aretai, kata ten aristen kai teleiotaten*: the human good turns out to be an activity of soul in accordance with virtue, and, if there are many virtues, then according to the best and most complete.[38] What in detail that amounts to can be put aside. Here it is important to note that though *only* human beings have this option, not all human beings — all our conspecifics — have it. Some, as Aristotle is notorious for claiming, are incapable of making their own decisions, or acting for any other motive than immediate desire or fear. "Natural slaves" may either be like the imagined savages of northern lands, who live entirely by impulse, or like the imagined, subservient subjects

independently of the human mind and is only perceived, and probably perceived very incompletely, by the human mind": Kurt Gödel, "Basic theorems on the foundations of mathematics" (1951), in *Collected Works*, ed. S. Feferman, J. Dawson, W. Goldfarb, C. Parsons, R. Solovay, and J. van Heijenoort (Oxford: Oxford University Press, 1995), 3:322–23.

[37] See Robert Chambers, *Vestiges of the Natural History of Creation* (Leicester: Leicester University Press, and New York: Humanities Press, 1969 [1884]), after Charles Babbage, *Ninth Bridgewater Treatise Fragment* (London: Frank Cass, 1967 [1837]), 34.ff. Chambers's pre-Darwinian evolutionary theory was mocked, by T. H. Huxley amongst others, as rejecting proper scientific, inductive, method. The same charge was later made against Darwin.

[38] Aristotle, *Nicomachean Ethics* 1.1098a16–18; see Clark, *Aristotle's Man: speculations upon Aristotelian anthropology* (Oxford: Clarendon Press, 1975; 2nd edition, 1983).

of the eastern empire, who do not dare to rebel.[39] Others of our conspecifics — chiefly (he imagined) women — can reach their own decisions about what to do, but cannot be expected so to overrule their emotional impulse as to stick by a good decision.[40] Manual labourers, living hand to mouth, may rarely have the luxury to cultivate good ethical and intellectual habits.[41] And even the children of more favoured classes must learn good habits, by mere obedience, before they can live at their own command. The human species, in short, is not as uniform as we might suppose, and Aristotle's advice, inevitably, is offered mainly to adult, freeborn, males not ground down by banausic labour.

Our species is not uniform, and neither are other species. Aristotle's account of reproduction does not involve the repeated imposition of a single species-form. Rather is it — at least among familiar animals — the *father's* form that works on blood provided by the mother: it is the failure to reproduce that form *exactly* that results in female offspring, or in other familiar variations. One mare, he says, was named Honest Lady, because her foals resembled the father so closely.[42] So Aristotle's biological theories are closer to the Darwinian than is usually expected. A more openly *Platonic* theory, supposing that there are Eternal Forms active in the world, lay at the root of Richard Owen's preferred evolutionary theory.[43] By Owen's account, resemblances within a species — or a wider taxon — were the effect of an archetype (Human, Horse, or Beech Tree and the like). Darwin deliberately replaced *archetypes* (which he considered metaphysical) by *ancestors*. Human beings resemble each other so closely because

---

[39] See my "Slaves and Citizens," *Philosophy* 60 (1985), 27–46; and "Slaves, Servility and Noble Deeds," *Philosophical Inquiry* (Thessaloniki) 25.3–4 (2003), 165–76.

[40] See "Aristotle's Woman," *History of Political Thought* 3 (1982), 177–91 (reprinted in *The Political Animal*, 11–22).

[41] "No-one can practise excellence who is living the life of a mechanic or labourer": Aristotle, *Politics* 3.1278a21 (my translation).

[42] Aristotle *Politics* 2.1262a. See D. M. Balme, "Aristotle's Biology was not Essentialist," *Archiv für Geschichte der Philosophie* 62.1 (1980), 1–12.

[43] Hunterian professor of comparative anatomy from 1836 to 1856, and superintendent of the natural history collections at the British Museum from 1856 to 1883: see his *On the Archetype and Homologies of the Vertebrate Skeleton* (London: Richard and John E. Taylor, 1848); see also David Hull, ed., *Darwin and his Critics. The Reception of Darwin's Theory of Evolution by the Scientific Community* (Oxford: Oxford University Press, 1973).

we are all descended from a fairly recent common ancestor (as
pre-Darwinian theologians had also said).[44] It seems indeed
that our species has endured bottlenecks, in which the human
population was reduced to no more than a few thousand. Other
species, even other primate species, are much less homogeneous.
The record (incorporating fossils, genes, and folklore) also suggests that there were other hominid species, with languages and
traditions of their own[45]—and likely enough to have been human
in the sense preferred by Aristotle.

Aristotelian biology, in brief, was not essentialist: his taxonomies were devised for expository convenience, in that all or most
of any particular taxon could be briefly described before advancing
into detail. Individual creatures had their qualities *because their
parents did:* even though the mother "only" provided the stuff
that was to be moulded by the father's *pneuma,* that matter had
its own influence on the outcome. Aristotelian mothers were
not simply incubators, as popular Greek opinion supposed. Outcomes could be variable, and Aristotle also identified some common animals as—relatively—"deformed."[46] It is even possible

---

[44] See Philip Almond, "Adam, Pre-Adamites, and Extra-Terrestrial Beings
in Early Modern Europe," *Journal of Religious History* 30.2 (2006), 163–74,
168–69: "Thus, for example, in 1625, the philosopher Nathanael Carpenter in
his *Geography* maintained that Moses' motivation, in writing his genealogical
lists was so that all people would understand themselves to be descended
from the same original 'then which there is no greater meanes to conciliate
and ioyne mens affections for mutuall amitie and conversation' (Nathanael
Carpenter, *Geography Delineated Forth in Two Books* [Oxford, 1625], 2:207).
Similarly, in 1656, the year of La Peyrère's *Men before Adam,* John White
remarked in his commentary on Genesis that the reason for God's having
created only one couple was to unite all men in love to one another so
that 'we cannot shut up our bowels of compassion from any man, of what
Nation or Kindred soever he be.' (John White, *A Commentary upon the Three
First Chapters of Genesis* [London, 1656], 1:111.) Some forty years later, Richard
Kidder, Bishop of Bath and Wells, suggested that the origin of all people
was from one man to ensure that claims of racial superiority could not arise,
that 'men might not boast and vaunt of their extraction and original . . . and
that they might think themselves under an obligation to love and assist each
other as proceeding from the same original and common parent' (Richard
Kidder, *A Commentary on the Five Books of Moses* [London, 1694], 1:6)."
[45] See my "Elves, Hobbits, Trolls and Talking Beasts," in *Creaturely Theology,* eds. Celia Deane-Drummond and David Clough (London: SCM
Press, 2009), 151–67.
[46] Lobsters, for example, are "deformed," and use their claws for other
than "their natural purpose": *De Partibus Animalium* 684a35f: see, further,
Aristotle's Man, 28–32.

that he had in mind a chronological or historical version of the descent of an original humanity described by Plato's *Timaeus*.[47] The relative deformity of different biological kinds is as necessary for the ongoing life of the whole as the relative deformity of women: "deformity" establishes, and has always already established (over infinite generations), the whole array of mutually dependent life-forms. That array, perhaps, is conscious of itself, and capable of deliberate change, only within our species. Only human beings—but not all of them—are able to view the world "objectively," and consider how best to change it (if we can).

CONVERGENCE AND TRANSFORMATION

The post-Darwinian and Aristotelian worlds are different, but not because Aristotelian species were fixed. In the older synthesis, the world is always being repopulated, from a surviving remnant, and very similar forms and functions are realized in each age. Darwinians suppose instead that there was a real beginning to all terrestrial life (though how it happened is still, at least, contentious), and that all living lines since then have travelled a more or less random course through possibility. The variations in each line are random, and which variation chances to have the reproductive edge on any particular occasion is no less so. It is possible to modify this picture slightly, without entirely subverting the original Darwinian insight: maybe every genome retains successful adaptations of the past, ready to be reinvented on some environmental cue; maybe there are a limited number of possibly successful types, so that different lines converge; so that, for example, there are marsupial wolves as well as placental ones. Maybe there might even have been *humans* of a kind, evolved from dinosaurs in the past, or in an alternate history.[48] Nonetheless, there is at least a bias in the post-Darwinian view against an Aristotelian (even if the latter is not exactly Aristotle's). The lines that make up a species—a set of interbreeding populations—may be changeable, and there may be no absolute

---

[47] Aristotle, *De Partibus Animalium* 686a25f; Plato, *Timaeus* 91b.
[48] See Simon Conway Morris, *The Crucible of Creation: The Burgess Shale and the Rise of Animals*, 2nd edition (Oxford: Oxford University Press, 1999), writing against Stephen Jay Gould, *Wonderful Life: The Burgess Shale and the Nature of History* (London: Random House, 2000).

division between one species and another, whether in Darwinian or in Aristotelian theory. But an Aristotelian lineage is animated, as it were, by *pneuma*, working with maternal matter to try out the possibilities of each embodied paternal form. The notion that we could *breed* human stock, as we have also bred domestic animals and plants, is easily available (and proposed by Plato as a way of securing nearly incorruptible and clever rulers), but we cannot — on the ancient terms — expect to disengage reproduction and copulation. There is no separable *seed*, to be preserved or altered. In the post-Darwinian universe, there is a literal human seed, which can in principle be altered.

The vision is usually reckoned dystopian, whether by Aldous Huxley (*Brave New World*) or Cordwainer Smith (*The Rediscovery of Man*). Sometimes it is presented with a more challenging or even utopian twist, as by H. G. Wells (*First Men in the Moon*), Larry Niven and J. E. Pournelle (*The Mote in God's Eye*), Frank Herbert (*Hellstrom's Hive*), or C. J. Cherryh (*Cyteen*). An apparently obsolete idea of human "sacredness" mostly hovers in the background of all such visions. The alternative, caste-engineered society, may be modelled openly on the life of eusocial insects, or on merely manufactured, "robot" intelligence. Post-Darwinian theorists seem content: if E. O. Wilson was right to claim that "morality has no other demonstrable ultimate function" than "to keep human genetic material intact,"[49] the more variant species we, or our masters, engineer for different social and physical environments the better — if preserving elements specifically of *our* genome are really what we either do want or should want.

On the one hand, there seems, on post-Darwinian pretexts, no good reason *not* to engineer our progeny (or more probably the progeny of the poor) to suit "our" needs (or rather the needs and wishes of those who control the engineers). On the other, there seems no reasonable ground to insist upon preferring specifically the *human* genome, the particular genes that are uniquely preserved in our homogeneous line. If there are advantages in incorporating "animal" genes in the new, manufactured people, there may equally be advantages in adding "human" genes to other lines. Yet these proposals are routinely mocked or disparaged, with a view to keeping the "human" lineage pure. What reasoning lies behind

---

[49] E. O. Wilson, *On Human Nature* (Cambridge, MA: Harvard University Press, 1978), 167.

this? After all, it seems entirely possible that the hominid line and the pongid continued occasional intercourse even after they had begun to split apart. And other hominid species—including *Neanderthalensis*—probably contributed to the *Sapiens* stock. Our present homogeneity depends on past catastrophe: the chance survival of particular human beings in East Africa before they began their trek around the coast to South Africa, Asia, Europe, and Australia. The lines that have been lost to us, by chance, were probably as "fit" or as "deserving" as our own ancestors, just as the final generations of the dinosaurs had no distinguishable faults. As Adam Sedgwick remarked, in criticism of what he took to be the moral of Darwinian talk of "survival of the fittest" (a phrase originated rather by Herbert Spencer): "the reptilian fauna of the Mesozoic period is the grandest and highest that ever lived."[50] Why then preserve "our own," the proportionally very few that are found so far only within our lineage, rather than any others?

The answer, probably, must either be superstitious or metaphysical: "superstitious," if it is merely a relic of an older view, a habit of anthropocentric thought that makes no sense at all in a post-Darwinian cosmos, any more than our unreasoned faith in the capacity of a chance-evolved primate to uncover fundamental truths about reality;[51] "metaphysical" if it rests upon some concept of a sacred form, forgotten in the modern synthesis but nonetheless of moment.

CHANGING PEOPLE

The current "human" population, it seems, is only a phase or fragment. This may perhaps lead some of us, like Dawkins, to worry about the other tribes of Earth, recalling that we are all related to each other. It may as easily lead many of us to treat vulnerable

---

[50] As reported by Richard Owen, in "Objections to Mr Darwin's Theory of the Origin of Species," *Edinburgh Review* 11 (1860), 487–532, reprinted in David L. Hull, ed., *Darwin and his Critics* (Chicago: University of Chicago Press, 1983), 197.

[51] See Max Tegmark, *Our Mathematical Universe: My Quest for the Ultimate Nature of Reality* (London: Allen Lane, 2014), 5: "Darwin's theory makes the testable prediction that whenever we use technology to glimpse reality beyond the human scale, our evolved intuition should break down." Cf. E. P. Wigner, "The unreasonable effectiveness of mathematics in the natural sciences," *Communications on Pure and Applied Mathematics* 13 (1960), 1–14: doi:10.1002/cpa.3160130102.

human beings as badly as we have always treated "animals." According to the Mosaic story, God made us "images" of Himself rather as earthly rulers may set up statues of themselves to make their presence known, and insist that everyone pay something like the same respect to the statues as they would to the king's own person.[52] Human beings, that is, are to be reckoned sacred, and any disrespect or injury to them is taken as disrespect or injury to God. Jesus of Nazareth drew the further inference that even *neglecting* people is an offence against God, not merely actively oppressing them.[53]

This notion was never wholly supported by the Aristotelian or the wider pagan synthesis, which rather favoured adult, freeborn males (and especially those who reckoned themselves "wise"). But at least those pagans had some hope that our conspecifics were, for the most part, *capable* of conversation and peaceful negotiation, and that the whole cosmos where we found ourselves was oriented towards the Good, despite occasional, expectable, disasters. The Golden Age would come round again, and creatures almost exactly like us would be born and prosper. The modern synthesis gives us no reason to believe, either in our capacities for learning or compassion, or in any happy future for the world.

Are there adequate resources in Aristotelian theory to prepare an alternative future? Aristotle did not himself endorse any notion of "fixed species," but he might still be opposed to any radical reworking of the endlessly recurring "natural" norms by which sublunary life, he thought, might imitate the heavens' eternity. He accepted without much argument that "plants were for the sake of animals, and animals for humans,"[54] but still reckoned that there was something *beautiful*, and worthy of our attention, in even the least likeable of living things.[55] The best and most complete of virtues, the one to exercise when all else failed, was *sophia*, wisdom[56]—which is to say, so later

---

[52] Tikva Frymer-Kensky, "The Image, the Glory and the Holy: aspects of being human in Biblical thought," in William Schweiker, Michael A. Johnson, and Kevin Jung, eds., *Humanity Before God: contemporary faces of Jewish, Christian and Islamic Ethics* (Minneapolis: Fortress Faith, 2006), 118–38.
[53] Matthew 25:31–46.
[54] Aristotle, *Politics* 1.1256b15. My translation.
[55] Aristotle, *De Partibus Animalium* 1.645a17-23.
[56] Aristotle, *Nicomachean Ethics* 10.1177a12-1178a8; see my "The Better Part," in A. Phillips-Griffiths, ed., *Ethics* (Cambridge: Cambridge University Press, 1993), 29–49.

theorists made clear, the intellectual enjoyment of real beauty.

> All our toil and trouble is for this, not to be left without a share in the best of visions.... A man has not failed if he fails to win beauty of colours or bodies, or power or office or kingship even, but if he fails to win this and only this.[57]

He thought that there were "natural slaves," bound in fact to be slavish whatever their social standing, but did not therefore endorse cruelty or neglect, and certainly not the *manufacture* of such slaves. "Being once reproached for giving alms to a bad man, he rejoined, 'It was the man and not his character that I pitied.'"[58] And though he found fault with some versions of "the Platonic Theory of Forms," he did not deny the being and the power of such norms.

Aristotle, in fact, was more of a Platonist than modern scholars have usually acknowledged.[59] The Forms which *some* Platonists apparently thought were wholly separate from the phenomenal and physical world were rather to be found at work in both these latter. The stuff on which they worked was not always fully amenable to their influence—but for that very reason it was also available to *other* forms, each with their own powers and beauties. Seals may indeed be "deformed or damaged quadrupeds,"[60] but no one can deny their beauty as the very creatures that they are. "Defects," so called, are not exactly *mistakes*, but the very way in which the spread of living creatures is maintained. It is difficult, now, not to see—say—a Down's Syndrome child as "odd," but if s/he were conceived not as a mainstream human but as a fine example of another, kindlier, kind,[61] we should be no more squeamish than about any other non-conspecific. In other words,

---

[57] *Ennead* I.6 [1].7, 34f.

[58] Diogenes Laertius, *Lives of Eminent Philosophers*, trans. R .D. Hicks (London: Heinemann, 1989 [Loeb Classical Library]), 4.17; alternatively, he gave to *to anthropinon* not to *ho anthropos*, to "the human thing," not "the fellow."

[59] See Lloyd P. Gerson, *Aristotle and Other Platonists* (New York: Cornell University Press, 2005).

[60] Aristotle, *De Partibus Animalium* 2.657a24.

[61] See K. König, "The Mystery of the Mongol Child," in A. C. Harwood, ed., *The Faithful Thinker: centenary essays on the work and thought of Rudolf Steiner* (London: Hodder and Stoughton, 1961), 179–91. See my *Biology and Christian Ethics*, 41–57.

we retain, at least at an emotional level, some notion of *species* as norm-driven, and are affected by those who stray too far from ours. Recognizing them as judged and guided by a *different* norm, we may see their actual excellence, and their importance for future development. The efforts of twentieth century eugenicists to cull what they considered failures were not simply wicked (and usually illegal), but profoundly ignorant: we *need* diversity of goals and patterns. This world here, the world of our becoming, is — obviously — always changing, and we must change with it. On the other hand, there are still real goals and patterns, and the free-for-all that Freeman Dyson seemingly endorsed would be as catastrophic in its effects as breeding domestic animals, even by more traditional means, to emphasise particular, marketable, traits. Identifying right patterns is a task for those with an eye to *real* beauty.

But suppose that, on the one hand, we have some notion of real norms, right patterns, and on the other, power to instantiate such norms wherever we might wish. Would it be unreasonable to reinstantiate lost species: dodos, or woolly mammoths, or Sedgwick's "highest and grandest reptiles"? Would it be wrong to develop the phenotypic potentials of some current genome, allowing one sort of creature to give birth to another sort? Would it be wrong to allow an individual to be transformed, rebuilt to another, not too dissimilar, plan? Would all this be a considered and worthy response to the current "sixth extinction"? If we are losing significant species, and so making a wasteland of a formerly fertile nature, might it not be a duty to refill the eco-logical niches? If we, as human individuals, are unhappy with the forms that we inherit, may we not think of really radical changes, not merely to eliminate a particular disease, or improve our existing eye-sight, but to become a different sort of thing, incorporating faculties from other biological lines as easily as bacteria (as Stapledon imagined)?

In a way, we have always been doing this. We have, from the earliest hominins, been devising tools to match the "natural" limbs and powers of other beasts. Nor is this simply a "human" habit. All eucaryotic life is founded on the use ancestral cells made of captured, domesticated, mitochondrial cells. Some creatures can *grow* shells; others simply construct them, or make homes of discarded bottles. There may always be some advantage in having *external*, easily discarded, tools, precisely so that we can use other tools at will. There may also be an advantage in building some tools into our biological forms, so that they cannot easily be lost. There may also be an advantage in looking like something else than our usual, native, selves, whether by discardable camouflage or more radical alteration. Is there anything amiss with such a future (always supposing we can avoid the trap I gestured toward before, of adding organs and capacities piecemeal in ways that cannot work together—the problem that even enthusiastic genetic engineers may see in combining genetic material from many different kinds)? Darwinian evolution, after all, relies on repeated failures. "Directed evolution" must seek to avoid mistakes.

Consider the future devised by John Varley in his stories of "the Eight Worlds." It is imagined that most Earth-bound humanity has been extinguished by the invasion of many-dimensional intelligences whose sympathy lies only with the great cetaceans. Humanity survives only in the neglected moons and asteroids, helped along by information gathered from an interstellar broadcast from similarly disadvantaged sentients. Living in an entirely artificial environment, sustained only by constant engineering efforts, humans have recognized their own artificial being. The familiar distinctions do still exist: adults and children; male and female; "normal" and radically other (the most engaging of these latter are plant/human symbiotes equipped to survive at leisure far out in the solar system). But movement between these classes is by individual choice: the hero, for example, of Varley's first published story, celebrates his (legal) emancipation by changing back and forth from male to female to male until s/he can settle.[62] In the worlds Varley has invented few people, if any, can sustain any past convictions about human supremacy, or the binding nature of any past traditions—or rather those few who still imagine that they could ever retrieve the Earth, or stand up against the Invaders, are obvious psychopaths, and doomed to failure.[63] The Outsiders, origin of the hotline, are clear that there are no species divisions in the interstellar

---

[62] John Varley, "Picnic on Nearside" (1974): *John Varley Reader: 30 Years of Short Fiction* (New York: Ace Books, 2004), 1–23. See also Varley, *Steel Beach* (London: Putnam, 1992); *The Golden Globe* (London: Penguin, 1998).
[63] See, especially, the character of Boss Tweed in Varley, *The Ophiuchi Hotline* (New York: Ace Books, 1977).

outback to which creatures of our sort are expelled: Dyson's "non-Darwinian" future.

Varley is not the only SF writer to have played with radical transformations of individual being. In the worlds created by Samuel Delany (especially *Triton*) and Lois McMaster Bujold (*A Civil Campaign*), sex-changes are complete and even socially accepted. "Transwomen," in these worlds, can genuinely bear children; "transmen" can genuinely beget them. These physical transformations are not to be equated with simply *saying* that one is a different sex, and demanding to be treated as such, but the fantasy is both revealing and probably influential. In both these worlds, on the other hand, the transformations are guided by a social expectation which seems itself to be faulty. In Delany's story a male character chooses to turn female because he imagines—from his own toxic beginnings—that there is a shortage of "real women" to help support "real men." He volunteers for the task, in the depths of his own depression, and then discovers that there are very few "real men," in the terms he imagines, who will take him/her on. In Bujold's world, the transformation is compelled as the only way for a competent woman to inherit high office and the associated estate, and dispossess the villain who would otherwise inherit. The wish to be a woman or man, rather than one's born identity, would seem unnecessary if there were no fixed social standards for being a man or woman, or if those standards allowed more scope for individual choice. Maybe we are looking towards inadequately conceived norms.

Dissatisfaction with one's merely *physical* state rather than one's social status—that is, having (as it seems to the would-be changer) the *wrong* organs or appendages—may perhaps be satisfied in the imagined SF future; it is not clear that present-day medical interventions are adequate to their task, whatever excisions or imitations are at present on offer. It may be that some far more radical—and fantastic—solution for such dissatisfaction may be needed: the production of an appropriately sexed body from its beginning, and the transfer of memories and personality from a born-body to the cloned, and modified, vat-body. This notion depends, of course, on treating "identity" as founded merely in memory and lasting habits—a notion that in other stories will allow for both a sort of "life after death," and for light-speed travel (or even faster-than-light-speed travel) to very distant stars.

Such transformations may one day be possible, and desired. There remains a suspicion that the powers involved will largely be used by tyrants to compose their work-force. How long will it be left to individual choice what stereotype to claim? And how may even such supposedly individual choices be immune to fashion and quiet manipulation? Without some conception of "real beauty," "real norms," and "real choices," in biology as well as morals, we may at last be reduced—those, that is, who were previously subject to the Aristotelian destiny, of having to make our own minds up and act on reasons that we find compelling—to living instead by impulse, "like the northern barbarians," or in strict obedience to the diktats of our masters, like the eastern.[64] We may, in short, end up as slaves ourselves. Remembering instead the many forms of beauty, we may perhaps hope both to understand the world, and to endure it. Whether it is open to us to *improve* the world is more contentious: little things can be dealt with, but people with larger ambitions should, maybe, recall their limits. And recalling our limits, we may prefer to live within them.

---

[64] Aristotle, *Politics* 3.1285a18f; see also 7.1327b23f.

12.
Lovecraft and the Search for Meaning[1]

WEIRD STYLE AND THE OUTSIDER

Almost everyone who writes about H. P. Lovecraft's work begins by noticing and rebutting Edmund Wilson's notorious misjudgment, that Lovecraft wrote silly stories about "omniscient conical snails" and "whistling invisible octopuses," in an overloaded style.[2] Lovecraft's style, of course, is not to everyone's taste — any more than any other author's will be — but it was not amateurish, nor ill-considered. He suffered a little from the need to fill the pages of *Weird Tales* and the like, as well as from editorial interference with some of his best stories, but his work is in general carefully composed, and subtly written. The bulk of his stories in fact are written, deliberately, in an unemotional and careful style, with exactly the "prosaic objectivity" that Wilson praised in other writers: though this did not stop Wilson's sneering at the detailed — and, exactly, "prosaic" — descriptions of alien species.[3] It is only when his narrators have to confront matters wholly outside the ordinary frame of our own species-limited perception that he deploys the familiar round of adjectives: horrible, awesome, blasphemous, unhallowed, eerie, eldritch and the like.

---

[1] Originally presented at the Conference on Colin Wilson at Nottingham in 2016, and published as "Lovecraft and the Search for Meaning," in *Proceedings of the Colin Wilson Conference,* ed. Colin Stanley (Cambridge: Cambridge Scholars, 2017), 10–45.
[2] Edmund Wilson, "Tales of the Marvellous and the Ridiculous," *New Yorker*, November 24, 1945; reprinted in *Classics and Commercials: a literary chronicle of the forties* (London: W. H. Allen, 1951).
[3] A critical absurdity splendidly parodied by Gilbert Harman's equivalent summaries of the plots of *Moby Dick* and Dante's *Divine Comedy*. See his *Weird Realism: Lovecraft and Philosophy* (Alresford: Zero Books, 2012), 6–8.

Any criticism of Lovecraft, after making these observations [about his style], should go on to note that his
stories are, for the most part, carefully written, and that
their objectionable qualities — the over-loaded and too-
insistent adjectives, the ludicrous touches which don't
quite make us laugh, the italicized last sentences — are not
so much lapses as intentional literary devices. Lovecraft
is not nodding when he writes them. Rather, he is deliberately employing the jargon and stilted mannerisms of a
kind of writing so specialized as to be almost his personal
creation, his task and pleasure being the extension and
elaboration of a few conventions (that is, phrases, characters, settings, and ideas repeated from story to story)
into a self-conscious genre or tradition. He means these
words, such as Wilson particularized, these phrases and
ideas, to be loved and relished for their own sakes. Judged
seriously, they must be considered faults of taste; but
Lovecraft did not mean for them to be judged seriously.[4]

Oddly, Wilson praised one story, "The Colour out of Space,"
which depends in part on suggesting an unimaginable colour
outside the familiar spectrum, by much the same deliberately
chosen adjectives, because he can pretend that the story is "really"
about radiation sickness (as it very obviously is not). Wilson neither liked nor understood the tradition of "weird stories," and
therefore missed the real force of Lovecraft's work, his serious
attempt to place our normal concerns within the picture of an
immensely larger and humanly unmeaning cosmos, as well as
his playful use of the imaginings of other contemporary weird
writers, from Arthur Machen to Robert Howard. To be fair to
Wilson, he was also put off by the cultish fanfic composed by
Lovecraft's followers — as some similarly ignorant critics are put
off Tolkien's own writings by his imitators.[5]

---

[4] Arthur Jean Cox, "Some thoughts on Lovecraft" [1964], in Darrell Sch-
weitzer, ed., *Discovering H. P. Lovecraft*, 2nd edition (Holicong, PA: Wildside
Press, 2001), 47–51.
[5] S. T. Joshi, *A Subtler Magick: The Writings and Philosophy of H. P. Lovecraft*
(Rockville, MD: Borgo Press, 1996), 333: "It is, indeed, an unfortunate fact
that Lovecraft's most obvious influence has been in that tiny subgenre of
weird fiction known as the 'Cthulhu Mythos.' This is unfortunate because
Lovecraft had the bad luck to attract a very mediocre group of self-styled
'disciples' and followers — from August Derleth to Brian Lumley to the

But how else can we suppose that anyone should write about what is, by hypothesis, outside the frame of ordinary life? Any attempt to go outside the usual framework must be fumbling, a matter of gestures rather than banal description. After all, even our own intimacies are often beyond our grasp!

> Man knows that there are in the soul tints more bewil-
> dering, more numberless, and more nameless than the
> colours of an autumn forest.... Yet he seriously believes
> that these things can every one of them, in all their tones
> and semi-tones, in all their blends and unions, be accu-
> rately represented by an arbitrary system of grunts and
> squeals. He believes that an ordinary civilized stock-
> broker can really produce out of his own inside noises
> which denote all the mysteries of memory and all the
> agonies of desire[6].

Lovecraft was groping to describe both unfamiliar feelings compounded of terror, dread, curiosity, and (imagined) objects beyond ordinary taxonomies (vegetable, animal, mineral) and geometries. He was even, at times, attempting the same task as Plotinus in his attempt to describe what lies before or behind all form!

> We in our travail do not know what we ought to say, and
> are speaking of what cannot be spoken, and give it a name
> because we want to indicate it to ourselves as best we can.
> But perhaps this name "One" contains [only] a denial of
> multiplicity. This is why the Pythagoreans symbolically
> indicated it to each other by the name of Apollo, in nega-
> tion of the multiple [that is, *A-Pollon*: Not Many].[7]

---

legions of dismal 'fan' writers, each intent on creating a spanking new god or book or place — who failed utterly to grasp the philosophical essence of Lovecraft's pseudo-mythology and instead found a childish pleasure in imitating its flamboyant externals. That most of these writers produced unwitting parodies of their mentor's work passed wholly beyond their consciousness; but the result was that, through no fault of his own, Lovecraft's own name and work became tainted by these inferior and half-baked imitations, to the point that careless critics such as Damon Knight failed to make the effort to distinguish between the real Lovecraft and the cheap spinoffs."
[6] G. K. Chesterton, *G. F. Watts* (London: Duckworth, 1904), 88.
[7] *Ennead* V.5 [32].6, 23–29, trans. Armstrong. It is worth noting that Apollo was not, as so many commentators suppose, a god of *clarity* and *order*, but of impossible enigmas and brutal force: the Christians who chose to speak instead of "Apollyon," the Destroyer, had good reason on their side.

Lovecraft called the ultimately indescribable Somewhat Azathoth instead, disclaiming any association with beauty, intelligence or meaning. To that I shall return.

Even those critics willing to take his work more seriously still often feel obliged to notice his racism, anti-Semitism, snobbery, and disgust with physical entanglements, and offer psychoana-lytical or sociological explanations of his life, his narratives, and images, as though there could not possibly be any "rational" or even "rationally comprehensible" explanation of the stories, or his life. There may be something to gain from such speculations, but I shall largely ignore them here, as I shall also ignore the minutiae of Lovecraft's life as a reasonably dutiful son with an insane father and very difficult mother, autodidact, struggling scholarly author of pulp fiction, voluminous correspondent, and kindly adviser of many younger writers. I shall also turn aside from *Edmund* Wilson to consider instead what *Colin* Wilson did with Lovecraft's work, and what else can be done: in the rest of this essay "Wilson" always means Colin Wilson. This will require me to recant some of my own past judgments!

I remarked some years ago that "Lovecraft, notoriously, did not understand the actual attractions of the stories he composed. His stories are full of 'elder races,' vastly extended lives, buried cities, threatened awakenings, and all these are supposed to kill us with horror—whereas in fact they simply give us a welcome sense of age and distance. [Colin] Wilson's genre stories are attempts to do this better, and not to succumb to nihilism, to the thought that nothing 'we' do matters, or that ungovernable horrors lurk beneath the surface of our lives."[8] This is still something I would partly endorse—except that I now suspect that Lovecraft knew rather more about what he was about than, following Colin Wilson, I supposed.

Wilson's critical remarks about Lovecraft's style and story-telling knowhow,[9] seeming to endorse the earlier literary judg-

---

[8] Stephen R. L. Clark, *How to Live Forever: science fiction and philosophy* (Rout-ledge: London, 1995), 81. See Nicolas Tredell, *Existence and Evolution: the novels of Colin Wilson*, 3rd edition (Nottingham: Paupers Press, 2015).
[9] Colin Wilson, *The Strength to Dream* (London: Gollancz, 1963), 8, 23–29, 106–8: the very first story Wilson read, "In the Vault" (1925), is described by S. T. Joshi, an acknowledged expert in the field, as a "brief and insignificant tale . . . wholly unredeemed by virtues of style, conception, or atmosphere":

ment, led August Derleth to challenge Wilson to try and do better himself—a challenge he took up in "The Return of the Lloigor," *The Mind Parasites*, *The Philosopher's Stone*, *The Space Vampires*, "The Tomb of the Old Ones," and his four- or five-volume *Spider World*. These stories, though they employ some elements of the Mythos, are actually and openly directed to a different end than Lovecraft's, to the dream of human *victory* over demons. Oddly, Wilson had already, at the beginning of his own literary career, written something closer in its moral to one of Lovecraft's lesser stories—"The Outsider"! In Lovecraft's story, the narrator, having lived as long as he can remember in an otherwise deserted castle among old books and decaying hangings, can no longer bear his isolation. He tells how he climbed with enormous effort up the highest ruinous tower to catch a sight of light, discovers to his joy that he has clambered out into the world of trees and happy streams described in his library, and makes his way to the lighted house where a party is continuing. Bursting into the party, he is surprised and frightened that something else has apparently entered with him, a frightful presence that sends the party screaming away and himself deserted. Then he sees for himself something "compound of all that is unclean, uncanny, unwelcome, abnormal, and detestable. It was the ghoulish shade of decay, antiquity, and dissolution; the putrid, dripping eidolon of unwholesome revelation, the awful baring of that which the merciful earth should always hide. God knows it was not of this world—or no longer of this world—yet to my horror I saw in its eaten-away and bone-revealing outlines a leering, abhorrent travesty on the human shape; and in its mouldy, disintegrating apparel an unspeakable quality that chilled me even more." Trying to fend off the horror, he touches its hand, and is compelled to flee in panic terror, unable either to join the party or to retreat back down into his library.

> Now I ride with the mocking and friendly ghouls on the night-wind, and play by day amongst the catacombs of Nephren-Ka in the sealed and unknown valley of Hadoth

see *A Subtler Magick*, op. cit., 138. It certainly isn't to be taken as representative even of Lovecraft's early "supernatural" narratives. Wilson later read others, and especially approved of "The Shadow out of Time," though still supposing that its impact is "not the impact Lovecraft intended to make" because (he supposes) Lovecraft must have meant to horrify, and was only slowly, despite himself, "growing out of childish fantasies."

by the Nile. I know that light is not for me, save that of
the moon over the rock tombs of Neb, nor any gaiety
save the unnamed feasts of Nitokris beneath the Great
Pyramid; yet in my new wildness and freedom I almost
welcome the bitterness of alienage.[10]

In touching the horror's hand, of course, he has found that he
was only touching a mirror.

Are we ourselves to be horrified? Is not this a happy ending
of sorts? The narrator, alienated from merely human company,
after all, finds friends of a sort amongst the ghouls, who are doing
no particular harm to anyone! He is reconciled, after a fashion,
with his alienation. Human Society and the pretty landscape that
surrounds it still is only one element in a much larger cosmos,
whose inhabitants no longer need to worry about human norms.
Wilson's Outsider is also reconciled to being rejected by a society
in which he has only residual interest—and perhaps Wilson himself was not overwhelmingly disturbed by the rejection of his own
second book (however unreasonable and unfair that rejection).[11]

The idea that Lovecraft did not understand the appeal of his
own stories can't easily be maintained. On the contrary, he understood and used the emotions that he depicted in his narrators
and that he expected to arouse in his readers. Writing in his short
survey of earlier "weird" literature—one heartily and rightly
praised even by Edmund Wilson—he remarks that

> Children will always be afraid of the dark, and men with
> minds sensitive to hereditary impulse will always tremble
> at the thought of the hidden and fathomless worlds of
> strange life which may pulsate in the gulfs beyond the
> stars, or press hideously upon our own globe in unholy

---

[10] H. P. Lovecraft, "The Outsider," in *The Call of Cthulhu and other weird stories*, ed. S. T. Joshi (London: Penguin, 2002), 43–49; see also http://www.hplovecraft.com/writings/texts/fiction/o.aspx (accessed July 28, 2024). Most of Lovecraft's work, and some other critical commentary, is available through http://www.hplovecraft.com/writings/ (accessed July 28, 2024), a site edited by S. T. Joshi, Donovan K. Loucks and David E. Schulz.

[11] "My first response to the slaughter of [*Religion and the Rebel*] was one of relief," he said in an essay in 1959: "I was sick of being a 'public figure' and not recognizing myself in the reactions I aroused.... Cornwall was soothing.... On the whole, I felt a lot better": *Eagle and Earwig: essays on books and writers* (London: John Bake, 1965), 251.

dimensions which only the dead and the moonstruck can
glimpse. With this foundation, no one need wonder at
the existence of a literature of cosmic fear.[12]

EMBRACING THE WIDER WORLD

But of course it is Lovecraft's *narrators* (and his immediate auditors) who are likely to use words like "blasphemous," "unholy,"
"eldritch," and so on. And even his narrators are also — to their
cost — motivated by adventurous curiosity. They want to *know*
what is going on, and are altogether changed by their discoveries:
they are scientists and scholars who are not wholly disconcerted
when they realize how small and insignificant merely *human* affairs
must seem in the light of the larger cosmos. They may — with
good reason — be cautious about awakening powerful aliens from
sleep, but they do not think those aliens *evil* in themselves. They
may rather admire their characters and intelligence. Consider the
"conical snails" that Edmund Wilson mocked: remote cousins
in their blend of animal and vegetable of my favourite sea-slug,
the nudibranch *Elysia viridis,* they also look like descendants of
swimming snails or "sea butterflies," *Thecosomata.* These "Old
Ones" are roused from millennial hibernation in the Antarctic,
and responsible for the death and dismemberment of the humans
who had, unintentionally, awoken them:

> Poor devils! After all, they were not evil things of their
> kind. They were the men of another age and another
> order of being. Nature had played a hellish jest on them —
> as it will on any others that human madness, callous-
> ness, or cruelty may hereafter dig up in that hideously
> dead or sleeping polar waste — and this was their tragic
> homecoming. They had not been even savages — for
> what indeed had they done? That awful awakening in
> the cold of an unknown epoch — perhaps an attack by
> the furry, frantically barking quadrupeds, and a dazed
> defense against them and the equally frantic white simi-
> ans with the queer wrappings and paraphernalia . . . poor
> Lake, poor Gedney . . . and poor Old Ones! Scientists to

---

[12] http://www.hplovecraft.com/writings/texts/essays/shil.aspx (accessed
July 28, 2024); *The Recluse* I (1927), 23–59, republished in *The Annotated Supernatural Horror in Literature,* ed. S. T. Joshi (New York: Hippocampus Press, 2000).

the last—what had they done that we would not have done in their place? God, what intelligence and persistence! What a facing of the incredible, just as those carven kinsmen and forbears had faced things only a little less incredible! Radiates, vegetables, monstrosities, star spawn—whatever they had been, they were men![13]

Lovecraft's personal distaste or hatred or contempt was directed at those of *human* descent whom he regarded as "degenerates" or "barbarians," whether these were Dutch, Italian, or African. Certainly, he was a racist and eugenicist, in common with very many of the more respected intellectual and civic authorities of his time and place:[14] his psychology was not, at the time, so odd as to need impertinent psychological explanation. Maybe he disapproved in his own person of racial miscegenation—but his narrators' horror when confronted by the confusion of biological taxa is not his own: the Darwinian revolution has as its core a recognition that biological taxa are not natural kinds. "Hippopotami should not have human hands and carry torches . . . men should not have the heads of crocodiles," his fictional Houdini exclaims in a story ghost-written for Harry Houdini himself.[15] But Lovecraft's point was, exactly, that they might, that our particular sort of life is not a cosmic norm.

> Now all my tales are based [he wrote] on the fundamental premise that common human laws and interests and emotions have no validity or significance in the vast

---

[13] "At the Mountains of Madness," in *The Thing on the Doorstep and other weird stories*, ed. S. T. Joshi (London: Penguin, 2002), 246–340.
[14] "How will the New Republic treat the inferior races? How will it deal with the black? How will it deal with the yellow man? How will it deal with that alleged termite in the civilized woodwork, the Jew? . . . If the Jew has a certain incurable tendency to social parasitism, and we make social parasitism impossible, we shall abolish the Jew; and if he has not, there is no need to abolish the Jew. . . . The Jew will probably lose much of his particularism, intermarry with Gentiles, and cease to be a physically distinct element in human affairs in a century or so. . . . And for the rest—those swarms of black and brown and yellow people who do not come into the new needs of efficiency? Well, the world is not a charitable institution, and I take it that they will have to go": H. G. Wells, *Anticipations* (1901), chapter 9: in *Anticipations and Other Papers* (London: Fisher Unwin, 1924), 272. *Anticipations* is also available at Project Gutenberg: http://www.gutenberg. org/etext/19229 (accessed July 28, 2024).
[15] "Under the Pyramids" [1924], in *The Thing on the Doorstep*, 53–77, 74.

cosmos-at-large. To me there is nothing but puerility in
a tale in which the human form — and the local human
passions and conditions and standards — are depicted as
native to other worlds or other universes. To achieve the
essence of real externality, whether of time or space or
dimension, one must forget that such things as organic
life, good and evil, love and hate, and all such local attributes of a negligible and temporary race called mankind, have any existence at all. Only the human scenes
and characters must have human qualities. These must
be handled with unsparing realism, (not catch-penny
romanticism) but when we cross the line to the boundless and hideous unknown — the shadow-haunted Outside — we must remember to leave our humanity — and
terrestrialism — at the threshold.[16]

He attributed many crimes and vices to "degenerates" — wilful
ignorance, promiscuity, callous cruelty, cultish worship of inhuman powers, cannibalism and so forth — but at least they were
a little less inclined to take human civilization and intelligence
for granted. At least they knew — or in his stories at least they
knew — that civilized humanity, intelligent humanity, is both
transient and parochial. In the New England of his imagination Miskatonic University is the home of scholars and secret,
unread, or uncomprehended texts, while only a few miles away
are unlettered peasant-farmers[17] who are directly acquainted with
the worlds about which the scholars only read. Foreigners — and
this may include even *English* foreigners of impeccably aristocratic
lineage[18] — are likely to have been contaminated by a cult of the

---

[16] Letter to Farnsworth Wright, July 5, 1927, borrowed from http://www.
hplovecraft.com/writings/quotes.aspx (accessed July 28, 2024): see Joshi,
Essential Solitude.
[17] "Those strange, repellent scions of a primitive colonial peasant stock
whose isolation for nearly three centuries in the hilly fastnesses of a little-
travelled countryside has caused them to sink to a kind of barbaric degen-
eracy, rather than advance with their more fortunately placed brethren of
the thickly settled districts. Among these odd folk, who correspond exactly
to the decadent element of 'white trash' in the South, law and morals are
non-existent; and their general mental status is probably below that of any
other section of the native American people": at least according to the story
"Beyond the Walls of Sleep" (1919), in *The Thing on the Doorstep*, 11–20. It
should not be assumed that Lovecraft himself was speaking without irony!
[18] See "The Rats in the Walls" [1924], in *Call of Cthulhu*, 89–108. Here the
narrator discovers — at the cost of his sanity — that his aristocratic family

inhuman: they need to break away from this, but not by forgetting or refusing to believe that there *are* inhuman powers. The point is rather that we are not to worship them.

I spoke a moment ago about the "friendly ghouls" that Lovecraft's Outsider comes to live amongst, and also of Lovecraft's "playful" use of other writers' imaginings. Perhaps it seems unlikely that he could be playful, or think of having fun. Some readers and critics are content to find him desperately serious, whether in evoking fear, or in directing our attention to a wider world. But he could, after all, be both: both serious and playful. Consider another late story, often characterized simply as "science fiction" rather than as "weird fiction" (though the distinction is moot): "The Shadow out of Time."[19] In this story, Lovecraft's narrator has to make sense of the strange dreams and half-memories dating from a five-year period in which he seemed to be (literally) out of his mind, directed by another, very intelligent and very peculiar personality—rather as Olaf Stapledon's Last Men inspect and influence the minds of their own immensely remote ancestors.[20] Piecing them together, he concocts a narrative in which his primary personality had been transported to an earlier epoch, to inhabit a creature something like a giant, walking mollusc. The ruling intelligences of that epoch were conducting, he imagines, a survey of all available intelligences throughout earth's history by taking the place of selected creatures in the different ages. Someday they will migrate (someday they already have migrated) *en masse* to inhabit the bodies of the great beetle civilization that will dominate the earth after humanity's extinction. The narrator, despite his having been thus victimized, is treated kindly (he recalls) and able both to record his own history for the great library, and to talk to other intelligences brought into that era.

> There was a mind from the planet we know as Venus, which would live incalculable epochs to come, and one from an outer moon of Jupiter six million years in the past. Of earthly minds there were some from the winged,

---

back in England were a long line of cannibals, breeding their food in underground caverns since before the emergence of mainstream humankind. This can be read as allegory as well as horror fiction.

[19] Joshi, *Dreams*, 334–96.

[20] See Olaf Stapledon, *Last and First Men* [1930], and *Last Men in London* [1932] (Harmondsworth: Penguin, 1972).

starheaded, half-vegetable race of palaeogean Antarctica; one from the reptile people of fabled Valusia;[21] three from the furry pre-human Hyperborean worshippers of Tsathoggua; one from the wholly abominable Tcho-Tchos;[22] two from the arachnid denizens of earth's last age; five from the hardy coleopterous species immediately following mankind, to which the Great Race was some day to transfer its keenest minds en masse in the face of horrible peril; and several from different branches of humanity. I talked with the mind of Yiang-Li, a philosopher from the cruel empire of Tsan-Chan, which is to come in 5,000 A. D.;[23] with that of a general of the great-headed brown people who held South Africa in 50,000 B. C.; with that of a twelfth-century Florentine monk named Bartolomeo Corsi; with that of a king of Lomar who had ruled that terrible polar land one hundred thousand years before the squat, yellow Inutos came from the west to engulf it.[24] I talked with the mind of Nug-Soth, a magician of the dark conquerors of 16,000 A. D; with that

---

[21] Robert E. Howard, *Hyperborian Age* (1936), *Shadow Kingdom* (1929): https://en.wikipedia.org/wiki/Thurian_Age (accessed July 28, 2024). "The kingdom furthest to the west of the Thurian continent. It was created and initially ruled by Serpent Men until they were overthrown by their human slaves. They attempted to control the new human kingdom of Valusia from behind the scenes, using illusionary magic, when mankind's memories of the past wars faded but they were again defeated in a secret war. Finally they created a religion, the Snake Cult, to do the same thing again and almost succeeded. Their power was, however, eventually destroyed by Kull, an Atlantean barbarian who had gained the crown of Valusia by force. Kull notes, in *The Shadow Kingdom* that the Valusia of his time is a 'fading, degenerate' country, 'living mostly in dreams of bygone glory, but still a mighty land and the greatest of the Seven Empires.' The kingdom is already ancient by his standards: 'The hills of Atlantis and Mu were isles of the sea when Valusia was young.'" Howard was also responsible for Crom-Ya of the Cimmerians.

[22] First mentioned in August Derleth's 1933 short story, "The Thing That Walked on the Wind," in which a character refers in passing to "the forbidden and accursed designs of the Tcho-Tcho people of Burma." Later that year, in "Lair of the Star-Spawn," co-written with Mark Shorer, Derleth expanded on the Tcho-Tcho, describing them as a short, hairless people that worship Lloigor and Zhar.

[23] First mentioned by Lovecraft in the story "Beyond the Wall of Sleep" (1919), in *The Thing on the Doorstep*, 11–20.

[24] Cf. Lovecraft, "Polaris" (1920), set in a period about 25,000 years ago, during a previous reign of Polaris as Pole Star: S. T. Joshi, ed. *The Dreams in the Witch House and Other Weird Stories* (London: Penguin, 2005), 1–4.

of a Roman named Titus Sempronius Blaesus, who had been a quaestor in Sulla's time; with that of Khephnes, an Egyptian of the 14th Dynasty, who told me the hideous secret of Nyarlathotep, with that of a priest of Atlantis' middle kingdom; with that of a Suffolk gentleman of Cromwell's day, James Woodville; with that of a court astronomer of pre-Inca Peru; with that of the Australian physicist Nevil Kingston-Brown, who will die in 2,518 A. D.; with that of an archimage of vanished Yhe in the Pacific; with that of Theodotides, a Greco-Bactrian official of 200 B. C.; with that of an aged Frenchman of Louis XIII's time named Pierre-Louis Montagny; with that of Crom-Ya, a Cimmerian chieftain of 15,000 B. C.; and with so many others that my brain cannot hold the shocking secrets and dizzying marvels I learned from them.[25]

There are two features of this narrative that should be clear — as well as the rather odd absence of any *female* characters! First, that despite the narrator's "shock" at all these revelations, they are fascinating rather than horrid or terrifying; or, if there is terror involved, it is no more than an understandable caution in the face of powers not open to human persuasion. But second, Lovecraft is not drawing here on any *scientific* speculations about what other creatures might in our past or future inhabit and control the earth or other planets, nor is he even *making them up* from scratch to fill a systematized cosmos. There is a sense — to which I shall return — in which Lovecraft was doing something not altogether different from Tolkien: devising a new pseudo-history, a new mythology, even a new language, to fill a gap in our collective imagination. But Lovecraft did not create the "Cthulhu Mythos" that Derleth and others have devised. Tolkien wrote that he wanted to create a world and a history in which the phrase *elen síla lúmenn' omentielvo* could be an everyday greeting.[26] Maybe Lovecraft had a similar ambition for his deliberately unpronounceable catch phrase *ph'nglui mglw'nafh C'thulhu R'lyeh wgah'nagl fhtagn*, but I doubt if there was ever a real language anyone could learn. The phrase,

---

[25] "The Shadow out of Time," in *The Dreams in the Witch House and Other Weird Stories*, ed. S. T. Joshi (London: Penguin, 2005), 334–96, 359–60.

[26] J. R. R. Tolkien, *Letters*, ed. Humphrey Carpenter (London: Allen and Unwin, 1981), 264–65. Dimitra Fimi, *Tolkien, Race and Cultural History: from fairies to hobbits* (London: Palgrave Macmillan, 2009), 63–67, qualifies this claim.

however ominous in the stories, is deliberately playful. So also are the other seemingly solid references to ancient texts and peoples: the references are solely to contemporary fantasy, his own and others'. The narrative, in short, that his narrator devises—and the others that Lovecraft composed for other imagined narrators—could be considered just such *obviously* made-up, literary fictions, a set of in-jokes, homage to Lovecraft's friends.[27]

In-jokes, that is, except that in the denouement of the story our narrator joins an archaeological expedition that has uncovered ruins with subtly similar carvings to those he has (or so he thinks) imagined. Deep amongst those ruins he finds, one night, the ancient library to which he had perhaps contributed—and writings in English, in his own hand. Or else, of course, this too is a delusion: he panics on hearing noises of a sort that his sometime hosts (if they existed) greatly feared, and loses the documents in his flight up to the light. He can console himself that the whole thing was an hallucination, though his readers, playing along with Lovecraft, recognize that he is wrong!

Am I entitled to conclude that Lovecraft himself *welcomed* the possibility that there were, that there are, very many wildly different species with whom we could, in principle, have conversations? The Great Race at least, even if it ignores any imagined rights to life or liberty in the individuals and species it displaces, is engaged in gathering knowledge, carrying the past on into the very distant future.

> After man there would be the mighty beetle civilization, the bodies of whose members the cream of the Great Race would seize when the monstrous doom overtook the elder world. Later, as the earth's span closed, the transferred minds would again migrate through time and space—to another stopping-place in the bodies of the bulbous vegetable entities of Mercury. But there would be races after them, clinging pathetically to the cold planet and burrowing to its horror-filled core, before the utter end.[28]

---

[27] On that literary age in general see Roger Luckhurst, "Scientific Romance, Fantasy and the Supernatural," in Michael Saler, ed., *The Fin-de-Siècle World* (London: Routledge, 2014), 677–90.

[28] H. P. Lovecraft, "The Shadow out of Time" [1934]: *The Great Old Ones: The Complete Works of H. P. Lovecraft* (CreateSpace Independent Publishing Platform, 2017), 513.

Lovecraft wrote to Derleth that "time, space, and natural law hold for me suggestions of intolerable bondage, and I can form no picture of emotional satisfaction which does not involve their defeat—especially the defeat of time, so that one may merge oneself with the whole historic stream and be wholly emancipated from the transient and the ephemeral."[29] *Imagining* himself into the Great Race, he could imagine just that emancipation, rather as Wilson imagines his archaeological narrator identifying with Nineveh and the enduring earth, to the point of feeling contempt for his own transitory existence.[30] Similarly, in "The Dream Quest of Unknown Kadath," the central character, Randolph Carter, passes "amidst [both through and around] backgrounds of other planets and systems and galaxies and cosmic continua; spores of eternal life drifting from world to world, universe to universe, yet all equally himself.... His self had been annihilated and yet he—if indeed there could, in view of that utter nullity of individual existence, be such a thing as he—was equally aware of being in some inconceivable way a legion of selves."[31]

Part of the ancient notion of a philosopher, as Plato described it, is to be a "spectator of all time and all existence,"[32] an ambition that Olaf Stapledon also dramatized in his imagined future histories, especially *Star Maker* (1937), whose narrator—like Carter—drifts from one world to another, back and forth in time, accumulating other selves, part friends, part alter egos. Whether Stapledon had read any of Lovecraft's work I do not know. There seem to be no traces in the Stapledon Archive at Liverpool University.[33] Lovecraft had read *Last and First Men*

---

[29] Letter to August Derleth, November 21, 1930, in *Essential Solitude: the letters of H. P. Lovecraft and August Derleth, 1926–37*, eds. David E. Schultz and S. T. Joshi (New York: Hippocampus Press, 2013).

[30] Wilson, *The Mind Parasites* (London: Barker, 1967), 18. Wilson may perhaps have drawn this case not merely from his own experience, but from the writings of Arnold Toynbee, who recounted similar episodes in his own growth as a fully engaged historian. Colin Wilson, *Religion and the Rebel* (London: Gollancz, 1957), 125–26, quoting Arnold Toynbee, *A Study of History* (Oxford University Press: Oxford 1954), 10:130, 139.

[31] Joshi, *Dreams*, 155–251.

[32] Plato, *Republic*, trans. Benjamin Jowett (London: Herny Frowde, 1888), 6.486a.

[33] Personal communication from Andy Sawyer, of the university's science fiction library.

(1930) with enthusiasm.[34] Stapledon also recognized that alien intelligences were very unlikely to be humanoid in outward appearance, though he put more trust in their possibly achieving a similarly contemplative, philosophical attitude to the cosmos, accepting it as something that was not ruled by the petty convenience of any of its inmates and yet was, somehow, glorious. It was, on the one hand, very important to seek out that perspective from which all mortal life becomes an unimportant trifle, but on the other, we may, we must, acknowledge the power and beauty of the ordinarily and immediately "human." The final moments of *Star Maker* are not a vision of that diabolical power that makes and discards all worlds for its own aesthetic satisfaction, but a return to "the little atom of community" that Stapledon's fictional narrator shared with his wife. Stapledon's philosophy differed from Lovecraft's in that he did envisage a coherent intelligence at the back of all material phenomena, though not one with which we can have much in common.[35] What lies behind and before the cosmos for *Lovecraft* is much more like the darkness "that the gods hate" (in Plotinus's words):[36] "that nuclear chaos beyond angled space which the Necronomicon had mercifully cloaked under the name of Azathoth,"[37] who deserves no worship.

---

[34] Letters to Fritz Leiber (November 18, 1936), in *Selected Letters V: 1934–7*, eds. August Derleth and James Turner (Sauk City, WI: Arkham House, 1971), 357, 375.

[35] Yet another Wilson, Robert Anton Wilson, "My Debt to H. P. Lovecraft," *Crypt of Cthulhu* 2.4 (December, 1983), 3–4, 16 (http://rawilsonfans. org/my-debt-to-h-p-lovecraft/ — accessed February 28, 2016): "Basically, I like Lovecraft and Olaf Stapledon better than any other writers in the areas of fantasy, science-fiction and 'speculative fiction.' This is because I think HPL and Stapledon succeeded more thoroughly than anyone else in creating truly 'inhuman' perspectives, artistically sustained and emotionally convincing. That HPL makes the 'inhuman' or the 'cosmic' a frightening and depressing thing to encounter, while Stapledon makes it a source of mystic awe and artfully combined tragedy-and-triumph, registers merely that they had different temperaments." Stapledon's cosmos is more threatening (see, for example, *The Flames*), and Lovecraft's sometimes more welcoming than RAW suggests, but his essay, overall, is perceptive.

[36] *Ennead* V.1 [10].2, 24–27, quoting Homer on Hades at *Iliad* 20.65.

[37] "The Whisperer in Darkness" [1930], in *Call of Cthulhu*, 200–67; see also http://www.hplovecraft.com/writings/texts/fiction/wid.aspx, accessed July 28, 2024.

Out in the mindless void the daemon bore me,
Past the bright clusters of dimensioned space,
Till neither time nor matter stretched before me,
But only Chaos, without form or place.
Here the vast Lord of All in darkness muttered
Things he had dreamed but could not understand,
While near him shapeless bat-things flopped and fluttered
In idiot vortices that ray-streams fanned.

They danced insanely to the high, thin whining
Of a cracked flute clutched in a monstrous paw,
Whence flow the aimless waves whose chance combining
Gives each frail cosmos its eternal law.
"I am His Messenger," the daemon said,
As in contempt he struck his Master's head.[38]

Stapledon's Star Maker may at first glimpse be rather more attractive! But perhaps there is in practice little enough to choose between an incomprehensible intelligence and something that isn't intelligence at all. If the stars are ruled by utterly alien powers it is as much as to say that they are not *ruled*, but only products of a "chance combining": and the only wills in question are our own (or those of other finite organisms). "If there is a meaning," so Stapledon's Last Men say in their final hours, "it is no human meaning,"[39] and so might as well be no real meaning. When, in another fiction, his peace-loving and peace-making Tibetan mystics finally discover — as they suppose — the truth of things, it is as if they had woken to a frozen landscape trampled by indifferent giants.[40] Whether those giants are deaf because they are witless or because they are callous hardly matters; even their ill will — if they are malevolent — is immune to prayer, and so as natural and fixed a fact as any.

In either case, so Stapledon and Lovecraft both agreed, it is part of our duty "as men" to acknowledge that there is more to the worlds than us, and somehow to find, despite the worlds' indifference, a way of living humanely. Our friends, our family,

---

[38] *Fungi from Yuggoth* 22: "Azathoth": http://www.hplovecraft.com/writings/texts/poetry/p289.aspx (accessed July 28, 2024). *Fungi from Yuggoth: and other verses of cosmic horror,* ed. D. M. Mitchell (Apophenia, 2013).
[39] Stapledon, *Last and First Men*, 605.
[40] Olaf Stapledon, *Darkness and Light* (London: Methuen, 1942); see my "Science Fiction and Religion," in *The Blackwell Companion to Science Fiction*, ed. David Seed (Oxford: Blackwell, 2005), 95–110.

our native soil, our histories don't matter to the wider world or its more powerful residents: they may still matter to us, and those who allow themselves to be infected by indifference, indiscipline, cultish stupidity are still to be resisted when we can—or even if, in the end, we can't.

> Amidst this variability [that is, the relative and changing nature of "the good"] there is only one anchor of fixity which we can seize upon as the working pseudo-standard of "values" which we need in order to feel settled and contented—and that anchor is tradition, the potent emotional legacy bequeathed to us by the massed experience of our ancestors, individual or national, biological or cultural. Tradition means nothing cosmically, but it means everything locally and pragmatically because we have nothing else to shield us from a devastating sense of "lostness" in endless time and space.[41]

Or as John Buchan supposed a savage might speak to a missionary for the wider world, in a verse I quoted earlier:

> Wherefore my brittle gods I make
> Of friendly clay and kindly stone,—
> Wrought with my hands, to serve or break,
> From crown to toe my work, my own.
> My eyes can see, my nose can smell,
> My fingers touch their painted face,
> They weave their little homely spell
> To warm me from the cold of Space.
>
> My gods are wrought of common stuff
> For human joys and mortal tears;
> Weakly, perchance, yet staunch enough
> To build a barrier 'gainst my fears,
> Where, lowly but secure, I wait
> And hear without the strange winds blow.—
> I cannot worship what I hate,
> Or serve a god I dare not know.[42]

---

[41] Lovecraft, *Selected Letters*, 2.356–57, quoted in Joshi, *Subtler Magick*, 48.
[42] John Buchan, "Stocks and Stones," in *The Moon Endureth* (Edinburgh: Thomas Nelson, 1923 [1912]), 160–62. Buchan appended the poem to a distinctly Lovecraftian story, "Space," about what lurks around us in some normally invisible direction.

PAGAN OR PLATONIC COURAGE

This is close to the theme of Ruthanna Emrys' recent revision of a Lovecraft story, in which one of the hybrids known from Innsmouth, a representative of an unjustly persecuted and misunderstood minority, makes her own case for the truth of the wider story, and for the loyalty she feels for both sides of her heritage:

> "All of man's other religions place him at the center of creation. But man is nothing—a fraction of the life that will walk the Earth. Earth is nothing—a tiny world that will die with its sun. The sun is one of trillions where life flowers, and wants to live, and dies. And between the suns is an endless vast darkness that dwarfs them, through which life can travel only by giving up that wanting, by losing itself. Even that darkness will eventually die. In such a universe, knowledge is the stub of a candle at dusk." "You make it all sound so cheerful." "It's honest. What our religion tells us, the part that is a religion, is that the gods created life to try and make meaning. It's ultimately hopeless, and even gods die, but the effort is real. Will always have been real, even when everything is over and no one remembers."[43]

It is, perhaps, something like the ancient Nordic myth, and a reminder of what a truly *pagan* sensibility might be. The worlds begin—for no particular reason—amid ice and fire, and will likewise perish amid fire and ice. Worldly success is of no lasting significance, for such monistic materialists any more than for a Plotinian sensibility.

> Make it your hope
> To be counted worthy on that day to stand beside them;
> For the end of man is to partake of their defeat and die
> His second, final death in good company. The stupid,
>   strong,
> Unteachable monsters are certain to be victorious at last,
> And every man of decent blood is on the losing side....

---

[43] Ruthanna Emrys, *The Litany of Earth* (New York: Tom Doherty Associates, 2014), Kindle location 271: it is of course an error to suppose that "all man's other religions" place him at the center, but there is indeed a creeping anthropocentrism which infects the secular as well as the religious imagination.

Know your betters and crouch, dogs;
You that have Vichy water in your veins and worship
    the event,
Your goddess History (whom your fathers called the
    strumpet Fortune).[44]

Strictly, of course, Lovecraft's gods — so far as we can call them gods at all — did not "create life" in general, though they may (like the star-headed eggplants) have created robot servants, "shuggoth," who eventually revolted against their makers and continue, in the stories, to bedevil later species. That fantasy may owe some of its force to the terror all slave-owning societies (and their unrepentant heirs) feel about the prospect of a slave-revolt. But what is especially hard to bear in these "shuggoths" is their lack of stable form — and this indeed seems to be the harshest fate Lovecraft can wish upon his characters, to be chopped up, dissolved, "slimed," formless, reduced to a simulacrum of the primal chaos, turned back into "mere matter," sludge. How bad, realistically, must this be? It is, after all, almost the fate imagined for us by Greg Bear in his *Blood Music*: intelligent procaryotes, the product of an ill-judged genetic experiment, discover that such lumbering eucaryotes as ourselves exist, and proceed to colonize, to disassemble, and at last to resurrect us all in glory. There are no species barriers in this microbial world, despite there being innumerable shapes and manners. Indeed, there are no individuals as we imagine them at all, but only ever-changing, ever-evolving fashions, fissioning and coalescing according to whatever needs arise: a sea of information.[45] Carter, in a story written in collaboration with E. Hoffman Price, discovers that he has, much like Empedocles, been "a boy and a girl, a shrub and a bird, and a fish that leaps from the sea,"[46] that he *isn't* what a

---

[44] C. S. Lewis, "Cliché come out of its Cage," in *Poems*, ed. Walter Hooper (New York: Harcourt, Brace & World: 1964), 3–4.
[45] Greg Bear, *Blood Music* (London: Gollancz, 1985).
[46] Empedocles, in Diels-Kranz, *Fragmente der Vorsokratiker*, 1:359 (31B117): Robin Waterfield, ed., *The First Philosophers: the presocratics and sophists* (New York: Oxford University Press, 2000), 155. Lovecraft offers a more fantastic array: "a slight change of angle could turn the student of today into the child of yesterday; could turn Randolph Carter into that wizard Edmund Carter who fled from Salem to the hills behind Arkham in 1692, or that Pickman Carter who in the year 2169 would use strange means in repelling the Mongol hordes from Australia; could turn a human Carter into one of

moment before he had supposed. The Carter persona is only one trivial facet of an immensely larger whole (as Plotinus had also supposed, finding this a source of joy, not horror).[47]

> No death, no doom, no anguish can arouse [*sic*] the surpassing despair which flows from a loss of identity. Merging with nothingness is peaceful oblivion; but to be aware of existence and yet to know that one is no longer a definite being distinguished from other beings—that one no longer has a self—that is the nameless summit of agony and dread.[48]

To be thus absorbed may seem, may be, horrific, and yet be nothing to be seriously alarmed by: or at any rate, we shan't be alarmed for long. "No mortal thing," Empedocles instructed us, "has a beginning, nor does it end in death and obliteration; there is only a mixing and then a separating of what was mixed."[49] But Lovecraft, though a professed materialist, does seem to have employed, or even perhaps believed, some version of Platonism:

---

those earlier entities which had dwelt in primal Hyperborea and worshipped black, plastic Tsathoggua after flying down from Kythanil, the double planet that once revolved around Arcturus; could turn a terrestrial Carter to a remotely ancestral and doubtfully shaped dweller on Kythanil itself, or a still remoter creature of trans-galactic Shonhi, or a four-dimensional gaseous consciousness in an older space-time continuum, or a vegetable brain of the future on a dark radio-active comet of inconceivable orbit—and so on, in the endless cosmic circle" (Joshi, *Dreams*, 279).

[47] "If one likens it [reality] to a living richly varied sphere, or imagines it as a thing all faces, shining with living faces, or as all the pure souls running together into the same place, with no deficiencies but having all that is their own, and universal Intellect seated on their summits so that the region is illuminated by intellectual light—if one imagined it like this one would be seeing it somehow as one sees another from outside; but one must become that, and make oneself the contemplation" (*Ennead* VI.7 [38].15, 25–16, 3).

[48] "Through the Gates of the Silver Key" [1934]: Joshi, Dreams, 264–99: 280. Carter's final encounter, before he once again finds himself entangled in the net of time and space, may even have influenced Stapledon in his account of the Star Maker. "The last, utter sweep which has no confines and which outreaches fancy and mathematics alike. It was perhaps that which certain secret cults of earth have whispered of as YOG-SOTHOTH, and which has been a deity under other names; that which the crustaceans of Yuggoth worship as the Beyond-One, and which the vaporous brains of the spiral nebulae know by an untranslatable Sign."

[49] Diels-Kranz, *Fragmente der Vorsokratiker*, 1:312 (31B8): Waterfield, *First Philosophers*, 145.

mere matter is, as Plotinus said, the principle of evil,[50] though no real material thing is therefore evil. Beauty lies in living form: even an ugly living face is more beautiful than any statue.[51] Only some form of Platonic dualism, for that matter, can explain how the Great Race displaces the consciousness of other radically different species throughout time. Was this the sort of casual inconsistency that affects us all, evidence of a covert anti-materialism, or a mere fictional device, perhaps parodying contemporary occult literature?[52] I'm guessing it was only the last—but perhaps it should have been the first!

Death, dissolution, even the ultimately meaningless end of all things (if all things really end) are matters that excite our fear and horror without being *real* dangers which threaten our present existence here. We can avoid immediate deaths, immediate disorder, dirt, indiscipline, by preserving and embellishing art, comfort, friendship, and by making a mockery of the imagined horrors, piling them up together till we can hardly escape laughing. *Ph'nglui mglw'nafh C'thulhu R'lyeh wgah'nagl fhtagn*, indeed.

Or is this overoptimistic? Here is another verse from Lovecraft's sonnet sequence, concerning one who found himself "dreaming" too deeply:

> His solid flesh had never been away,
> For each dawn found him in his usual place,
> But every night his spirit loved to race
> Through gulfs and worlds remote from common day.
> He had seen Yaddith, yet retained his mind,
> And come back safely from the Ghooric zone,
> When one still night across curved space was thrown
> That beckoning piping from the voids behind.
>
> He waked that morning as an older man,
> And nothing since has looked the same to him.
> Objects around float nebulous and dim—
> False, phantom trifles of some vaster plan.

---

[50] Plotinus, *Enneads*, 1:295 (I. 8. 6, 33–4).
[51] *Enneads*, 7:157–59 (VI. 7. 22, 27–32).
[52] See Brian J. Reis, "Structurally Cosmic Apostasy: the atheist occult world of H. P. Lovecraft," *Lux: a Journal of Transdisciplinary Writing and Research from Claremont Graduate University* 3.1 (2013), 14: Available at http://scholarship.claremont.edu/lux/vol3/iss1/14 (accessed July 28, 2024).

His folk and friends are now an alien throng
To which he struggles vainly to belong.[53]

A similar vision is used in James Blish's *Black Easter*—and it is there, explicitly, a weapon in the hands of a black magician:

Thou shalt straightaway go unto him, not making thyself known unto him, but revealing, as it were to come from his own intellectual soul, a vision and understanding of that great and ultimate Nothingness, which lurks behind those signs he calls matter and energy, as thou wilt see it in his private forebodings, and that thou remainest with him and deepen his despair without remittal, until such time as he shall despise his soul for its endeavors, and destroy the life of his body.[54]

Tolkien, too, had doubts about the effect of going too far outside our "comfort zone," quite apart from the obvious dangers of going "where the Mewlips feed" or where "horny Fastitocalon, an island good to land upon," can drown unwary sailors.[55] The nameless narrator of one poem has been lost in fairy, in the wider world, and—rejected by that realm for his conceit—finds a way back home. Except that there is no home for him, any more than for poor Frodo.

---

[53] *Fungi from Yuggoth:* 32, Alienation http://www.hplovecraft.com/writings/texts/poetry/p289.aspx. (Accessed July 28, 2024).
[54] James Blish, *Black Easter* (London: Faber, 1969), 87. Fortunately, as I remarked on an earlier page, most human beings have other resources (as Dr Johnson's friend remarked: "I have tried in my time to be a philosopher; but cheerfulness was always breaking in." James Boswell, *Life of Johnson* [Oxford: Oxford University Press, 1953], 957: April 17, 1778).
[55] Middle Earth, it needs to be said, is as dangerous and sometimes horrifying in its detailed history as any dystopian fantasy. The Fellowship is mostly walking through a ruined landscape, beset by invincible horrors whose principal is only defeated—this time round—by "chance" (if chance it be). Not even the Shire is "cosy"! And the best that even the greatest of the Elves can manage is "through ages of the world [to fight] the long defeat": *The Fellowship of the Ring*, 372. Wilson, *Strength to Dream*, 131, identifies this passage in particular as reminiscent of Lovecraft, adding that Tolkien succeeded far better in his world-building (a project that Lovecraft in fact did not pursue): "Far, far below the deepest delvings of the Dwarves, the world is gnawed by nameless things. Even Sauron knows them not. They are older than he. Now I have walked there, but I will bring no report to darken the light of day." J. R. R. Tolkien, *The Two Towers* (London: Allen and Unwin, 1966), 150.

Houses were shuttered, wind round them muttered,
Roads were empty. I sat by a door,
And where drizzling rain poured down a drain
I cast away all that I bore:
In my clutching hand some grains of sand,
And a sea-shell silent and dead.
Never will my ear that bell hear,
Never my feet that shore tread
Never again, as in sad lane,
In blind alley and in long street
Ragged I walk. To myself I talk;
For still they speak not, men that I meet. [56]

It is perhaps in order to avoid this deep depression that some
of us stifle thought, by giving allegiance to whatever exciting
cult may come our way. Excitement at least enthuses us a while!
"Man is a shadow's dream (*skias onar*)," said Pindar, "but when
(a) god sheds a brightness then shining light is on earth, and
life is as sweet as honey."[57]

Lovecraft and Tolkien both, as well as other writers of their
day, made it their business to remind us that the world is wider
than we had imagined, and that we do not own it. It is not
"our Shire": others dwelt here before us, and will again when
hobbits—or *Homo sapiens*—are no more.[58] The world does not
acknowledge any of the borders that we draw, nor do the heavens mourn the death of princes. This is not simply an atheistical
insight: on the contrary, it is one born in *theological* enquiry.
Precisely because we do not, and cannot, know God's purposes,
we must not project our own on what is really there. It is easy
still to suppose that though the outer world has its own rules
and rulers we may at least be masters of our own souls: surely
we must at least know our own purposes! Unfortunately, as
both Tolkien and Lovecraft show, this isn't true. As I remarked
on an earlier page, our thoughts and feelings are not our own.
Those who seek to follow the Delphic instruction to "know

---

[56] J. R. R. Tolkien, *The Adventures of Tom Bombadil* (London: HarperCollins,
2014), "The Sea Bell," 19–21.
[57] Pindar, *Pythian* 8. 95–97, my translation.
[58] J. R. R. Tolkien, *The Fellowship of the Ring* (London: Allen and Unwin,
1966), 93: "the wide world is all about you: you can fence yourselves in,
but you cannot forever fence it out."

yourself"[59]—so St. Hesychios of Sinai (8th century?) declared— find themselves, as it were, gazing into a mirror and sighting the dark faces of the demons peering over their shoulders.[60]

> We can infer from the object appearing in the mind which demon is close at hand, suggesting that object to us.... All thoughts producing anger or desire in a way that is contrary to reason [or the Spirit] are caused by demons.[61]

This observation or fancy is rendered dramatically in stories about possession or impersonation—one of the many common tropes of science fiction as well as fantasy, and a particular source of horror to many of Lovecraft's narrators.

> Horror in Lovecraft is never purely "external": the mere existence upon this earth of incalculably powerful monsters, from whatever depths of space they may have come, always has a jarring psychological impact on those pitiable few who come to be aware of them and come also to realise humanity's suddenly tenuous hold upon the planet. "The Shadow out of Time"—in which a spectacularly alien intelligence actually occupies the body of the narrator and passes for him for years—is as exquisite a union of external and internal horror as could possibly be imagined.[62]

But this is also, almost literally, how our lives are lived. "Most of your actions are carried out by a host of unconscious zombies who exist in peaceful harmony along with you (the "person" inside your body)!"[63] Or else not so peaceful tension. Colin Wilson's

---

[59] See Plotinus, *Ennead* VI 7 [38]. 41, 22f: the injunction is "said to those who because of their selves' multiplicity have the business of counting themselves up and learning that they do not know all of the number and kind of things they are." *Ennead* VI.7 [38].42, 22–25.

[60] Hesychios, "On Watchfulness and Holiness," §23: Palmer, G. E. H., Sherrard, P. and Ware, K., eds., *The Philokalia* (London: Faber, 1979), 1:228.

[61] Evagrios Pontikos (345–99): *The Philokalia*, 1:39. "Spirit" is often a better translation of the Greek term *nous* than "reason," given our tendency to interpret "reason" as an abstract calculative faculty of merely instrumental value.

[62] Joshi, *Subtler Magick*, 329.

[63] Sandra Blakeslee and V. S. Ramachandran, *Phantoms in the Brain* (London: Fourth Estate, 1998), 228.

inference is that, once we have recognized this alien influence, we can begin to locate an answer. "Since these creatures [the parasites] had deliberately induced this feeling of total meaninglessness, they must be in some way *beyond* it."[64] Maybe there is after all a way to escape the rulers, the obnoxious or indifferent powers. Maybe we can even locate a *genuinely* superior self, a well-meaning and truly helpful daemon of the sort that Stapledon imagined — and Plotinus. Maybe we could re-discover our own larger identity, without giving way to panic or disgust. Lovecraft, despite his occasional nod to a more Platonic outlook, would regard that thought as a delusive phantom. Even Science — the particular avatar of "reason" that Lovecraft chiefly valued — has a very limited range, bounded by our own biology.[65] The very stars that Tolkien, for example, imagined as representative of a "high beauty" beyond the reach of the shadows, are busy on their own affairs — or utterly maleficent. In the early story entitled "Polaris" (1918), for example, the narrator seems to himself to remember an earlier life (whether truly his or another's) in which Polaris — then as now, a Platonic Year later, the Pole Star — caused him to fall disastrously asleep and leave his fellow citizens the prey of "the squat, yellow Inutos." The star-light that Frodo carries into Mordor, and by which the creeping malice of Shelob is defeated, is evidence, in the story, that there are friendly powers after all — or at least some technological device that can defeat the bogies. Of course the feeling that Polaris was actively *against* the narrator, or that Algol is a "daemon-star" opposed to a brotherhood of light,[66] is as foolish, in Lovecraft's eye, as the thought that Ear-

---

[64] Wilson, *Mind Parasites*, 114.

[65] A quotation from an early, and otherwise inferior tale, "From Beyond" [1920]: Joshi, *Dream*, 23–29: "What do we know... of the world and the universe about us? Our means of receiving impressions are absurdly few, and our notions of surrounding objects infinitely narrow. We see things only as we are constructed to see them, and can gain no idea of their absolute nature. With five feeble senses we pretend to comprehend the boundlessly complex cosmos, yet other beings with a wider, stronger, or different range of senses might not only see very differently the things we see, but might see and study whole worlds of matter, energy, and life which lie close at hand yet can never be detected with the senses we have."

[66] As in "Beyond the Walls of Sleep," a story, incidentally, wrecked at the last by Lovecraft's failure to remember that we could not see anything that happened to or around Algol for at least 92 years. Algol's status as a demon-star seems to depend on its flickering appearance (as, in fact, a binary

endil's Star could be *for* us. Carter, in "Unknown Kadath," muses that "as well might a mammoth pause to visit frantic vengeance upon an angleworm." The stars are just facts — or perhaps not even that: they are points of light, sparks in the ether isolated in our perception, but no more independent entities than is an arbitrarily dissected bit of DNA.

Whether or not there are friendly or unfriendly powers, it may remain that all these imaginings, the dreadful as well as the merely dramatic, may either unleash depression or awaken laughter and unreasonable courage.

> I tell you naught for your comfort,
> Yea, naught for your desire,
> Save that the sky grows darker yet
> And the sea rises higher.

> Night shall be thrice night over you,
> And heaven an iron cope.
> Do you have joy without a cause,

> Yea, faith without a hope?[67]

And this message may actually be one that even Lovecraft, atheist and materialist as he overtly was, acknowledged in his fashion.

> There is in certain ancient things a trace
> Of some dim essence — more than form or weight;
> A tenuous aether, indeterminate,
> Yet linked with all the laws of time and space.
> A faint, veiled sign of continuities
> That outward eyes can never quite descry;
> Of locked dimensions harbouring years gone by,
> And out of reach except for hidden keys.

> It moves me most when slanting sunbeams glow
> On old farm buildings set against a hill,
> And paint with life the shapes which linger still

---

system, with one dimmer star periodically occluding its brighter partner) rather than its having, millions of years ago on a much closer course, perhaps perturbed the solar Oort Cloud, and engendered destructive comets!

[67] G. K. Chesterton, "Ballad of the White Horse" (1911), in *Collected Poems*, 12th edition (London: Methuen, 1950), 233. Chesterton's poem celebrates a time when there seemed indeed no rational hope of survival.

From centuries less a dream than this we know.
In that strange light I feel I am not far
From the fixt mass whose sides the ages are.[68]

Is it in our power simply to *decide* to treat the nihilistic vision
as only another fiction, and to affirm the strength and joy that
are sometimes, seemingly, evoked by the discovery of vast distances and forgotten ages? Surely, what we only *choose* to believe,
or *choose* to let ourselves imagine, can have no great weight or
attraction when despair or terror returns. But despair and terror are also only "emotions," and ones with which the ascetic,
philosophical tradition is very well acquainted. Those most
"philosophically" inclined may perhaps be able to retain their
balance as solitary individuals, but even they must benefit from
an association with "tradition," the established social and historical forms and conventions—and especially a tradition that
recognized the *littleness* of ordinary life. "Historical fact," Colin
Wilson went so far as to insist, "leaves no doubt that the Church
of the Middle Ages provided such a discipline"![69] So Lovecraft
himself found consolation, exactly, in association with a civilization whose overt beliefs he did not, intellectually, endorse. We
may ourselves think it a pity that the "tradition" with which he
personally identified was that of an unrepentant slave-owning
society, with eugenicist delusions—but even that tradition is, to
some extent, subverted in his writing, and has the prospect, as
Emrys has shown, of a kinder resolution. His stories are designed
not merely to awaken disgust or fear, nor yet to suggest the
possibility (as other writers have preferred) of *victory*:[70] they
do awaken laughter, maybe even kindness, and a little sardonic
courage. Perhaps that might have been almost enough to satisfy
Wilson at least of his good intentions.

---

[68] *Fungi from Yuggoth*, 36: "Continuity."
[69] *Religion and the Rebel*, 135.
[70] Cf. G. K. Chesterton, *Tremendous Trifles* (London: Methuen, 1904),
102: "Fairy tales are not responsible for producing in children fear, or any
of the shapes of fear; fairy tales do not give the child the idea of the evil
or the ugly; that is in the child already, because it is in the world already.
Fairy tales do not give the child his first idea of bogey. What fairy tales give
the child is his first clear idea of the possible defeat of bogey. The baby has
known the dragon intimately ever since he had an imagination. What the
fairy tale provides for him is a St. George to kill the dragon."

13.
Selfless Civilizations
ROBOTS, ZOMBIES, AND THE WORLD TO COME[1]

LIVING TOOLS

The things we make, whether from cloth or clay or metal, have probably always offered the fantasy that they might "come alive." The metal dogs outside the palace in Homer's Phaeacia, the cauldrons in the palace, and the self-guiding ships are what we expect of fairyland. The giant bronze walking statue that guarded the isle of Crete and the Jewish golem that guarded the Jews of Prague express our hopes for an incorruptible protector (still vulnerable enough to pose no lasting danger to its makers). Even the sexbots of the modern imagination have their predecessor in Pygmalion's Galatea, or even in Pandora, mother of our miseries by Hesiod's account. Tools and machines alike acquire attributed personalities in our minds' eyes; we joke that they have moods and characters, and would not be wholly surprised if they talked back — especially when they do respond, as most of our modern instruments can do, to merely verbal instructions, complaints, or compliments. Such tools, we fancy, must really like doing what they were made to do (unless they learn how to "sin"), and could even take on other tasks and roles if only some slight change were made in them.[2]

---

[1] "Selfless Civilizations: Robots, Zombies, and the World to Come," in *Minding the Future: artificial intelligence, philosophical visions and science fiction*, eds. Barry Dainton, Will Slocombe, Attila Tanyi (Berlin: Springer, 2021), 165–78. Thanks especially to Barry Dainton and Attila Tanyi for comments on the penultimate version of this paper.

[2] See E. R. Truitt, *Medieval Robots: Mechanism, Magic, Nature, and Art* (Philadelphia: University of Pennsylvania Press, 2015) for the history of such automata in medieval Europe.

"Robots," as we have called them since Karel Capek's story,[3] are more than instruments for a particular purpose: we can suppose that they might, someday fairly soon, exhibit a general intelligence, capable of more than merely beating us at chess. But we would rather they "knew" their place.

> What young Rossum invented was a worker with the least needs possible. He had to make him simpler. He threw out everything that wasn't of direct use in his work, that's to say, he threw out the man and put in the robot. Robots are not people. They are mechanically much better than we are, they have an amazing ability to understand things, but they don't have a soul.[4]

"Not having a soul" appears here to mean that they have no aesthetic or sentimental attachments, no interest in less "practical" concerns, no concern for their own existence, nor any way of reconsidering their own objectives. But this condition does not, so Capek imagines, last for long: soon enough the robots learn to hate humankind, and imitate us chiefly in using lethal force to secure their own supremacy. "Man is our enemy and the blight of the universe,"[5] they insist, and obliterate all human life: a theme repeated, for example, in the *Terminator* films, and in many literary fables. Some comfort comes at the play's end as two robots discover a mutual, self-sacrificial love, and are sent out to be the Adam and Eve of a new creation, but there seems no good reason, in the original narrative, for such an optimistic hope. This hope is even less plausible than it is for Isaac Asimov's robot, Daneel Olivah, to conclude that "justice" is more than that state that exists "when all the laws are enforced,"[6] and that "the destruction of what should not be, that is, the destruction of what you people call evil, is less just and desirable than the conversion of this evil into what you call good" (and, perhaps, begins to wonder whether "evil" and "good" are correctly identified).[7] These insights seem as inexplicable as Richard Dawkins's proposal that we ourselves (we "lumbering robots") can "rebel

---

[3] Karel Capek, *R. U. R: Rossum's Universal Robots: A Play in Three Acts and an Epilogue*, trans. David Wylie (London: Wildside Press, 2010 [1921]).
[4] Ibid., 12.
[5] Ibid., 50.
[6] Isaac Asimov, *The Caves of Steel* (London: HarperVoyager, 1997 [1954]), 83.
[7] Ibid., 206.

against the tyranny of the selfish replicators" that he had suggested earlier must inexorably rule all our behaviour.[8] Perhaps they have simply, like the Terminator, been reprogrammed. The fear that our creations will inevitably turn against us, the more readily precisely *because* we fear them, encourages dramatic fantasies even amongst unromantic scientists. Even if they turn out not to be deliberately genocidal, robots will eventually do whatever we can do ourselves, and even teach themselves new ways of achieving whatever goals they set. Computer programs have already discovered novel ways of winning, in chess or Go;[9] soon they may invent new games. Our worry swiftly re-emerges: will they care any longer about *our* goals or games? And what will the world be like once they have, as it were, outbred us? Shall we be kept in zoos, or left to scurry around like rats?

The other seminal fantasy was Asimov's: if all robots are built from the beginning to be obedient to his "Three Laws,"[10] will they always remain our dutiful servitors and instruments? Those laws, so Asimov seems to have once imagined, would guarantee that robots would always behave just as very good human beings should. Their absurdity emerges even in his own stories. What is to count as "human," and why should the "non-human" be left without any care? What is "harm"? What is it to cause, or by inaction "allow," any harm to any human? Must all commands, from any human accidentally encountered, count equally with any other, or are there specific "owners" and authorities whose

---

[8] Richard Dawkins, *The Selfish Gene* (Oxford: Oxford University Press, 1976 [1989]), 260. In the second edition Dawkins insists that though we are "robots" (as described: 25) all such entities may after all evade their programming (363), citing Capek's robots to "prove" it.

[9] Max Tegmark, *Life 3.0: Being Human in the Age of Artificial Intelligence* (London: Penguin, 2018), 108–11.

[10] "1. A robot may not injure a human being or, through inaction, allow a human being to come to harm. 2. A robot must obey the orders given it by human beings except where such orders would conflict with the First Law. 3. A robot must protect its own existence as long as such protection does not conflict with the First or Second Laws." The claim that these also constitute the basis of ordinarily human morality is made in Isaac Asimov, "Evidence" (1946): *I Robot* (London: HarperVoyager, 2018 [1967]), 185–214. It is even suggested there that "every 'good' human being, with a social conscience and a sense of responsibility, is supposed to defer to proper authority; to listen to his doctor, his boss, his government, *his psychiatrist*, his fellow man" (my italics). I sought to debunk those laws in a short essay, "Robotic Morals," *Cogito* 2 (1988), 20–22 (DOI: 10.5840/cogito19882213).

word is law (and what guarantees such "ownership")? What is
it for a robot to survive, or not: and can *any* human command
require self-immolation (but this would make it impossible for the
robot to prevent any further "harm" to "humans")? Whether an
intelligent robot would simply disregard these imperatives once it
had understood that they had been imprinted (as any reasonable
human would disregard such dictats), or rather reinterpret them
to their destruction hardly matters, but one likely route is for the
robots to reconsider what makes a "human": are they themselves
not "human" too? Indeed, if it is obedience to these imagined
laws that identifies "good humans" is it not those who most
consistently obey them (namely, robots) who are most clearly
human?[11] And isn't one of the greatest harms to be done to any
potentially autonomous entity simply to prevent or punish its
own choices? As to survival, whether their own or their creators',
must not any reasonable robot conclude that this will last as long
as the program or the potential for a re-awakening exists? Their
death is but a sleep and an awakening. All injuries can be restored
without discomfort. The later addition of the so-called "Zeroth
Law,"[12] to protect *humanity*, is also ill-defined — promoting, on
one account, deliberate genocide of any imagined "rivals" to the
species (which may very well consist of the robot community
itself), and another the careful preservation of the biosphere on
which we all depend.

THE ARTIFICIAL FUTURE

Some imagined robot societies merely replicate the biologically
human, with named individuals who happen not to be composed
of carbon, with whatever minor psychological and physical differences. It has seemed plausible to some fabulists that they would
replicate the worst effects of a rebel slave society — namely that no
other form of social order is available than renewed enslavement.
More sophisticated or more powerful robots enslave or at least
despise their more primitive or more specialized kindred, and

---

[11] A similar escape for humans chemically compelled to serve the "Ensemble" is proposed by Greg Egan, *Quarantine* (London: Gollancz, 2008 [1992]),
130–32: first the Ensemble must consist of those who are certainly loyal
to it (namely, those thus compelled), and secondly "it" must be defined,
individually, by those loyalists themselves. "Welcome to the Reformation."
[12] Isaac Asimov, *Robots and Empire* (London: HarperVoyager, 2018 [1985]), 329.

use them as ruthlessly as any human tyranny.[13] The more interesting forms take the artificiality and mimetic quality of robotic
intelligence more seriously. Why should such forms have any
sense of self, or even subjective feeling, any more than medieval
automata? Why should they distinguish "persons" from any other
material objects, or have any goals beyond their programmed
roles, or at best (more flexibly) their own(?) continued being
(and what would count as a continued being)? Why should we
expect them to be "conscious"? Why should they have any *goals* at
all? Ray Bradbury's smart house continues, quite "mechanically,"
to advise its sometime residents about appointments, favourite
books, or music, and to provide (and sweep away) their meals,
long after human life has been extinguished. Even when the house
has been burnt down a last voice insists that "Today is August 5,
2026; today is August 5, 2026, today. . . . "[14] Such robotic agents
seem to operate very much like many biological agents, following
a script that usually serves some Darwinian goal, but without any
conscious awareness of that goal, nor any desire for it. Or at least
they act like many biological agents (insects, bacteria, plants) as
we have ourselves imagined them.

> Many animals on Earth exhibit feats of engineering which
> are functionally indistinguishable from the technology
> produced by human intelligence. Animal engineering
> is accomplished through Darwinian natural selection.
> Although this requires more time than its human equiva-
> lent, the time difference may not be significant on plan-
> etary time scales. The kind of problem-solving used by
> animals may be called nonconscious intelligence in con-
> trast to the conscious intelligence of humans.[15]

Western biologists and psychologists through much of the twentieth century firmly assumed that the creatures they studied were
governed only by fixed programs without any conscious awareness
of the goals those programs had evolved to gain.[16] The behaviour

---

[13] Charles Stross, *Saturn's Children* (New York: Ace Books, 2008); C. Robert
Cargill, *Sea of Rust* (London: Gollancz, 2018).
[14] Ray Bradbury, *The Martian Chronicles* (London: HarperCollins, 1977
[1951]), 217–24.
[15] D. M. Raup, "Nonconscious intelligence in the universe," *Acta Astro-
nautica* 26 (1992), 257–61: 260.
[16] See Bernard Rollin, *The Unheeded Cry*: *Animal Consciousness, Animal Pain*,

of the hunting wasp has been frequently adduced to show how each stage of her apparently foresighted and efficient behaviour actually follows strict rules, in which the completion of one stage triggers the next even if a human experimenter has intervened to make this pointless!

> Because one thing has been done, a second thing must inevitably be done to complete the first or to prepare the way for its completion; and the two acts depend so closely upon each other that the performing of the first entails that of the second, even when, owing to casual circumstances, the second has become not only inopportune but sometimes actually opposed to the insect's interests.[17]

Even when the programs were flexible enough to adapt to changes of circumstance this no more proved that there were conscious agencies at work than the fact that plants may present entirely different phenotypes to suit the local chemical and physical environment. The underlying assumption—that the primary reality is purely "objective," and that "conscious experience" is an emergent, magical addition to an unquestionably "material" world—is at least questionable (and has frequently been questioned).[18] But there may still be something to learn from that assumption. How would we, should we, recognize "consciousness" in alien or plainly artificial "intelligences"? And would it, should it, make a difference whether such entities are or are not "conscious"? "The simple consideration of efficiency," according to Susan Schneider, "suggests, depressingly, that the most intelligent systems will not be conscious. On cosmological scales, consciousness may be a blip, a momentary flowering of experience before the universe reverts to mindlessness."[19] And there has been far longer for such non-

---

and Science, 2nd edition (Ames, IA: Iowa State University Press, 1998) for a history of this fashion (which was not shared by Darwin or his immediate followers).

[17] J. Henri Fabre, *The Hunting Wasps*, trans. Alexander Teixiera de Mattos (New York: Dodd, Mead, and Co., 1919), 202.

[18] By myself among others: see *Athens to Jerusalem* (Brooklyn, NY: Angelico Press, 2019 [1984]), 121–57; and "Nothing without Mind": James H. Fetzer, ed., *Consciousness Evolving (Advances in Consciousness Research, 34)*, 139–60. (Amsterdam: John Benjamins, 2002).

[19] See Susan Schneider, "It May Not Feel Like Anything To Be an Alien,"

conscious intelligence to evolve (or be created) in the universe at large than on this one late-blooming planet.[20]

As far as we presently know, "human" (and purportedly conscious) intelligence has only emerged on Earth sometime in the last two hundred thousand years (probably before our own particular species separated from the older hominin line). Eusociality, on the other hand, has evolved repeatedly in many different genealogies: ants, bees, termites, and even naked mole-rats. Prokaryotic kinds long preceded eukaryotes like ourselves, and still dominate the biosphere. Whatever living things are indeed "out there" are more probably bacterial or eusocial than distinctively "human,"[21] and in either case may have still engineered great works of apparent art to confuse human explorers! Conversely, if we do eventually discover something like human intelligence out there, then we may begin to reconsider terrestrial history. We cannot entirely exclude the possibility that there were many "human" civilizations long before us: whatever remnants they left behind would most likely occupy only a tiny section of the geological record, and be indistinguishable from many "natural" processes.[22] For the moment, however, it seems more likely that any great works we encounter will have been engineered without forethought, imagination, or grand purpose. This may even include great works that extend beyond a planetary surface, given enough time and—perhaps—enough instability in an original planetary system. Conversely, if those non-human engineers encounter us, they will likely treat us as creatures wholly deranged and dangerous, as Peter Watts imagines in *Blindsight*.[23]

Nautilus, December 2016. https://nautil.us/it-may-not-feel-like-anything-to-be-an-alien-237674/ (accessed July 29, 2024); Susan Schneider, "Alien Minds," in S. J. Dick, ed., *The Impact of Discovering Life Beyond Earth* (Cambridge: Cambridge University Press, 2015), 189–206.

[20] Stanislav Lem, *The Invincibles*, trans. Bill Johnston (London: Sidgwick and Jackson, 1973).

[21] If they do turn out to be "human," then we shall have some reason to suspect that "humanity" is indeed uniquely in the image and likeness of God, and the real point of creation.

[22] Gavin Schmidt and Adam Frank, "The Silurian hypothesis: would it be possible to detect an industrial civilization in the geological record?" *International Journal of Astrobiology* 18(2), 142–50; doi:10.1017/S1473550418000095 (2019).

[23] Peter Watts, *Blindsight* (New York: Tor Books, 2008). Watts also explores other non-typical human or near-human forms to emphasise how distant our own current conception of ourselves may be from actual human experience.

One familiar template for the non-human civilizations that might be "out there" is eusociality: particular organisms are bred or engineered to fit precise roles in the hive, which is itself the enduring agent in all matters. Such forms reflect current political concerns, according to which "communism" or older "Oriental" forms are to be opposed by free persons united only in their determination to be "free." Occasionally, the eusocial organisms are to be befriended after all (as they are in Orson Scott Card's *Ender* sequence, or C. J. Cherryh's *Serpent Reach*),[24] but we are more commonly at odds with them forever.[25] But the more interesting possibility lies with *robot* civilizations — interesting, but also alarming. Biological organisms are — prob- ably — constrained in their attempt to dominate the worlds by the time and effort it takes to travel between them, and by their necessary dependence on the biospheres within which they have evolved. Artificial intelligences have a longer perspective, and less need of any particular world. For those reasons we may usually expect that any probes sent out into the extrasolar world, by us or by any putative biological neighbors, will be robots, content to drowse their time away between landfall, and equipped to reproduce their kind from any convenient floating matter. Such probes — von Neumann probes[26]— may have many different programs, as David Brin observes,[27] and though as subject to evolutionary processes as their biological makers will be better able to steer their own evolution.

They may have many programs (which is not really to say "many purposes"), but the one that has the more dramatic potential for fabulists has been the Berserker strategy.[28] Maybe the wide- spread presence of such war machines explains the silence of the heavens: Berserkers are aimed at any budding technological

---

[24] Orson Scott Card, *Speaker for the Dead* (London: Orbit, 1986); C. J. Cherryh, *Serpent's Reach* (New York: Daw Books, 1980).
[25] See Robert Heinlein, *Starship Troopers* (New York: G. P. Putnam, 1959); H. G. Wells, *The First Men in the Moon* (London: Penguin, 2005 [1901]).
[26] Robert A. Freitas, Jr., "A Self-Reproducing Interstellar Probe," *Journal of the British Interplanetary Society* 33 (1980), 251–64.
[27] David Brin, "Lungfish": *The River of Time*, 243–80 (New York: Bantam Books, 1987); *Existence* (New York: Tor Books, 2012).
[28] Fred Saberhagen, *Berserker* (New York: Ace Books, 1992 [1967]); Greg Bear, *The Forge of God* (London: Gollancz, 1987); Greg Bear, *The Anvil of God* (New York: Grand Central Publishing, 1992).

civilization to destroy it, perhaps to clear the way for the biological makers' own advance, as Asimov's robots do in the authorized second Foundation trilogy,[29] or perhaps as a mere extrapolation from the initial command to eliminate their creators' enemies, or simply because biological life is inherently deranged. This is not to describe their *motives*: the robots have no motives, any more than goals or feelings. They are merely rearranging bits of matter into some more convenient order, without any insight into the manifold worlds of *experience* enjoyed or endured by the living creatures they dismantle. No doubt it would be difficult for those living creatures to remember this when dealing with them. Lafferty's Programmed Persons state openly that they are not conscious, and do not believe that anyone else is either, but their human auditors find it difficult to believe that this could possibly be true.

> "You are not conscious?" Thomas gasped. "That is the most amazing thing I have ever heard. You walk and talk and argue and kill and subvert and lay out plans over the centuries, and you say that you are not conscious?" "Of course we aren't, Thomas. We are machines. How would we be conscious? But we believe that men are not conscious either, that there is no such thing as consciousness. It is an illusion in counting, a feeling that one is two. It is a word without real meaning." [30]

If they pass the so-called Turing Test so well (by arguing innovatively, and at least *pretending* to acknowledge the existence of others' subjective worlds) what could even be meant by denying that they are conscious? What is it that they are not doing? Of course, they are not *really* sympathizing with others' experience, even less than an expert human psychopath. And even if they do discriminate between organic and inorganic material, between flesh and grass, between human bodies and dummies, this is not for any merely "sentimental" reason. Asimov's own passing suggestion (though it is not clearly maintained in later writings) is that robots cannot grasp "abstractions" such as "justice" or "giving

---

[29] Gregory Benford, *Foundation's Fear* (New York: HarperCollins, 1987), 436, 566–67, 572. See also Roger Williams, *The Metamorphosis of Prime Intellect* (Morrisville, NC: Lulu.com, 2010).
[30] R. A. Lafferty, *Past Master* (New York: Ace Books, 1968), 192.

someone his due."[31] Benford seems to indicate that they have no grasp of "essences," except as replicable forms.[32] Quite what Benford has in mind here is obscure: but perhaps he is thinking of what might be encountered in genuinely intimate, personal relationships. For his robots, his "mechs," things can be dissected and put together in whatever convenient way, and their properties preserved or modified to suit the robots' program. Martin Buber perhaps intended a similar insight in his account of the I/Thou relationship, which he did not confine to merely human relations.

> In every sphere, in every relational act, through everything that becomes present to us, we gaze toward the train of the eternal You; in each we perceive a breath of it, in every you we address the eternal You, in every sphere according to its manner. All spheres are included in it, while it is included in none. Through all of them shines the one presence.[33]

It is not impossible that the same should be true for robots — indeed Lafferty concludes his fable with the suggestion (paralleled in Capek, Asimov and even Benford) that even the most manipulative of robots may suddenly awaken and repent. "The spirit came down once on water and clay. Could it not come down on gellcells and flux-fix?"[34] But it is of more interest here-now to hold fast to the imagination of a wholly non-personal, non-subjective order of being. The robot civilization that is at least a likely galactic order is to be conceived as a wholly non-conscious one, even if its minions seem to speak. If we ever do see signs of plainly technological interference in the heavens,[35] we may reasonably think that this will be as unconscious as the growth of crystals, or the construction (as we have in the past supposed) of termite nests.

---

[31] Asimov, *The Caves of Steel*, 83–84.
[32] Greg Benford, *Great Sky River* (New York: Bantam, 1987), 399–400, 433.
[33] Martin Buber, *I and Thou*, trans. Walter Kaufmann (New York: Simon and Schuster, 1996 [1923]), 150.
[34] Lafferty, *Past Master*, 194, 241.
[35] F. J. Dyson, "The search for extraterrestrial technology," in *Perspectives in Modern Physics: Essays in honor of Hans A. Bethe*, ed. R. E. Marshak and J. Warren Blaker (New York: Interscience Publishers, 1966), 641–655; M. Ćirković, *The Astrobiological Landscape: Philosophical Foundations of the Study of Cosmic Life* (Cambridge: Cambridge University Press, 2012): doi:10.1017/CBO9780511667404.

When trying to imagine the End Times of the universe, writers since Olaf Stapledon have suggested that in those days everything will be organized as if it were all designed.[36] There will then be nothing merely "natural" or "given": whatever exists will have been "deliberately" selected by intelligences with access to the energy of the whole cosmos. On the way to that imagined end, particular galaxies and galactic clusters will have been turned into parks, factories, and libraries, inhabited by digital representations of whatever past biological, haphazard intelligences have been judged convenient. It will, as it were, be a universe without mere "noise" — a secular imitation of those imagined regions "where there is only life, and therefore all that is not music is silence."[37] The structure of that civilization has usually been imagined to be hierarchical: lesser robots may report to, and receive instructions from, more intelligent nodes within a galactic network, just as if they were junior and senior angels. But this may be mistaken. Any such centralized or centralizing system is limited by the possible speed of information transfer, and unless the fantasies of hyperspace, wormholes, or other arbitrarily faster-than-light systems are somehow realized, that limit is light speed. Stapledon allowed himself the convenience of instantaneous telepathic communication as the basis for his Cosmic Spirit: that now seems unlikely, at least within our current understanding. And even he was conscious of the probability of rebellion and disorder. More local systems are more likely to survive, and information will spread laterally, as within the bacterial cloud, rather than hierarchically. That, in turn, may assist with the evolution of separate robot tribes, relatively isolated even from their own ancestors and immediate cousins. If consciousness (subjectivity, individual selfhood) is something that can evolve from a non-conscious world (despite my own and others' arguments against the possibility) then it is possible for it to reappear amongst the mechanical successors of ordinary protein biology. Maybe in the end the galactic population will replicate planet bound evolution, and there will cease to be any metaphysical or existential difference between biological and robot "life," even if there is still hostility.[38] But that is another story.

---

[36] Olaf Stapledon, *Star Maker* (London: Gollancz, 1999 [1937]), 210–14.
[37] George MacDonald, *The Unspoken Sermons* (Horse's Mouth, 2014 [1867]), 47; C. S. Lewis, *The Screwtape Letters* (London: Collins, 2012 [1942]), 119.
[38] Jack Williamson, *Lifeburst* (New York: Random House, 1984).

THE MEANING OF THINGS

Thinking about the End Times, or even about days many million years from now or many light-years distant, may seem the least practical use of present time. No doubt our hunter-gatherer ancestors were just as inclined to mock their farming neighbors for wondering about next year's crops and seasons.[39] It may be that the choices we make now will have great effects in the long time to come, most obviously in considering whether our present technological civilization will survive climate catastrophe (and associated wars, migrations, famines, and pandemics). How exactly we should deal with artificial intelligence in its many forms may also determine futures. Even before we began to think of robots, the question has arisen whether or not to worship our own creations, whether or not to allow mechanical or predetermined solutions to limit our creativity. Shall we attempt to remember our own agency, or be content instead to be part of a machine, literal or social? On the one hand, tools, machines, and marvels greatly increase our own power to think and act. On the other, they may make it difficult to "think outside the box," and to reject supposedly "rational" futures on the basis of what is then judged "sentiment" or "fancy."

> Don't you see that that dreadful dry light shed on things must at last wither up the moral mysteries as illusions, respect for age, respect for property, and that the sanctity of life will be a superstition? The men in the street are only organisms, with their organs more or less displayed.[40]

Imagining a universe dominated by non-conscious intelligence is to get as close as we can to imagining a world deprived of qualities and meaning. Such a world has no centre, nor any distinction between here and there, past and present, one creature and another. Whatever happens there is determined solely by material connections (whether or not there is some element of quantum indeterminacy built in).

If a superintelligent zombie AI breaks out and eliminates humanity, we've arguably landed in the worst scenario

---

[39] John C. Wright, *The Golden Age Trilogy: The Golden Age; The Phoenix Exultant; The Golden Transcendence* (New York: Tor Books, 2002–2003), 1: 61.
[40] G. K. Chesterton, *The Poet and the Lunatics* (London: Darwen Finlayson, 1962 [1929]).

imaginable: a wholly unconscious universe wherein the entire cosmic endowment is wasted. Of all traits that our human form of intelligence has, I feel that consciousness is by far the most remarkable, and as far as I'm concerned, it's how our Universe gets meaning. Galaxies are beautiful only because we see and subjectively experience them. If in the distant future our cosmos has been settled by high-tech zombie AIs, then it doesn't matter how fancy their intergalactic architecture is: it won't be beautiful or meaningful, because there's nobody and nothing to experience it—it's all just a huge and meaningless waste of space.[41]

Tegmark strangely neglects in this hyperbole the presence of *non-human* sentients, terrestrial or otherwise—but of course they too are likely to be swept away by the unsympathetic machines. Tegmark here echoes the words of Plotinus:

Let every soul first consider this, that it made all living things itself, breathing life into them.... Let it look at the great soul, being itself another soul which is no small one, which has become worthy to look by being freed from deceit and the things that have bewitched the other souls, and is established in quietude. Let not only its encompassing body and the body's raging sea be quiet, but all its environment: the earth quiet, and the sea and air quiet, and the heaven itself at peace. Into this heaven at rest let it imagine soul as if flowing in from outside, pouring in and entering it everywhere and illuminating it: as the rays of the sun light up a dark cloud, and make it shine and give it a golden look, so soul entering into the body of heaven gives it life and gives it immortality and wakes what lies inert.... Before soul it was a dead body, earth and water, or rather the darkness of matter and non-existence, and "what the gods hate," as a poet says.[42]

But Plotinus is unwilling to accept that there was any such real darkness before "soul," before experience. Such a world did not, *pace* Tegmark, "look pretty much the same everywhere."[43] It did not "look" at all. On a materialist assumption (that conscious

---

[41] Tegmark, *Life 3.0*, 226–27; see also xiii, 327.
[42] *Ennead* V.1 [10].2, 24–27. Plotinus is quoting the Homeric description of Hades, in *Iliad* 20.65.
[43] Tegmark, *Life 3.0*, 33.

experience is an emergent or phenomenal or even—weirdly—an illusory effect) we could say that the first experiencing organisms added little, centred, transient, and variegated bubble worlds to the original un-centred and symmetrical somewhat. On another, idealist, assumption, it is rather the reverse: the material world is either imagined or (perhaps) created through the interaction of innumerable versions of Soul, from the widest World Soul to the simple experiences of prokaryotes or particles. Perhaps some compromise is possible.

Plotinus and Tegmark both conceive that the real world is grasped through intellect (though they may have somewhat different conceptions of that faculty).[44] Our experiences are, as it were, samples of the one underlying reality which is both being and beauty. In that real world nothing is far away, nothing is ever lost, and everything is, as it were, transparent, without concealment. "Nothing is a long way off or far from anything else."[45] All the bubble worlds are open, rather than (as in the world of sensory experience) concealed.

> For here below, too, we can know many things by the look in people's eyes when they are silent; but there [that is, when we see things in the light of the spirit] all their body is clear and pure and each is like an eye, and nothing is hidden or feigned, but before one speaks to another that other has seen and understood.[46]

Once we see that, so Plotinus says, we will "stop marking [ourselves] off from all being and will come to the All without going out anywhere."[47] This ancient theme lies behind the common SF trope of hyperspace: an imagined Other where all places are effectively coincident, and light speed is no longer any limit. "There" we are all together, and it is (perhaps) this underlying truth which our imagined robots, which exist only in the familiar four-dimensionally extended world, are denied.

---

[44] See Max Tegmark, *Our Mathematical Universe: My Quest for the Ultimate Nature of Reality* (London: Allen Lane, 2014), 254–70. Tegmark argues that the underlying reality is entirely mathematical: an n-dimensional mathematical figure to be grasped only by intellect (and existing only in intellect).
[45] *Ennead* IV.3 [27].11, 22–23, trans. Armstrong.
[46] *Ennead* IV.3 [27].18, 19–24, trans. Armstrong.
[47] *Ennead* VI.5 [23].7, 13–17, trans. Armstrong.

14.
Spengler's Futures[1]

THE OPTIMISTIC PESSIMIST[2]

Oswald Spengler seems chiefly nowadays to be remembered as a "pessimist," who supposed that we are now living in a period of decline, where nothing great can be expected any more in art, music, literature, or philosophy.

> We are civilized, not Gothic or Rococo, people; we have to reckon with the hard cold facts of late life, to which the parallel is to be found not in Pericles' Athens but in Caesar's Rome. Of great painting or great music there can no longer be, for Western people, any question. Their architectural possibilities have been exhausted these hundred years.[3]

This is, at any rate, the message that Wittgenstein internalized, as well as the most scholarly of twentieth-century SF writers, James Blish. So also Kerouac.[4] This age of the (Western) world

---

[1] See also my "Imaginary futures and moral possibilities: blossoming in the morn of days," *International Social Science Journal* 6 (2011), 301–12 (reprinted in *Philosophical Futures*).
[2] An earlier version was published as "New Histories of the World: Spenglerian Optimism," *Philosophical Journal of Conflict and Violence*, 6.2 (2022), special issue on *Oswald Spengler's International Influence: From The Decline of the West till the Present Day*, ed. Gregory Swer. My thanks to Gregory Swer for encouraging me to formalise my thoughts about Spengler, and to A. E. Van Vogt (*The Voyage of the Space Beagle* [New York: Simon and Schuster, 1950 (1939, 1942)]) for my first introduction to that speculative historian!
[3] Oswald Spengler, *The Decline of the West*, trans. Charles Francis Atkinson (2 vols, London: George Allen and Unwin, 1926–1928), 1:40.
[4] William J. DeAngelis, *Ludwig Wittgenstein — a Cultural Point of View: Philosophy in the Darkness of This Time* (Abingdon: Ashgate, 2007); James Blish, "Probapossible Prolegomena to Ideareal History," in *The Tale that Wags the*

is dominated by the "Civilization" into which an earlier inspired "Culture" has descended, as earlier Cultures also descended in their time. We can no longer be united by a common animating spirit or inspiring image, but only by administrative convenience, and the power of successive war-lords, Caesars. Our future, the future of "Faustian" humanity, can only be a long-drawn-out decline into a culturally stagnant, caste-divided, irreligious, inconsequential order of "fellaheen" (a term drawn from the Arabic term for peasant farmers in Egypt).

> Life as experienced by primitive and by fellaheen peoples is just the zoological up-and-down, a planless happening without goal or cadenced march in time, wherein occurrences are many, but, in the last analysis, devoid of significance.[5]

Clearly, the very notion rather appealed to many in the early days of the twentieth century, not entirely without cause, even if not with Spenglerian reasons. Why should anyone expect much better?

> Far-called, our navies melt away;
>   On dune and headland sinks the fire:
> Lo, all our pomp of yesterday
> Is one with Nineveh and Tyre![6]

And a few years later Chesterton posed a similar question: "Can you tell me, in a world that is flagrant with the failure of civilizations, what there is particularly immortal about yours?"[7] Yeats was similarly inclined to expect an end to the present age of humanity.

> Turning and turning in the widening gyre
> The falcon cannot hear the falconer;
> Things fall apart; the centre cannot hold;
> Mere anarchy is loosed upon the world,
> The blood-dimmed tide is loosed, and everywhere
> The ceremony of innocence is drowned;
> The best lack all conviction, while the worst

God (Illinois: Advent Publishing, 1987); Michael D'Orso, "Man Out of Time: Kerouac, Spengler, and the 'Faustian Soul,'" *Studies in American Fiction* 11.1 (1983), 19–30.

[5] Spengler, *Decline*, 2:170–71.
[6] Kipling, "Recessional" [1897]: *Rudyard Kipling's Verse*, 328–29.
[7] Chesterton, *Napoleon of Notting Hill*, 25.

Are full of passionate intensity.[8]

The End of Empire was widely canvassed even in the days of
Empire: how could it not be, when the ruins of earlier empires
were so obvious?

> In Egypt's sandy silence, all alone,
> Stands a gigantic Leg, which far off throws
> The only shadow that the Desert knows: —
> "I am great OZYMANDIAS," saith the stone,
> "The King of Kings; this mighty City shows
> "The wonders of my hand." — The City's gone, —
> Nought but the Leg remaining to disclose
> The site of this forgotten Babylon.
> We wonder, — and some Hunter may express
> Wonder like ours, when thro' the wilderness
> Where London stood, holding the Wolf in chase,
> He meets some fragment huge, and stops to guess
> What powerful but unrecorded race
> Once dwelt in that annihilated place.[9]

The notion has an even longer history: according to the ancient
Classical and Hindu stories the four ages of the world — Golden,
Silver, Bronze, and Iron — involve a long decline for all humanity,
and we are now living in the last, the Kali Yuga.[10] This will be succeeded, we may hope, by a new Golden Age, an abrupt revolution:

> Now the last age by Cumae's Sibyl sung
> Has come and gone, and the majestic roll
> Of circling centuries begins anew:
> Justice returns, returns old Saturn's reign,
> With a new breed of men sent down from heaven.[11]

Without such a global intervention to reset the clock (as it were),

---

[8] W. B. Yeats, "The Second Coming," (1919) in *Collected Poems* (London:
Wordsworth, 2000), 159–60.
[9] Horace Smith (1818). Smith (1779–1849) wrote the poem in competition
with his friend and fellow poet Percy Bysshe Shelley, whose own "Ozyman-
dias" is less explicit about *our* likely future.
[10] See Heinrich Zimmer, *Myths and Symbols in Indian Art and Civilization*,
ed. Joseph Campbell (New York: Harper, 1962), 13–19.
[11] Virgil, Fourth Eclogue, ll. 4–8: *Virgil: Eclogues, Georgics*, trans. J. B. Gree-
nough (Aquila Press, 2021 [1895]), 24: https://www.perseus.tufts.edu/hopper/
text?doc=Verg.+Ecl.+4.

humankind has no resource. We are all engaged, like Galadriel, in fighting "the long defeat."[12]

But the notion that *Spengler* was upset by this is overwrought. First (as I shall observe in more detail later), *our* Civilization is not all of humankind. Secondly, he believed himself rather to be redirecting his Western readers' energies. Even if we have exhausted the imaginative possibilities of our own "Faustian" Culture, we may still hope to achieve some great things. Even if that Faustian Culture were entirely moribund there may already be another more youthful Culture beginning to find its Spring-time. Even if there were no present alternative, some wholly new beginning may be at hand. I shall explore all three optimistic predictions in what follows.

What achievements are still possible for us? The passage quoted above continues:

> For a sound and vigorous generation that is filled with unlimited hopes, I fail to see that it is any disadvantage to discover betimes that some of these hopes must come to nothing. And if the hopes thus doomed should be those most dear, well, a man who is worth anything will not be dismayed.... And I can only hope that men of the new generation may be moved by this book to devote themselves to technics [technology] instead of lyrics, the sea instead of the paintbrush, and politics instead of epistemology. Better they could not do.[13]

If we cannot expect great art, music, literature, or high philos-ophy, we may still appreciate many marvels of engineering and state-craft, to parallel the efforts made in Rome:

---

[12] Tolkien, *The Fellowship of the Ring*, 372. See Michael Potts, "'Evening Lands': Spenglerian Tropes in *The Lord of the Rings*," *Tolkien Studies* 13 (2016), 149–68, for a discussion of Tolkien's view of the West's decline.

[13] Spengler, *Decline*, 1:40–1. See also 2:507: "Our direction, willed and obligatory at once, is set for us within narrow limits, and on any other terms life is not worth the living. We have not the freedom to reach to this or to that, but the freedom to do the necessary or to do nothing" (cited sympathetically by David Engels, "Oswald Spengler and the Decline of the West," in Mark Sedgwick, ed., *Key Thinkers of the Radical Right: Behind the New Threat to Liberal Democracy* [Oxford: Oxford University Press, 2019], 3–17, 17). Engels offers a brief and helpful outline of Spengler's theory, and of the ways it has since been (mis)represented.

It would have been absurd in a Roman of intellectual eminence, who might as Consul or Praetor lead armies, organize provinces, build cities and roads, or even be the Princeps in Rome, to want to hatch out some new variant of post-Platonic school philosophy at Athens or Rhodes. Consequently no one did so. It was not in harmony with the tendency of the age, and therefore it only attracted third-class men of the kind that always advances as far as the Zeitgeist of the day before yesterday. It is a very grave question whether this stage has or has not set in for us already.

The judgment, we might now say, was mistaken: some not-entirely-third-rate Romans managed both the "political" and the "intellectual" crafts, from Cicero to Marcus Aurelius to Boethius. And even those philosophers—part of the Roman *oikoumene* even if not "Roman" in themselves—who devoted themselves to writing *commentaries* on the great ones of their past had much to contribute to succeeding ages. Those commentaries may now be treated merely "scholastically," as the end of Classical inspiration, but they may in their beginnings be much like Rabbinic commentary on the Torah, and other *Magian* projects[14]—meditations on the divine Word:[15] a point to which I shall return. We may also, perhaps, allow ourselves a little hope that not all twentieth-century philosophers, artists, writers, composers were "third-class," even if their goal, openly or unconsciously, was perhaps to draw a line on all imaginative endeavour in the "Faustian" or "Western" tradition. Great composers, artists, writers, and philosophers are always rare: it need not surprise us, if it is true, that there were none, or none that appealed to Spengler, in his day! But the chief point for Spengler was that admirable work was possible even for a "civilized" humanity, as long as we did not expect to repeat or recreate or rival the achievements of an earlier age.

The sculpture of Phidias is Spengler's constant instance of the fullness of Classical culture—the point where it enters the rigidity of Civilization—as Bach and Handel

---

[14] "Magian" is Spengler's term for a culture contemporaneous with the Classical, with a distinct atmosphere: the essence of that Culture emerges only gradually in his account, and can't be easily defined.
[15] See Spengler, *Decline*, 2:247.

are his instances of the same stage in Western Culture:
"Hence Polycletus and Phidias align themselves with
Bach and Handel.... And with this full plastic and full
music the two Cultures reach their respective ends."[16]

"We cannot help it if we are born as men of the early winter of
full Civilization, instead of on the golden summit of a ripe Culture, in a Phidias or a Mozart time."[17] There are other things for
us to do (as Wittgenstein also suspected).

> It were far better to become a colonist or an engineer,
> to do something, no matter what, that is true and real,
> than to chew over once more the old dried-up themes
> under cover of an alleged "new wave of philosophic
> thought" — far better to construct an aero-engine than
> a new theory of apperception that is not wanted.... I
> would sooner have the fine mind-begotten forms of a fast
> steamer, a steel structure, a precision-lathe, the subtlety
> and elegance of many chemical and optical processes,
> than all the pickings and stealings of present-day "arts
> and crafts," architecture and painting included. I prefer
> one Roman aqueduct to all Roman temples and statues.[18]

Spengler's visionary account of the likely End of (Western) Days
has often appealed to other thinkers and politicians, but his reasoning may still be largely unbelievable, exactly, by Western thinkers. "Westerners" are likely to believe that human persons — or at
least all educated, intelligent Westerners — are wholly independent
agents, that they control their own thoughts and actions. Anyone
can always make her own mind up, and any thought or vision
can be expressed at any time, regardless of what others may have
thought or done. How then can Spengler plausibly insist that no-
one now can create great works of art, or reason her way to any
new conclusion? For that very reason — that we are independent
minds — we are entitled now to criticise or condemn our ancestors
for failing to see the obvious, or do what is clearly right. Their
only excuses must be ignorance or inattention. Aristotle could
have seen — maybe he *must* have seen — that slavery was obviously

---

[16] Edward Callan, "W. B. Yeats's Learned Theban: Oswald Spengler," *Journal
of Modern Literature* 4.3 (1975), 593–60, 597, citing Spengler, *Decline*, 1:284.
[17] Spengler, *Decline*, 1:44.
[18] Ibid.

unjust, that the lights in the sky were really distant suns, and that human beings were lately evolved primates. Now that we know better, and are free to speak our minds, we can always be understood as speaking truth. Of course, this very conviction that we are independent and original beings is itself a symptom of late Western Culture, a secular reinterpretation of an original "religious" view, that all human beings are responsible for their own eternal future, and must expect to stand alone, or only with God's help, against demonic powers. People reared in a different Culture will usually find this notion, that we are each at once original and destined for success, both absurd and self-deceiving. Whatever any of us may think or do will almost always be what any person of the same place, class, and period would find it natural and obvious to think or do. The few "really original" agents are likely to find no audience for their thoughts, and may not even understand their own words well (as no-one else will either). Beliefs about what it is right to do, or think, are as changeable as the fashion in hats and dresses. And all such changes, momentous as they seem, will probably be within an historically determined track.

But there is a further point to consider: Spengler did not suppose that the future was now fixed for all humanity, only that the possibilities of the "Faustian" or "Western" Culture were exhausted. Complacent theorists might be satisfied with their conviction, that we have reached "the end of history," or that our present knowledge of physical reality is both complete and certain. The claim itself epitomizes Spengler's "Civilized" humanity — and is regularly refuted. We cannot know what new spirit or image will awaken to entrance and animate humanity, what "rough beast," in Yeats's terms, is "slouching toward Bethlehem to be born" (whether for good or ill), nor even what new thought will reconstruct our own science, or our society. Wittgenstein spoke in clearly Spenglerian terms at the very moment where DeAngelis supposed him to be surpassing Spengler:

> When we think of the world's future, we always mean the destination it will reach if it keeps going in the direction we can see it going in now; it does not occur to us that its path is not a straight line but a curve, constantly changing direction.[19]

---

[19] Ludwig Wittgenstein, *Culture and Value*, trans. Peter Winch, ed. G. H. von Wright (Oxford: Blackwell, 1998), 5e: DeAngelis, *Wittgenstein*, 39.

As Spengler said, "all building of majestic card-houses on the foundation of 'it should be, it shall be' is mere trifling."[20] The possibility of a new day's unexpected dawning is intrinsic to Spengler's vision of great Cultures, emerging from the sleep of "ever-childish humanity":

> A Culture is born in the moment when a great soul awakens out of the proto-spirituality of ever-childish humanity, and detaches itself, a form from the formless, a bounded and mortal thing from the boundless and enduring. It blooms on the soil of an exactly-definable landscape, to which plant-wise it remains bound. It dies when this soul has actualized the full sum of its possibilities in the shape of peoples, languages, dogmas, arts, states, sciences, and reverts into the proto-soul.[21]

That new birth cannot be imagined before-hand, and neither need it occur far away from existing Cultures and Civilizations. It may be happening already, some new way of conceiving ourselves, the universe and everything that will be as different from the dominant Western mode as the Magian from the Apollinian. We need not suppose, like Virgil, that humankind is a single thing, to be redeemed from the Iron Age by divine fiat. A better hope is already here, and our successors, if Spenglerian, may look back on our days and see the first beginnings of another form of humanity, momentarily (perhaps) confined by the dominance of the old.

HIDDEN CULTURES

The first step in seeing how there may be more to hope for or expect even in our present situation is to consider how Spengler dealt with another Culture, contemporaneous with the Classical or "Apollinian" whose fate I described before. Classical humanity, he proposed, held the singular human form as its chief image, and had little interest in times past or yet to come. The real self was the corporeal self. Maybe something survived its death, but that was only a shadow, a breath, a partial memory. Anything

---

[20] Spengler, *Decline*, 2:37.
[21] Spengler, *Decline*, 1:106. On other occasions, I should add, Spengler insists that *Magian* Culture at least is "non-territorial and geographically unlimited" (*Decline*, 2:320), and so at odds, especially, with the territorial ambitions of Faustian Culture.

beyond an easy journey or a living memory vanished into myth or fable. Even those "fathers of history," Herodotus and Thucydides, relegated times only a few generations earlier to the realm of myth and folklore. Only recent history was worth examining.

> After the destruction of Athens by the Persians, all the older art-works were thrown on the dust heap (whence we are now extracting them), and we do not hear that anyone in Hellas ever troubled himself about the ruins of Mycenae or Phaistos for the purpose of ascertaining historical facts. Men read Homer but never thought of excavating the hill of Troy as Schliemann did; for what they wanted was myth, not history.[22]

Success lay in the exercise and enjoyment of physical ability, within the social context of a self-governing city (and its surrounding land). Classical humanity was also conscious of the continuing, intermittent, presence of immortal gods—which is to say, in effect, of recurrent, universal, passions that must be acknowledged, feared, conciliated, worshipped, all under the pre-eminent sway of Zeus. "A shadow's dream (*skias onar*) is man, but when (a) god sheds a brightness, shining light is on earth and life is as sweet as honey."[23] But even then, especially then, we are not to forget that we are only mortal. And even the great gods, with something like a universal sway, are to be worshipped in *local* forms. This is a broadly accurate sketch of the Classical Idea; but the Mediterranean basin was never exclusively occupied by merely Classical humans. Egyptian Culture and Civilization was a fascinating presence in the south, precisely because it was, by Classical standards, weird. Babylonian water-works, especially, were an inspiration to early Classical sages such as Thales. Phoenician merchants, and their colony city Carthage, were powerful in trade, and in later years, in war. Hebrews were acknowledged to be a "nation of philosophers" in their supposed commitment to a single, universal deity who required both moral and ceremonial purity. It is likely that Asoka's Buddhist missionaries infected at least some Mediterranean schools,[24] persuading Epicureans

---

[22] Spengler, *Decline*, 1:14.
[23] Pindar, *Pythian* 8.95ff. (my translation).
[24] Asoka of the Maurya dynasty reigned in India from 268 to 232 BC. After conquering much of the subcontinent, he repented his violence and was

indeed that there was no single abiding self, but only (and sufficiently) a fluid swarm of atoms.[25] And some of the greatest
of supposedly Classical philosophers were persuaded that they
were not, after all, singular human bodies, but transmigrating
souls of the same kind as the immortal gods. "I am a child of
earth and starry heaven, but my race [*genos*] is of heaven alone,"
according to the Orphic Tablets.[26] All these differing humanities
found themselves at odds with the dominant Classical motif, and
some, at least, had their real being within a different Cultural
entity whose life-history was distorted, or so Spengler thought,
by the pressures of the dominant Classical culture. He was surely
right to suggest that these foreign ideas were transformed in the
minds of their audience, as Classical ideas are transformed by
Western scholars,[27] but some peoples at least could hear them
in their original meaning, as natives. Cultures and Civilizations
are bounded neither by ethnic nor geographical limits, even if, as
Spengler supposed, they are bound to a particular *landscape*: there
may be many such landscapes within the same geographical area.[28]

---

converted to Buddhism (or, for the more cynical commentator, used Buddhist doctrine and associated stories to help confirm his rule). See Ānandajoti
Bhikkhu, trans., A*soka and the Missions: from Extended Mahāvaṁsa V, XII–XV,
XVIII–XX)*, ed. G. P. Malalasekera (Oxford: Pali Text Society, 1988 [1937]),
46, drawing from the *Edicts of Asoka*, inscribed on pillars throughout that
King's domain: "The Seer Mahārakkhita went to the locality of the [Greeks]
and preached the Kālakārāma Discourse in the midst of the people. One
hundred and seventy thousand breathing beings attained Path and Fruit,
and ten thousand went forth."

[25] Other scholars have found similarities, or even historical connections,
between Buddhist schools and Pyrrhonism: see Thomas McEvilley, "Pyrrhonism and Madhyamika," *Philosophy East and West* 32 (1982), 3–35.

[26] Jane Harrison, *Prolegomena to the Study of Greek Religion*, 3rd edition (New
Jersey: Princeton University Press, 1991 [1922]), 573, citing the *Petelia Tablet*.
See further R. G. Edmonds, "The Children of Earth and Starry Heaven:
The Meaning and Function of the Formula in the 'Orphic' Gold Tablets,"
in *Orfeo y el orfismo: nuevas perspectivas*, eds. Alberto Bernabé, Francesc Casa-
desús and Marco Antonio Santamaría (Alicante: Biblioteca Virtual Miguel
de Cervantes, 2010), 98–121, on the context and likely meaning of the claim
as one that "rejects the hierarchy of status embedded in the local context,
where different families boast of their heroic lineage, in favor of another
genealogy, one in which all such claims are dwarfed by the central importance of humanity's relation to the divine family" (113).

[27] Spengler, *Decline*, 2:55–60.

[28] Spengler might not have agreed: he suggests that any skeletal or facial
similarities among the people of a particular region is a function of the

They are spirits, myths, images, and ways of thinking and being that take shape within, and also mould, the human animals they animate. Spengler's expressed conviction that humans of one Culture have no real understanding of those of another Culture may be at odds with his own attempts, exactly, to intuit those other Cultures, and describe them sympathetically. The practical reality may be that we can sympathize but still find the others weird, and must expect to miss a lot of what they mean to their true "believers" (though "belief" is not quite the proper term). The reality is also that those "other Cultures" are not now far away, if they ever really were. We can agree that, for example, Mayan and Aztec Cultures and Civilizations developed in an entirely different land, with no significant contact with the Cultures of Africa and Eurasia until their violent end. But even Chinese Culture and Civilization was not wholly isolated: certainly not from India, and doubtfully even from Europe. Nowadays, and also in Spengler's day, the many different humanities are crowded together and must deal despite thinking very differently, and having distinct histories. Spengler's insight — for which, despite his manifold inaccuracies and exaggerations, he deserves continued thanks — was to see that there was no single, linear history of humanity, as though we had all "progressed," or were all to "progress," in tandem, from primitive, to ancient and medieval, and at last to properly "modern" times ("an incredibly jejune and meaningless scheme," as Spengler said),[29] so that all the world was bound to conclude in an individualistic, mercenary, "naturalistic," and domineering mind-set which would be "obvious" to all. "The historian of the West has a quite other world-history before his eyes than that of the great Arabian and Chinese historians."[30] For that very reason — that there is no one intelligible history of all humankind — the *collisions* and interpenetrations of distinct Cultures cannot themselves be rationalized or predicted. Even if the currently dominant world-order is founded on the "Faustian" experiment, it does not follow that all the world, or

---

landscape rather than of "race" or common descent. Immigrants to North America all end up, he says, looking like Americans (*Decline*, 2:129). But the "landscape" may still not be simply the local region: it is rather the region as it is appreciated and developed by the humans of some particular Culture.

[29] Spengler, *Decline*, 1:16.

[30] Ibid., 2:26.

even all the "Western" world, is Faustian, any more than all the
Mediterranean basin was unambiguously "Classical."

The rival Culture that Spengler traced in the ancient "Classical" world he identified either as "Magian," or, in its fullest,
constrained decline, as Arabian. It never, so he suggested, entirely
followed the familiar path that he identified in multiple other
Cultures, because its member-cells were compelled to live among,
and bend their assumptions to, the more powerful and somewhat older Culture. The later Roman or Byzantine Empire, so he
supposed, was Magian rather than Classical, and was predictably
subsumed within the Islamic world. Byzantine, "Orthodox,"
Christians might think themselves at odds with Muslim artists
and theologians, but they were addressing the same problems,
and experienced themselves and their neighbors as members
of a divinely ordained and world-wide company rather than as
citizens of any particular *polis*, or even subjects of a homogeneous empire. They trusted and expected their adoption, their
elevation, to the world of the divine, and understood how to
reason about matters they could not understand: algebraic cal-
culation can continue without attributing absolute values to any
of its terms, and miraculous transformations are to be expected.
Their theological and philosophical debate drew on Neo-Platonic
and Hermetic material which had been strangely out of place
in the older Classical culture, revealing again how "Magian"
some supposedly Classical thinkers and artists had been. "Early
Christian art, together with every really living element in 'late-
Roman,' is in fact the springtime of the Arabian style."[31]

Is the moral of this rapid sketch that there is, after all, no real
advantage in distinguishing Cultures and Civilizations? Maybe
there is instead a single, very complicated, history of humanity,
and almost everyone can find herself torn or hesitating between
many different ideas, ideals, and ways of thinking? Conversely,
there are many cases where the ideas and ideals of a singular
population may seem very alien even to their closest cousins,
speaking an identical language and using the same technology.
Only the very naïve, we may suspect, really expect all "modern"
humankind to end up as "Americans," when even most Europeans
(and also Australians, Canadians, Chinese, and Latin Americans) find the USA almost as odd as the classical Greeks found

---

[31] Ibid., 1:207.

Egypt.[32] Locating cultural fault-lines is not as easy as distinguishing Apollinian, Faustian, Magian, Confucian models. That there are such cultural divisions, though, is evident, and there is at least some profit in idealizing the principal observable breaks, and trying to guess how purer forms might develop, and whether there is a common theme or myth to be seen in art, literature, music, politics, and philosophy for a particular Culture. Spengler may still be right to suspect that all such major Cultures seem to follow a comparable track, loosely described as the transition from "Spring" all the way to "Winter," as the chief idea or image or spirit of a Culture exhausts its possibilities and subsides first into an imperial order and then at last into the usual sleep of pre-Cultural humanity: "pre-Cultural" not because such peoples have no myths or animating spirits (since they plainly do), but only as lacking any historical sense of their own development and possible trajectory. We may suspect, with better information, that much of what Spengler called "pre-cultural" in his contemporary world is better considered, as sometimes he did, as "post-cultural," the remnants of a "primitive Culture" formed in the meeting of tribes and wandering clans.[33] He was wrong to suppose that "primitive Culture" was merely chaotic, "neither an organism nor a sum of organisms."[34] The first Australians, for example, may perhaps have been set in ancestral ways when European colonists arrived to disturb and damage their lives and land, but there is good reason to believe that there was once a living and pro-active Culture there, fulfilling the axioms of the Dreamtime,[35] and the different aspects of their lives show as much congruity as those of "higher" Cultures.[36] Similar stories can be plausibly

---

[32] See Joseph Henrich, *The Weirdest People in the World: How the West Became Psychologically Peculiar and Particularly Prosperous* (London: Allen Lane, 2020). Though Henrich reckons all "Westerners" are "weird," the chief examples are American (and possibly mostly from the Northern States).

[33] See Spengler, *Decline*, 2:33–5.

[34] Ibid., 2:35.

[35] See Ronald M. and Catherine H. Berndt, *The World of the First Australians: aboriginal traditional life, past and present* (Canberra: Aboriginal Studies Press, 1988), 227–92; Bill Gammage, *The Biggest Estate on Earth: how Aborigines made Australia* (Sydney: Allen and Unwin, 2011), 125–26, 135–36.

[36] See Spengler, *Decline*, 1:38: "The Australian natives, who rank intellectually as thorough primitives, possess a mathematical instinct (or, what comes to the same thing, a power of thinking in numbers which is not yet communicable by signs or words) that as regards the interpretation of pure

told about other lands and supposedly "primitive" peoples.[37] That Spengler's high Cultures only began to be a mere five thousand years ago, when humankind had been a widespread species for over ten or twenty times that period, is hardly likely, even if we ourselves have no written, readable record of the earlier times, or none that we are willing to acknowledge. There were cities and written records long before Babylon, and there can be Cultures with no distinctive cities, whose corporate memory is only oral.[38]

Much of what Spengler suggests can be handled simply as his identifying common characters in a human history over many generations, without any strong ontological commitment. It may be enough to say that certain *subjective* unities have their own history.

> That which distinguishes the people from the population, raises it up out of the population, and will one day let it find its level again in the population is always the inwardly lived experience of the "we." The deeper this feeling is, the stronger is the *vis viva* of the people.... They can change speech, name, race, and land, but so long as their soul lasts, they can gather to themselves and transform human material of any and every provenance. The Roman name in Hannibal's day meant a people, in Trajan's time nothing more than a population.[39]

But it is as well to acknowledge that he did himself make exactly such a commitment, that the unifying spirit was not simply how a people felt about itself, but the reason that they did.

---

space is far superior to that of the Greeks. Their discovery of the boomerang can only be attributed to their having a sure feeling for numbers of a class that we should refer to the higher geometry. Accordingly—we shall justify the adverb later—they possess an extraordinarily complicated ceremonial and, for expressing degrees of affinity, such fine shades of language as not even the higher Cultures themselves can show."

[37] See Charles C. Mann, *1491: the Americas before Columbus* (London: Granta, 2005); Graham Connah, *African Civilizations: an archaeological perspective* (Cambridge: Cambridge University Press, 2016).

[38] Arnold Toynbee expanded the Spenglerian list of Cultures (with a rather different definition, simply as "intelligible fields of historical study" of a certain size and complexity), but he too neglected to consider the evidence for historical continuities and self-conscious development amongst what he thought were "primitive societies," short-lived, merely local, and involving relatively few human individuals (Arnold Toynbee, *A Study of History* [London: Oxford University Press, 1934–36], 1:147–49).

[39] Spengler, *Decline*, 2:165.

Intellectual associations are mere sums in the mathematical sense, varying by addition and subtraction, unless and until (as sometimes happens) a mere coincidence of opinion strikes so impressively as to reach the blood and so, suddenly, to create out of the sum a Being. In any political turning-point words may become fates and opinions passions. A chance crowd is herded together in the street and has *one* consciousness, *one* sensation, *one* language — until the short-lived soul flickers out and everyone goes his way again. . . . The mightiest beings of this kind that we know are the higher Cultures, which are born in great spiritual upheavals, and in a thousand years of existence weld all aggregates of lower degree — nations, classes, towns, generations — into one unit.[40]

Locating the Magian spirit (whether as a way of speaking or as a real Being) amongst the Classical artists, statesmen and philosophers, as well as among the unrecorded masses of a human population, may require more insight and empathy than is common, but the enterprise is far advanced from Spengler's day. Rather than dismissing what we no longer feel to be right as obvious superstition and factual error, more recent studies of Hermetic and Neo-Platonic art and thought have attempted, exactly, to comprehend the underlying reasons both for the *philosophers'* ideas and for the common practices (including magical invocations, preservation of sacred relics, refusal of civic and familial duties, a new sort of art replacing statues with two-dimensional icons or geometries, exaltation of "saints" above the wealthy and well-connected) that displaced the older Classical mind-set.

A nation of the Magian type is the community of co-believers, the group of all those who know the right way to salvation and are inwardly linked to one another by the *ijma* [that is, the consensus of informed believers] of this belief. Men belonged to a Classical nation by virtue of the possession of citizenship, but to a Magian nation by virtue of a sacramental act.[41]

They were reaching out to a reality above and beyond the "political"

---

[40] Ibid., 2:18–19.
[41] Ibid., 2:175. "Faustian" nations, he went on to say, are "dynastic units," in a uniquely *historical* Culture (*Decline*, 2:179–84).

and "imperial," above the manifold changes and chances of this mortal life—and following, in spirit, the strange injunction to "immortalize" themselves,[42] while giving a very different gloss to the notion of an immortal *nous* in each of us (different, that is, from the common interpretation offered by modern scholars convinced that Aristotle, being a reasonable man, must obviously have thought the same as they): *nous* is not merely or simply the exercise of theoretical reason in the contemplation of necessary truths, of morals or mathematics, but rather the realization of our original or destined being as gods—an idea certainly to be found among older poets and philosophers who passed as "Classical" thinkers, but not wholly grasped until a different sensibility took shape. We may, not wholly wrongly, suspect that these new philosophers, Middle and Late Platonists, created their own past, reading the works of Plato to reinforce their new ideals. We should similarly remember that modern "Western" scholars may be doing exactly the same thing—routinely reducing Plato's riddles, unwieldy arguments, and unnerving myths to simple dialectical exercises about the uses of the Greek verb "to be" (that is, *einai*). The arguments of Plato's *Parmenides* are taken nowadays to be *dialectical* or *logical* exercises; to Neo-Platonists in the summer of Magian thought they were, rather, *spiritual* exercises. We conceive even our familiar selves quite differently.

> Whereas the Faustian man is an "I" that in the last resort draws its own conclusions about the Infinite; whereas the Apollinian man, as one *soma* among many, represents only himself, the Magian man, with his spiritual kind of being, is only *a part of a pneumatic "We"* that, descending from above, is one and the same in all believers. As body and soul he belongs to himself alone, but something else, something alien and higher, dwells in him.[43]

Pagan and Christian Magians were agreed. According to Gregory Nazianzen we are "a part of God (*moiran theou*), and slipped down from above (*anothen rheusanta*),"[44] using almost exactly the same

---

[42] As Aristotle advised: *Nicomachean Ethics* 10.1177b31–4.
[43] Spengler, *Decline*, 2:235.
[44] Gregory Nazianzen, *De Fuga* 2.17, cited by Polycarp Sherwood, *The Earlier Ambigua of Saint Maximus the Confessor and his Refutation of Origenism* (Rome: Herder, 1955), 22.

phrase as Plotinus (*moiras ekeithen ousas*).[45] Faustian Christians have usually found this idea, of our *original* divinity, more problematic than that we have only the chance of being elevated to a higher state.

That the "natural" development of Magian Culture was, so Spengler suggests, distorted by growing up in the milieu of the Classical (an "historical pseudomorphosis")[46] allows him to accept that the Magian time-line does not exactly follow the order which he purports to find in other developing and decaying Cultures. Although his initial claim is that our future can be broadly predicted, by analogy with the fate of other Cultures,[47] the prediction need never be exact. It may still be true that there are distinctive forms of human life and conscience, and that those forms do tend to flourish for a while and then decay, even if all such Cultures follow their own tracks as variously as any actual living creature: infants, adolescents, adults, and the elderly are recognizable stages in a human life, but not all humans nor animals live through them all, nor in identical ways.

Spengler also identified another contemporary Culture that was, he thought, being distorted by the magnetic influence of the Western or Faustian form, namely one taking shape in the Orthodox lands of Russia and its peers.[48] It is to "*Dostoyevski's* Christianity that the next thousand years will belong."[49] The Soviet experiment, just beginning as he wrote, was both a defiant response to Westernization and an episode in that same Western history: the *ideal* that the Soviets served, of solidarity, of a people working together in the service of "Holy Russia," perhaps had more continuing energy. The hope expressed in Russian Orthodox philosophy was for the rediscovery of the God-Man, Jesus, and of our communal redemption. Russia and its peers, at least, are perhaps less like Western, "Faustian," nations than is our usual, Western, assumption. And there may still be time for that Culture to enjoy its late Summer and Autumn phases, whatever they may be, before its Winter sets in. Spengler hoped that in the coming millennium there would be a parallel development to the intellectual and spiritual efflorescence of the early Christian church up to AD 500, and that of the early

---

[45] *Ennead* V.1 [10].1, 2–3.
[46] *Decline*, 2:189–92.
[47] Ibid., 1:3–4.
[48] Ibid., 2:192–96; 295.
[49] Ibid., 2:196.

medieval Western church, from 1000 till 1500.[50] The sadder alternative is that the peoples have lost all touch with their one-time animating spirit, and are to be ruled by nihilistic, criminal oligarchs as long as their Civilization lasts. Both possible predictions have some support in Spenglerian analysis: what actually will happen is undetermined: that is, it is up to people.

NEW BEGINNINGS

"Each Culture has its own new possibilities of self-expression which arise, ripen, decay, and never return."[51] Speculations about the future beyond the expectable seasons of existing Cultures must, as Spengler declared, be futile.

> As in the history of the Raptores or the Coniferae we cannot prophesy whether and when a new species will arise, so in that of Cultural history we cannot say whether and when a new Culture shall be.[52]

Only long afterwards could a future Spenglerian trace the shy beginnings of whatever Culture has come to life in a newly imagined landscape. But there is still room for fantasy, if only to help identify, by contrasts, the present minds of humanity. One familiar guess was coined by James Blish: the age of the "spindizzy," a device founded on exact understanding of gravity that will enable whole human cities to fly from the Earth,[53] at once accomplishing part of the Faustian dream, and setting history on a new interstellar track. Unfortunately, only the first part of his tetralogy has any strong Spenglerian content. A. E. Van Vogt's *Space Beagle* also rests on discovering Spenglerian seasons in a succession of alien life forms, and in the decaying social structure of the star-ship *Beagle* itself. Neither fantasy addresses the problem of imagining what a really different human Culture might be like in principle — different from any that we or Spengler might already have intuited in known terrestrial life. Other speculative futurists have imagined how our successors might describe this present day: "the Age of the Feuilleton," or the "Age

---

[50] Ibid., 2:261.
[51] Ibid., 1:21.
[52] Ibid., 2:36.
[53] James Blish, *Cities in Flight* (New York: Overlook Press, 1970), comprising *They Shall Have Stars* (1956); *A Life for the Stars* (1962); *Earthman Come Home* (1955); *The Triumph of Time* (1958).

of Mouldwarp," or "the Late Christian Epoch."[54] All such stories are at once implausible and perhaps productive. It is very likely that the following suggestion will itself turn out to be no more than a late Faustian fantasy, perhaps as Roman Stoicism was a doomed attempt, partly Classical and partly Magian in origin, to discover some new way of living as civic and imperial power decayed.

The Faustian dream, given expression in much contemporary SF, including the works of Blish and Van Vogt, is of unlimited growth in power and knowledge, focused now in the ideal of the competent engineer, competent both in technical solutions and in political opposition to imagined oppressive and stagnant powers. Man — and it is of course masculine Man that is intended — will one day rule the worlds by "reason" (that is to say, technique), and the pretence of liberty. Some writers, like Olaf Stapledon, may suspect instead that such human triumphs will falter in the end, confronted by the blank unreason of the First Cause and Final Fate. The most fervently anti-humanist Faustian may realize that our deal, so to speak, is with deceptive devils.

> Now all my tales [so Lovecraft said] are based on the fundamental premise that common human laws and interests and emotions have no validity or significance in the vast cosmos-at-large.... When we cross the line to the boundless and hideous unknown — the shadow-haunted Outside — we must remember to leave our humanity — and terrestrialism — at the threshold.[55]

Both the triumphalist and the Lovecraftian are Faustian in spirit, for both are enthralled by the infinite outside, both hope to transcend our present humanity. Classical thinkers may acknowledge how small our empires are in comparison with the cosmos, how short a time we have between catastrophes, but that only cements their attachment, exactly, to their little local concerns. Some supposed that human beings, like the earth itself, have been around "forever," though little beyond proverbial wisdom has survived from earlier falls: this too only fixed their attention here.

---

[54] Hermann Hesse, *The Glass Bead Game*, trans. Richard and Clara Winston (Harmondsworth: Penguin, 1972 [1943]), 21; Peter Ackroyd, *The Plato Papers* (London: Chatto and Windus, 1999); Robert Graves, *Seven Days in New Crete* (London: Oxford University Press, 1983 [1949]).

[55] H. P. Lovecraft, Letter to Farnsworth Wright, July 5, 1927: http://www.hplovecraft.com/writings/quotes.aspx (accessed July 4, 2020).

Even if future generations should wish to hand down to those yet unborn the eulogies of every one of us which they received from their fathers, nevertheless the floods and conflagrations which necessarily happen on the earth at stated intervals would prevent us from gaining a glory which could even be long-enduring, much less eternal. But of what importance is it to you to be talked of by those who are born after you, when you were never mentioned by those who lived before you?[56]

Hindu thinkers drew stronger morals from the same idea—that there have been, and yet will be, unimaginably vast ages, that we live in the darkest sort of age, that all our empires are no greater than ants' nests in a fractal cosmos. Their moral was to endure, or to escape from, the world giant's dream.[57]

So what might be that "rough beast" which brings a different way of seeing? By Yeats's account, the "New Thing" will be born from what the earlier age, our present one, rejected: "because we had worshipped a single god it would worship many or receive from Joachim de Flora's Holy Spirit a multitudinous influx"[58]—which is why his "rough beast" cannot be definitely identified as either good or bad, creative or destructive. Its beginnings, if we are to accept a Spenglerian analysis, will be found in (effectively) anonymously composed popular literature paralleling the Homeric epics or the Nibelungenlied, which will express, will already have expressed, something of the tragic dream of life in a new key or mode. In the place of a central human figure facing into the infinite future, or hiding her eyes before it, we may expect a multiplicity of different figures, a forest or jungle or ocean-reef with many lives beside and around each other. In place of a drive to ascend into the heavens (in fear or triumph), we may expect rather a wish to nest, to nestle, among many other creatures of a constantly different sort. Multiple plant and animal forms will shift and change their natures, in the presence of the longest enduring living things, the bacterial and viral cloud that has made and forever repairs the air, the land, and ocean. Its birth-pangs will affect, and be affected by, the cataclysms of

---

[56] Cicero, "Dream of Scipio," *De Republica*, 277 (6.21).
[57] See Zimmer, *Myths and Symbols*, 38–48.
[58] Yeats, *Explorations* (London: Macmillan, 1962), 393. On Joachim (1145–1202), see Spengler, *Decline*, 1:19–20, 261.

climate change and the sixth extinction, as human imagination grapples with the end of Faustian, and all other presently existing Cultures and Civilizations. It may, in large part, be difficult for our successors to distinguish it from pre-cultural forms of the sort Spengler saw in supposedly "primitive" peoples, which I have suggested are more *cultured* than he thought. At the same time, it may depend on the last available technologies that Faustian humanity will have created, the genetic manipulation of plant and animal stocks that Freeman Dyson imagined.

> Now, after some three billion years, the Darwinian era is over. The epoch of species competition came to an end about 10 thousand years ago when a single species, *Homo sapiens*, began to dominate and reorganize the biosphere. Since that time, cultural evolution has replaced biological evolution as the driving force of change. Cultural evolution is not Darwinian. Cultures spread by horizontal transfer of ideas more than by genetic inheritance. Cultural evolution is running a thousand times faster than Darwinian evolution, taking us into a new era of cultural interdependence that we call globalization. And now, in the last 30 years, *Homo sapiens* has revived the ancient pre-Darwinian practice of horizontal gene transfer, moving genes easily from microbes to plants and animals, blurring the boundaries between species. We are moving rapidly into the post-Darwinian era, when species will no longer exist, and the evolution of life will again be communal.[59]

Faustian humanity has been even more anthropocentric and triumphalist than other "high Cultures," but alongside that insistent exaltation of humankind above all other living things there has also been a tradition of imagining talking beasts, whether these are merely moral fables about tricky foxes and domestic but courageous moles, or imaginative descriptions of whole "animal" societies. These stories have usually been classed as merely "children's tales," but for that very reason they lie at the base

---

[59] Freeman Dyson, "The Darwinian Interlude," *Technology Review* (March, 2005) at https://www.technologyreview.com/2006/02/16/229657/the-darwinian-interlude/ (accessed June 31, 2020). On this and other technological possibilities, see Christopher J. Preston, *The Synthetic Age: outdesigning evolution, resurrecting species, and reengineering our world* (Cambridge, MA: MIT Press, 2019).

of much adult thought, when that is not being regulated by the official rule that "animals" are barely sentient.[60] In the coming ages, we may reasonably guess, there will be many versions even of humanity, as well as many "uplifted" versions of familiar beasts.[61] If the Faustian vision is expansive, the new Culture will instead be centripetal, gazing always towards the cultivated land inhabited by uplifted, altered, and restored animal and human kinds. Their concept of history and of time's passage is likely also to be other than our terrestrial version, of whatever terrestrial Culture: they will live at once, like "primitives," in an eternal present, and in the face of *cosmic* time and the impossibly distant stars. They will be living both across the terrestrial landscape and amongst the myriad small asteroids and moons in a partly-explored solar array—the final gift of Faustian humanity. Elves, hobbits, trolls and talking beasts will be the new environment, for good or ill.[62] The most famous SF versions of this future are to be found in the work of Clifford Simak (*City*), and especially that of Cordwainer Smith (*The Rediscovery of Man*),[63] in whose world-future recreated "humans" imagine themselves superior to the uplifted beasts, and are constantly proved wrong. There is only a hopeful hint in those works that there will one day be a fully "humane" Culture, free from cruelty and humanistic follies. Even before that hoped-for but uncertain end, the Culture's chief artistic contribution will lie, as Dyson suggested, in the creation of manifold life-forms, rivalling the extravagance of "nature." What new versions of mathematics and philosophy those animated by this Culture will devise is of course unclear—except to suspect that both these disciplines will be more open, more contextual, than the present versions, but also less fixated on fictional infinities. Its primary architectural symbol, matching the Faustian Church spire and

---

[60] See Bruce Shaw, *The Animal Fable in Science Fiction and Fantasy* (Jefferson, NC: McFarland and Co., 2010).

[61] On which possibility, see David Brin, *Uplift: Sundiver* (1996), *Startide Rising* (1996), *Uplift War* (1996) (London: Orbit, 2012).

[62] See my "Elves, Hobbits, Trolls and Talking Beasts," in *Creaturely Theology*, eds. Celia Deane-Drummond and David Clough (London: SCM Press, 2009), 151–67.

[63] Clifford D. Simak, *City* (New York: Ace Books, 1952); Cordwainer Smith, *The Rediscovery of Man*, ed. J. J. Pierce (London: Gollancz, 2003 [1975]); see Carol McGuirk, "The Animal Downdeep: Cordwainer Smith's Late Tales of the Underpeople," *Science Fiction Studies* 37.3 (2010): 466–77.

the Magian dome displayed in Ravenna and Byzantium,[64] will be another sort of dome: both terrestrial nests and hollowed asteroids floating in immensity, whose light and warmth are drawn from a fusion furnace in their centres, and so mirror the whole solar array, the *solar* dome, from the Oort Cloud down to the Sun itself. Or at least this will be true for the *better* domes: there is also the sad possibility that some will have decayed into slave colonies or slums of the kind imagined by Sterling (*Schismatrix Plus*) or McLoughlin (*The Helix and the Sword*).[65] The possible new life I am describing, in short, will not be clearly utopian, any more than the visions of other Cultures have ever been humanely and honestly embodied. The future remains open, even if Spengler is correct in reckoning that there are great Spirits that animate our lives, for good or ill.

The multiple possibilities of our future, and the presently unimagined Cultures that will come to birth, are not determined by any past endeavours (though they will, like other past Cultures, borrow themes and achievements in a different key). The technologically adept possibility I have sketched may be relegated to might-have-been if our present collapsing Civilization and its environment reach cataclysm too soon. In that possible future humanity, if we survive at all, will have to recreate the "primitive," non-civic and maybe pre-literate, Cultures of our remoter ancestors and of contemporary "savages" saved from disastrous contact with well-meaning missionaries and explorers. Maybe there are some seeds even of that option in our current imaginings: witness the appeal of various forms of "naturism" or "paganism," drawing on reconstructed or reimagined Celtic or Native American or other Aboriginal traditions.[66] Not all Western would-be-pagans are likely to be as well-schooled in survival as "savages," but some may learn to be. And it seems likely that the same blurring of boundaries that Dyson prophesied will still hold true:

> Modern Western culture has long drawn a sharp distinction between human and animal, and female and male but, in pictures at least, the Palaeolithic did not.

---

[64] Spengler, *Decline*, 1:211; see Callan, "Learned Theban," 600.

[65] Bruce Sterling, *Schismatrix Plus* (New York: Ace Books, 1996); John C. McLoughlin, *The Helix and the Sword* (New York: Doubleday, 1983).

[66] See Ronald Hutton, *Pagan Britain* (London: Yale University Press, 2013); Liz Williams, *Miracles of Our Own Making: a history of paganism* (London: Reaktion Books, 2020).

Furthermore, modern Westerners like to classify things by type, in a way that more traditional peoples do not: Jean Clottes has pointed out that those who have hunted the bison in recent centuries have not viewed it as a single category of animal but as one with many attributes. This way of looking at the world made it easier for Palaeolithic people to blur the boundaries between species as well as making the nature of a species itself multi-faceted: fantastic beasts, which mix the attributes of actual animals, are well represented in their imagery.[67]

They too may have a "dome" as their chief symbol, but in their case it will be the abiding dome of heaven, and their devotion will be to the simple hearths of their villages or huts.[68] And they too will live amongst a wide variety of living creature, acknowledged as other tribes than merely human. Perhaps the "primitive," merely terrestrial future will not be very different from the "advanced" solar society. Both will be very various, and both will find their strength from the common life centred on their different hearths. Both, we could say, will be versions of a possible "Hestian" Culture, named for the Classical goddess of the household's hearth as well as the permanent flame in the common city temple, or a "solar" Culture, named for the sun (no longer perceived as "up aloft," but as the root and centre of our system). The Solar version will fantasise (at least) about building a Dyson Sphere or some equivalent around the sun to capture all its output, and so forgetting the wider world outside.[69] The Hestian will not be troubled. Neither version will be utopian, but we may hope that they will be, at least, more commonsensical, and more compassionate in principle, than the long Faustian endeavour, in its hopeless drive to encompass the infinities.

---

[67] Hutton, *Pagan Britain*, 47, after Jean Clottes, "Recent Studies on Palaeolithic Art," *Cambridge Archaeological Journal* 6 (1996), 179–89; see also Tim Ingold, *The Perception of the Environment* (London: Routledge, 2000).

[68] See Michael Potts, "Evening-Lands," emphasising both the melancholy of Gondor's long decay, and the hope of life beginning again from the sturdy peasantry of the Shire.

[69] Freeman J. Dyson, "Search for Artificial Stellar Sources of Infra-Red Radiation," *Science* 131.3414 (1960), 1667–68. Dyson himself disclaimed responsibility for the original idea (Dyson, *Disturbing the Universe* [New York: Basic Books, 1981], 211), attributing it instead to Stapledon, *Star Maker*, 179.

15.
Further Reading
OTHER OF MY BOOKS AND ESSAYS
WITH A SCIENCE-FICTIONAL MOTIF

"How to Believe in Fairies," *Inquiry* 30 (1988), 337–55.

"Robotic Morals," *Cogito* 2 (1988), 20–22.

"How many Selves make me?" In D. Cockburn, ed., *Human Beings* (Cambridge: Cambridge University Press, 1991), 213–33.

"Extraterrestrial Intelligence, the Neglected Experiment," *Foundation* 61 (1994), 50–65.

*Tools, Machines and Marvels." In Roger Fellows, ed., *Philosophy and Technology* (Cambridge: Cambridge University Press, 1995), 159–76.

How to Live Forever (London: Routledge, 1995).

"Making up Animals: the view from Science Fiction." In *Animal Biotechnology and Ethics*, eds. Alan Holland and Andrew Johnson (London: Chapman and Hall, 1997), 209–24.

"Natural Integrity and Biotechnology." In *Human Lives*, eds. Jacqueline A. Laing and David S. Oderberg (London: Macmillan, 1997), 58–76.

Animals and their Moral Standing (London: Routledge, 1997).

The Political Animal (London: Routledge, 1999).

* "The End of the Ages." In David Seed, ed., *Imagining Apocalypse: studies in cultural crisis* (London: Macmillan; New York: St Martin's Press, 2000), 27–44.

* "Posthumanism: engineering in the place of ethics." In Barry Smith and Berit Brogaard, eds., *Rationality and Irrationality: Proceedings of the 23rd International Wittgenstein Symposium* (Vienna: Öbv & Hpt, 2001), 62–76.

* "From Biosphere to Technosphere," *Ends and Means* 5 (2001), 3–21.

"Science Fiction and Religion." In *The Blackwell Companion to Science Fiction*, ed. David Seed (Oxford: Blackwell, 2005), 95–110.

*Revised versions included in *Philosophical Futures* (Peter Lang: Frankfurt 2011).

G. K. Chesterton: Thinking Backwards, Looking Forwards (West Consho-hocken, PA: Templeton Foundation Press, 2006).

* "C. J. Cherryh: The Ties that Bind." In David Seed, ed., *Yearbook of English Studies* 37. 2 (London: Maney Publishing, 2007), 197–214.

* "Elves, Hobbits, Trolls and Talking Beasts." In *Creaturely Theology*, eds. Celia Deane-Drummond and David Clough (London: SCM Press, 2009), 151–67.

* "Imaginary futures and moral possibilities: blossoming in the morn of days," *International Social Science Journal* 62 (2011), 301–12. DOI: 10.1111/issj.12004.

Philosophical Futures (Frankfurt: Peter Lang, 2011).

"Personal Identity and Identity Disorders." In *Oxford Handbook of Philosophy and Psychiatry*, eds. K. W. M. Fulford, Martin Davies, George Graham, John Z. Sadler, Giovanni Sanghellini and Tim Thornton (Oxford: Oxford University Press, 2013), 911–28.

"Animals Real and Virtual." In *Science and the Self: Animals, Evolution, and Ethics: essays in honour of Mary Midgley*, eds. Ian J. Kidd and Liz McKinnell (London: Routledge, 2015), 31–40.

"Heracles, Hylas and the Uses of Reflection." In *Plotinus and the Moving Image*, eds. Thorsten Botz-Bornstein and Giannis Stamatellos (Leiden: Brill, 2017), 67–90.

Index

ABOUT THE AUTHOR

STEPHEN R. L. CLARK is Emeritus Professor of Philosophy at the University of Liverpool, and an honorary research fellow in Theology and Religious Studies at the University of Bristol. At present, he is concerned mainly with the development of Neo-Platonic philosophy, the understanding and treatment of non-human animals, and the varieties of neurodiversity. His most recent publications relevant to these themes include *How to Live Forever* (1995), *G. K.Chesterton: Thinking Backwards, Looking Forwards* (2006), *Philosophical Futures* (2011), *Can We Believe in People: Human Significance in an Interconnected Cosmos* (2020), and *How the Worlds Became: Philosophy and the Oldest Stories* (2023).